YOUNG BEAUTIFUL FLAT

DAVIDE LONGO

YOUNG BEASTS AT PLAY

*Translated from the Italian
by Silvester Mazzarella*

MACLEHOSE PRESS
QUERCUS · LONDON

First published in the Italian language as *Così giocano le bestie giovani*
By Narratori Feltrinelli, Milano, 2018
First published in Great Britain in 2022 by

MacLehose Press
an imprint of Quercus Editions Limited
Carmelite House
50 Victoria Embankment
London EC4Y 0DZ

An Hachette UK Company

A CIP catalogue record for this book is available
from the British Library.

ISBN (MMP) 978 1 52940 821 8
ISBN (Ebook) 978 1 52940 822 5

10 9 8 7 6 5 4 3 2 1

Designed and typeset in Adobe Caslon by CC Book Production
Printed and bound in Great Britain by Clays Ltd, Elcograf S.p.A.

"Well, boys, the city's yours now.
But let's go further.
If you possessed the whole country,
and this city stood for the whole of Italy,
what would you do with Italy then?"
"Not much, but it would be entirely serious,"
was Johnny's answer.

BEPPE FENOGLIO: *Johnny the Partisan*

PART ONE

First Prologue

Five young people are walking along a pavement in the suburbs.

Two o'clock in the morning. A black leather jacket; a beige corduroy trench coat; a grey overcoat too short for the boy wearing it; a parka; a dark knitted sweater. The boy in the overcoat has a bag on his shoulder. The bag is magenta in colour, halfway between red and blue; there are two white numbers stamped on it. Walking beside him is the only girl. She is wearing the sweater and is more relaxed than the others.

They turn into a narrow, badly lit street. The windows of the surrounding houses and apartment blocks show no lights, the shutters of the shops are closed, and nothing can be heard but a tram passing down Corso Giulio.

"Perhaps we should think again about this," the boy in the overcoat says. The girl takes his hand. No-one slows down or lifts their eyes from the pavement.

A shabby old two-storey building has three lattice windows overlooking the road, and an oval sign above its front door that is difficult to read. No lights or sign of movement from the inside.

"Give the bag to me," says the boy in the leather jacket.

The boy in the overcoat holds the bag out to him, and its clasp opens with a snap.

"Edo and Luciano, you two watch the windows. Nini and I will throw them in. Stefano, go to the corner and keep an eye on the road."

Stefano slings the now empty bag back on his shoulder. The girl and the others wait for him to move as instructed. He limps to the corner, then looks towards the far-off lights. After a few seconds comes a soft explosion followed by the sound of breaking windows, then a second, even softer explosion.

The boy at the corner turns and the other four run towards him, while behind them yellow reflections begin to spread across the asphalt. He too begins to run. After a few metres the others catch him up. Their collective steps strike the road loudly.

Expectant, precise and unambiguous.

That is how young animals play, before they discover their claws were never meant for playing.

I

"Stop! No way through."

Arcadipane takes the cigarette from his lips and stares at the massive figure in a yellow cape blocking his way. A man much taller than himself, even with his boots buried in the mud.

"Why not?"

The man gives this question some thought. An imprecise question that gives Arcadipane time to observe a nose bent to the right from some ancient fracture, oriental cheekbones, and a not entirely unattractive scent of mixed aniseed and tobacco. The man looks about thirty or thirty-five years old.

"They told me not to let anyone through," insists the man from under his hood, raising his voice to be heard against the rain.

Arcadipane puts his cigarette back between his lips, but the filter is now full of water. He throws it away and watches as it disappears into the mud, the raindrops striking it as precisely as a hammer hitting the broad head of a nail.

"They told you . . . who told you?"

The subconscious mind of the man registers authoritative overtones in this question and passes this information to his conscious mind, which has second thoughts about this little thickset guy with no umbrella, whom he has just seen get out of a well-kept Alfa Romeo Quadrifoglio, looking inoffensive both in physique and rank.

"It was the man in the raincoat who told me, the commissario," the man says, turning to indicate something. "He said not to let anyone through."

Through the veil of rain Arcadipane can distinguish the backs of four motionless figures gazing intently at the ground. Not far off are a bulldozer, a lorry and a crane. In the background the mountains and the sky seem as if made from some identical substance: melancholy, inert, suffocating, nostalgic, passive and moribund. "Bloody hell," he thinks. "Here we go again." He searches his pocket for a sucai* lozenge amid the fluff at the bottom. He puts the sweet into his mouth and begins to chew. Gradually, the lump blocking his throat dissolves. He becomes newly aware of the cold, of the acidity of the coffee he drank half an hour earlier at a motorway snack bar, and of the reason he is now here.

"What are you building here?" he asks.

"We're not building anything."

"Then what are you doing?"

"Laying cables."

"What kind of cables?"

The man puts his hands into his pockets without answering. Arcadipane knows when he is beaten. Unwillingly, he slips his left hand into the sheepskin jacket his in-laws gave him and produces the necessary document. The man looks from the identification pass to Arcadipane, and then back at the pass again.

He opens his arms as if to say, "How was I to know?"

Arcadipane knows the man is really thinking, "Why the hell couldn't you have said you were police in the first place?" But 366 similar investigations have taught him that even people

---

* Sucai is the word the Piedmontese use to describe a lozenge typical of their region; they are black cubes covered with sugar and taste of sweet liquorice.

with nothing to hide never reveal to the police the first thing that comes into their heads. Or even the second. Don't deceive yourself: rubbish bins can't empty themselves, or, as Bramard would say: the truth never thrusts itself forward; you have to work hard to find it.

"Well then, what are these cables you are laying?"

"Electric cables," the man says, "for the railway."

Arcadipane looks around: grassland and rice fields as far as the eye can see, and a kilometre away the embankment for the new high-speed railway, with a Frecciarossa train passing as silently as a finger over velvet; Milano to Torino in fifty minutes. Much further to the west, a ruined farmhouse. There's nothing else.

"But it wasn't me who found them," the man says.

"Oh no? And who did find them, then?"

"My cousin Nicolae."

"Your cousin Nicolae. And you are?"

"Roman."

"Roman," repeats Arcadipane, shifting his gaze to the group behind this big guy. "So one of those men is your cousin. And the other two?"

"The short one's Vincenzo. The other's the boss, Signor Coletto. But we called him later."

Arcadipane nods, searching for the man's boots with his eyes. Nothing visible above the mud but the plastic-covered end of one of the laces. Who knows what those things are called? If they have any name at all, Mariangela would be sure to know it. So would Bramard. They are the only people who know such things.

"Have you anything else to tell me or shall I go and talk to Signor Coletto?"

The man scratches his several days of blond beard.

"The boss said he needed someone with a licence to operate

a crane, so I made a copy of my cousin's. But now I'll get into trouble."

"And . . ."

"As soon as I got to Italy, I did four months for assault. The boss doesn't know that. He only wants clean people."

Arcadipane looks down at his own reddened hands, swollen with cold. And at the ribbon round his finger to protect the skin from his wedding ring. He knows this evening he will go home to the woman so much more wide awake than himself who was prepared to take him on, and he will tell her what has been happening, and even before he can have a shower, they'll be between the sheets together.

He knows this is one of the effects seeing a dead man has on him. Even a man like this one.

But what other people don't know is that the effect doesn't last. Even the dead become a habit if they are what you do for a living.

"Last year," he tells Roman, "we arrested a man who had watched the woman next door bury something in her garden regularly on the sixth day of every month. He decided this must be her pension. So one day when he needed money, he went to the old lady, smashed her head in with a monkey wrench and started digging. Do you know what he found?"

Roman stares at him with the bland if hostile expression of one who, only recently arrived in Italy and nervous and lonely, does everything his friends suggest he should, such as getting into fights in bars, staring at displays of naked girls and longing to acquire a used BMW; until some little woman more wide awake than him decides for some reason of her own to take on this country bumpkin who wakes each morning slobbering onto his pillow and thirsting for milk.

Arcadipane gives him the answer: "What he found was three hundred and twelve little ceramic dogs. They had been coming to her in the post once a month."

But Roman's mind is far away, concentrating on heavy structural steelwork, on levers and presses, counterweights and pulleys.

"Well, what shall I tell him, then? About the licence and . . . everything else?"

Arcadipane pauses before replying.

"Can I give you a bit of advice?"

The other nods.

"First, never hide anything unless you have a reason for it. And secondly, if you assume other people are more intelligent than you are, you'll find you won't make many mistakes. Now could you please get out of my way?"

Roman moves aside. Arcadipane places his shoes in the massive prints left by the man's feet and presses on. Another twenty metres of water and mud to reach the little group beyond him.

"Good evening, commissario."

Arcadipane settles beside his assistant Pedrelli without bothering to answer his greeting. He has no need to look at the man to know he is fifty-one years old and weighs as many kilos. He has bristly hair and a chronic ulcer, and they have had nothing in common for the last sixteen years.

"And our men?"

"I sent them away to buy nylon sheets," Pedrelli says. "The director and I have had the idea of building a shelter and pumping the water away from the area where we made the find."

Arcadipane looks at the "director", Signor Coletto, in his waterproof trousers and practical windcheater; he had always thought those guys with beauty spots on playbills advertising Piedmontese comedies didn't exist in real life, but clearly . . .

"We have a pump we can attach to the caterpillar," Coletto says. "But so long as the trench keeps filling with rain . . ."

Arcadipane nods, struck by the man's accent. He moves on to the two wearing yellow capes: Nicolae is a little fatter than his cousin but of the same basic type, but the other man, Vincenzo, is about fifty, lean, malarial, and Sicilian enough to know keeping your mouth shut is not a sin.

"So?" Arcadipane says, indicating the hole full of water these four men are keeping an eye on.

Pedrelli pulls out a notebook, but two big blue circles suddenly explode on his page of carefully written notes. He quickly puts the notebook away again and reverts to memory.

"Towards twelve o'clock, the worker Nicolae Popescu noticed a human cranium where they were digging and told the operator to stop. They called Signor Coletto, the foreman, who came over to have a look and then informed us."

Arcadipane scans the faces under the hoods. No-one denies this or adds anything to it. He turns to the foreman.

"Then why didn't you call the carabinieri? There's a police station not far from here."

"My son-in-law's a policeman." The other man shrugs. "He says that's always the best thing to do."

Arcadipane looks down into the pool, which is the size and colour of a small dining room. The water in it is still rising, and the rain is marking the pool with a whole alphabet of small shapes.

"Are they under there?"

"No, commissario. The usual procedure in such cases is to leave things where they are, but the workers thought that, left on the spot . . ."

"Well?"

"We moved them into the container," summarises the man who looks as if he has had malaria.

Arcadipane follows his gaze to the grey prefabricated structure. There is no tree, bush or other vegetable presence of any sort near it that the rain could either attack or nourish.

"When was the last exam for promotion to commissario, Pedrelli? A year ago?"

"Last February, commissario."

Arcadipane reaches into his pocket, pulls out a sucai, and throws it into his mouth. At that moment the slow interregional train clatters past. This one takes an hour and fifty minutes to reach Milano.

"Next time I'll be sure to fail that exam myself," he says, making off, "since you are so anxious to call yourself commissario."

2

Kneeling on the floor of the container, Sarace taps the thigh bone, the iliac crest and the ischium with his ballpoint pen, then lifts a couple of vertebrae closer to his myopic eyes, which are magnified by his blue-tinged lenses.

He examines with detachment those structures that once held life in its most intense, soft and mysterious form, exploring inside them, turning them over and extracting a sound like hollow wood, before putting them back on the blanket.

"A fine collection, don't you think?" He indicates the whole set of bones.

Arcadipane, crouching opposite, looks at the long arm and leg bones laid out by the workmen together with a pelvis, spine and cranium to give some idea of a complete figure. On one side is a little pile of small bones they had no idea what to do with.

"Like Andorra and Liechtenstein," Sarace remarks. "If you have no interest in banks, you never know where to find them on the map."

Arcadipane rubs his hands on his wet trousers, trying to restore a little warmth to thighs made numb by the cold and his awkward position kneeling on the floor. In addition to himself and Sarace and the arbitrarily assembled collection of bones in front of them, the container they are sitting in is furnished with a bare desk, a basket, an unlit kerosene stove and a small cupboard. On the walls are two maps of the area with cadastral surveys sketched in felt pen. Not a place where anyone would wish to spend the weekend.

"Well?"

Sarace pulls off his latex gloves, screws them up in a ball and throws them into the basket beside the desk.

"Male, young, dead. Since the cranium has a precise hole in the occipital region, it is not hard to imagine that the last thing he would have heard would have been a point-blank shot."

Arcadipane, after ten years' experience of working with Sarace, knows the man never likes to hazard premature guesses, but he also knows that at weekends Sarace sings with a group called The Disciples of Boom and doesn't give a damn what anyone thinks of his hairstyle. But even so he ventures to ask: "When do you think it happened?"

"1986," Sarace says. "A Tuesday in late spring."

Arcadipane watches him snigger and slips his pen back into his raincoat pocket.

"For all I know," Sarace continues, "this man may equally well have been dead twenty years, or maybe eighty. It all depends on how deep down he was found, on the humidity, the nature of the ground, and whether he was inside a coffin or any other sort of box. Do you still have that woman Alessandra working in your lab?"

"Yes."

"Not a pin-up to go on my calendar, but she certainly knows her job . . . Take our friend to her with a bit of the soil in which he was found, and something may emerge. It's always difficult with bones but you can always hazard a guess. So long as you take the trouble to complete the correct form."

Arcadipane looks up.

Once sure of his attention, Sarace leans towards the leather

19

bag sagging at his side like an elderly and dysplastic cocker spaniel.

"This is the official form on which we record discoveries that may date back to the war years." It has four pages. "Fill it in, put the bones in a box, attach the form to the box and send the whole lot off to the appropriate office, where they will check to see if it relates to any reports of disappearances in the area during the war or shortly afterwards. If no attribution can be found, we'll just have yet another unknown death on our hands. On the other hand, if we can find a descendant who would like to fill an empty space in the family vault, the bones can be given a fine funeral. Either way, you and I are now free to go home and have a nice shower."

Arcadipane looks at the bones. They are not white or even yellow, but a pale pistachio green.

"You think they could really . . ."

"Eight times out of ten."

Arcadipane rubs his temples and the nape of his neck. For some days now he has had the feeling of a heavy book pressing on the base of his skull between two nerves at the back of his neck.

"A bloody awful day." He raises his shoulders. "Still, it may be worth . . ."

Sarace waits to see whether Arcadipane has got the point, and if he has, to give him time if he wants to change his mind. Then, with a weak smile, he rises to his feet.

"Mariangela and the children?" he asks, beginning to change out of his work clothes.

"They're all fine."

"And Mariangela's taking exams at the moment?"

"Every six months. That's how it works. Incidentally, she keeps asking me to say thank you."

Sarace smacks his lips as if to dismiss that as nothing, then, carefully protecting his elaborate hairdo with one hand, he lowers an oilcloth hood over the voluminous glittering banana-like structure on his head. Even under the neon light, his angular face still has the happy-go-lucky sheen of the years when he first started working on his appearance.

"I'll take the car and get the stuff. Shall I send you Pedrelli?"

Arcadipane nods.

When Sarace opens the door, the container is suddenly filled with a din of machinery, of voices insisting something must be moved, of heavy rain still beating down, and of the wailing of an old-style rip-start engine determined not to start; then the door closes after him, and Arcadipane is once more aware he is alone between four silent walls.

He goes to the desk, rests his bottom against its smooth edge and pulls out his cigarette packet. It is damp, making it difficult to light a cigarette. The bones lie on the floor, silent, enigmatic and pistachio green.

The remains of some soldier, whether fascist or partisan, he thinks, but young and with his head full of bullshit, and then what happened? Right or wrong, just destined to rot away in the ground . . . "Bloody hell."

Reaching into his pocket, he realises he is weeping and pauses. For a good couple of minutes, he enjoys the feeling of warm tears on his face though they are already cold by the time they get down to his neck, then he dries his nose on his sleeve, takes a visiting card from his back pocket and dials the number on his mobile.

"Yes." A woman answers.

"I'm looking for Doctor Ariel."

"That's me and I'm not a doctor."

Arcadipane takes a slow breath.

"It's all quite normal," the woman says before he can answer. "Tartara likes to imagine your face when you realise I'm a woman. In any case he's an old fool with his best years long behind him. But he did warn me you would ring. You're the one with the strange name, aren't you? The policeman?"

"Arcadipane."

"Arcadipane. You know, seventy-five per cent of phone conversations occur between people who will never in fact speak to each other on any other occasion. However, I'm on call at the moment, so I can't discuss your problem now, though it sounds interesting. Would you like to make an appointment?"

A knock on the door. Arcadipane blows out smoke and puts his hand over the phone.

"Just a moment!"

When he brings the phone back to his ear the woman asks, "Are you crying?"

"No."

"Have you been taking drugs?"

"No."

"So do you want this appointment?"

More knocking.

"Come in, Christ, come in!"

Pedrelli opens the door and enters.

"What's going on?" the woman asks on the phone.

"Nothing. Just my work."

"Are you hitting someone?"

"Why on earth should I do that?"

"But that is what you do, isn't it? You drive with the horn blaring, take fingerprints and hit people to make them speak. 'Own up, you bastard! Your friends have already given you away. Do you want them to get you locked up for twenty years?'"

Arcadipane stares at Pedrelli who is staring at the bones on

22

the blanket while the bones are staring at the neon light suspended from the ceiling.

"I'll see you tomorrow at four p.m.," says the woman. "My address is on the card that man Tartara gave you. Don't be late, we'll only have fifty minutes." She rang off.

Arcadipane smooths down the few hairs that form a crown round his head, as if just coming home after a long walk in a howling wind.

"Please excuse me, sir," Pedrelli begins. "I had no idea . . ."

Arcadipane lifts a hand to stop him.

"The ditch?"

"Almost reclaimed."

"Check if anything jumps out of it: personal objects, clothes, cartridge cases, anything."

"Certainly, commissario."

Arcadipane studies the Savoyard elegance of his deputy, which neither tiredness, soaked clothes nor muddy shoes can compromise.

When they first met, Arcadipane was twenty-three and already Bramard's right-hand man, while Pedrelli was a junior police officer two years older than him, who had just been sent to their office to be given something to do after being transferred to Torino from Genova. Arcadipane had watched him perform the first jobs he had been given efficiently and taken note of his short hair and clean, pale face, a real lesson. Then they had made him Arcadipane's deputy as part of the ritual round at headquarters.

"Did you put in a request for a cretin?" Arcadipane had asked Bramard when they were alone together.

Bramard had poured himself some tea and continued scrutinising some files without answering. But that evening, setting off as usual without saying goodbye, Bramard had left open on his desk *The Encyclopedia of the Dog*, a book it was his habit to consult religiously after each interrogation and in free moments. "Tomorrow have a desk prepared here in the office for the new man," he had said as he put on his coat.

Bramard, a man Arcadipane would never understand but who would teach him everything he would ever learn about people and their criminal tendencies, had then gone home, while he himself had got up and gone over to Bramard's desk.

The encyclopedia was lying open at a page showing a brown dog with nothing proud, intelligent or threatening about him. An ordinary dog, in fact, of medium size.

"A frank, well-behaved dog," he read in the book, "stable and well balanced, an effective cowherd and a wonderful companion, always at his master's side, if a little shy of strangers. Despite his delicate and unobtrusive manner, he is afraid of nothing, and thanks to his tenacious nature, can even prove himself a daring hunter. If you desire to teach him sweetness and patience, you will find him extremely receptive to being trained."

Arcadipane now observes Pedrelli standing there in front of him: dripping with rain, eyes lowered, short hair, face still lacking in distinction. Exactly as he always had been, except that now both were twenty-seven years older.

"Do you know what I used to say when I went as Bramard's deputy to on-the-spot investigations?"

Pedrelli looks up interrogatively.

"That I was the person responsible," Arcadipane says, extinguishing his cigarette against the sole of his shoe. "When others know you're the person responsible, they pay attention to you."

"Just imagine," Pedrelli grumbles. "That can't be the case . . . When you and I have been putting up with each other all these years."

Arcadipane forces a smile. So what? He looks through one of the container's two little plexiglass windows: just above the line of the mountains, a break is now dancing in the clouds, like a yellow candle in the dark depths of a church.

"Thirty years," he muses.

Thirty years of murders, inquests, competitions, retirements, colleagues, heaps of paper, new arrivals, changes of office, false tracks, reports, sentences, delusions, witnesses, children, the occasional commendation, trials, bouts of bronchitis, newspaper articles, antacids, impressions, blowouts, disciplinary reports, autopsies, interceptions, political quarrels and endless, sleepy, opiate hours of waiting when there's absolutely fuck all you can do except wait.

"Commissario."

The clouds close. Even that single candle at the far end of the church has gone out.

"Commissario?"

The rain is still falling, beating more heavily than ever on the container roof.

"Commissario, sir. The foreman wants to know when they can start work again."

Arcadipane looks at the bones on the grey blanket.

"Tell him to piss off. Now let's you and me go and have some coffee."

3

Once home he goes straight to the kitchen, opens the fridge and drinks a mouthful of fizzy water straight from the bottle. There's a note on the table. "At supper we wanted to discuss something very important, but you didn't come home. Can we talk at breakfast? Very urgent. Loredana and Giovanni."

Arcadipane tries to prop the note back against the fruit basket where he found it, then goes silently to his room, undresses and lies down on his back with his hands behind his head, happy to rest his upper body.

"What's the time?" Mariangela asks, with a half yawn.

"It's already after two."

Without moving, she lays her hand on him.

"You're frozen. You must have been out all day in the rain."

He pulls his legs back a little so as not to touch the big, soft buttocks under her nightie.

"Rain?" he says. "It was twenty degrees, I even caught a bit of sun."

She giggles, making the mattress vibrate. No need to tell her again the story of his 366 on-the-spot investigations . . . she knows all about that.

"What do those two want?" he asks.

"Let's keep that as a surprise for you. But you've had a hot shower, haven't you?"

"No."

"It would help you to relax."

"And where would that leave me?"

She says nothing. It is a big bedroom, not overcrowded with furniture: a four-seasons wardrobe, two not-quite-antique chairs and a chest of drawers. Everything more than twenty years old except the bedside lamps. Bought at IKEA. "We need some lighting with a mobile stem."

"What does that mean?"

"It means I read at night, and you don't."

"If I smell bad, I'll go and have a shower."

She slips a thumb into his pants.

"Not now, you'll make too much noise," she says, grasping his genitals as if to prevent him getting out of bed. "Have you eaten?"

"We were working out of town. I ate on the way back."

"Absolute rubbish, I'm sure."

"A motorway snack bar. The usual thing."

"I left you some . . ."

"Yes, I know, I put it in the fridge. Is all OK here?"

"Everything's fine."

"Then shall we go to sleep now?"

She nods, rubs her head on the pillow and pulls her hand out of his pants. He concentrates on the weak glimmer of the little chain round her neck. As her breath gradually grows slower, a strip of light climbs the sheet and the merino-wool blanket they bought at a demonstration when the children were still small and begins to cross the well-worn parquet as far as the cleft dividing the shutters of the French window. Beyond them are the apartment blocks, cars, signboards and pavements of this neighbourhood, where he has been living since boyhood.

About a year ago, a petition was lodged to double the number of local street lamps for the sake of security. He knew it would achieve nothing, but he signed it all the same. He was reluctant to take the trouble simply because it was his job. "In any case it will lead nowhere," he had told himself.

But within ten months they got forty-five new street lamps. Energy-saving ones that gave a yellow light.

Now, in order to be able to sleep, residents with old-fashioned shutters had to adjust them or replace them with roll-up blinds, at their own expense. Just what he had expected. Some people moved away. Territorial groups began forming in the area: Albanians, Romanians, Nigerians, even Chinese. When you move one piece on the chessboard . . . The only long-established residents who did move were five or six tarts past their first youth, since, with these powerful new street lamps, potential customers now needed no more than a glance to detect the artifice required to draw attention to essential parts of their bodies previously in need of no special support. Of course, they still had affectionate clients who had known them for years, but when you have lost 30 per cent of your income . . . So they were forced to move a little further out, to new, less brutally lit areas. Younger tarts from the east were moving in to take their places. Who wouldn't prefer a window near the centre of town to the suburbs? For them, the new street lights wouldn't be a problem for a good few years.

"Tired?"

"Exhausted."

In a rustle of viscose and cotton, Mariangela turns towards him. She reaches into his pants again and gazes at the stubble on his cheeks, his high forehead and his large south-Italian eyes.

"Why can't you sleep?"

"I don't know."

"Was it nasty today?"

"It's never pretty when they call us out."

"But some occasions must be worse than others."

28

He puts his hand heavily over hers, as if to close her words with a full stop.

"Same as usual," he says, shaking his head.

They study each other's faces a few centimetres apart, half buried in the pillows. The shadow falling on her face helps conceal the passing years; the flesh of her lips is still compact, her eyes are still capable of wildness above a nose more sharp than powerful.

"Was Loredana's light still on when you came in?" she asks.

"I didn't look. Why?"

"She's been studying. Maybe working too hard."

"She chose the classical line, and she has to take it seriously."

"But she should also get out and take more exercise. She's fifteen. The doctor never insisted she score an all-round grade of eight."

"If he had done, we'd be asking him to look at that other genius too."

"Don't be so wicked."

"But you were the one who was angry about it."

"And not you?"

He tries to shrug. Which is not so easy when you're lying down.

"For a policeman to have a son who can't pass his exams is par for the course. But for a teacher . . ."

Mariangela scratches her knee, then puts her hand back inside his pants.

"We should speak to the football coach."

"Why? Hasn't he just had a word with the boy?"

"Giovanni came back from that meeting with such a face I didn't like to ask. I'd just been arguing with Loredana. Now she wants to give up carbohydrates."

"What can I do? Tell the man to come and see me just

because I have a gun? After all, he's the coach. In any case they'll have already made up their minds."

"About what?"

"About who the best players are. They'll be in the squad and the rest will make up the reserves."

"What would that mean?"

"It could mean a quality team and promotion, possibly to Division D."

"But the boy's a good player, isn't he?"

Mariangela's husband holds up two fingers. She looks at him questioningly.

"Is he too small?"

"How do you mean?"

Her eyes continue to question him. Wild black eyes beneath a patina of domesticity.

"The boy's small," Arcadipane says, again holding up two fingers. "At that level physique is important."

She fixes her gaze on a point on his chin. For all he knows, she could be questioning his genes.

"But with guts like his, he can certainly develop into a good player. Maybe even to a professional standard."

"When?"

"How do you mean, when?"

"About the squad and the reserves. When will they tell him?"

"The championship has only just started, there's still time for things to change."

He is aware of an arm moving under the bedclothes. She is shifting her heavy breasts to make herself more comfortable. They have been sagging like udders for several years now. He loves them pressing against his back and shoulders, but only so long as she does not expect him to do anything more active.

"With Giovanni's personality, he could give up football altogether," Mariangela says.

"He'll never do that."

"But what if they set him back another year at school?"

"Why should they?"

"We could bribe him to give up football, to stop playing"

"He won't give it up."

"Why are you so sure?"

"Because he's a pit bull terrier, he'll never give up football."

"I don't like you calling him that."

"That's what his friends call him. He likes it."

"But please don't call him that at home."

"Alright."

"Giovanni's such a nice name."

"Of course." He reaches over to kiss her cheek. "Now go to sleep, you have to get up so early."

She leans over just far enough to accept his kiss, then falls back on her pillow. He puts his hand on her head and keeps it there. Just as well she doesn't have fine bones, or they would have been crushed long ago, after so many years together. But look: there's not even a scratch on her skin.

"It must be five years since I last saw him naked," she says. Having just shut his eyes, he opens them again.

"Who?"

"Giovanni? And you?"

"Why should I see Giovanni naked?"

"But if you're telling me he's small . . ."

"I meant he's short in stature, not that he's small in any other respect."

She scratches the side of her nose and stares at him.

"So we have no idea what that part of him looks like?"

"None at all. In any case, what does it matter?"

31

"I just mean, we're his parents, and we have no idea what he looks like now."

He stares at her. "I expect one day some woman will take an interest in that aspect of him. Now can we go to sleep?"

She shuts her eyes, lifts her chin a fraction, and begins breathing more slowly.

He continues to gaze at her, knowing she's putting the pieces back into the box even though the puzzle isn't yet finished. Piece after piece, before she goes to sleep. A procedure that needs discipline. Which she has, and always has had. Everyone loves her for it. A calm woman, tolerant and extremely disciplined. While he on the other hand has always been a pain in the arse who never knows when to stop, when it's time to put away the pieces of the puzzle and close the box. But she always knows what to do, or if not, she does nothing at all.

"It's not we who pursue our cases," Bramard had said one day, "the cases pursue us." Early one foggy morning they had been eating ham sandwiches outside a food shop that had just raised its blinds.

"Can I ask you something?" Arcadipane now asks Mariangela, without opening his eyes.

The noises their bed made were a code they had themselves created with their own four hands. The result of twenty-eight years' hard work. Now it was the night shift.

"What do you call that plastic bit on the end of your shoelaces? You know, that hard bit of plastic that sometimes snaps off."

"It's called an aglet."

He smiles without putting his hand in front of his mouth, which he would never do by day. His teeth are so ugly. Healthy, but there are just too many of them. Big gnashers carelessly thrust into his jaws. A disaster. Sometimes he thinks he should

32

get a dentist to sort them out, but there seems no point. Time, money and pain. Like trying to hide a heap of rubble behind pretty curtains.

"How on earth do you know that word?"

"It was in a film with Tom Cruise. But how is Corso Bramard these days? Have you seen him recently?"

"No. But what was that film with Tom Cruise?"

"A film for young girls, you wouldn't like it at all. Bramard's living with a new partner and her children now, isn't he?"

"I think so. Why wouldn't I like the film?"

"Because you wouldn't. Can we have them to dinner some evening?"

"They live out in the country."

"They must be accessible by road."

"I don't know. You know how he is. Come on, let's go to sleep now."

He shuts his eyes and listens to her breathing and the ticking of the clock in the kitchen. The one on the dresser which they didn't even bother to change when the clocks went forward "because no-one ever looks at it".

The strip of light between them on the bed is extinguished for a moment as their neighbour's cat walks along the windowsill on his way back from a tour of the apartment block. In a moment he will come in through the flap cut by the Olivero family next door into their French window, and which goes click-clack every time the cat goes in or out. The man's in insurance. Once many years ago he was arrested and taken to what in those days was still known as a centre for faggots, in that age of public decency, obscene acts, and who knows what else. An unbelievable mass of documents was needed just to send the whole lot of them home again the next morning. They'd found the man in bed with a boy everyone knew as "the painter"; when Pedrelli asked him why he was called that, he had said "Would you like to see my brush?" One of those stories people used to tell at colleagues' retirement dinners and their children's marriages and suchlike occasions. Like "Remember that trattoria where they used to serve cat meat?" or "the time a dead man was deposited by the flood on a bench by the embankment?" Until finally there would no longer be anyone left who dated back to that time, and you would even begin to wonder whether such stories had ever been true.

Now he can feel Mariangela's hand caressing his forehead, his closed eyelids, his coarse cheekbones, his primitive jaw and his enormous ears. In fact, his whole crappy old face.

"Vincenzo?"

"Yes?"

"What's the matter?"

"Nothing. Maybe it's what I ate at the motorway grill."

She does not move and says no more. He imagines her searching for the words she needs to use to explore, find out and get to know; but a few seconds later her breathing has slowed to a gentle rhythmical puffing and blowing. When he looks at her, he sees her lips are slightly open. She is asleep.

He slips from under the bedclothes and follows the yellow strip of light to the corridor. The doors of the children's rooms are ajar, their lights off. He goes into the bathroom and, without turning on the light, sits down on the toilet.

The night beyond the window is fragmented by the street lights. No car can be heard, not even a siren.

He leans against the wall, the tiles cold against his head. A sound of flushing from the floor above is the sign that Carlo Merlo is getting ready to go out and open his newsagent's shop.

"Half past three, bloody hell!"

Arcadipane reaches into the washing machine and pulls out his muddy trousers. Fumbling in the pockets he finds one last sticky sucai pastille.

He puts it into his mouth and begins chewing.

4

"Shall I wake him?"

"Not a great idea. Have you picked up your art card in the corridor?"

"You've already asked me that. But why can't I wake him now?"

"Wait till this evening. You can survive that long, can't you?"

"Of course. *Has anyone actually seen him?*"

"It's not as if he's having a good time."

"It's half past seven already. Perhaps he can only rest when he's in bed."

"Have a go, then."

"No. He'd take it badly. Could he be trying to avoid us because of something you said to him?"

"I've said nothing to him!"

"You must have done, stop trying to be clever. What are you laughing at?"

"I don't need you to tell me when I can laugh."

"But you want it too, don't you? Why should I be the only one to make an effort?"

"Why not?"

"He's always like this. When Papà's not here, it's me this and me that, then when something has to be said, the boy sticks his tail between his legs, it's always me . . ."

"Fucking cunt . . ."

"Giovanni, watch your language, you're not on the training ground now."

"That's alright, just let him talk, blah, blah, blah ... he doesn't even know what the words he's using are supposed to mean ... it's not as if they were performing *Jerusalem Delivered* ... the psychological Mongols!"

"Go on, put words in my mouth, tell me I'm not up to it!"

"Now you're starting to exaggerate. And you're late, you need to get a move on."

"Mamma, couldn't you ask him?"

"I've already said what I think."

"That's not thinking."

"Why not, it's what Switzerland always does, and see how well they're doing. No, don't chuck that in with the plastic, can't you see it's a tetra pak?"

"I'm going to wake him up."

"It's getting late now. But you could phone him during the day, if you like."

"On the telephone?"

"Why not? You do everything on the telephone."

"Yes, but he'll just say he's busy and ring off."

"He may really be busy, have you ever thought of that?"

"Mamma, where are my shin pads?"

"On the radiator, are you packing your bag already?"

"I'm going to Andrea's today, there's training at six."

"Can you give me a lift to school?"

"Psychomongols can't drive, didn't you know that?"

"Please. I was just joking."

"The scooter's out of order."

"Of course, what a coincidence. I'm off now."

The door slams.

"You could have given her a lift, couldn't you?"

"How could I do that if my scooter's out of order?"

"Then you'll be late yourself."

"Yes, yes, I'm off now. In fact, I can probably catch the twenty-six. Though it only passes when it feels like it."

"If I had to be there at seven fifteen, don't you think I'd be there in time?"

"Just relax, Madonna! What's got into you this morning?"

The door slams again. The sound of the coffee machine is followed by the silence of a woman drinking. Then coffee cup into dishwasher and heels going down the corridor. Door opening. Silence.

"In any case, I know you're not really asleep."

"Uh-huh."

"But this evening try and stay in, OK?"

"Yes, yes."

Sounds of steps receding, keys, a door shutting.

Arcadipane pushes the bedclothes back from his chin, takes off his socks, throws them in the laundry basket, then takes clean ones decorated with diamonds from a drawer and puts them on.

He walks down the corridor in his vest and pants holding his mobile phone. The kitchen is tidy. Mariangela does not like to go out leaving crumbs on the tablecloth.

He looks in the kitchen cupboard for his moka coffee pot. Instead of finishing to dress while the coffee is heating, he stares at the horrendous jigsaw with the missing piece that Loredana ate when she was two years old. They put a frame round it as a joke. And Mariangela has always said, "Anyone who eats in our kitchen will know us well enough to understand."

The moka machine rumbles. Arcadipane lets it continue because he likes the noise . . . Then his mobile squeals.

"Yes, Pedrelli, what is it?"

"Sorry to ring so early, commissario, but they've phoned from the dig to say they've found more bones."

"Tell them to put them in a box, and send someone to fetch them."

"Yes, commissario, but it seems there's an awful lot of them."

"What do you mean, an awful lot?"

"The foreman says more skulls."

Arcadipane is silent. The shutters are open. The day outside is nothing like yesterday. No sun, but a high sky and perfect weather.

"Then send Lavezzi and Mario to fetch me. Meanwhile, you go there with three men, tell them to stop digging and isolate everything. I want the photographer too. And warn Sarace."

"I've just called him. He'll come as soon as his hairdresser has finished with him."

Arcadipane rings off and reaches down to scratch an itching testicle.

This reminds him that Lavezzi says there's a technique from Thailand in which they yank on your balls: it hurts like hell but afterwards feels like heaven. Underpants and tight trousers can cramp your bollocks, and apparently yanking them helps to . . . But you have to be careful, Lavezzi says . . . because there's only two places in the city where they know how to do this properly; everywhere else it's just "bollocks", as Lavezzi puts it, and you risk ending up in A & E with something you won't find easy to explain.

Arcadipane pours his coffee and pulls his hand out of his pants to scratch his beard.

5

The day before, with all the rain, it had not been easy to find the place.

Leaving the village, which was the closest reference Pedrelli had been able to give him on the phone, he had gone down a couple of cart tracks that led to farms where an old man had threatened to set the carabinieri on to him and a young lad had meaninglessly waved a newspaper in his face. How he finally got to the right place, he would have been unable to say. On the other hand, while touring the fields in the rain, he had been haunted by the memory of the last time he and Mariangela had enjoyed screwing each other. A sudden painful thought forced him to pull over for a few minutes to eat a couple of sucai lozenges before setting off again.

"Turn right," he now directs Lavezzi, recognising a trattoria among a clump of houses.

Lavezzi turns right. A young man of few words and little education, but far from stupid. He keeps five or six smurfs on his desk, changing them once a month, unexpected in one who lives behind his parents' bakery and is an assiduous frequenter of prostitutes. Contradictions that make him an able and by no means disagreeable policeman. Especially because he does so little talking.

On the other hand, Mario, sitting behind him, is old enough to remember the Po when people still bathed from the sandbanks below Piazza Vittorio.

Mario is also the only one in the car today who has actually shot anyone – a Prima Linea Marxist terrorist, during an armed robbery back in the seventies. The man had been firing at random with a sub-machine gun. They transferred Mario for a few years to a small town in central Italy to save him from becoming a target. As soon as he came back to Torino, he got straight back to work without boring everyone to death with "the time when I . . ." or "what can any of you lot know who have never . . ." Now he keeps quiet and lets his white hair do the talking. Safe in the knowledge, of course, that those who never saw the sandbanks in those days are from another race: they would never understand.

"Turn here, then straight on," Arcadipane says.

Lavezzi takes the cart track. The car threatens to fall apart because the narrow unpaved road is thick with mud and these new Fiats are a very poor replacement for the old Alfas. Lavezzi slows down and holds the car firmly to the track. Running alongside them is an irrigation trench. None of the three has the least inclination to have to be towed.

The top of the crane appears in the distance, then the bucket of the bulldozer, seven or eight cars, and the container where Sarace had put the bones.

"It's clear we aren't the only ones here," Lavezzi says.

Arcadipane recognises a Land Rover that belongs to a journalist from a Torino newspaper. An innocuous bore. Someone who does too much thinking when he would do better printing the first thing that comes into his head. If you have a dirty cellar, best not to keep your salami there too long.

They stop in the muddy area that is now used as a parking space. There is also a blue van of the sort used as a hearse, the foreman's pickup and three or four marked police cars.

"Let's find out which way the wind is blowing," Arcadipane says.

They get out and head for the yard, where some twenty people are scattered about. Arcadipane has on the same jacket as yesterday, left to dry overnight on the radiator, but not his wet shoes. He's wearing moccasins, having nothing else available.

As he heads for what seems to be the heart of the action, he notices two men talking and smoking with Nicolae and Roman, the Romanian cousins. All four seem to be hugely enjoying themselves.

"Commissario!" Pedrelli is approaching.

Arcadipane stops to wait for him. Mario and Lavezzi stop too, but stand a little to one side.

"I tried to get you on the phone, but there was no answer." Pedrelli shakes his head. "As far as I can make out, everything will go with the people from Milano."

Arcadipane looks round himself. It's like the end of a birthday party, with the dirty plates still on the table together with a tray carrying a couple of fritters that the children have fingered and no-one wants because the cake tasted better.

"What people from Milano?"

Pedrelli indicates a tall guy, whose thick hair is too long, directing three men in white overalls who are working in a large pit that was not there the day before. They have attaché cases, a small flag or two, and some stretchers and large metal boxes.

"That's Commissario Nascimbene," says Pedrelli. "He and his men specialise in this kind of thing."

Arcadipane notices the foreman Coletto not far off talking nineteen to the dozen to the journalist he noticed earlier. A meeting of minds. Lighting a cigarette, he goes to a white tent where the man with too much hair is directing the orchestra.

"Nascimbene," the man introduces himself. "Excuse me for not getting in touch with you before, but it's like a battle at sea.

You have a rough picture of the enemy, but until they start firing at you, you have no idea what you're up against."

Arcadipane briefly returns the man's handshake and studies the pit where the three technicians are scratching about with their heads bowed. Not a particularly deep pit, but wider than it was yesterday.

"What have you found?"

Nascimbene has shoulders like clothes hangers and large teeth. A beanpole of a man who enjoys tennis and will keep his decent figure into old age. He contemplates the dig with no great satisfaction.

"Ten or a dozen skeletons," he says. "We've widened the excavation by some six metres and found nothing else. Normally that would mean that there is nothing else."

He pulls a packet of chewing gum from the pocket of his trench coat and offers it to Arcadipane, who indicates no thank you, he is smoking. Nascimbene unwraps a piece of gum and puts it into his own mouth.

"You'll never believe how much there often is to find." He shakes his head. "Only last year we came across five lots. With one exception, all stuff from the war."

"And the exception?"

"That was in a small village near Verona." He scratches himself above the eye with his chewing gum packet. "The carabinieri called us in because they had found some bones in a field. We dug up twenty-five skeletons, many of them with crucifixes round their necks. See that man in boots?" He points to one of the three in white overalls. "He's dug out sites the size of football pitches in Bosnia. With two hundred, even three hundred corpses. It was he who explained that this lot were monks. 'What do you mean, monks?' I asked him. 'With all these bricks lying around,' he said, 'there must have been a monastery here, or something of that kind.' 'Quite likely,' I told him. 'Let's just put it all back and go home.' Then last week the doctor responsible for the official analysis told me: 'The crosses date back to the Middle Ages. And so do the bones. It must be the crypt of some old abbey no-one even knew existed.'"

Nascimbene puts the packet of chewing gum back into his pocket.

"That's a one-in-a-million example, though. Otherwise, it's usually partisans and fascists, accounts settled during or after the war. Some old man still alive around here probably knows who these people are and who killed them, but so far no-one has said anything . . . And even if they do discover something, how can you start legal proceedings against the dead? Or elderly survivors living their last days in a hospice? Or even identify everything from a scientific medical-legal point of view; just imagine the mountain of paperwork that would involve . . ."

Arcadipane thinks about this. Nascimbene smiles.

"Satisfied?"

Arcadipane shakes his head; there is something he doesn't understand.

"Well, at least we've set your mind at rest!" Nascimbene scratches a beardless patch on his cheek, perhaps the scar from an old burn. "Just think if you'd been forced to open a file."

Arcadipane treads his cigarette into the mud and looks up at the high-speed tracks, where for the moment no train is passing. Beyond the embankment, now that the mist has cleared, the tops of lorries can be seen passing on the autostrada.

"Is that where the bones are now?" He nods towards the white tent behind them.

Nascimbene shakes his head. "No, they're already in the van. No point in worrying about it now. We'll wrap the lot up and take them away. Then we can examine them at leisure and see whether anything else is involved. So long as you have nothing against it, I'll also release the whole site now. The director's impatient to get on with his work. Sorry if I was responsible for you coming all the way out here for nothing, but it's always best to talk face to face, don't you think?"

Arcadipane unenthusiastically shakes the hand Nascimbene holds out to him.

"Oh, I was forgetting one thing," Nascimbene says. "Can you also send on to us the bones that were found yesterday? I left the address with your assistant. No particular reason, but . . . for the sake of completeness! We don't want you having to hang on to someone's leg when we've got the head . . ."

Arcadipane does not smile.

"OK," he says.

Turning towards his own men, he indicates they can go back to their cars now. All move off except Pedrelli, who waits for him.

"Shall I tell Sarace we won't be needing him?" Pedrelli says.

Arcadipane nods and takes a few steps, then suddenly turns towards the blue van. The police officer guarding its closed doors is talking on his phone. Probably to some girl since he is swinging about and patting his hair.

"Well?" The man looks first at Arcadipane, then at Pedrelli. He has never seen either of them before.

"You're supposed to be on duty," Arcadipane tells him. "What the fuck do you mean by chatting on your phone?"

The policeman takes his mobile from his ear and slips it into his pocket, without taking his eye off the two others. A young man with a fresh face.

"The bones are in this van, aren't they? We'd like to take a look."

The policeman slowly opens the van door.

45

Inside are about twenty open metal boxes, each around thirty centimetres high. The bones in the boxes have been divided into legs and arms and so on. Arcadipane heads for the box of skulls. He counts them quickly. There seem to be eleven or twelve.

"OK, you can close the van again now."

Arcadipane starts back towards the cars without glancing at the dig from where he knows Nascimbene is watching him.

"Hello?" The journalist intercepts him. "What can you tell me?"

"What do you expect me to tell you? It's nothing to do with us."

They walk side by side for a moment. The journalist smells of deodorant. Arcadipane himself has forgotten to put any on. Who knows what he smells of now?

"Come on, you must be able to tell me something!"

Arcadipane glances over at the two plain-clothes men still laughing and joking with the Romanians.

"Go over and talk to them." He indicates them with his chin. "Not the labourers, the other two. They know everything."

"Really?"

"Absolutely."

The journalist moves away. Reaching the cars, Arcadipane gets into the Fiat where Lavezzi and Mario are waiting. Lavezzi starts the engine. He could have said "Quite a trip today", or "A morning completely wasted", but in fact he drives on in silence because he loves prostitutes but has few words. As for Mario, everyone knows he saw those sandbanks . . .

Arcadipane dials the number of his office.

"Put me through to Alessandra," he says as a message to whoever will eventually take the call, no matter who it may turn out to be.

He waits, staring at the car on the embankment in front of him: a crappy Peugeot driven by Pedrelli with his narrow head.

"Yes?"

"Alessandra? Arcadipane here."

"Good morning,"

"Listen. Those bones they brought in yesterday. Have you had time to look at them?"

"The box is here, but I haven't opened it yet. They said it wasn't urgent."

"OK. But have a look."

"What exactly do you want to know?"

"I'm not quite sure."

"Then I'll start with the basics."

"Always the best place to start. I'll pass by about six."

"I don't know if I'll have had time by then . . ."

Arcadipane rings off, puts his phone back in his pocket and adjusts the car's temperature. They are still in their jackets and the sun has been beating down on the car for the last half hour.

"Do you know what we were saying earlier?" Surprisingly, it is Lavezzi speaking.

"No."

Lavezzi turns to Mario.

"That there's a singer called Mario Lavezzi." He smiles.

Arcadipane fixes his eyes on the road.

"With big teeth," adds Mario from the back.

Arcadipane lights a cigarette and lowers his window a finger's breadth.

"Pity this is such a short journey. Your conversation is so stimulating."

47

6

He knows this area. Solicitors, directors, gynaecologists, insurance agents, dentists, well-off families with unearned incomes and lots of property; subsidiaries of big companies, possibly something shady about them though nothing extreme. He knows this from the wooden front doors with their brass bells and permanent nameplates.

Above a certain financial level, allowing for the passing of time, nothing is merely provisional. While below that level, everything is provisional, and you get used to that.

The building he has to find turns out to be an impressive one. No stucco or beaten ironwork unlike those near it. Everything about it is heavy and grey. Marble pillars and windowsills, concrete banisters, handrails and railings, grotesque human faces above the windows.

He checks the time: five minutes to four. The street is still clear. Not many pedestrians, most of them obviously students. The polytechnic is not far off. Some of the students look Chinese and there's a college a couple of blocks away. "Bloody hell!" He puts a sucai in his mouth and throws away his cigarette because the mingled taste of tobacco and liquorice is disgusting. On the glass front door of the building is a would-be-artistic metal plaque. Most of the bells just have numbers without names or words suggesting "surgery" or anything like that.

It has started raining again. Just lightly. No sign of it on the pavement yet, but you can begin to see it on the windscreens of parked cars.

Beyond the front door a figure crosses the entrance hall from right to left: a man the same height as Arcadipane and just as compactly built, and who walks in almost the same way. It's almost as if Arcadipane is watching himself reflected in the glass. Reaching the wall, the man turns and goes back the other way, pushing a broom.

Arcadipane knocks. The man, in overall and slippers, comes to the door.

"Who are you looking for?"

He speaks with an indefinite country accent. He has black bushy brows and white hair that sticks out in all directions.

"Doctor Ariel," says Arcadipane.

The man gives him a stare.

"Top floor."

No sooner has Arcadipane been admitted than the man disappears through a side door from which emerge the sound of a transistor radio and a crash of crockery.

The lift proves to be locked. "Bloody hell," Arcadipane grumbles, starting up the stairs.

On the first floor a dentist's and an apartment, on the second an apartment and an insurance firm, and from then on apparently no further commercial premises.

Reaching the top, Arcadipane undoes two buttons on his jacket and takes a deep breath. The corridor before him is weakly lit by a photoelectric cell. One door is marked by the name "Ariel" on a sheet of paper.

He knocks.

"Come in."

49

He finds a small flat with three internal doors under a mansard roof. The closed door could be a bathroom, and the half-closed one possibly a bedroom. Through the third door, in a sort of small living room, a woman is sitting with her back to him, her brown hair spread over the back of her armchair. Opposite her is another similar armchair, and there is also a low table between the two chairs, and a bookcase.

"If you'd like some tea, help yourself," the woman says without turning.

Against the wall on the right on a low piece of furniture he sees a kettle, two electrically heated plates, and three non-identical cups.

"If you don't want tea, please sit down and we'll start."

Arcadipane walks round the woman's chair, across a long-haired carpet, and sits down. The deal chair swings briefly under his weight, then quickly settles. The only light in the room comes from the curtainless window facing him. The hillside beyond the window is like a carapace secreted by the city from its glands. Arcadipane is physically aware of this but would not have known words like carapace and secreted.

"We shall meet five times," the woman begins. "Three times this week and twice next week. That might not seem much to you, but things either work or they don't, at least that's what I've always believed. Don't you agree?"

Arcadipane nods, his eyes fixed on the window, though aware that the woman has lifted a cup from the table between the two chairs and taken a sip.

"I expect you know that king penguins choose their partner at first sight. They stay faithful for life and if one of the two dies its partner falls into a kind of catalepsy until a killer whale or polar bear swallows it. But in our case, I shall give you assignments to do between one meeting and the next. You will be free to do them or not, as you please. Payment and any problems will be up to you. Is there anything you want to ask?"

"How much do you charge?"

"You don't beat about the bush, do you? A hundred euros for each session."

"A hundred euros."

"I know that seems a lot, but I've decided I need to be well paid for what I do. In any case, if the course works it will be money well spent from your point of view, and if not, you'll just have yet another reason to complain. Agreed?"

"Alright, what must I do?"

"To begin with, don't ask silly questions like that. You may be embarrassed, but remember you're not a child. This is the plan: today I'll do the talking, and next time you'll do the talking. After that we'll see. Now listen, and only stop me if anything I say is not right."

He is aware of the woman putting her cup down on the table.

"You are fifty years old."

"Forty-nine."

"Don't be so pedantic. If I were a fortune teller, you would be paying much more. You are forty-nine years old, and till now you have always controlled your life without finding a great deal to say about it. Those who live differently annoy you, people who talk loudly in church or make long confessional phone calls to their friends. People who have not grasped the fact that there is only one thing to understand: that life is what you see, or at the most what you do. Nothing more exists than that."

She pauses, as if to see whether he has taken in what she is saying. Arcadipane says nothing.

She goes on. "So people condemn you as insensitive, coarse, rough and egoistical, a sort of wild man who has been given clothes to wear and taught how to press buttons on a telephone.

I allow myself to say this because I'm sure you have always criticised yourself for being ignorant. You know this perfectly well and what has caused it, just as you know the origins of your own body and face. I have watched the children of the rich in Piazza Bodoni. Kids of sixteen and seventeen whose curly hair seems specially designed, physically well proportioned, with perfect teeth, symmetrical faces and amber-coloured skin. Anthropological evidence, even if no-one would ever dream of putting it in those exact words. Evidence of the cruel truth: that anyone beautiful but poor can mate with someone rich in an exchange of genes, just as someone rich but ugly can mate with someone beautiful who needs money. Thus, those who are beautiful and rich in the long run can make lots of money. Merely because they happen to be rich as well as beautiful.

"But as for you, what you see when you look in the mirror each morning is something quite different. What you see is that century after century the poor and ugly couple with others who are also poor and ugly. Look a little lower down and something else is written in very small letters; look closely and you can read, 'And they were ignorant too, every one of them'. But you didn't come here for comfort. You did what was within your range: you managed to snare a wife more beautiful and better educated than yourself, got a qualification and fathered children who will raise the status of your family. How many children have you got? Three, four?"

"Two, of . . ."

"No matter . . . They are bound to be better looking than you are and better educated, and will probably be richer and happier too. Most men of your generation and with your background end up overcome by depression, victimisation, violence, alcoholism, mysticism, coprophagy, dementia or some other form .

of dependence. Even if you spend twenty minutes in front of a gambling den; I'm sure you know what I'm talking about. You have not fallen into any of these traps for three reasons: you have higher-than-average intelligence, you have found an occupation that suits you, and you possess shining*. Do you know what shining is?"

"No."

"Do you understand Piedmontese dialect? Have you ever heard of *gheddu*? To have *gheddu*?"

"No."

The woman reaches to the table beside her and takes a couple more sips from her cup. Even though she has not stopped speaking for ten minutes her breathing remains regular and her voice steady, showing no trace of anxiety or exhaustion. Without looking at her, Arcadipane hears the tinkle of her cup presumably touching what must be a button or a belt as she lowers it again.

"You realise that bottled water together with grubs for fishing, ice cream and cocaine are the main elements that bring primary material to the consumer? I have thought a lot about it and am sure that I am getting close to something really big. Yes, sir. You love your work even though it's exhausting and it damages you. It functions as your teddy bear, like a blanket when you sleep. It can comfort you with both erections and cuddles. Like vaccinating yourself with a little bit of typhus to avoid catching something much worse. Which brings us to the point."

---

* In Italy, the word "shining" is known from the films of Kubrick, in which it is translated as "*luciccanza*", meaning intuition, or the ability to see things that escape others; Ariel uses the word as an equivalent of the Piedmontese word "*gheddu*", which has no real Italian counterpart, but means knowing how to survive in any situation, or having practical and inventive intelligence.

He imagines he hears the woman stretch her neck, or it may have been something else that squeaked.

"Your problem began a year and a half ago? Or was it two years? To begin with you took no notice though it's something that can kill people like you. But it got progressively worse. You will have noticed that your sense of humour was no longer shielding you. Holes appeared that needed to be stitched up to repair them. Finally, even your work began to suffer: things escaped you, you no longer managed to focus as you did before, and worse still, even when you do focus, your work no longer speaks to you, and even if it does say something it no longer interests you. Your shining is extinguished, or at the very least overshadowed. Not that anyone has complained; the problem is not with others, it is you yourself who can't accept the fact that you are losing your grip. But do you know what the most amusing aspect of this is? That even this is not the real reason why you are here."

"No?"

The woman reaches for the kettle and pours a little hot water into her cup. Arcadipane detects the smell of marijuana.

"You are not a person who would ever do anything so humiliating as to come here because your life was going to pieces, which leaves three alternatives: either you can't get an erection anymore, or you're having panic attacks, or uncontrollable fits of weeping."

"I don't get panic attacks," Arcadipane answers with a confidence that must register with her.

"Which leaves alternatives one and three. With your wife, presumably."

"With my wife what?"

"I expect you've been having problems screwing your wife?"

"Yes."

"In what way has it been going wrong?"

"How do you mean?"

"How does your wife explain it: too tired, migraine, overwork, midlife crisis. Either way, I'm sure she assumes there's another woman. They always assume that, you know?"

"There is no other woman."

"Pity. It would do you good to find out whether having sex with someone else would help. At least then we'd have some idea what we're talking about. Why not try a prostitute? I imagine, in your job, that would cost you less than coming to see me. What do you say, do you feel up to it?"

Arcadipane reaches into his pocket, impelled by the urge to put a sucai into his mouth.

"And what effect does the other thing have?"

"What other thing?"

"When you feel a need to weep. What effect does that have? Can you show me?"

Arcadipane, without turning to look at her, stretches out his hand to show the sucai lozenge on his open palm.

"I thought they didn't make those things anymore."

"There's a grocery store where . . ."

"No matter. Have you talked to your wife?"

"What about?"

"About your instrument going on strike."

"No."

"Quite right. It would be pathetic, and it's nothing she doesn't already know. Most varieties of Viagra are made from the guano of seabirds, you know. The better ones contain other natural substances, but mostly . . . There are some people who haven't screwed anyone for a lifetime and occasionally that makes them weep, even though for them it's not a tragedy that trying to overcome the problem never produces results. Sure you wouldn't like some tea?"

"No, thank you, maybe a coffee."

"Coffee? That would be like bringing sharp knives into a kindergarten. Now listen to me. We're getting near the end of our session, and you need to remember what I'm telling you. This summer I went to the seaside, to a place where you had to go down a lot of steps to reach a couple of square metres of dirty sand crowded with people. It was pointless, but I was the guest of friends with a small girl. A child neither pretty nor pleasant. One day they asked me if I could look after her for five minutes while they went off to a snack bar on the beach for a coffee. I agreed, because I realised how hard it must be even for the parents to have such a child on their hands all day long . . . So I took the girl down to the water's edge, taking care to protect her from being overwhelmed by small boys. About ten metres away there was a man of about sixty, a Nordic type, with white hair but a still-athletic figure. He was crouching at the edge of the sea trying to build a tower with four large stones entirely different from each other in shape. It would have been clear to anyone that four such stones could never make a tower. 'Utter nonsense even to try,' I told myself. Then the child Camilla called to me: she wanted to go a little further out to play in the waves. So we did that. Then one of the small boys started throwing wet sand. 'Hey,' I shouted at him. 'Move a bit further away.' When I turned, I saw the stones had actually been balanced in a remarkable achievement of weight and counterweight. One or two stuck out as if on the point of falling over but the construction stayed firm even when waves struck it. I looked for the Nordic builder and saw that he was now bathing with some adolescent girls as if he had never achieved anything at all. 'Life has taught you something, Ariel,' I told myself. 'Wonderful.'"

She drank.

"Is that the end of the story?"

"No, not at all. I just need a moment to catch my breath."
She drank some more.

"Then I turned back to Camilla. After a while I looked again and saw there were two Filipino boys, a big one and a small one, throwing handfuls of sand at the balancing stones. I looked for their parents and saw they were a short distance away, smoking and watching the boys but saying nothing. At that moment the unlikely tower fell. The parents continued smoking; it meant nothing whatever to them. 'There, Ariel,' I told myself. 'Now life has taught you another lesson. Horrible.'"

"In fact . . ."

"Don't interrupt! My friends came back. We sat down and began chatting. 'Now I'll tell you about the tower,' I thought, but when I turned to point it out what I saw was the two small boys crouching with their fathers and uncles and trying to rebuild what they had just knocked down. They discussed it, experimented, and offered reasons. 'In just a short time, Ariel,' I told myself, 'you have been forced to change your mind three times and you have been surprised three times.'"

Silence reigns in the room. Arcadipane wonders whether to turn and look at the woman but at that moment he is distracted by shreds of fog forming over the hills he can see through the window, almost fluorescent in the fading light.

"On Thursday I shall want you to tell me a story about when you were a child or young boy. Perhaps the last time you broke down in tears. A nice twist of the heart! And you must make your story last the full hour, because I shall say nothing. At three thirty."

Arcadipane gets up, takes his wallet from his pocket and opens it.

"Leave the money in the little bag near the door and open the

57

window a little before you leave. I've certainly earned it today! My armpits are all sweaty."

Out in the street he finds the same light drizzle as when he arrived. For no apparent reason he feels exhausted and wishes he could lie down. Across the road there is a bar, apparently a rather elegant one. There are no traffic lights or marked pedestrian crossing, so he holds up a hand to protect himself as he crosses the road. In the bar, he sits down at the table nearest the window and orders a double espresso and a slice of cake. As he bites into the cake it occurs to him that he has not the least idea what the woman looks like. Is she fifty or seventy? Does she have a long face or a square one? Is she fat or slim, light-skinned or southern? Was she wearing a wedding ring? Trousers or a dress? Firm little tits sticking up or great loose boobs spreading over her belly? He was with her an hour. A hundred euros! And he knows nothing whatever about her. "Bloody hell!"

A moment later he has fallen asleep with his chin on his chest, and a trickle of saliva dripping onto the fine sheepskin jacket his in-laws gave him.

7

He drives into the courtyard and looks for a free corner to park the Alfa.

Some of his people, just arrived, are gabbling at the exit at the back of the old four-storey buildings that form the police headquarters. One is having a stretch, one is throwing away a cigarette end, and one is already stowing holster and gun in the glove compartment of his car.

Arcadipane is familiar with their quick movements, and the lazy way they discuss anything inessential.

Quite different from when they come back after making an arrest, or from a raid that is the climax of months of investigation, or from a shoot-out. Though even then they would hang about the courtyard leaning on their cars and smoking, but their words would be few and far between. Mostly they would simply stare at each other.

Like resting your weight on your woman after making love, he reflected. You both know that sooner or later one or the other must move and the returning world must draw you apart. But you both prolong the moment, as if building a trench round yourselves. Then finally one of you slithers to one side, or forces the other to, letting the rest of the world back in. Bloody hell!

Arcadipane searches his pocket for one of the sucai lozenges he bought loose that morning while Lavezzi and Mario waited for him in the street with the engine running. He chews it as he moves towards the door.

In the entrance hall he is hit by the unhealthy heat characteristic of all public buildings: central heating on full blast, emphasising the smell of old furniture and inadequate cleaning. Going down to the basement he passes familiar faces, responding minimally to their greetings. In the gents he struggles to pee into a urinal. His short, thick penis makes him think of a potato forgotten amongst the embers of a fire. Then he shakes it and cradles his balls in his hand, like a purse weighed down by a few fifty-cent coins. Bloody hell!

Someone else come in. He turns to see Pedrelli at a basin emptying a packet into a small glass.

"Antacid. Would you like some?"

Arcadipane shakes his head. "My stomach's the only part of me still in good order." He washes his hands in the other basin and throws a little water over his face.

"If you have no further need of me, I . . ." Pedrelli begins, putting away his glass.

"That's fine, you can go, I'm just going in to see Alessandra for a minute, then I shall be off too."

He waits for Pedrelli's footsteps to die away, then goes to the door. He's in the corridor when his mobile rings.

"Hello."

"Arcadipane? Nascimbene here."

He does not respond.

"Nascimbene. You remember. This morning. The trench."

"Yes. What is it?"

"Tomorrow one of my men will be in Torino to give evidence in court. He could pick up the packet of bones while he's there. That'll speed things up, what do you think? Name of Capello. I've told him to ask for you by name, OK?"

"I'll make sure they get it ready."

"Thanks, have a good day."

"I will."

Arcadipane puts his mobile back in his pocket and knocks at the lab. No answer. He puts his ear to the door. No sound from inside. He goes in.

During his lifetime he has been into seven or eight laboratories. They are all alike, or if they don't all look the same, at least they have the same smell. Not disinfectant or anything worse, as you might suppose, but a smell of ironmongery: screws, nuts, bolts and new equipment that perhaps in many cases has never yet been used. Clean, as smells go, even if not necessarily to everyone's taste. It probably comes mainly from the furniture and the machines, even though laboratories with ancient machines and furniture smell exactly the same. The secret is not to waste time thinking about it, and to save any guesswork for a time when it might come in useful. In other words, very seldom.

There is no-one in the room, but the neon lights are on, and an extractor is running above a small glass basin. An almost inaudible drip. The liquid inside the container is blue.

Arcadipane notices that the bones have been laid out on a small table in the middle of the room, just like in the container at the yard, except that whoever did it this time does know where Andorra and Liechtenstein go. The bones seem to be shinier than they were before. Perhaps someone has washed them, or at least wiped them with a rag.

"So, we meet again," he tells the bones.

The skull stares back in silence, the great cavities for its eyes lit by a reflection from the metal surface of the table. Arcadipane clasps his hands behind his back and walks round the lab: a computer, test tubes, a "heater" for prints, a refrigerator, microscopes, bookshelves, books and a writing desk. On the desk, among heaped papers, are two photographs. In one Alessandra Sabatini is with a bald man of about seventy in glasses, who is wearing what looks like a bowling shirt. In the other she is on a beach holding a plump small girl. All on the beach apart from Alessandra and the little girl are in bathing costumes.

"Her niece," Arcadipane speculates, "or the child of a friend."

Apart from the fact that she is not married and presumably has no children, all he knows of Alessandra is that at the end of her day's work, she gets into an olive-coloured Ford Fiesta and heads for the ring road with her radio tuned to the LatteMiele pop-music station. He imagines she must live in Alpignano, Caselette or Brandizzo, one of those suburbs where no-one knows their neighbours. An attic flat or a two-room ground-floor apartment. No dogs, that would be too much trouble. A cat at most. Her evenings would be no problem. She finishes work late, and he imagines her heating food for herself and eating it in front of the TV. But he can't imagine her weekends at all. Probably she reads and goes for walks and disentangles string for her cat.

While Arcadipane is studying a poster above the desk advertising a concert by a rock group called Nomads, Alessandra opens the door behind him.

"I thought this lot must all be dead by now," he says against the muffled hum of the extractor, pointing to the five musicians on the poster.

"The only one left of the original line-up is Beppe," Alessandra says. "The others came in later."

"Which is Beppe?"

"The one in the middle."

Arcadipane examines Beppe, who resembles the more famous pop singer and entertainer Gianni Morandi. Alessandra's trainers squeak on the green rubber floor as she moves a trolley.

"He looks the youngest."

62

"It's his hair," she says. "He's actually sixty-two now."

Arcadipane shakes his head to show he would never have guessed it. He turns to look at Alessandra, who is standing near the table with the bones, as always in the same shirt and shapeless jeans. She is studying a black exercise book, her leather waistcoat identical to the one Beppe is wearing on the poster.

"Have the bones told you anything?"

"Just possibly," she says, her eyes still on the exercise book.

Arcadipane goes nearer. Alessandra continues reading. She has the poor skin of an adolescent and the thinning hair of an old woman. She probably cannot do much about either, but gives the impression she could if she took the trouble.

"Shall we start with what I am certain of?" she says.

"Let's do that."

Alessandra puts down the exercise book and moves to the short side of the table.

"The pelvis is masculine, and the forehead and jaw suggest Caucasian race. The femur is a long one. Based on the table of comparison I use, that of Trotter and Gleser, his height must have been between one eighty-five and one ninety. Other tables may add or subtract a centimetre or two, but that is more or less where we are."

"Tall," Arcadipane summarises, unable to take his eyes off the little rolls of fat on Alessandra's neck.

"The extremity by the breastbone," she indicates the collarbone, "is usually completely formed by about the age of twenty-five. Here this is not quite the case, so I would put his age at between twenty and twenty-five. The coronal suture, which crosses the skull, is in fact still visible, so he was certainly under thirty."

"Under thirty."

"Yes, but we must listen to Sarace. He's the forensic

63

pathologist. I'm merely a chemist, even if I do have a master's degree in osteology."

"Osteology . . ." repeats Arcadipane, running a finger over the skeleton.

"Yes, I've always been interested in bones."

"You have always been interested in bones. Why?"

Alessandra gives him a sharp look to see if he is being serious, then takes off her latex gloves, goes to the desk, opens a drawer and takes out a book. She props it up on a corner of the table, not far from the cranium. Arcadipane studies the book's white cover.

"Bin Bass," he reads.

Alessandra moves the book a centimetre or so closer to herself, perhaps just because he mispronounced the name.

"In the eighties he got the University of Tennessee to give him a hectare of land and started placing cadavers there to discover what happened when they decomposed in different conditions: among leaves, under the earth, in sand, in the boot of a car, in the sun, in snow, in water, sprinkled with lime or wrapped in plastic. In this way he was able to help the police solve hundreds of cases. When I was in the States, I wrote to the university secretary asking to see this. He is considered the greatest forensic pathologist in the world. He had no reason to give a damn about me; after all, I was a mere nobody. But even so . . ." She indicates the desk.

Arcadipane turns to look at the photo of the man in the overalls, his face as jovial as the manager of a retirement home. When he turns back Alessandra is staring at a few lines written in ink on the first page of the book.

"To my Italian groupie," she reads, "or rather, to my friend and brilliant colleague."

Arcadipane studies her smile. It seems to have become the smile of a younger woman, slimmer and more beautiful. Which could be a good thing, if it were not for the fact that this woman is still imprisoned in Alessandra's body.

"The people from Milano are convinced that this skeleton dates from the war." Arcadipane nods at it. "What would your American doctor say?"

Alessandra closes the book and shuts off her smile.

"We have no fragments of skin or hair, so we're dealing with bones that have been buried for decades. But as Bill would say, with bones it's easy to make serious mistakes, so one should never jump to premature conclusions without testing for carbon or at the very least for fluorine and nitrogen."

"What can you do?"

"Nothing. It would require a specialised laboratory and patience."

"How much patience?"

"A few weeks. So long as they are prepared to authorise it. It'll be rather expensive."

Arcadipane runs his finger along the edge of the table. Cold and smooth. He contemplates the bones. They look less like pistachio now. More like parchment. Like the curtains in his bedroom.

"What have you been writing there?" he asks, indicating the pages of the black exercise book, crowded with sloping hand-writing.

"Nothing." Alessandra shrugs. "Just a few notes."

Arcadipane leans his head to one side.

"Imagine we're in a bar. Off duty."

Alessandra gives him a diffident look.

"I'm only guessing."

"Guessing." Arcadipane echoes her. "Imagine an off-duty chat."

She hesitates for a moment, then takes a pen from the pocket of her waistcoat and points at the middle of the right thigh bone.

"There's an old fracture at this point. Bearing in mind the degree of calcification, the fracture can have no connection with his death, but at the sides there are some little nicks, see?"

Arcadipane stoops to get a better look.

"Little holes."

"At regular distances, as if caused by the screws for a metal plate."

"A plate?"

"A plate for the surgical reduction of a fracture. If the subject died not long after the operation to remove the plate, this would all make sense: fracture healed, the holes made by the screws not yet completely calcified."

"Does this tell us when he died?"

"No, but I don't think they did this kind of operation during the war. You'd have to ask an orthopaedic surgeon to be certain."

Arcadipane crouches to peer at the bone from another angle.

"How long is it going to take you to finish telling me what you're thinking? Because I've got to let them know at home if I'm going to be late back."

Alessandra does not smile, but shows neither annoyance nor embarrassment. This is why her colleagues do not warm to her. People are happier with people who weep, make faces, roll their eyes and throw themselves on the floor. Behaviour easy to interpret. But her failure to be like this in no way displeases Arcadipane.

Bramard was another of the same type. One night a drug addict accused of killing his girlfriend got hold of a screwdriver and, goodness knows how, managed to smuggle it into the interrogation room. The first piece of evidence to suggest a case of mental infirmity. For ten minutes Bramard watched the man

66

shout, roll around on the floor and smear the room with his blood, just as one can watch a river flowing without expecting it to reveal anything new. Finally, the guy begged him to call help because he was losing blood. That was what Bramard was. Like a tree. A tree has nothing happening inside it, to all appearances. When in actual fact a great deal is going on. But you cannot discover that just by glancing at the tree, or even by pressing your ear against it. Only time is relevant. So long as the tree's leaves do not turn yellow, and so long as in springtime its branches continue to grow a couple of centimetres nearer the light, it is alive. As simple as that.

"They found this in the same hole," Alessandra says.

Arcadipane glances at a small object she has taken from a box.

"A rivet?"

"A rivet-like button. It has the word 'Rifle' on it. Probably came off a pair of jeans."

"So?"

"The Rifle company dates from 1958, so if the man was wearing Rifle jeans, he must have died at least fifteen years after the end of the war. Maybe even later than that, since the brand is still sold today."

"And he would have been wearing those trousers?"

"One can't say."

"One can't say."

"The button could equally well have found its way into the ground nearby in a thousand other ways." Alessandra shrugs. "As I told you, these are just guesses."

Arcadipane balances the little copper-coloured object in the palm of his hand. It is light, empty and smooth. Qualities that are not easy to ignore. The moment passes.

"Put our friend here in a box," he says. "Tomorrow some people from Milano will be coming to pick him up."

Alessandra takes the button in her fat fingers and puts it back in the box. At that moment, the jerky rattle of a no.13 tram shakes the courtyard, penetrating the basement windows and pervading the room. Then the physiological ticking of instruments takes over the laboratory again. Alessandra peers over her glasses at Arcadipane.

"What's the matter?"

"You have a bit of cake on your collar."

Thinking back over the stresses of the day, as a small compensation Arcadipane goes off to give hell to the people upstairs.

8

There is an evening hour when even prosaic large buildings that advertise things like bread, shoes, pizza and trousers, look as if chromium-plated and adorned with sequins. At this time of day, it is also difficult to detach oneself from the road, because exhaust fumes mixed with a salty tang rising from the River Dora make one feel that every breath could be one's last, every place other than where one actually is to be undesirable, and melancholia to be unbelievably sweet.

This is what Arcadipane is vaguely aware of as he drinks beer and eats crisps leaning on his car, an Alfa Quadrifoglio, in front of the bar nearest his home in the suburban district where he has lived for so long.

In the outdoor space before him four lads and a girl are doing the same. Two of the boys and the girl are already familiar to him, having been involved in bicycle scams and other minor fiddles. They recognise him too but pretend not to since such meetings can lead to conflict, and no-one wants to be hit by the last bullet fired in the film and die during the closing credits.

Much better to enjoy the hour, this last scrap of summer, over watery beer. A month from now it will already be dark at this time, and the far-off mountains beyond the main street will no longer be visible, giving way to the flashing of traffic lights. They have a beauty of their own too, but it is a beauty that can wait.

His mobile rings. Mariangela.

"Nearly home," Arcadipane tells her.

"Does that mean now," she says, "or that we can expect you in three hours?"

"I'm just coming. I'm already downstairs."

"Glad to hear it."

Arcadipane throws the kids in the outdoor area a last glance and makes a move. Pavement, waste bins, the main door of the apartment block where he lives. Going in he passes the Merlo family and greets them politely; then the lift, the landing, his keys and the corridor.

"Ciao." This is Giovanni emerging from his room neatly dressed in his tracksuit. He has shaved and moves on, his face evermore adult at seventeen.

"Ciao," Arcadipane answers.

The boy enters the kitchen, takes a rice cracker from the table, which has already been laid, and turns back to his room. At that moment, Loredana comes out of the bathroom, sees the rice cracker in her brother's mouth and looks daggers at him, but says nothing, except "Ciao, Pa" to her father before disappearing into her own room.

"Bloody hell, a united front," Arcadipane reflects. "Things are getting really serious."

Pulling off his coat, he steps into the boiled-wool slippers the children gave him three years ago for Christmas. At first, he hadn't been much impressed to be given slippers, especially such ornate ones, but to his surprise he has grown fond of them. They are comfortable and never make his feet sweat, even in summer. They are also the only grey item of clothing he possesses. And the only thing decorated with three-dimensional flowers.

"Dinner!" Mariangela calls from the kitchen. "Come and sit down!"

Normally, this initial announcement does no more than

remind the boy that he still needs to wash his hands, and the girl that she has forgotten to phone a friend, or the boy that he must get something from his room, while the girl flies off the handle because no-one but herself has arrived on time . . . but this evening, for a change, after only two minutes all four are sitting in their places.

"Not a good sign," Arcadipane tells himself.

In the centre of the table is a pan full of orecchiette, traditional ear-shaped pasta handmade by Lucetta, the Puglia mother of one of Mariangela's colleagues. A woman who has been going blind for the last seven or eight years, so that every time it's a case of "let's enjoy the orecchiette because this must be the last time she'll be able to make them". But then the old woman kneads the dough and gets out her rolling pin, and from the penumbra of her glaucoma relentlessly produces orecchiette yet again.

"Well, then?" Arcadipane starts, preferring to get these out of the way so as to keep his mouth free for tucking into the turnip tops.

The eyes of the two children follow the movements of their mother with undivided attention as she fills their plates. Then a little olive oil must be added, and for Giovanni a little paprika . . .

"I think you wanted to tell me something, didn't you?"

"Yes," concedes Loredana, but first she turns to her mother. "You've given me too much."

"Eat what you can," says Mariangela dismissively.

Arcadipane loads his fork and thrusts it into his mouth. He has always gobbled his food in huge mouthfuls. "He does it to attract attention," his mother had always commented critically. Whereas his father, known as Antonietto or little Antonio because he weighed only fifty kilos and came from a family of tinkers that he had left to work in a factory, would take a different line . . . "The boy will stop of his own accord," he would

71

say, himself eating steadily, "when he realises he's making himself ill."

"You remember what we were talking about last year . . ." Loredana begins.

"No, I can't say I do."

Loredana crushes a rice cracker.

"A dog," she says, taking the plunge. "We decided we really want a dog."

Arcadipane thinks fast and decides on the sticking-plaster approach.

"No," he says firmly. "Now please pass the paprika."

Giovanni does this automatically, his eyes on his plate. In any case, no-one has mentioned his name, or his training, or football, or scooters, or even the coming weekend. For him the family is simply an object that, like his shin pads, is inconvenient and smelly and hampers his movements but, things being as they are, must be worn and can protect him from certain painful blows. Though playing without shin pads is cooler.

"Who are you playing this Sunday?" Arcadipane asks.

"Monza."

"A strong side?"

The boy helps himself to a big forkful of food.

"Not bad . . . third . . ."

"Well, if they're third . . ."

"Excuse me, Papà, but why not?"

Arcadipane looks at his daughter. He pours himself some wine from the half-litre carafe on the table.

"Because now's not the right time."

"That's what you said last year. But Mamma says we can discuss it again now."

Mariangela's small smile is neutral.

"Papà."

"Yes?"

"Can we discuss this calmly?"

Arcadipane glances at Mariangela, who nods to her daughter to speak.

"Well then," says Loredana, going back to her prepared speech. "Seeing that you're always out, and Mamma has so much to do already, I can guarantee that Giovanni will help me look after the dog. We've already agreed that. In the morning, I'll take the dog before school, and in the evening, Giovanni will take it after supper. On the weekends, we'll take turns."

Arcadipane looks at Giovanni, who is refilling his plate. The boy seems to indicate yes with his head, but it could equally well be a conditioned reflex of chewing.

"And Tiziana has said she'll look after it during the holidays. She has a garden, and her family love dogs. They have two already. One more would be no extra trouble, Tiziana's mother says."

"Have you discussed it with her mother?"

"Only in general. Now let's hear what you have against it, because it's only right that we look at the question from all angles."

Arcadipane helps himself to more orecchiette. These damned school debating groups. He swallows a mouthful of wine.

"But the vet—"

"The dog can be our Christmas present from both of you, and we'll pay for any vaccinations it needs out of Nonna's money. We'd also like it to be properly obedience-trained, which will mean six Saturday afternoon lessons behind the Auchan supermarket. We've saved up money for that too."

Arcadipane aims a sidelong glance at Giovanni, who at the word "money" switches his eyes to a point on the horizon, as any nomad worth his salt would do when forced to negotiate.

Then he goes back to eating. The boy must really have given in on the subject of money.

"What about dog hairs?"

"The dog will sleep with me, and I've already promised Mamma I'll vacuum my room every day. But in any case, Weimaraners have short hair and don't shed much anyway. Papà, they're lovely dogs, and it won't give any trouble, I promise."

"We'll have to think about it."

"No!" Loredana raises her voice. "I know what that means!"

Arcadipane sets his jaw.

"OK, then no, we don't even need to think about it."

He immediately notices the change in the atmosphere when he expresses a view Mariangela does not "share". She now takes the pan containing the last few orecchiette from the table and goes over to the gas cooker. Giovanni's eyes follow the pan, then he turns back to concentrate on the few still left on his plate. Mariangela brings over the next course, meat loaf.

"It will certainly be a considerable responsibility," she says. "And you two are beginning to spend more and more time away from home. I think this is what worries Papà. If you take anyone to live in your house, even a dog, you must make sure you have the time and inclination to look after them. Otherwise, it would make more sense, even from the dog's point of view, to leave it to lead its life somewhere else."

Arcadipane adds nothing to this and does not even pull a face. He gives Mariangela's words time to take effect. She has put the matter so beautifully, sensibly, logically and clearly. But it's no good. Loredana collapses in a heap.

Ever since she was a small child, she has had a habit of huddling up in disapproval and displeasure; a sort of Maginot Line, like a small insect, extremely effective in combining

74

defensiveness with tenderness. Some criminals have the same habit. These are usually petty thieves, the kind one can establish a familiar relationship with. They have to be small and skinny: being plump does not have the same effect. Nor does being tall. To huddle up in this way, people must have something of the child in them, and their offence has to have been little more than a prank, not anything involving drugs, physical injury or blood. Though forgers and writers of blank cheques can achieve it. And those who swindle old people are experts at collapsing in a heap. They begin by moving their eyebrows in a particular way and the rest follows automatically . . .

"Vincenzo?"

"Yes?"

"Do you agree?"

"Agree what?"

"I was just saying that at the kennels they always need volunteers to take the dogs for walks and look after them. Couldn't Loredana go there sometimes?"

Arcadipane looks longingly at the meat loaf getting cold on the table. If someone has collapsed in a heap, it doesn't look good if everyone else goes on eating as if nothing has happened. Giovanni is passing the time by cleaning his plate with bread.

"If she has the time."

"I don't want to go to the kennels!" Loredana says, her voice that of someone who has just climbed a couple of flights of damp stairs from a cellar. "I want a dog here and now so I don't feel so alone!"

Mariangela puts a hand on her daughter's shoulder.

"You feel alone?"

"I don't just feel alone, I am alone!"

"That's not true."

"Papà's out all day, and when you come in at about two, you

75

spend all your time correcting homework. And when Giovanni isn't at school it's like he's not even here at all . . ."

Her brother looks at her. "Rubbish!"

"I'm sorry you feel alone, but we do spend a lot of time together, you and I," Mariangela says. "We talk, we sew, we go shopping and you have your friends."

"Only Teresina." Loredana is almost in tears.

"What about Carlotta, Sara and Elisa? You're constantly chatting to them on the phone."

"Only about nonsense things." Now Loredana *is* crying.

Arcadipane is aware that things are veering out of his control. Getting up with relief, he takes the big knife from the drawer and begins to cut the meat loaf. Giovanni pushes his plate over to his father. Mariangela continues to stroke Loredana's head which has dropped to her chest while great tears flow through the make-up on her eyes.

"Are you sure this is properly cooked?" Arcadipane asks, noticing pink inside the meat loaf.

Loredana leaps to her feet, dropping her fork and making her plate with its remaining orecchiette and turnip tops bounce on the table.

"You think of nothing but eating, any of you!" she screams, then pushes her chair back with a blow from her leg and runs off. Her footsteps echo down the corridor. The door of her room slams, then her stereo can be heard: Irish music.

"Of course it's cooked," Mariangela says, making no attempt to hide the reproof in her voice. "It's got ham in it!"

Arcadipane lets the knife continue slicing halfway through the meat, finishes the job without pleasure, sits down exhausted, and lets his arms drop by his sides.

He has had to deal with a mad psychologist, the waste of a hundred euros, a weeping daughter, a pea plant that won't grow straight and a wife who is beginning to loathe him, with nothing but a pocketful of lozenges between him and his next flood of tears!

He watches Giovanni filling his plate, carefully avoiding the carrots.

"Have you both come to an agreement about this?"

Giovanni shrugs.

"It's alright by me."

"What's alright?"

"Getting a dog."

"Your sister says you're involved in it too and have also contributed money. That's a bit more than 'alright by me'."

Giovanni looks from him to his mother.

"This meat loaf is very tasty," he says.

Mariangela, taking some herself, smiles at the compliment.

"Well?" Arcadipane asks.

"Loredana's the one who wants it. 'It's alright by me' means I'll do my bit, but that's all."

Arcadipane looks up quickly; something in him has been alerted.

"Why does your sister say you're never at home? You go to school on Tuesdays and on Thursday afternoons. What do you do the rest of the time if you're not at home studying?"

"I *am* at home studying."

Arcadipane looks at Mariangela.

"Is he here studying?"

"Among other things," she says, cutting the meat loaf into small pieces and, scarcely opening her lips, forking the pieces into her mouth two at a time. A strategy Arcadipane has never understood, though he knows she would be happy to explain its meaning and its beauty and advantages to him with methodical patience. Which is precisely why he has never asked her to.

77

"Well, if you're not studying what are you up to?"

Giovanni straightens his back.

"Nothing!"

"If I find out you've been telling me tales . . ."

"What d'you mean, tales?"

"I don't know." Arcadipane raises his voice. "If they're nothing but tales, how can I know what they are?"

Giovanni looks at him.

"But there's no sense in that," is all he says.

Arcadipane fixes him with a look he never normally uses at home. Even Mariangela has seldom seen it, and then only when she has been picking him up from work or meeting him in a café not far from his office, moments when he has been a bit slow to put his eyes back like pistols into their holsters, so to speak. Which is why she now keeps quiet and does not intervene in her usual fashion to improve on what her husband has been doing rather less well than herself.

"Have you finished your meal?" Arcadipane asks Giovanni, determined to get on with eating his own food.

Giovanni says nothing.

"If you've finished, you may leave the table."

The boy gets to his feet, takes his plate to the sink and goes out of the kitchen.

Arcadipane helps himself to a slice of the meat loaf and cuts it into four. He puts one piece into his mouth. The silence is broken by the sound of him eating.

"Why don't you want them to have a dog?" Mariangela asks him.

"Are you really asking me that?"

"Of course I am!"

"Because you know it will be up to you and me to look after it!"

78

"Of course it will be up to us, me in particular."

"And during the holidays the mother of . . . that girl will find some reason why she can't take it."

"Then we shall just have to take the dog with us when we go away."

"And have you any idea how much vets cost?"

Mariangela holds her napkin in both hands, wipes her lips, then places it neatly next to her place at the table, where she has been eating and dispensing samples of her grace and patience.

"I agree," she says, then she switches to a different tone. "Now tell me the real reason why you don't want them to have a dog."

Arcadipane looks at the orecchiette left on Loredana's plate; the green at the top has lost its fine marine fluorescence and reverted to the same plain green as everything else that is born of earth and ultimately returns to it.

"Because they piss and crap and die," he says.

"That's what I said when you insisted on us having a second baby." Mariangela smiles. "But that never held you back."

"But now I'm fifty and I'm tired. And I don't want to quarrel."

"And I, for my part, have no intention of just being the one running along behind."

"I've never asked you to run along behind."

"But if a person runs away, it leads to someone else running after them; you should know that, it's your profession."

Arcadipane puts his hand into his pocket, then remembers he is at home. He reroutes his fingers, which already have a little sugar on their tips, from the sucai lozenge to his cigarettes. He takes a cigarette that has already come out of the packet, and places it on the table.

"Do you know what 'shining' means?"

"Yes." Mariangela nods. "Do you?"

"No, but I know it's something I haven't got anymore."

79

Arcadipane has no idea what the expression on her face may be telling him, because her eyes are fixed on the cigarette as though the matter were between him and that two-coloured cylindrical object.

"Are you having problems at work?"

"I don't know."

"Can I help you in some way?"

"I don't even know that."

They say no more. Arcadipane feels an extreme weariness that he can't explain. Something starting from his feet and rising up to his ears. He doesn't even want to go and lie down, just to have someone to take him in their arms and deposit him on a deckchair by the sea, and even take off his shoes for him. And send everyone else away. He longs to be alone.

"I'll go and see Loredana," his wife says. "You have a cigarette. We'll clear the table later."

Arcadipane nods. They both get up. She heads into the flat, and he goes out to the veranda. They kiss each other on the cheek, and neither would have been able to say who offered their cheek first and who their lips. They slip separately away.

The veranda is a balcony that they have closed off with a glass partition and a folding door that they always keep open, making it into a terrace. From there they can see much of the city, and they can also see what the city no longer is, but they can't tell exactly where the city now ends. But they pay little attention to this because the outline of the mountains dominates the view and the rare lights that mark it out steal away what remains visible. Apart from the Sacra di San Michele, a place where he has never been.

His phone begins vibrating in his pocket.

Arcadipane checks the number. An unfamiliar one.

"Yes?"

"Good evening, this is Questore Appendino."

So much for beaches, deckchairs and taking off his shoes.

"Good evening, questore."

"Good evening, commissario. Please forgive me calling at such a late hour, but I shall not take up much of your time. It's about the trench at Chivasso, they rang me this afternoon."

"Then they will have told you that the matter has been handed over to Milano."

"An excellent decision. We have specialists, so for heaven's sake, let's make use of them."

"Naturally."

"Good. Let's pass on the relevant material to them as quickly as possible. Making sure everything is consistent in timings and method. Without anyone having to start asking for anything. There has never been a better occasion to give proof of our willingness to co-operate, don't you agree?"

"We have already made an agreement with Commissario Nascimbene."

"Perfect, then all that remains for me is to reiterate my great respect for you and wish you every success in your work."

"And the same to you."

"Of course, goodnight."

"Goodnight."

Now, with Mariangela, he watches a thriller from the eighties which he has already seen the beginning of three times. This time too, by the third commercial break he has fallen asleep on the sofa, his head propped on her legs. Towards the end he wakes up during the shoot-out, at which point Loredana comes in and curls up against him. Arcadipane puts a hand on her head and the girl closes her eyes. They stay like this till the closing credits, when the girl gets up and goes to her room.

"Come and sleep now," says Mariangela, also getting up and

leaving Arcadipane alone, his head below his legs which are raised up on the arm of the sofa.

The questore never phoned me at all, he decides.

He looks at his reflection on the TV, now switched off, and reaches out, feeling a need to stroke something more interesting than the carpet.

9

"Chivasso. Early on Tuesday morning, men working in heavy rain on a site for the high-speed railway (will we ever be able to claim it's finished?) unearthed a mass grave containing the remains of a dozen bodies. 'Yet another sad inheritance from the last war,' commented Commissario Nascimbene, head of the police task force specialising in such matters. 'Even today such discoveries are not uncommon,' added the investigator, 'discoveries that, even after the passage of sixty years, yet again lay bare the wounds of wartime conflict. The bones of partisans, soldiers, fascists and innocent civil victims of reprisals, people whom it is our duty to try to identify through research and analysis.' A painful duty indeed; the exhausted face of Nascimbene after his exacting day of discoveries in the area speaks volumes about how difficult it is, at such a late stage, to give names to the victims. Not to mention the task of tracking down those who were responsible for their deaths. But perhaps it is just as well that . . ."

Arcadipane closes the newspaper he has just found lying open on his desk and reclines in his chair.

One side of his office is lined with shelves, one is dominated by the window, one the door, and the fourth by a sofa which looks as if someone once left a red-hot pan on it. It's old and ugly, but whenever he tries to order new furniture . . . perhaps it matters that the armchair once belonged to Bramard and that, earlier still, Petri used to take forty winks on the sofa, though the rest means nothing much. The only item personal to Arcadipane is the ashtray, which now needs emptying: a black marble object with three brass inserts for parking your cigarette. A wedding present, unbelievably – the sort of thing you might expect to find in a Bulgarian brothel. There's a knock on the door: Pedrelli.

"Commissario, there's an officer here from Milano. I tried to find out what he wants, but he insists on talking to you in person."

"Send him up. What's the meaning of this newspaper? Are you trying to take the mickey?"

Pedrelli inclines his head like a dog making a valiant effort to understand, but Arcadipane is already out in the corridor.

The people at the desks in the outer office, watching him pass, hastily open folders, skim through minutes and attack the keys of their computers as if still typing on the old Olivettis. Not that they had been twiddling their thumbs before, it's just that at the sight of Arcadipane they suddenly feel they must be seen to be active. Natural enough when the ball reaches your part of the field – unlike great players, who never relax their concentration even when it's nowhere near them. Though some, like Bramard, seem to pay no attention even when the ball is coming straight at them, but then . . . zap! It's like being born with three nipples; more likely to be a problem than any sort of advantage – unless you happen to be a circus performer or a policeman.

The man from Milano has climbed the stairs.

"My name is Capello, Nascimbene has sent me to—"

"Yes, yes, but we have to go downstairs again."

"Commissario?" Pedrelli puts in.

"What is it?"

"If I may . . ."

"Quickly, Pedrelli. We're in a hurry."

"I didn't quite understand . . . about the newspaper?"

"What newspaper?"

"You were telling me about … a newspaper … maybe I wasn't paying attention … but in the heat of the moment … I don't understand what that was about."

Arcadipane waves him away with a gesture implying it doesn't matter, and heads down the stairs, the officer from Milano walking beside him: a man of medium build about thirty years old, with unremarkable hair, but incredibly wide nostrils.

"How did it go in court?" Arcadipane asks him.

"In court?" The man seems confused. "Oh, you mean the evidence. Nothing much. It's just they keep you waiting so long."

Arcadipane slows down imperceptibly, thinking fast. He searches his pockets for a key.

"Get yourself a coffee from that machine over there. And get me one too, macchiato, in my case. I'll get you the box and be back in a minute."

"It really doesn't matter …"

"No trouble at all." Arcadipane holds out the key to him more insistently. "The coffee's terrible, I'm afraid, but it doesn't cost much."

The man makes an effort to smile. Heading for the machine, he looks back a couple of times as Arcadipane crosses the corridor with short, urgent steps and opens the door of the laboratory without knocking.

Alessandra, sitting in front of her microscope, half turns towards him on her revolving stool. Her lab coat is open, revealing a waistcoat, denim shirt, and the inevitable shapeless trousers.

She points at a packet on the table.

"The person who's taking it has to sign for it," she says, turning back to the microscope.

Arcadipane takes a few steps towards the middle of the room. The large box has been tied up with string and sticky tape and

85

marked with a pen and rubber-stamped. Beside it is the sheet of paper needing a signature.

"Was it you who put that newspaper on my desk?" he asks.

Alessandra continues to stare into her microscope and says nothing. It is hot in the laboratory, the smell of hardware mingling with something that reminds him of dead flowers in a cemetery when he was a child.

"Throw them in the bin," his mother used to say when they changed the flowers on his father's grave. And he would run to the rubbish bin, holding at arm's length what had once been alive and fragrant but now stank of rot and decay . . . "Bloody hell!"

He puts a sucai into his mouth and chews it, staring at the box of bones. When he has established that the bone he wants is there, he looks at Alessandra, who is still working at her microscope.

"Can you find me a large envelope?" he asks.

Without a word she gets up and goes to a cupboard to get one, the sort of envelope they use for exhibits, and takes it to Arcadipane. She watches him strip the sticky tape off the package, open it and take out the thigh bone.

"No," she says. "That's the left thigh bone. What you want is the one from the right leg."

Arcadipane puts it back and takes out the right thigh bone, which he slides into the envelope.

"Is that everything?" he asks.

Alessandra rummages in the bottom of the box, finds the rivet-like button and puts it into the envelope with the thigh bone, then they close the box taking care to make sure that the marks on the tape are all in the right places, and when they have done this Arcadipane picks up the box and sheet of paper and leaves the laboratory with them.

A few minutes pass, during which Alessandra stares at the

bulging envelope on the table, then the door opens and Arcadipane puts the signed receipt down beside the envelope.

"I can't trust anyone upstairs," he says.

Silence, except for the ticking of instruments. The shape of a parked car can be made out beyond the frosted glass of the laboratory's little window. A door slams.

"There *is* one person you can trust," Alessandra says. "But, unfortunately, she's someone you don't like."

"How much do I dislike this person?"

"Rather a lot."

Arcadipane stares at her.

"No, not that woman," he says.

Alessandra shrugs.

"Unless you can think of someone else . . ."

Arcadipane takes the envelope and holds it out to her.

"But you'll have to do the talking."

Alessandra ignores the envelope and goes back to her desk. She takes three sheets of paper from a drawer, staples them together and returns.

"Here's a copy of my notes," she says. "You'll find they are perfectly clear."

He turns the side pocket of his sheepskin jacket towards her. Alessandra folds the papers and slips them into it.

"And the newspaper on my desk?"

"All fat girls are bitches, everyone knows that."

An hour later he is sitting at his usual table at the trattoria ten minutes' walk from the police station. The place is full of all sorts as always, since it serves local offices, shops, a market, art galleries, expensive houses and even a couple of blocks of flats.

"What can I bring you?" the waitress says.

Arcadipane orders horse steak with fried artichokes, and Pedrelli chooses cappelletti in broth. The girl says OK without writing it down and goes off to the kitchen.

"Do you remember that girl when she was a child?"

Arcadipane watches the proprietor's twenty-year-old daughter disappear through the curtain, a diamond in her incisor and their order committed to memory. He studies the pictures on the walls: ancient photos of comic actors. Totò. Sordi with spaghetti, Fabrizi with a chop, and the French footballer Platini, eating with a group and staring out, well-tanned, from behind his autograph signature.

"One evening this summer I came here on my own," Arcadipane says. "Mariangela was out with the children, and I didn't want to eat at home."

Pedrelli cautiously lifts a grissino breadstick to his mouth and leaves it hanging there like an antenna that can tell him where to go to solve his problem.

Arcadipane signals to the proprietor's older daughter, who is preparing coffee and bitters and writing out bills behind the counter. "They put me to sit with a little man a few years older than you and me, dressed for work with his white hair tied behind his head. The sort of guy who does large paintings on walls . . ."

"Murals, you mean."

"Something like that . . . Anyway, we exchanged a few words: work, family, children, the usual. He had no children, but was just back from a job in Sassari where he'd had five academy students as his apprentices. Twenty-year-olds who arrived early in the morning, worked hard and went home in the evening, while he'd fixed up a small camp bed for himself in a corner of the store. Good at their work, he said, well-trained and intelligent, then . . . on the last evening . . ."

Arcadipane leans across the table as if what he is about to say must be said in confidence. Pedrelli does the same.

"On that last evening they all went out to a pizzeria, then after kisses and hugs, he went back alone to the store and lay down on his bed. He had no sooner turned off the light than he heard noises from the yard. There's nothing anyone can steal, he thought; perhaps one of the kids has forgotten something. Then the door opened, and what do you think happened?"

Pedrelli lets the grissino continue to dangle from his mouth.

"It was one of the girls, forty years younger than himself. Without a word, she took off her clothes and slipped into the bed with him. To begin with he lay as still as a dead fish, but then, with the girl's lovely smooth skin against him . . . if life insists on giving you presents, as the saying goes . . ."

The waitress puts their food down in front of them and goes off without so much as a "*buon appetito*". A few seconds slowly pass, filled with the silent scent of meat and broth, then Arcadipane pours himself some wine and begins to eat.

Three men from the gasworks sitting near them are discussing the midweek football matches: Chievo 1-1 Torino, Juventus 1-1 Catania. Arcadipane, being a southerner, favours Juventus, while Pedrelli supports Torino because he is himself from Torino, but the real fact of the matter is that neither team means a damn thing to either of them.

"Is something wrong with your food?" Arcadipane asks his deputy, watching him constantly move the cappelletti about on his plate as if arranging them for a photographer.

Pedrelli puts one politely in his mouth and chews it deliberately and sadly, as if in hospital.

"A few years ago," he says, "our Nicoletta got a crush on someone."

"Oh yes?" Arcadipane uses his fork to strip a last mouthful of horsemeat from the bone. He imagines his son doing dirty work in the middle of the pitch and understands the pleasure.

"A crush on who?"

"Morsetti."

"Who's Morsetti?"

"You know, the ice-cream manufacturer."

Arcadipane picks up his bone with both hands and starts working on it.

"Well, if she'd married him, it would have been like winning the lottery! Was it the older son or the younger one?"

"Neither. The father."

"The father? He must be sixty if he's a day . . ."

"He was sixty-four."

Arcadipane watches Pedrelli load his spoon with another cappelletto and slowly and sadly begin to chew it. The bone in Arcadipane's hand, which in other circumstances might still have been able to give him some pleasure, suddenly seems irrelevant. He puts it down and looks to see whether there is anything more appropriate on his plate. A couple of artichokes. He starts cutting these into very small pieces.

"Not that I could have done anything about it," Pedrelli says. "The girl was twenty-two. In some sense one can understand even if . . . the roadster car, a weekend on his boat and in Venice."

"But isn't the man married?"

"Of course. But he started talking of divorce, and even of setting Nicoletta up in the firm with his children. Those were terrible months, commissario . . ." Pedrelli gestures with his spoon as if to prove that he left no stone unturned. ". . . And what with all the arguments and shouting, it put Delia off her food and I couldn't get any sleep . . ."

"Why did you say nothing about it at the time?"

Pedrelli stops torturing his cappelletto.

"It was the moment when Commissario Bramard . . . so many things were going on that autumn. In any case that's just how I am with my private life: I lock the door on it and throw away the key. Luckily, my sister had been going through some problems with her husband . . . a total crisis. Doctors, pills, no end to it. Sometimes all you need is someone to listen . . ." Pedrelli looks down at his plate. "But if people get to hear about it . . . It would almost have been more acceptable if I'd gone to a sorcerer."

Arcadipane takes a hush puppy from the basket on the table and breaks it open. A hard crust but soft inside. He puts it into his mouth with the last piece of artichoke.

"And how did that work?"

Pedrelli gives Arcadipane his dogs-can't-understand expression.

"I mean, if you go to a psychologist," Arcadipane says vaguely. "How does that work?"

Pedrelli swallows a spoonful of broth to cover the word he has managed to avoid pronouncing.

"You sit down and talk to him. He gives you advice. Nothing special."

"And what advice did he give you?"

"To let things take their course. He said you can't control everything, especially people. You have to accept what happens, welcome the positives and accept the negatives. Learn to be detached."

"And then . . . ?"

"So that's what we did." Pedrelli nods. "'So you're going out now, are you?' I would say to Nicoletta. 'Have a good time!' As if it were nothing. After a couple of weeks of that, Nicoletta came home in tears. Morsetti's children and their mother had intervened. The scandal was ruining the image of the firm, and if was not stopped divorce would be the least of it! Their shares would be taken away from them, the car, the boat and even their house by the seaside. Nicoletta was upset for a few days, but not for long, then went back to her studies, and next summer she met Matteo. They've been an item for two years now."

Arcadipane checks his mobile for messages. With the look of someone who has for a moment forgotten his own pain and then been suddenly reminded of it.

"Should we go now?" Pedrelli asks.

Arcadipane says no hurry, but looks towards the serving counter, hoping to intercept the older daughter and order a coffee.

"I'm glad we had this talk," Pedrelli says.

Arcadipane nods absent-mindedly.

The girl at the counter is putting profiteroles on a plate: she looks much like her sister except that the upper half of her body is much more substantial and the lower half noticeably slimmer. It occurs to Arcadipane that the girls should swap occupations, the elder should become the waitress and the younger should go behind the counter. While trying to attract the girl's attention, he hears a long breath followed by a sharp suck. Pedrelli, who is looking down at his plate with moist eyes.

"It may not be much to you," his deputy says, looking up, his chest rising and falling under his khaki sweater, "but . . ."

Arcadipane studies the corner of the handkerchief Pedrelli is blotting his tears with before going back to his broth, which must by now be cold. And he understands.

It has taken him forty years to learn how to do well the only two things he had ever had any talent for: being a policeman and being a husband. And now he is probably no longer a success at either.

For everything else that life had to offer: communicating in general, opening himself to other people and sympathising with them, eating well, loving other women, understanding art, remembering films, getting his teeth straightened, finding the right words, patting himself on the back, finding positive aspects of things other people enjoyed like sauna, Sundays, the natural world, and washing his feet before going to bed; for all these other aspects of life it is now too late.

That is the meaning of old age: it's when you no longer have enough time to get good at doing anything new.

II

The police stations in the Barriera district represent purgatory, and in purgatory you don't have much choice: you can either relax and wait, or you can gnaw your own liver and wait. Though even purgatory offers seats in both gallery and stalls, not to mention toilets that have to be cleaned. All you need take into account is how you get there, who sent you and why. Besides, there are people who have made their homes in Barriera. People squirming like babies in their mothers' bellies between piles of paper and petty thieving.

They have added a bit of extra emotion, these immigrants who come and go, presenting false names, false documents, false addresses and false genders, and lying about their ages. It all gives an impression of increased movement. Of more varied delinquency, but when it comes to it ... And you may add that all tarts are confident, all drug addicts are informers, all receivers of stolen goods are collaborators, and every thief is ready to tell you about a colleague who knows about another colleague, and who knows a colleague who turns out to be the person you first spoke to ... You can even dress up as a sailor if it pleases you, since when it comes down to it, a lake is not a sea.

Arcadipane throws away his fag end and rings the bell. The guard inside checks his computer screen before opening the door.

The next ten minutes piss you off in exactly the same way as when you go to see relatives in the country, with all their how are you doing, and how are you not doing . . . and you at least must certainly be enjoying yourself . . . and at least here you can breathe . . . and so your son's in the army, bloody hell, better if he were a faggot . . . yes, I know, but the competition . . . and mozzarella cheese from the south . . and now they want to tax the mobile home you keep on the beach . . . and how are Juve doing . . . and the son of my cousin, no obligation . . . and that impudent cow you sent us, what on earth gave you that idea!

Leaving the main building by the back door he shakes off the last of his old acquaintances, forcing himself to cross the courtyard unaccompanied. Calm down. Take a deep breath. And go over it again: I say this, she says that, then I say it's in her interests to . . . In any case what does she have to blame herself for? Shorten the lead, lengthen the lead, play the father, play the friend, the superior, the jailer, the priest. Is it his fault that such talent has ended up inside such a stupid fucking head? Does he need to have a ring in his nose and a pierced tongue before she'll listen to him?

Crossing the yard, he firmly grips the envelope under his jacket. The storehouse is a shack that dates back to the sixties: four concrete walls, a convex roof, large windows and industrial shelving up to the ceiling. Not so much as a partition inside, apart from two cubicles that serve as toilet and storeroom.

He knows this because when he first joined the police, he was condemned to spend two winter months as an "assistant" in a space that was usually reserved for supplies. Incidental and temporary work, but useful later on when he wanted to complain about the cold in the shack and the *Regulations for Registration and Distribution* as a threat for . . .

"I told you they're defective! What possible use can such returned goods be to you?"

Arcadipane slows down. The fire door is open, but the interior from where he is hearing the man's voice is in shadow. There's a bench against the outer wall for those waiting to be seen. Arcadipane sits down on it.

"Did you need an application form?" the man inside says. "Here's one, already signed by a senior officer. And look me in the eyes when I'm speaking to you!"

Arcadipane stands up to get a better view of this man. He is standing at the counter, a great beast from the riot squad, his shaven head more grey than black, his high-visibility blue jacket marked POLIZIA. Behind him are shelves, a ladder and a yellow section from a forklift truck.

"The return goods." Her voice comes from behind the riot cop.

The man neither moves nor replies. Such people are trained not to react on impulse. They intimidate you by staring at you in silence without moving. This is the first thing you learn in the riot squad: turn your back once too often, and you'll be smashed by a club or stabbed by a knife and end up as much use as a pile of shit. So study the object of your attention, sum him up, reason with him if you can, and attack him if you have to.

The man bends over calmly and now Arcadipane can see her beyond him: elbows on the counter and eyes on a monitor. She is chewing gum and, as always, her eyes are painted black and she has a small spoon fixed to her ear, a ring in her nose, and one side of her head is shaved. The only difference is the blue uniform sweater that makes her look less mad if slightly unwell.

The man stands up, plants an unlaced Anfibio boot on the counter, and moves a little to one side.

"If you have to wear these boots for hours as we do," she says, tapping the toe of her own boot, "eventually the seam is bound to cut into your foot. They no longer have the old boots in stock, only this new model. Now that I've shown you what's wrong with it, I'm putting in a request to the authorities to be kind enough to let me have another twenty pairs of the old style."

She takes her eyes off the monitor for a moment, glaring at him in her usual manner, calculated to make men want to smash her face in or fuck her on the spot, or probably both.

"The return goods," she says again.

The man's shoulders start shaking.

"I told you those boots are defective!" he says. "What the fuck do you care whether I take them back or chuck them in the bin . . . ?"

Isa suddenly lifts her leg and bangs her foot on the bench.

"You don't throw them in the bin. You sell them for forty euros in the shop for military wear at Porta Palazzo, and they can then sell them on for ninety-nine or ninety in the shop, or online for eighty-five plus postage. And in any case, it's not your feet the boots have been hurting, it's mine."

The man stares at her foot, hidden inside an Anfibio boot just like his own. Isa lowers her foot and turns back to the computer, still chewing gum.

"You know what I think?" the man says.

She pays no attention.

"If you put your hand in," he says, inserting his hand slowly into the boot, "I bet you'll find a seam at the end just the same as in this one."

She gives the hint of a smile, then suddenly things happen very fast.

Arcadipane would not have been able to say whether the sharp-edged paperweight had come from her pocket or from a drawer. All he knows is that it is now inside the toe of the boot, and that the noise made by its sharp edge cutting through its leather sole, and perhaps through the man's hand as well, continues to resound between the walls.

As the riot cop hurries out of the shack, Arcadipane looks him in the face: never seen him before.

The man takes a few quick steps into the yard, then stops abruptly and takes his hand out of the boot: the cut is bleeding, but not badly.

"Bloody bitch!" he shouts.

Pulling out a handkerchief, he tries to bandage his hand.

"You sodding bitch!"

A police officer appears with a cup of coffee at one of the windows on the second floor. The two men look at each other, but neither shows any sign of recognition. Then the man with the coffee draws back in and the riot cop continues to walk with one bare foot and the boot under his arm as far as the back entrance to the main building, through which he disappears.

Arcadipane puts a sucai lozenge into his mouth and gets up from the bench.

Isa gives him a casual look. He moves forward, keeping a twenty-centimetre gap between himself and the counter. He takes the envelope from under his jacket and places it on the flat surface. Isa gives him another brief look.

"Just get me out of this place," she says.

"Just get you out of this place what?"

"Whatever it was you came to ask for."

"Meaning?"

"Officially, I'm not allowed to be in here, so you forcing me to be here is against the rules. If you've come to me despite that fact, you must be after something pretty big. Though that's your business. All I need is to get out of this place."

Arcadipane thinks, I've still got time.

"There's a thigh bone in this envelope," he says, making no attempt at discretion.

"A thigh bone?"

98

"A thigh bone and a button. We need some research: asking round hospitals, searching archives. Alessandra has written it all down for you."

The girl reaches for the envelope and pulls it closer. The scars between her wrist and cuff are too precise to be casual but too superficial to be serious. Arcadipane cannot remember if she already had those scars when he last saw her.

"I want to come back inside," she says, "and I want my pistol back too."

"Why not? Then we'll have a collection and you and De Rita can get married. After all, you're already on pretty intimate terms with him, since you all but gouged out his eye!"

"He should have kept—"

"He should have nothing! At forty he deserves a quiet life in the office till he retires. Or have you not yet understood how much staying at his desk could mean to him, since you yourself would rather be out and about?"

She pushes the envelope away from her and turns back to the screen. Arcadipane lights a cigarette. For a few seconds they ignore each other.

"If you do this job, I promise to put in a good word for you."

No response.

"What did you think? Did you expect me to come here like a knight on a white horse to rescue you? It's not me who makes the decisions."

"It was you who had me put in here in the first place."

"I just wanted to save your arse. Don't you realise that at the first chance the others would have looked away and left you in the shit?"

She looks straight at him, then pulls the envelope towards her, opens it and looks inside.

"Give me two weeks," she says. "I won't come in here. I'll

work on my own account. If I get you what you want and say sorry to De Rita, you must take me back, otherwise I'll have to come back here."

Arcadipane finishes his cigarette with long, slow puffs, then goes to the door and throws the fag end into the courtyard. A couple of other officers are also smoking, leaning against the front wall. A third joins them, coming down the fire-escape ladder, so heavy that it groans at every step.

"You can have one week," Arcadipane says.

Isa taps on her keyboard. Then she turns the screen to show him the article about the pit found at Chivasso.

"Two weeks."

He looks at her: how old can she be now? Twenty-nine? Thirty? Thirty-two? How does she spend her pay? Cigarettes, pot, computers? Does she have a home where she can cook and sleep in clean sheets? And what does she do when she's not here in this warehouse where he has put her? Does she talk to other people? Have sex? With a man? With a woman? Has he created a hell for himself by getting it into his head to try and help sort out this particular girl's life? Just because her father was a policeman killed when she was still a small child? Because of the way he died? Because Elia Mancini, never mind what people said about him, had after all been one of his colleagues? So, should he, Arcadipane, really want to inflict on himself having to teach this girl how to make her way in the world? Him of all people? Him and his sucai lozenges?

He looks at the drops of blood in the courtyard shining like tiny reflectors in the sun. A riot cop's blood.

"OK, ten days, but no pistol. And speak to me politely. Bloody hell."

Three football pitches: one for eleven players, one for five and one for seven, marked out some twenty years ago next to the heavy old quadrilateral prison that is now a museum facing the new law courts, which are all lightweight tiles and glass.

Arcadipane gets out of his car and goes towards a bench near the exit Giovanni will emerge from. He does not want to watch him play or even talk to the other parents; just let him know he's there and that he'll take him home in the car.

Sitting with his back to the road, he lights a cigarette. He has been smoking since he was sixteen. Not much at first, but as soon as he could afford it at least a packet a day. He has never asked himself why or what for; all he knows is that when smoking he reflects deeply on the fact that he is smoking.

Giovanni comes from the door with his jacket, his club kitbag and his *Serpico* hat.

Arcadipane raises his hand, but the lad, already smiling, is looking in quite another direction.

With his hand up and his cigarette hanging from his lips, Arcadipane follows the direction of the boy's eyes and sees a girl sitting on a motor scooter at the side of the road, with one crash helmet hanging from her arm and another fastened to the handlebars.

As soon as Giovanni is close enough the girl, slender and beautiful, pulls him close and kisses him on the mouth. Her first kiss soon turns into a second and eventually a very long third one.

Arcadipane is shocked from his knees to his balls.

The two young people talk with their faces close together, then Giovanni glances at the time and towards the little kebab booth in the middle of the gardens and indicates yes.

Arcadipane spends the next half hour motionless, smoking and watching his son and the girl eating, kissing and talking intimately, as they sit at one of the five tables near the little booth.

When they go back to the scooter and put on their helmets, he trails them professionally to the block of flats that has been his home for the last thirty-seven years. The young couple stay outside necking continuously for seven minutes and forty seconds, except when they stop to look closely at each other as if to make sure they really do both exist.

Then the girl leaves with a slight wave of the hand, and Giovanni goes inside.

When the timed light on the stairs goes off, Arcadipane starts his car and drives towards the outskirts of the city, passing sheds, car parks, factories, premises for sale and warehouses. A half-hour journey during which he eats three sucai, allows himself to weep, and in his confusion switches on the windscreen wipers instead of wiping his face.

It is a quarter past ten when, driving back to the centre through an area dead during the evening, he goes into a little pub as bare as a church vestry, a place where he used to go occasionally with Bramard when they finished work late and did not want to lay heads teeming with the day's problems straight down on their pillows. Then came a time when Bramard used to go to drink there on his own, after Michelle and their little girl had been killed. At least everyone thought that was what he was doing, and Arcadipane would pass by to pick him up in the middle of the night. He never needed to call "Commissario!" more than once for Bramard to get up and come out. A moderate drinker, never out of control. In those days the pub had belonged to Pieter Moderno, and the girl who served at the tables had been the city's first black waitress.

Now the place is run by a girl of mixed race, with no-one ever speculating whether she might be the daughter of Pieter and the waitress. What matters has always been that the place is open all night, but different from other pubs open all night, in that no-one ever comes to sell things there, nor is there ever any former communists, would-be artists, drug addicts, fascists, or men in search of sex or tarts. The customers are all men and women with homes of their own postponing having to tell their partner "Here I am" or "Just let me sleep" or even "Let's discuss it in the morning". This is why it is such a quiet place, with no-one wanting to talk or make a pickup, or even to drink very much; they just want to be sad and experience their sadness alone without looking for sympathy.

Arcadipane spends an hour over a single beer, then leaves. It is not a beautiful evening. The sky is dull, the air full of smog and the temperature at that hopeless level that makes you sweat if you keep your jacket on and shiver if you take it off.

Walking quickly past the two blocks between him and the spot where he has parked his car, he fiddles among his thoughts in much the same way as he places his feet, a bit here and a bit there: the bones, the plaque, the rivet-like button, the psychologist, the hundred euros, the guard at the door of Isa's shack.

His mobile rings. Obviously Mariangela. He lets it ring.

The phone refuses to stop ringing.

He looks to see who it is.

And it isn't Mariangela.

13

When her teeth are near the food, she lets the tinfoil slip off it and grabs a mouthful. Without dirtying her hands or even needing a napkin, as if the only thing she has ever done in her life is to sit in a crappy street eating kebabs near an outdoor restaurant full of Arabs, sitting blankly in little armchairs that smell of mould, smoking and drinking tea.

Two even pass near her. Twenty-year-olds, all jeans and jackets, trying to move like bulls but looking more like rabbits. Isa doesn't even deign to look at them, and they pedal past her with lowered eyes.

It is as if they all understand that to touch her would be like sticking their hands in a shredder: a lot of fuss and you'd come away with part of yourself missing. Except those like the riot cop and De Rita, men who assume the world has been created in their own image and exists for their own amusement.

What surprises her though is that up till now no-one has made a serious attempt on her sexually. Lurking outside where she lives, armed not with a gun but with a chain or stick or with a couple of friends. And here she is! On a crappy road, late at night. Arabs, drug addicts, not another woman in sight, and she's on her own. She even lights a cigarette. As calm as if she owned the place.

Arcadipane stretches his neck which he has been holding at an awkward angle to get a better view from his rear-view mirror, then gets out of his car and goes over to her.

"Have you come to a decision?" she says.

"About what?"

"For at least half hour you've been sitting in that car fucking watching me."

"I was on the phone. I never noticed you at all. And in any case, I think we decided you would keep a civil tongue in your head when you speak to me, didn't we?"

Isa shrugs, her fine teeth as higgledy-piggledy as the thoughts of a child in her second year at primary school.

Arcadipane guesses the cost of her kebab and small can of beer, the remains of which will probably stay where they are until the next time the street is cleaned. They are at the meeting place of three roads. A few passers-by hug the walls, turn corners and go through front doors. It is not yet one o'clock, though night seems already well advanced.

"Wasn't there anywhere else we could have met?" Arcadipane says.

"What's wrong with meeting here?"

"It's a shithole of a place and, worst of all, everyone here knows everyone else."

"They sure know me, because this is where I live," Isa says, pointing at a block of flats covered with tiles, prominent among the smaller buildings.

The bar door opens. A pockmarked young man emerges with a tray, observes them without interest, and disappears into the oily fog of the outside area.

"Well?" Arcadipane inserts a cigarette between his lips.

"Do we have to do this here?"

"It was your idea to meet here! Or do you want me to come up and admire pictures of you as a child?"

Isa gets up and takes the only road that leads slightly uphill. Arcadipane waits a few seconds till it seems unlikely that she is heading in any definite direction, then joins her. In silence, they cover fifty metres to an arch and come out into a square, where there is a market every weekday morning and all day on Saturdays. At all other times, like now, there is nothing there at all. They start walking round it in an anticlockwise direction. Sometimes in the evening you still see a few people looking for parmesan, mozzarella, chocolate or salami. Tourists in shorts with male handbags who have read in their guidebooks that this is the biggest open market in Europe. Mostly Japanese, Germans and Americans. A sad picture, even a desperate one. Luckily, at this hour there aren't even any pickpockets around to fuck them over. But you're not likely to see French or Spanish people here. The Mediterranean quickly deflowers that sort of tourist virginity. In any case, on this particular evening there happens to be no-one in the square at all.

"I've had the bone looked at," Isa says.

"Who by?"

"Let's make an agreement. I won't fuck with you by asking why if you don't you fuck with me by asking how."

Isa's long legs make short work of the perimeter of the square. Arcadipane's shorter and stouter legs struggle to keep up with her.

"The holes in the bone," Isa says, "were drilled for a metal plate of Swiss design used in hospitals in Torino, Milano, Firenze and Bologna starting in 1972. After seven years they moved on to another product, also made in Switzerland."

By the light of the street lamps, the rectangular flagstones look almost organic.

"Between 1972 and 1979, in the three hospitals in Milano and two in Torino that used them, four hundred and twenty-six oblique fractures similar to this one were set. More than half of these patients later had their metal plates removed. If we exclude those who are still alive now and those for whom a death certificate exists, the number is reduced to two."

"Two."

"From Torino and Milano. In Firenze and Bologna everything is on paper. You'd have to go there yourself to check that out."

"And the two names?"

"One is Erico Costela, born in Brazil in 1937. He came to Italy in 1969 and returned to his home country in 1976. There is no information on him after that date. He was only one metre sixty-five tall."

"And the other?"

"Stefano Aimar, born in San Damiano Macra in 1952, height one eighty-six. First operation in May 1972 after a motorcycle accident, plate removed in 1974. His last known address was in Via Bava, in an attic flat he shared with another student of philosophy like himself, but from October 1974 he's nowhere to be found."

"Nowhere to be found by who?"

"By us."

"You mean you and me?"

Isa nods. "Doesn't Via Lampredotti mean anything to you?"

"No."

"Or Andrea Gonella?"

Arcadipane stops to think.

"Not that name either."

Isa rolls herself a cigarette with tobacco from a packet Arcadipane has not seen before. Her fingers work with a particularly feminine efficiency. He notices her thumbnails are stained with scooter oil.

"On the morning of the twenty-first of October 1974," she lights her cigarette, protecting the flame with her hand even though there is no wind, "someone threw two Molotov cocktails into a neo-fascist MSI premises in Via Lampredotti. This Gonella had been slow to put away the papers he was working with and had stayed late. Aimar's name was mentioned in the investigation file."

"But they didn't find him where he was meant to be living?"

"No, nor anywhere else either."

"Neither then nor later on?"

"No."

Arcadipane slows down to use the toe of his shoe to prod something shining in the gap between two stones. An anchovy stuck in the pavement like a piece of pyrite. The air is still full of a smell of the fish that the hydrants and spatulas of the police have been unable to clear away.

"How did his name crop up?"

Isa puts her hands in her pockets and lifts her shoulders.

"It seems there were four of them that evening. One was Edoardo De Maria, a student studying history. He came from a well-off family; his father owned four private institutes and his mother had an active interest in rest homes. For some reason, De Maria's name was the first to become known, but by the time the police made a move to arrest him, he had already escaped to France. From there, helped by his family's lawyers, he agreed to give himself up in return for a minimal sentence."

"And for giving the names of the others?"

"Yes."

"Who were Stefano Aimar and ..."

"Maria Nicole Bo – she too came from a good family – and Luciano Cau, a twenty-eight-year-old man already known for subversive activities."

"Four in all."

"Four."

A figure on a bicycle appears on the lane for trams and

coaches that crosses the square. Arcadipane follows it with his eyes until it disappears behind the wooden handcarts in the deposit area. The squeaking of pedals stays in the air for several seconds before it's muffled by the cotton wool of the night. A bell in a nearby tower strikes one. It isn't cold, just damp.

"What happened to the others? Apart from Aimar."

"De Maria surrendered to the carabinieri at Ventimiglia in November '74. He was given sixteen months for conspiracy. After that he went back to his studies and has since had a university career; for the last ten years he's been a professor of history here in Torino. Cau, on the other hand, went underground as soon as he knew they were after him. His name surfaced years later in the Milanese section of the far-left Lotta Continua. Arrested in '81, he got life for two murders and three robberies, and did twenty-three years without ever opening his mouth about Via Lampredotti or anything else. He was given a conditional discharge in 2002 and his sentence was annulled in 2004, and he has been working for several years since then in a co-operative outside the city. Maria Nicole Bo, Aimar's girl, disappeared at the time and no-one knows anything more about her."

"So she was never found."

"No, but if she was the victim of a fascist vendetta, it could be that her bones are in that trench with Aimar's."

Arcadipane agrees this could be possible, but claims it would not explain the fact that there are ten more bodies, not including the one said to be from Milano, nor a dozen things that he can't remember for the moment; but he does feel that this disturbs the picture Isa is painting.

An old man in a dressing gown comes out onto a balcony on the third floor to water his plants. The splash of the water hits them like an explosion of fireworks. Arcadipane and Isa go back the way they came, following the same route.

"Anything else?" says Arcadipane once they are back outside the kebab bar.

Isa looks at the sign above it, which has now been switched off. A little smoke and a couple of silhouettes still float over the outside area. She sits down on the same step as before. The tinfoil, the cigarette ends and the tin can are still in the same place.

"Did you know anyone called Petri?"

Arcadipane nods. Petri had been senior commissario when Arcadipane first joined the police. He had been captured by the British in Africa during the war and spent a year as a prisoner of war in India. After that he never drank anything but sparkling mineral water. He had insisted on always having a full bottle on his desk. A good policeman. He retired a few years later and Bramard took his place.

Isa tongues the little metal ball inside her cheek.

"Petri started working on the Via Lampredotti case, but after a couple of weeks the file was passed to the politicians." Isa stubs out her cigarette on the step and pushes the fag end into the tinfoil that contained the kebab. "I tried to get into those archives before when I was looking for something about my father, but there was nothing in the digital material and you can't get at the original papers, if they even still exist. This doesn't prove that there's necessarily any mystery involved. It's just that some of this information might be useful simply because so few people know about it."

Arcadipane looks at her and it occurs to him that what she has said is wise, wise and bitter, and if he had not been such a shit himself, he would have asked her to roll him one of her special cigarettes, just to try it, and then would have sat down beside her: the boss and his best agent sitting together on a step in the ancient and multi-ethnic and rather dangerous heart of the city by night, both silently smoking their last cigarette, having moved the pieces a little further on than allowed for by the rules of the game, thus getting things ready so they can start work with a clear head the next day.

But, instead, he takes one of his own cigarettes, lights it and stays on his feet, because for him it is too late even for that. He has no talent and no time left for learning. Too late. He's just a shit on his feet and Isa's just a turd sitting there on the step.

"This was in the files of the flying squad," she says, pushing a sheet of paper towards him. "It was signed by the head of the political police at that time, Romano Fiore."

"Never heard of him."

"It's a request to release an agent who had been chosen to follow up the Via Lampredotti case. It was probably Petri who had it put in writing."

Arcadipane's face reveals nothing but extreme exhaustion and the need for a sofa to lie on and time to file away the pieces of the story already in place. Was this a good moment to add anything more? And in particular, anything not obviously relevant? Anything merely bureaucratic? Isa is still holding the sheet of paper out to him. Arcadipane can see that there are no more than three or four lines written on it. He takes it from her.

"I the undersigned Romano Fiore, head of the political police . . . date . . . request . . ." Arcadipane lets his eye run over the name of the agent to be seconded, comes to the end of the request, reads the date, place and signature, then sits down on the step.

"A bit of luck finding this, wasn't it?" Isa suggests.

Arcadipane thinks he would once have thought "Yes, by God!" with a light of revelation beginning to shine in his head. But now he feels nothing. And the worst part is that so much of him will never be seen again, like the hair on his head and his erect cock; so much that might once have enhanced a young man, though an old one rather less so.

"No," he says finally.

"Why not? He could have talked with a witness at the time and seen the reports, otherwise what would have been the point of seconding him?"

Arcadipane puts a sucai into his mouth and looks back at the road where they have just been walking to and from the square. Cars parked on both sides, dirty pavements, overflowing rubbish bins. A baker's shop, a mini-market, a shoemaker.

"No," he says again. "This is where the story ends."

Isa waits a few seconds, then starts smoking again. That's what's so beautiful about her. She doesn't give a damn. There may be other beautiful aspects of her that he is not aware of, or that have nothing to do with her work. Perhaps she is like those orchids that flower once in ten years. But this is certainly not that special day.

"I'll sort out that business about where you're working," Arcadipane says. "But don't expect a miracle from one day to the next."

Isa gets up and stretches, her jacket pulled aside to reveal a flat white stomach and a filigree of blue veins on the tense skin of her hip.

"Do you want the bone back? If not, I have a friend who owns an industrial press."

Arcadipane says that would be fine. "So long as you get rid of it."

He watches her go to where her scooter is chained to a post, take off the chain and start the scooter with a single kick of the pedal.

"At least she does have one friend," he reflects.

14

"Her name was Marta and she came from outside Torino. She had been with Renato, but they had split up after he came back from a holiday boasting of the girls he had had in Trento. But she made no fuss about this. She was different. Her father was a dentist, and her mother worked at a herbalist's shop in the Sassi area. They had an apartment there just because it had a thirty-metre terrace, and they could not afford one that big nearer the city centre. But they did their shopping locally and had their breakfast at Gingino, while like everyone else her father washed his car at the fountains and Marta used to hang out at the park benches.

"She wore her hair long with jeans and boots and smoked pipe tobacco rather than cigarettes. She seemed bigger and more foreign. Other girls tried to copy her. One or two stopped wearing bras, but there was something about Marta that they could not replicate. She and Renato had first met at the park benches, where he would come after work. He was bigger than the rest of us, rode a motorbike and lived in Mappano, and he had been working in a nightclub in Corso Brescia since he was fourteen.

"When she left him without making a fuss, he didn't make a fuss either. No-one saw him for several weeks, but eventually he reappeared with a new girl on his motorbike.

"Marta did not go with anyone else for several months. Then

she and I became an item. I was eighteen and she was seventeen. I was in my last year studying accountancy, had neither a car nor a motorbike and was not good-looking, but anyone from that district knows such things can happen. You just have to be in the right place at the right time, as I was.

"We mixed with the others around the benches, and sometimes went to the centre of town, to bookshops or the cinema, or to places where she could read communist newspapers. 'One day you'll hit me with a truncheon,' she used to say. I was already thinking of joining the police, but we never quarrelled about that.

"When I asked her to come with me for two days at the seaside, she said 'OK' and her parents made no objection; she had already been on holiday by herself in England.

"I was familiar with the town of Andora in Liguria, because as a child I used to go there each year for a week to stay with my uncle and aunt. I could remember a hotel on the beach, with white steel balconies and little tables in front. And I decided that would be ideal for us. We started out early one morning from Porta Nuova. Marta had a coat and a big leather bag like a seasoned traveller. I suppose we did the sort of things two young people together always do, but I cannot visualise us now as we must have been then.

"When we arrived at the coast it was overcast and drizzling. We left our bags at the hotel and went to the pier. We were both smoking, I had cigarettes and she had her tobacco.

"She suggested we go for a walk.

"'Good idea,' I said. 'And I know where to go.'

"When I was a child my uncle Cece and his wife owned two butcher's shops, an abattoir near the new stadium, and other businesses that dealt in horsemeat. They were the only rich people in our family and every summer they invited their three nephews to the sea, since their brothers had lent them the money to buy their first shop.

"They had an apartment in a block of flats called Albatros, above the Due Citroni restaurant. You couldn't see the sea from this apartment, but it was only five minutes away. We used the Tortuga bathing establishment, third row. Over the years we grew close with my grandparents who came from Poirino with our cousins, a boy my own age and a girl with hairs on her back that turned black when she came out of the sea. My grandfather was witty and set us riddles like, 'What's the one thing all else depends on? Its name, of course.' Each year I had forgotten the answer, so I continued to think it a very clever joke. My grandfather was still working. He'd been driving a lorry for the same firm for forty-five years.

"On the beach one evening, before we all went off to have supper, each family in its own accommodation, he told us how once when reversing his lorry in the company yard, he had run over and killed his boss's small son under the wheels of his trailer. He still wept when he thought of it, and his wife put her hand on his knee. But since it had been an accident, the boss didn't sack him. The little boy was called Marcellino and he wasn't quite three years old. Aunt Cetta also wept. Once a year my grandfather and his boss, Marcellino's father, would go out alone together to a distant restaurant where no-one knew them, and drink enough wine to get tipsy. Then the boss would thrash him in the car park. At work the next day he would weep and ask my grandfather's forgiveness, and my grandfather, in tears himself, would protest, 'Not at all, the thrashing did me good too.' As we sat on the sand listening to him, we had a feeling that him telling us this must be a unique moment that would never come again. And, in fact, he did only tell the story once in all the summers we sat there close together under our parasols.

"What we especially looked forward to each year was an expedition to a local sanctuary because on the way we had to pass a military base which had two radar antennae that could even be seen from the beach. We would also pass open jeeps and lorries driven by soldiers in green uniforms. So I would wear some green trousers that had been bought in the market and my brown sports jacket. I would strut a few metres in front of my uncle and aunt, believing anyone who saw me would think, 'Look, there's one of the soldiers from the base.'

"I expect I was remembering that when Marta and I passed the signboards denoting the military zone, but I may be wrong. We were going to sleep together that night for the first time. We had touched each other at her home once or twice in the afternoon when her parents were out at work but had never taken off our clothes. We could easily have had sex, since I knew she had done it with Renato. But, in fact, we never did. I don't think she ever tried to stop me; I just think we both felt there was a boundary, and for the moment we wanted to respect it.

"Now that we were naked together under the bedclothes in our hotel room, she was calm. 'That's quite normal,' I told myself. 'She's done it before. All I need do is relax.' But for some reason it didn't go well. First, I couldn't get an erection, then I had an emission at the wrong moment. After that, with us both still naked under the sheet, Marta began chattering as if nothing had happened at all, and when she eventually fell asleep, I went into the bathroom, opened the window and sat down on the toilet bowl. Outside it was raining, and the lights of the radar were shining. I remembered how I had walked near the base long ago when I was a child in my green trousers and brown jacket, and how no-one could ever have taken me for a soldier since I had only been seven years old, and how everyone would have been aware of that except myself. And that was the last time I wept."

"Until your present crisis began," the woman says.

On the hills that Arcadipane has been staring at while speaking, a football appears, or what might be an aerostatic probe, and eighteen seconds later it passes the right-hand edge of the dormer window on a diagonal trajectory. Only two days have passed since his first appointment with Ariel, but the season is already sucking light from everything.

"You must be tired now," she says.

He feels like laughing: a fisherman has caught a fish, gutted it and thrown the guts into the sea and this woman asks him if he's tired. But he does not laugh. He's too tired for that. He can hear her drinking from her cup. When he came in, he noticed an ashtray and the remains of a joint on the little table between the two armchairs.

"You have five more minutes. Do you want to say anything else? Maybe tell me how things finished with the girl?"

"No."

"Just as well. In any case, we know that having spent the rest of the night weeping in the bathroom, you came out in the morning and screwed her repeatedly, till they knocked on the door to tell you both it was time to give up the room. After that, in a matter of weeks, the affair ran its course, as I don't need to remind you. No doubt Marta will have gone on to better-educated men, to university studies, to drugs, to travelling, to interior-design journals and voluntary service in Africa. But let's concentrate on you, since it is you and not Marta who is paying for this. Have you said 'no' during the last few days?"

"In what sense?"

"A 'no' with a meaning, not just a response to brush aside someone who asks you for money or wonders if you want sugar in your coffee. But 'no' to something big you are sure you won't change your mind about. Have you said any 'noes' of that sort or not?"

Arcadipane folds his hands in his lap, in what he imagines must be the same position Ariel is holding her own hands. He thinks.

"Yes, I have."

"Oh, marvellous." She gives a snort. "Homework for next time, then: take at least two of those 'noes' and turn them into 'yeses'."

"Which would cause a hell of a mess."

"Do you think you come here to have fun? But you should know that this is merely something for inexperienced green-horns. I am almost ashamed to ask you such a question. Now you can go."

For the first time, Arcadipane allows himself to look at the woman; she turns out to be a girl with rather conventional brown eyes, brown hair tied back behind her head, olive skin and lips a shade darker. The sleeves of her blue men's shirt are rolled up, and there is a blanket over her legs because in this attic it is always chilly autumn. A young girl. She is beautiful, yes, but just a young girl.

"I'm twenty-seven." She laughs as he gazes at her. "Maybe still too young to be explaining specious stories to you."

He feels no need to speak because he has already answered her by moving his shoulders, his jaw and, despite himself, even his pelvis. She has a childish nose, and teeth which could be those of the Madonna if the Madonna were to smile. He finds a sucai and puts it in his mouth.

"You're mad," he says, getting up.

At the door he takes two fifty-euro notes from his wallet and leaves them in the expected place. He knows she is watching him over the back of her chair, but does not turn. Going out, he closes the door behind him.

In the entrance hall the unsociable caretaker watches him, leaning against the jamb of the door with his mop and woollen rag. Arcadipane crosses five metres of waxed seventies marble, in his confusion pulling the handle twice before realising he should be pushing it, and finally reaches the road.

There is a single fragment of black cloud at the end of the avenue, with the rest of the sky blue. "A largely cloudless sky," as the radio forecast insisted that morning in the car. "Though by the weekend it may be different."

Going down the steps to the pavement, he becomes more aware that his mind is not working properly. He can't remember where he left his car. Or did he come by public transport? And if so, when could he have been listening to the radio? Should he go back home now? Or go to the city centre? Or call Pedrelli? Or is Pedrelli due to call him? And what about that bone and Via Lampredotti? And where will Giovanni be playing on Sunday? And who is Nascimbene? And what the hell does everyone want from him?

He crosses a moderate flow of traffic and goes into the bar on the other side of the road. He orders an iced coffee and shuts himself in the toilet.

Throwing a handful of what seems to be boiling hot water into his face, he lets some drop on his shoes, the floor and the collar of his shirt. When he feels the water reach his navel, he becomes even more confused, wet and upset.

"Will you have your coffee at the counter, or do you prefer to sit down?" asks the waiter when Arcadipane emerges from the toilet.

He takes the ridiculous triangular glass he is given, and without answering, carries it to the table near the window, throws himself onto the overstuffed chair and takes a sip. Why did he ask for cold coffee? What ought to be hot is not good cold. Hot and cold are not the same thing. And he's been given a macaroon too! He takes his phone and calls the most familiar number on it.

"Oh!" she says.

"It's me."

"I know it's you! What's going on?"

"Nothing. Just saying hello. Are you at home?"

"It's eleven o'clock on Thursday. I'm at school."

"Why did you answer if you're at school?"

"Because it's the second break now. But what's the matter?"

"What's the matter? Why should anything be the matter? And the children?"

"They must be at school too, unless you know more than I do. Are you in the centre or out of town?"

"Out of town."

"What are you doing? Tell me."

"How can I tell you? In a moment you'll have to be back in class!"

She thinks.

"We could have a bite to eat after school, if you like. The kids can look after themselves at home."

"Look after themselves, just imagine! By selling the furniture, I suppose. In any case, I'm in a bar. Having an iced coffee. It's very good too."

"Good for you. Don't worry."

"What is there for me not to worry about?"

"Nothing, everything's fine. The kids may seem a bit up and down, but I keep my eye on what's going on. We're lucky. They're on the right trajectory."

"Trajectory? What are you talking about? Why are you being so confusing today?"

"Never mind. Let's talk about it later calmly at home, alright? Now do whatever it is you have to do. But keep calm, mind."

Through the window of the bar, Arcadipane sees quiet traffic and a few passers-by. Drops of rain are beginning to hit the pavement, wetting the cars, the leaves and the steps of the house opposite.

"Vincenzo?"

He sees the caretaker throw open the door of the building he has just left and a moment later Ariel emerges. A few large drops of rain immediately strike her open raincoat and blue man's shirt. She stops, balancing on crutches, her big black shoes giving her a precarious foothold, then looks up.

"Vincenzo? I can't hear you!"

Then she begins moving again, taking the first step at a rush, and the second almost through inertia; then the third nearly throws her forward, stunted legs swinging under her coat like the clapper of a bell.

Now she has reached the pavement, on her feet in the rain. She looks first right, then left. A couple of people who happen to be passing slow down, but even if she has no hat or umbrella and with her crutches cannot raise her hands to protect herself, she does not give the impression of someone in need of help. So the passers-by don't stop, and even the caretaker has gone back into the house.

"Are you still there, Vincenzo?"

Ariel goes off to the left, firm little breasts shaping her wet shirt. Arcadipane watches her laborious and erratic progress. She terrifies him, but he also sees her as in some way belonging to him.

"Vincenzo?"

She opens the door of a nearly new Golf the colour of white coffee, throws her shoulder bag on the passenger seat and her crutches into the back, and leans for a moment on the canopy as if anxious to take in a little more air before shutting herself up in the car. Its coachwork is bubbling with splashes that hide her face. Then she gets in, starts the engine and drives away.

"Vincenzo?"

"Yes."

"Ah, there you are! I couldn't hear you just now."

"I'm still here."

Silence.

"I love you, Vincenzo, so please try not to get shot, or sign any cheques, or fall in love with another woman before this evening. Then we'll be able to sort everything out, alright?"

"Yes." He rings off.

Two or three people have come into the bar to get out of the rain. They order coffee or mineral water to pay for their shelter. Things that don't cost much.

Putting his hand into his pocket, Arcadipane finds the metal rivet button. Stroking its raised five-letter inscription, he feels an infinitesimal movement inside him that reminds him of his old hunger. Nothing much, just the faintest hint of returning appetite.

15

He stares at the magnetic quartz clock on the dashboard. The guy on the phone said five, but he has now been waiting in the excavated car park for at least half an hour, asphyxiated by the stink of manure, diesel and stale water typical of the countryside.

He lowers his window and studies the bell tower of a village not far away, insects flying over fields of threshed maize, and the tremor of sunflowers in a nearby garden. He is twenty kilometres from Torino now, but there is no trace of the storm that struck the Alfa on the way out. In any case, everything always comes late in the countryside.

He lights another cigarette and scratches his knee. He is creating a hell of a mess and he knows it. He has deliberately chosen to go out of town to give himself time to reflect and change his mind, but instead . . .

In his rear mirror he sees a red Renault Kangoo draw up, the only person in it the driver.

Here goes, he tells himself.

The guy parks on the opposite side of the open space, raising a cloud of dust. He gets out and opens the boot of his car. As Arcadipane can see from a distance, he is wearing overalls and a pair of well-worn ancient jeans, neither of them too clean.

The guy grasps a heavy sack of what could well be pet food and tucks it under his arm, while using his free hand to close the car door. He seems slim, but there must be more to him than meets the eye. You'd have to be strong to tuck a bag that must weigh at least thirty kilos under your arm.

Arcadipane gets out of his car.

"Hi," he calls to the other man, whose curly hair is covered with dust.

They shake hands and together make their way towards a gate in the fence. Dogs start barking from the far side.

"Normally, we're not open on Friday afternoons, but I had to come in to do a bit of cleaning. On Saturdays there's always a mass of people here."

He has a full set of teeth, though they all seem to be in the wrong places. He also has a finger missing. Arcadipane asks himself if this is a job reserved for the handicapped; if word got round that all you needed was to cut off your finger, the hospitals would be better prepared for it.

The guy opens a shed on the left and dumps his sack.

"OK, let's go," he says.

They walk along a concrete path. On one side, a small field has been stripped almost to bare earth, while on the other is the shed that contains the kennels, with cages visible in the distance.

"She tells me she has no special requirements."

"I see."

"And no previous experience."

"No matter. In questions of this kind one must be guided by instinct. But she does live in the city, doesn't she?"

"In the very heart of it."

"Then let's make sure we avoid anything unsuitable. I don't want to see you hurrying back here again in a month or so."

The first cage contains two large animals that show little interest in their visitors.

"The one on the left is already eight years old and not the most pleasant of animals. Grew up in the street, one of the old school. And cunning with it, a bit too much so. In his case you'd have to bear that in mind. The other, definitely not, he doesn't like strangers. Or to put it another way, he doesn't really like anyone."

They walk on. In the second cage a small white dog with curly hair comes to the bars and barks, as if in celebration. Two others, more cautious, also come forward. Half-size. The guy sticks one of his nine remaining fingers through the bars and strokes their damp noses.

"The little white one, Dorina, is an excellent dog. Two years old, neutered and used to living in a flat. She doesn't need much exercise, will sit happily on a sofa and likes everybody. The hound here is also a dog of good character, but needs plenty of exercise. So for anyone short of time . . . Then there's Alfred, a very good dog, six years old. He needs more confidence, but he has a very warm personality. Possibly a little deaf. Deaf dogs sometimes howl in the night. Which wouldn't do in a flat, of course. But you can't go wrong with Dorina. I'd put her in pole position."

"OK."

"See some more?"

"Yes, please."

In the next cage a small muscular backside protrudes from a dog basket.

"Not this one," is all the guy says, moving on. "And here are two half-husky siblings. The boy has problems with other males, but the girl is ready for adoption. She too has been sterilised, a good year old or more and used to everything. They came from Sicily in circumstances I won't bother to explain. The one in the dog basket would suit an experienced owner. There's a trace of Czech wolf in him. They are territorial dogs that need a lot of exercise, the right food, and a strong owner interested in sport. With the right approach they can give great satisfaction, but if you go about it in the wrong way, you're finished. No offence, sir, but I don't really see him as the right dog for you."

Arcadipane turns back.

"What about that one in the cage by himself?"

"His owner seems to have been a painter. When the old man died, his nephew brought the dog here, but he's minus a hind leg, more than ten years old and half blind. We keep him separate because otherwise he bites other dogs, even puppies. Unfortunately, even dogs can sometimes have a nasty character."

Arcadipane smokes and looks at other cages.

"What happens if after a time no-one adopts any of these dogs? Do you have them put down?"

The man stares at him, horrified.

"Are you quite sure you want to own a dog?"

"Why do you ask?"

"We never kill dogs here. Dogs that don't get adopted can stay until they die a natural death. Volunteers take them out for walks in the country three times a week. They get food and medical care and can play, and though they are confined in cages, they are of course living in the country."

Arcadipane looks around, still smoking.

"I'm glad you don't kill them."

"No, we never kill them. Would you like to think the matter over a little longer? It's not a decision to be taken lightly."

"I know. But let's go on."

They reach an area with cages on both sides. Some of these contain litters. The mothers are lying in shady corners out of the wind, and not far from bowls of water that seem to have a little weed growing in them. They are supervising their puppies, which are exploring and playing. The roof panels, grilles and concrete paths around here emanate sleep and somnolence. Nearly all the mothers have their tongues hanging out.

"This is where we keep puppies with their mothers. If you see anything you like, just raise your hand and we'll stop. Tomorrow, when children come with their parents, the puppies will be the first to go. Sometimes we have to protest because the children want puppies that are still suckling, and that may also need to be taken away to be dewormed. But feel free to look round a bit for yourself, and in the meantime, I'll give them some water. Don't hurry, just 'look for your counterpart' as my old master used to say."

Arcadipane asks himself who the hell a man working at the kennels could have had for a master. The guy heads back to the storage area while Arcadipane studies a cage with the words PALMIRA & SONS written on it. The mother inside is part hunter and part wolf. She has five puppies: two black, two white and one brown. The brown one is sitting facing the wall. When Arcadipane says "Tzé" to it, the puppy turns, lowers its snout and looks at him as if through bifocal spectacles.

"Well, Professor, which of you lot is the best, you yourself or one of your brothers and sisters?"

Professor gets up and goes over to his siblings, as if to consult them, but they ignore him and go back to their games. Arcadipane watches them, thinking over the many things he has experienced during the last few days.

The other guy is now on his knees, refixing a rubber pipe that has come loose from the kennels' external tap. He has put on a pair of gloves. When he hears Arcadipane coming, he turns and screws up his eyes against the sun.

"Well, have you made up your mind?"

16

For the last thirty years, perhaps longer, he has not driven down this road, but thirty years ago he did take it many times and nearly always for the sorts of reasons one never forgets. Which is why he does not hesitate at the roundabouts, even if last time he came this way there were none, and he soon finds himself back among piles of red earth that tractors have already dug over. He passes a lorry-drivers' restaurant where he remembers eating with Bramard, a cemetery already abandoned even then, and a castle half-hidden behind tall trees and a kiln, where he turns right. He checks the time to see if this could be a suitable hour to call. He knows that in those days the man used to eat early, but now of course . . .

The road narrows. He is forced to stop and mount the grass verge at one side when he meets a tractor with a manure-spreader and an old woman in a small car who inspires scant confidence. By now it is half past seven. Perhaps he can make good use of the time . . . even if this would be his second balls-up of the day, following his visit to the kennels. Though maybe this time, if he doesn't hurry, things will go differently.

He enters the trattoria, pushing his way through anti-fly strips. At a couple of tables people are already eating. "These bloody Piedmontese," he tells himself. "Mariangela wouldn't even have got round to heating the water yet."

He sits down at a table laid for one. The place has not changed much. For one thing, the table is still covered with the same wedding gauze as before, and infested with the same flies.

A woman approaches from the kitchen. Clearly, she does not recognise him. Not surprising, since she has only seen him a couple of times before, and that was thirty years ago.

"Well, what are we going to eat?" she asks in a strong local accent.

"Do you have carp?"

"Not today. Not when the warm weather is past."

"But it was quite hot today."

"If you give me a day's notice next time you come, I'll make sure we get some in."

Arcadipane does not even glance at the menu in his hand. He only came in here at all to have a moment to think. But since he *is* here . . .

"How about meat?"

"The cold meat's over there and you can help yourself. Or there's chops, grilled sirloin, liver and trout fresh from the fish tank. Unless you fancy frogs."

"Frogs, please."

"Frogs, then."

"And a half-litre of white. But first I'll have a quick look at the starters."

He watches the woman walk away: still beautiful despite tired arms, hair tightly pulled back, and breasts beginning to sag. He tries to visualise her at seventeen, when he knows Bramard had her in a field during some local festivity: his first woman. One of the few confidences Bramard ever shared with him, as he did one evening long ago over a meal in this place. It's unbelievable, but he can still remember everything Bramard said to him. And all the things they did together.

Now, after eating, he goes to the counter to ask for his bill and a coffee.

"Did you enjoy the frogs?"

"Yes, very much."

The woman leans across the counter to look down at the dog and her overalls fall open revealing a slight décolletage.

"Shall we give your friend something to eat too?"

"No, thanks very much, that won't be necessary," says Arcadipane.

She leans back behind the counter again, making no attempt to cover her décolletage. "I know dogs are just animals," she says, "but they can still cause trouble."

Ten minutes later Arcadipane takes a cart track that branches off from the road, and after a couple of bends, recognises the farmhouse at the top of a hill. The building still forms an L to the south, but otherwise seems to him in some sense to have changed. When he stops in the yard, he sees the roof has been restored and the front is now white, and there are vases of flowers on the stairs leading up to the kitchen, and geraniums in the windows.

"You wait here," he tells the dog.

Getting out of the car, he goes towards the steps. It's nearly half past eight now, but daylight is still clinging to the white walls. On the other hand, the mountains in the distance are blue. Between the house and the mountains lie some sixty kilometres of typical Piedmontese fields.

He knocks. The woman who answers the door is Elena. He knows who she is, even though he has never seen her before.

"Good evening," he says.

"Good evening."

Her fair hair has been pinned back behind her ears where it is longest. Not even the duster over her shoulder, or her singlet and Bermuda shorts can disguise the fact that she is Eastern European and beautiful.

"I'm Arcadipane, an old colleague of Corso's."

"Vincenzo?"

"Vincenzo."

"He's in there." She points with her chin.

The roofed area opposite the house, which used to contain an ancient tractor and other rubbish, has now been enclosed and the arches on the second floor have been glazed over. Where grass used to grow between the bricks there is now a creeper. Organised greenery, a deliberate design.

"Your friend's up to something," Elena says, looking at the Alfa.

Arcadipane turns to see a dark shadow clinging to the head-rest and wriggling about.

"Excuse me," he says, rushing back down the stairs.

Opening the car door, he finds the dog with a piece of padding still in its jaws.

"Come out!" he commands in a stifled shout.

He would like to give the animal a kick up the bum, but aware that Elena is watching him, heads for the farm annexe with the dog following.

At the top of the stairs, he shields his eyes with his hands from the sun's reflection off the glass in the door. Bramard is sitting at a rough table, opposite a small boy with his hair cut as if from under a bowl, a striped T-shirt and no obvious desire to be getting on with whatever he is supposed to be doing. At the far end of the room, a girl of about twelve is reading in an armchair. The three sides of the room that are not glass are lined with books.

Knock, knock.

Corso turns, and something he was about to say to the boy

remains trapped between his lips. He shows no surprise, only his familiar distant wooden expression. When Arcadipane opens the door, the small boy jumps to his feet.

"Just say that one more time," Corso tells him, "and we'll check it again before you go to bed."

"But I know it!"

"So do I. That's why we have to check it."

The small boy throws the exercise book into his small school bag.

"Who's that man?" he asks, nodding towards Arcadipane.

"A friend. And when you learn to ask questions properly, you'll find out more."

The child purses his mouth, as if to imply he couldn't care less, and hoists the satchel onto his shoulder.

"Ani!" he calls loudly to the girl.

She shakes her head without taking her eyes off the page she is reading.

"You can take the book with you," Corso tells her.

Ani shuts the book and calmly swings her legs and feet down from the armchair. Her body may resemble a tube of toothpaste, but it is clear that there is something powerful inside her, for the moment under control.

"How is it?" Corso asks as she passes him.

"Very beautiful, thank you," and she pats the cover of the book.

The two children mill round Corso, then go out.

"What sort of animal is that?" they hear the boy asking his sister as they go down the stairs.

"Boh!" is all the answer he gets.

Through the windows they can be seen cutting across the yard. The boy has stolen her book. She catches him up and snatches it back from his hand. Shoving each other, they climb the stairs and disappear into the house.

"What happened to that dog's paw?" Corso asks.

Arcadipane looks at the man who used to be his boss and who still, despite his shorter hair and more mellow eyes, has the same enigmatic expression. Corso's shoulders are more compact, as if his muscles have relaxed, but he is still just as tall and his movements no less athletic.

"I don't know," he says. "I haven't had him very long."

"How long is not very long?"

"A couple of hours."

Corso looks at the dog sitting close to Arcadipane's feet.

"But he's following you. What's his name?"

"*Trepet.*"

"What does that mean . . . ?"

"I don't know. It could be the name of a painter, I suppose."

"How is it written?"

Arcadipane takes from his pocket a booklet the guy at the kennels gave him and passes it over.

"*Tre pé,*" Corso says. "That's Piedmontese. It means three feet."

Arcadipane takes back the booklet and puts it in his pocket without comment. The dog breathes heavily as if worried, then farts and relaxes.

"Are you still teaching at that school?" Arcadipane asks.

"Still there."

"Still part-time?"

"No, full-time nowadays. Things have changed a bit."

Arcadipane looks towards the house where Elena is beating a small mat out of the window.

"How is it with the children?"

"Ani's easy. She already knew a little Italian, and she likes school and reading and made new friends immediately. But Matei's only just beginning to find his feet. He was closer to their father. School doesn't appeal to him much. I try to help him along."

"And Martina?"

"She came a couple of times in the early days: she wanted to see how her mother was doing and get to know me and so on, but then she went away all at sixes and sevens. I haven't seen her or heard from her for a year. Her father left her an apartment and some money. As far as that goes she's independent. In June, after she matriculated, she wrote to me, and we spent a few days together climbing in the mountains round Basel. We've agreed that she will never be what she could have been, but she will still be able to make something of herself. Now she's gone back to the Ivory Coast with the non-governmental organisation she works for. And your kids?"

"Giovanni plays football and if he doesn't make a cock-up of things, he'll pass his exams this year. Loredana's chosen classical studies and is going great guns, but she's putting on weight."

"And Mariangela?"

"Fine. She understands the children. She's teaching, and she keeps me going."

"So you two didn't divorce after all?"

"No."

"Are you ill?"

"No."

"Have you started taking bribes?"

"No."

"Then why have you come here now?"

Arcadipane takes a few steps towards the big windows. Trepet follows him, then collapses a metre away. He lifts his single back leg to lick his testicles. He is like the sort of log one hopes will fit into the fireplace, because otherwise one has no idea how to reduce it to a suitable size to put on the fire.

"Have you heard about those bones found near Chivasso?"

"I read something about it in the paper."

"It began as our case, then people from Milano got involved. I don't know how, but they've made up their minds that the bones must date back to the Second World War."

"In the paper it says that they're specialists."

"That's what the questore said when he called me at nine in the evening to make sure I was co-operating with him. Next day one of the Milano people came to our HQ to collect some exhibits we had kept back."

"But . . . ?"

"I deliberately held on to a thigh bone."

"A thigh bone."

"A thigh bone."

Bramard says no more. Arcadipane puts his hands in his pockets and watches Matei, out in the courtyard, kicking a red football against the wall of the house.

"Can one smoke here?"

"Come with me, let's go out."

They cross the yard as Matei celebrates scoring a goal by running around with his arms out. The ball comes to rest, unattended. A sound of puncturing can be heard and the puff of escaping air.

"What the fuck are you doing?" shouts the little boy.

"Matei!"

"He's made a hole in it, this *mânji!*"

"Take another ball from the garage." Corso strokes the boy's head but keeps walking.

Dog and child look at each other for a few seconds before Matei sets off for the garage. Trepet pisses briefly on the now deflated ball, then runs after the men, who have by now turned the corner.

"Are you making wine?" Arcadipane asks, pointing to the orderly rows of vines on the hillside.

"No. The vines were allowed to go to rack and ruin for too long. But maybe in a few years' time. What's all this about a thigh bone, then?"

Arcadipane describes Alessandra's discovery. In mid flow he stops himself.

"And there was this too."

Bramard takes the Rifle rivet button and turns it about in his fingers. There is a smell of grass and a smell of burnt wood from the chimney.

"Then why invent a story about bones from the war?"

"Would you prefer to walk on dried-out shit, or on shit that may still smell of something?" Arcadipane says, putting the rivet back in his pocket. "Twelve people killed in wartime doesn't need much explaining; but twelve in the nineteen seventies, that's another matter . . ."

Corso turns towards the upper part of the hill. The vines on the summit are still catching the last of the light, but just as he becomes aware of this, they suddenly vanish into shadow. Trepet is crouching at the men's feet. He has a white streak on his head, like an old dandy in a dancehall.

"How long did it take her to find out the name?"

"Who?"

"You know who. If you haven't spoken to higher authorities, you won't have been able to use interior resources. So you took the bone and brought it to her. That's what I would have done. How long did it take her?"

Arcadipane scratches his knee.

"Half a day."

"And . . . ?"

"Do you remember Via Lampredotti?"

"I do."

"It seems the bones must have come from one of those four."

"Aimar?"

Arcadipane searches for Corso's eyes, but in the rapidly increasing darkness he cannot see anything.

"How do you know?"

Corso lifts a wax match to the Gitanes between his lips. The match goes out, leaving a red glow.

"Because he was the only one of the five with a limp."

"Five? The file only mentions four."

On the municipal road a small lorry passes at double the speed limit, making a noise known even in the dark to policemen and thieves of the old school, because it used to be the speed bank couriers would drive at. From the house come children's voices and the smell of supper.

"How about a bite to eat?" Corso asks.

Arcadipane lights one of his own cigarettes and shakes his head.

"Then I'll go down and tell them not to wait for us," Corso says.

Arcadipane watches him cut across the vineyard with the confidence of a man putting his feet down as he gets out of his own bed. In spite of the two cigarettes, the vineyard still has a smell of its own, as does the earth and Trepet too.

PART TWO

PART TWO

Second Prologue

Five young people in an attic with a sloping roof. Night-time outside the dormer window. A man is sitting on the floor with one leg bent at an acute angle, leaning against the divan that also serves as a bed. He is wearing a leather jacket and the hand holding his cigarette is supported by his knee. He's the oldest of the group.

"Are you sure?" he asks calmly.

The boy walking round the room has his hair cut in a bob that follows the natural shape of his skull and the faintest hint of a beard. He has a beige corduroy trench coat and a plump red face.

"Of course I'm sure," he shouts. "I've been there since yesterday! Exactly the same cars!"

"Keep your voice down," says one of the three who are sitting at the table, taking tobacco from the pocket of his parka.

The boy in the trench coat watches him calmly roll himself a cigarette. He looks at the other two at the table: a girl who is a classic beauty and a tall boy who looks like a singer-songwriter.

"They even have a two-way radio in their car!" He spreads his arms. "Who do you think they can be?"

The girl's expression doesn't change. She has pulled off her sweater and hung it over the back of her chair. The boy, still in his grey coat, has a gloomy expression.

"Luciano, what do you think?" the man sitting on the floor says.

Luciano lights the cigarette he has finally finished rolling. A puff of smoke rises to the curved top of the dormer window.

"They can't be much in the way of coppers if they let themselves be fooled by someone like Edo. And anyway, how did they come to think of him?"

"Because someone must have seen us, of course!" says the boy in the trench coat angrily. "And if there was a witness, we're all fucked up, every one of us! My car's outside and tonight I'm off to France. If anyone wants to come with me . . ."

"What would be the point of that?" the boy in the parka says. "What could we do in France?"

"I don't know, but at least we'll be able to keep out of sight. Then there's my people . . . and there's Spain, and South America. We can surely find some way to disappear."

"Fine for those with money," the girl says.

The boy in the trench coat spins round.

"Why, haven't you got plenty of money yourself? You'd better be careful: even if it suits you to play at being working class, we all know who you really are!"

The girl smiles. The rain still tapping on the window is almost inaudible.

"We'll just have to give ourselves up," the boy who looks like a singer-songwriter says.

The first to turn on him is the girl.

"And you can shut up!"

"No!" The boy in the leather jacket intervenes. "Let him speak."

The boy in the grey coat looks at his hands. He knows he won't manage to say much before someone interrupts him. So he must choose his words carefully.

"We could never have known there was a man there. If we hand ourselves in, we can . . ."

142

"Don't you ever read the papers?" The boy in the trench coat raises his voice. "Isn't it obvious which way the wind's blowing? They won't give a fuck that we didn't know that. We'll be locked up and that'll be the end of us. The place is full of fascists. We wouldn't last two days."

"Our comrades who are in there are surviving well enough," says the one in the parka.

"That's because they have a proper organisation behind them, they're not poor fools like us!"

"Edo's right about that," the girl says. "What's done is done. It's stupid to think it'll be enough for us just to say sorry."

A bus passes in the street five floors below. Its rumble is gradually swallowed up in the rain.

"This extenuating circumstances business," the man in the sheepskin coat says. "Was that just your idea?"

"What do you mean?" says the boy in the grey coat.

"Did you think it up yourself, or did someone else put it into your head?"

The boy in the grey coat glances round to judge the expressions of the others. The girl beside him looks distant.

"You don't have to be a lawyer to understand that there are extenuating circumstances in a case like this."

The man in the leather jacket extinguishes his cigarette on the tiled floor.

"I wanted to wait a while before raising the subject, but now the discussion has taken this turn . . ." He raises his other knee and leans his other arm on it. "What we are dealing with here is something organised and extensive. We are a group taking serious action. Our colleagues are willing to welcome us in and give us something to do, and I'm not just talking about picket lines or blocking some fascists. We don't need more student nonsense. But we do need to be sure of ourselves. No more talk

143

of family, friends and university. There can be no turning back now."

The attic is silent and full of smoke, while the rain seems to be beating more heavily on the window.

"You can count me in," the girl says.

The boy in the grey coat puts his hand on her arm.

"Let's wait a few days, maybe Edoardo . . ." But the girl has already pulled her arm away.

"And what do you say, Luciano?" the boy in the leather jacket says.

The boy in the parka pulls a fragment of tobacco from his lip and shakes his head.

"I'll be disappearing, but I have contacts already. Each man for himself. Then we'll see."

"Edo?"

The boy in the trench coat does not know where to put his hands. He was unsure of himself when the discussion started, and he is now even more so. And there are not many places in this attic where he can rest his eyes apart from the eyes of the others.

"I'm going to France," he finally finds the courage to say. "I think that's best. We have to give things a chance to settle down. Then later we want to—"

"We've got the point." The man in the jacket cuts him short. "And what about you, Stefano? Will you go to France with Edo? Or are you going to go with Luciano? Or do you still plan to give yourself up to the police?"

Stefano looks at the girl, but her eyes are on the man in the leather jacket. She shows no trace of the fear and indecision the boy at her side hopes for. Nothing but confidence, readiness for action, and something even more terrifying that makes him feel insignificant, simple-minded and cowardly.

"I'll go where Nini goes," he says.

17

"Have the neighbours said what the smoke was like? Was it more brown or more black?"

"More black," Petri said.

The doctor allowed himself a few seconds to assess the room, about ten square metres now reduced to a splash of charcoal; then scratched his nose, which he had plugged.

"Based on my own experience, I would say the fire must have started down below. The man was probably up here, perhaps asleep, and hearing the bottles explode may have run to the stairs, but the petrol would have already set the linoleum alight and filled the ground floor with smoke. Assuming he couldn't reach the door, he would have gone back upstairs. He knew about the iron bars, of course, but he may have thought he had more time or that someone would come to his rescue."

Corso Bramard looked at the stairs up which the flames had travelled, and at the floor, on which a sticky layer, still warm, bore the imprint of their shoes.

"But in fact that's not what happened at all," the doctor continued. "The fire rose up quickly, attacked the carpet and in a few seconds all the oxygen –" he waved a hand to indicate *was finished* – ". . . had been replaced by carbon dioxide, hydrocyanic acid and sulphur dioxide, all things you can't breathe. That's why his mouth is between the bars: he was desperate for air. The only good thing is that in fires like this people hardly ever die of burns. When the flames reached him, he was probably already dead. Not much in the way of consolation, but in our job, we have to take what we can get, don't we?"

Corso looked at the dead man grasping the window bars: his skin dark red and his hands swollen, the odd scrap of cloth still sticking to a body that had lost all its hair. The feet in their shoes were stuck to the floor, as if the fire had grabbed him by the ankles to hold him back. The stink of what the doctor had named hovered invisibly in the air, stinging eyes and nostrils.

"Is this the first death you've seen?" Petri asked Corso.

"The first in a fire."

Petri signed a few documents, using the bag the doctor was holding up as a desk.

"Thank you, Domenico," Petri said. "We'll meet again tomorrow at HQ."

The doctor looked at his wristwatch.

"Later today, you mean," he corrected. Once his hat had disappeared down the stairs, all that was left in the room were the sounds made by three firemen testing the strength of the floor. From below they could hear the blows struck by one of their colleagues busy testing the ceiling down there in the same way.

"You lot go downstairs," Petri said.

The three firemen gave him sidelong looks, wondering whether or not to take orders from a policeman. Petri's impassive face convinced them, so they collected their equipment and went down. Going to the second window, the one the victim had not tried to open, Petri lit a cigarette.

"Take a good look," he said. "Even if we search for a glass that's half-full rather than half-empty, you're never likely ever to see anything worse than this."

Thrusting his hands into his pockets, Corso studied what was left of the man's lips, ears and nose. The eyes, dried up and still fixed on some point across the road, were the only thing that still retained their original colour: blue. Everything else had been reduced to a colourless mineral.

He went over to Petri at the window to share the clean air that his superior had pulled rank to be the first to breathe.

The windows, which had exploded in the heat, were now letting in cool night air and the hum of the crowd down in the road. Corso looked first at those beyond the security barrier, then up at those in pyjamas at the windows and on the balconies of nearby flats. Probably the very people who had heard the man shouting for help and then watched him burn without being able to do anything about it, apart from calling the police and the fire brigade. A dozen phone calls, starting with an anonymous tip off from a phone booth: "There's a fire in Via Lampredotti . . . with a man shut inside." It had come too late: in fifteen minutes the fire, primed with petrol, had ruthlessly destroyed the small house packed with wood, paper and synthetic materials. And with it a man who'd had no chance to escape.

A confusion of voices came to them up the stairs.

"So much for a moment of peace," Petri said, extinguishing his cigarette on the windowsill and returning its remains to his pocket.

Suddenly the room was filled with people who had no idea what to do but felt the need to rush round pretending to do something. Petri started allotting jobs: testing for false floors or empty walls, listing significant objects like weapons, papers and photographs. "Please," he added to no-one in particular, "will someone cover that dead body with a sheet, but don't touch it, there are people coming who will deal with it."

When Petri went downstairs, Corso stayed by the window, ignoring the looks colleagues now busy in the room were giving him.

He was watching the street where police were using a tape to hold back inquisitive onlookers, while a woman from the evening paper was talking to the leading fireman. The man answered questions by shaking his head and spreading his arms, then went back to propping himself solemnly against the fire engine.

Turning back into the room, Corso looked at the dead man, whom no-one had yet covered. He calculated the angle of the head and the direction in which the man had been looking, then studied the small houses opposite. All much like the house he was in now: at most two or three storeys, relics of a time when this area had been a village and not yet part of the city. He could see the entrance to a warehouse at street level, two other doors, two shops and the roll-up shutter of what could be a garage.

He headed for the stairs, but a police sergeant barred his way.

"Where do you think you're off to? Can't you see there are things to be done here?"

Corso held his gaze. The man was about thirty, of middle height, slim, with a curved back as though someone had given him a push when he was a small child and he had never tried to straighten it since.

"Bramard!" At that moment Petri's voice came up to him from the lower floor.

The sergeant smiled, revealing that his teeth were his best feature.

"Remember, when a sergeant farts, constables have to enjoy the smell." Then, with an automatic nod of the head in Bramard's direction: "Get on with you then, little Papà needs you."

Downstairs, firemen were still poking about in a clutter of blackened ruins. Only the metal skeletons of an armchair and an umbrella stand were recognisable. Several shapeless lumps were still giving off smoke and heat.

"We can throw this stuff away," Petri was saying, staring at a huge pair of shoes standing on the floor in a few centimetres of black water. He looked at Corso. "Well?"

"Nothing," Corso said.

"No ideas?"

"Afraid not."

"Take a bit longer to look around. There's no hurry. Don't forget, even at Moncalieri things started by being . . . then you noticed those marks."

Corso took a few steps towards the door, the stairs, and the wall, against which there must have been a bookcase. Then he went back to his starting point.

"It happened like the doctor said."

Petri stared at him.

"Then I shall promote that doctor to be my special guard. Anything to avoid being fucked over by the powers that be. You know how communists get on the questore's wick."

"But I'm not a communist."

"Then why not dress like a Christian, for Christ's sake? Even in uniform you look like you've come straight from a funeral. And that hair and moustache. Get a razor! Iron your uniform! The sergeant reported you to me twice last month. Do you think we're in America here? Where people can go to work in blue jeans?"

Corso gave Petri the same stare as he had given the sergeant earlier: his expression in no sense hostile but almost sleepy, his lack of respect emphasised by his shirt with its eccentric collar and the fact that, though he was still only twenty-three years old, he was considerably taller than everyone else at police HQ.

"Now be off with you!" Petri burst out suddenly. "Go and have a walk outside, then at least you won't be fucking us all up!"

Corso passed between a couple of colleagues, who were explaining to a girl in a dressing gown that they had been the first to get into the house. On the pavement opposite, the crowd was beginning to thin out. It was two in the morning now, and those on an early shift would soon have to think about getting to work.

A car appeared in the road. No horn or siren, just the driver leaning out of his window and stating without conviction: "Out of the way, I have to get through . . ." The car was a Giulia like the police cars, though coloured green and with nothing written on it. The officers lifted the cordon, and the car went to park near the firemen's vehicles. Three men got out of it: the driver, together with a man of about forty with a moustache, corduroy trousers, short boots and a heavy jacket, and another man about ten years older, his thick white hair combed with a parting. Under his open coat this older man was wearing a dark double-breasted suit.

They glanced briefly at the letters MSI on the door of the house, now almost completely obscured by the smoke, and went inside.

Corso walked on along the pavement towards the crossroads at the far end of the road. Every so often someone turned to look because of his police uniform, but no-one spoke to him. He reached the point where Via Lampredotti met the main street at a small area containing two benches, three rubbish bins, a fountain, a public urinal, a telephone box and a tram stop with the tramlines running on to form the spine of the main street. Turning, he looked back at the blackened house two hundred metres away. Its appearance reminded him of someone who has had rather too much to drink, but is nonetheless determined not to be left out of the group photo. By now someone had put a sheet over the dead body.

Corso went back down the road, this time studying the main entrances and doorbells that he passed, finally stopping in front of the garage he had earlier noticed from above. There was a hole in the roll-up shutter, with a handle and a handwritten notice with the name *Tiziana*.

He turned back towards the burnt-out house.

Petri and the white-haired man were staring at him from a window on the upper floor.

18

"Who's that man who's just arrived?"

"The one with white hair?"

"Yes."

"You don't know who that is?"

"No."

"That's Fiore, our political chief."

"I thought the police political chief was called Fava."

"At one time he was. But now it's this guy."

Alberta came up to them.

"Everything OK?"

"Everything's fine."

The girl went back to the cash desk where Pieter was sitting, intent on a crossword or some similar puzzle. His real name was Pietro Moderno, but he had been living in Amsterdam for many years before coming back with a young black girl, money to invest in a bar, and a new name for himself. Alberta was not the woman's real name either, but she was the only black waitress in Torino and her real name was probably too difficult for local people.

"What's this Fiore like?" Corso asked.

Petri took a swig of beer.

"Do you read the papers?" he said. "Are you aware of what's happening?"

"I do read the papers."

"Then you must be able to imagine it."

Apart from the two of them, there were four people in the bar, all sitting at different tables. Quite a crowd, seeing that it was five in the morning. The other unusual feature was that one of the four was a woman and no-one was pestering her. Perhaps because none of them, including the woman, was either drunk, drugged up, an artist, politically restless or without a home to go back to – all needs it would have been difficult to satisfy in a bar at that hour. This was why Petri went there, though it was far from the centre and wasn't even on his way home. It was only the second time Corso had set foot in the place.

"Do you know anything about fishing?" Petri asked.

Corso realised this must somehow relate to their previous conversation.

"You know what they throw into a river when there's a sheat-fish gobbling up all the other fish?"

"No."

"Pike. And do you know why they do that?"

"No."

"Because pike are insatiably hungry and have eight hundred hooked teeth, that's why. A pity no-one ever realises that the result is just to fill the river with pike."

Corso drank the rest of his small glass of beer.

"Tomorrow morning," Petri said. "You go will go back to the fire with Gianni and Ottavino. You will listen to what people are saying. See if there's any movement near the site. We need to know whether anyone has seen anything, and if anyone is saying anything. Pozzacco and I and the others will check out the guy's family and occupation."

"But I've already applied for leave for tomorrow morning."

Petri studied with intensity the two inches of beer still

remaining in his own glass, and finally waved his hand: suddenly he had remembered.

"Then you can join them a bit later," he said. "In any case they'll have enough to keep them busy for a while."

"Alright. I'll be off now, then. Goodnight."

"How are you going to get home? Walking?"

"Walking."

"Good for you." Petri nodded. "It might jog your memory."

The road before Corso was long, straight and silent. A classic city road at five in the morning, the steady, sleepy murmur of the river as it flowed through this isolated area, not so much a sound as a sort of magnetic attraction. A magnet that consisted of millions of cubic metres of non-stop water in muddy motion. On the other three sides, contrasting with the river, the city's atrophied limbs were beginning to stir: street-sweepers, milk lorries, newspapers, the first timid vessels of public transport of the new day. Corso estimated his walk home: a quarter of an hour. Then how long it would take to go back to Via Lampredotti: about half an hour. He decided on the latter.

When he reached the open space with its urinal, kiosk, two benches and overflowing rubbish bins, he found the bar there just opening. The man behind the counter was switching on his coffee machine. He gave the impression of a man who had barely escaped from some very ugly situation, perhaps because of the scar that had half closed one eye, distracting attention from his dress and the rest of his general appearance.

"Coffee?"

"An Americano, please."

"What's that?"

"Normal coffee in a large cup, then you add hot water."

"That's a new one on me."

The man was good enough to throw away his first effort,

but the second, which he placed on the counter, was no less disgusting. Corso dunked a ready-made brioche in it, paid the very small sum the proprietor asked, then headed down Via Lampredotti.

The ribbon isolating the burnt-out house was now obstructing nothing but the pavement directly outside it. A paper notice attached to the wall announced that the property was under "judicial attachment" and quoted the relevant laws. Two workers heading for the tram stop gave it a summary glance and walked on, talking of quite other matters. News of a crime lasts no longer than the fish wrapped in the newspaper that reports it.

Corso went to stand in the angle made by Via Lampredotti and a smaller road named after some irrelevant village, and smoked a couple of cigarettes there to give the impression that he was waiting for someone. Before he could light a third the shutter of the garage he was watching opened.

The woman who emerged had clearly never been beautiful even when young. Corso imagined soft buttocks inside her loose trousers and breasts sagging under her coat, which was in any case too short for her. Apart from her fiery red hair and heavy earrings, and the early hour, she looked like any other woman of sixty out to do her shopping.

He followed her to the tram stop and then onto the tram itself, taking it as far as the last houses of the Barriera district, six-storey blocks built during the fascist era to accommodate workers at the nearby electrical power station, now long condemned as substandard property, and mostly sublet. The woman spoke to nobody throughout her journey and did not even say good morning to a man who came out while she was searching for her keys and held the door open for her.

When she vanished through the main door of the block,

Corso glanced at the time on the wristwatch of a man who happened to be walking beside him. He still had enough time to go home, read a couple of chapters, and make himself some decent coffee.

19

"Shall we discuss D'Annunzio?"

"Not me."

"Not you?"

"D'Annunzio shouldn't even be on the syllabus. We all know what kind of man he was. What about you, Paolo? You liked him."

"I can't say I liked him, but I had to read something of his for my final exam at school."

"Very good. What did you read?"

"The thing he wrote on strips of paper when he temporarily lost his sight, the book with the black cover . . ."

"The *Notturno*. Shall we talk about the *Notturno*, then?"

"I didn't like it."

"No?"

"No, it was too . . . old-fashioned."

"Well, of course . . . his models. Are there other writers you feel closer to?"

"Ungaretti."

"Good, a careful study of Ungaretti will never do you any harm. What can we say about Ungaretti?"

"He was born in Egypt in Alexandria and died quite recently. He also lived in Paris. And in Brazil. 'M'illumino d'immènso' is his most famous poem."

Silence.

"Could you add anything to that, signorina?"

"Ungaretti . . . won the Nobel Prize for poems he wrote about the First World War. 'M'illumino d'immenso' is his most famous poem, in which he illustrates the precarious nature of . . . the meaninglessness of capitalist war which exploits poor people as cannon fodder. Then there's 'Ed è subito sera', also about the precarious nature of life."

"In effect just what Primo Levi says. He lives near my home, in Corso Re Umberto."

The students were silent, the atmosphere vacillating between boredom and satisfaction. The teacher contemplated the four students who had said nothing at all, then began leafing through the book before him as though he did not know it, despite the fact that he had written it himself.

"D'Annunzio, Ungaretti, Levi and Quasimodo too, because 'Ed è subito sera' is actually a poem by Quasimodo, signorina . . . I think we've made a good digression on the early twentieth century . . . recognising that the general vision is—"

"I've forgotten my student passbook." The speaker was one of those who had not said a word up to that point.

The lecturer used his palm to remind himself what he must remember to convey from the left side of his skull to his right ear. His sparse hair, smoothed down with hairspray, neither approved nor disapproved.

"That's a formality." He smiled. "We can sort it out later; in the meantime, let's deal with those who do have their passbooks with them . . ."

This operation took only a few minutes, after which the seven students said ciao and headed for the door. When they had gone, the lecturer slipped off his jacket to reveal extensive areas of sweat under his armpits. His figure seemed unexpectedly athletic for his job and for the way he wore his hair. This was probably the result of rowing, by which since childhood he had strengthened his shoulders and forearms, and which had helped him find friends in the exclusive circle of those active on the river.

Now he contemplated the pen between his fingers, as though that implement must obviously be responsible for everything that had been happening. Beyond the windows stood the Mole, that massive local headquarters of radio, and the television building, with its greater expanse of glass. Together, they blocked out whole areas of blue sky. It was only when the lecturer relaxed his back against his chair that he noticed there was someone else still there, watching him from high up at the back of the auditorium.

"Well?" he said.

Corso got to his feet and descended the thirty-six steps, stopping a metre from the lecturer's desk.

"Good morning," he said. "I've come here to take the exam for the course."

"Good morning," the lecturer answered. "Your companions have just finished. But if you have your student passbook with you, I'll be happy to sign it."

"I'm not an official member of the seminar," Corso said. "I just want to take the exam for my own benefit."

The man glanced towards the door, as if afraid someone might come in and surprise him in an improper attitude. He seemed reassured by the buzz from the corridor and the far-off echo of a bongo drum.

"Very well," he said, getting back into his jacket. "Please sit down, and we'll see what we can do."

Forty-two minutes later, the lecturer signed the student passbook Corso pulled out of the pocket of his jeans.

"Your book's nearly full," he commented, leafing through the pages, "and with excellent grades. Have you decided who you would like to write your thesis for?"

"No," Corso said.

"If the twentieth century interests you, I'd be happy to be your supervisor."

Taking his passbook back, Corso laid on the desk a form complete with his full name, grades and personal data. The teacher studied it, uncertain whether to touch it or not.

"I need this for my leave of absence," Corso told him, anxious not to waste words.

The man nodded, continuing to read the document, line by line, until he reached the rubber stamp at the end.

"Though I imagine it's not easy doing things this way," was his only comment as he provided the necessary signature.

Corso left him and descended through two floors full of young people smoking, chattering, eating and kissing. A few, more isolated, were reading or watching the others while trying not to be seen doing so. An occasional puff of wind from the large half-open windows struggled with a smell of sweat and grass in the indoor warmth. Perhaps this was why Corso imagined the day outside must be even colder and brighter than it seemed. The air was limpid enough to confer a mathematical clarity on the confusion of bodies, voices, clothes and bicycles.

He spent a few seconds contemplating this, then hoisted the bag that contained his uniform onto his shoulder and moved towards the toilet near the bar to change into his police clothes.

"You know there are people here who have given their butt to get where they are?"

He became aware that a boy had caught up with him halfway down the stairs and was now blocking his path. It was the one who had spoken of D'Annunzio and *Notturno* in the seminar. There was another boy on the left of this one, and behind him a third.

"So the question is," the one behind said, "are you a cop or a scab, or just a bloody stupid idiot?" Corso judged from this boy's manner that he was not giving satisfaction, so lit himself a cigarette, and began to stare through the window at the Mole, whose design never failed to amaze him. The world was full of perfect things together with so many more that were less than perfect.

"What do you keep in there?" the nearest boy said, touching the bag with Corso's uniform in it. "Your pistol? Your truncheon? Or haven't they trusted you to get your hands on anything like that yet?"

Corso took a long, calm, thoughtful pull at his cigarette, not for courage but simply because he had needed that lungful of tobacco ever since he had come into the building that morning. Other students were going up and down the stairs, but none of them seemed to be taking any notice.

"As I see it," the boy who had been the first to speak said, poking a finger into Corso's face, "those sideburns of yours can't possibly be professionally acceptable in a policeman. What do you say? Shall we shorten them a bit for you?"

"Some other time," Corso answered. "I have to go now."

The three stopped for a moment as if paralysed, then the boy in front cut the air with two long fingers as if with scissors and laughed. When the one behind him turned away towards the terrace, the other two followed.

Corso relit his Gitanes: there may have been a lump inside it. One thing he loved about Gitanes was that sometimes something in them reminded him of a piece of wood. When he looked up again, he saw the three boys leaning on the banister and talking to others. Some of those others were from the seminar, while others were new faces. And some of the new faces were girls.

Suddenly he knew that one of the unknown girls was *her*. And instantly realised she would go on being *her* for ever.

20

He left the gents in his uniform and crossed the hall.

A boy and girl who were arguing in front of the jukebox paid him no attention but everyone else stopped whatever they were doing to follow him with their eyes. Because he had gone into the toilet in plain clothes.

The coffee he had ordered and paid for before getting changed was waiting on the counter. He swallowed it quickly and went out while the jukebox blasted out the first solo of "Europa".

His trained eye recognised the car at once, even though it was crammed into the space between yet another bar and the copying office. Seeing him pass in uniform, kitbag on shoulder, his young contemporaries looked around to check whether he was alone.

The best thing at such times was to escape quickly but not too quickly, because he hated any kind of snatching, hurrying, charging, or anything resembling agitation. Someone at central office had said that a few years earlier things had been different, but Corso was too young to know. In any case the young never believe that anything can ever have been any different in the past, while the old are only too certain of the opposite.

He rounded the corner and got into the car. Inside it, Petri was smoking. How bourgeois can you get: a father giving his son a lift in his Alfa Romeo Alfasud. The car was ultra bourgeois.

"What's happened to you?" Petri asked.

"Nothing."

"What do you mean, nothing? Your eyes are popping out of your head!"

Corso was still dreaming of *her*, aware he'd been thinking of nothing else ever since the moment he had caught sight of her.

"I didn't want to be late!" He glanced at himself in the mirror.

"You said twelve! It's still two minutes to. Relax; life is usually longer than you think, and even if that proves not to be so, it's still usually best to keep calm."

Petri started the engine, reversed so as not to cross the main entrance to the university, and drove rapidly towards the River Po. When they passed Pieter's bar neither of them acknowledged the fact that they had been there together only a few hours before.

"The dead man," Petri said, "is Andrea Gonella, thirty-two, an accountant who worked for a firm manufacturing enamel for packs of tinned food at Settimo. A card-carrying member of the party for years but not much of a militant, a man more at home behind a desk than out on the square. In fact, his wife says he only called in at the party office twice a week to check their accounts. Normally, he would not have been there on a Sunday, but yesterday he had to record a number of donations. The only people who knew he was there were his wife and a couple of comrades who left at about eleven. They kept the money in a metal cash box. Fifty thousand lire, not much. No weapons or documents. The typical guy in the wrong place at the wrong time. Why did you call me in? Has the Madonna been speaking to you in your sleep?"

Corso began speaking as they were crossing the bridge over the River Dora and by the time they turned into Corso Giulio he had already finished what he had to say. Petri listened, limiting himself to a final solemn "about what your colleagues have discovered", a sign that what Corso had been saying had not vanished entirely into thin air.

Then Petri asked, "Why are you wearing your uniform?"

"Regulations."

"When you're with me, I'm the regulations. Change back. You are more use to me in plain clothes."

They parked at the corner where Corso had smoked two cigarettes under the meaningless street name. Someone passed carrying shopping bags full of vegetables, a crate of Martinone pears and four Japanese persimmons. A bit further along they were closing down the market. The district had few pretensions, though it did aspire to a certain modest dignity. A few steps more and they were in front of the closed shutter.

"Here?" Petri grumbled, pointing. Corso nodded.

Petri knocked, assuming an attitude of respect.

No response.

He knocked again, more insistently, then called out "Signora Tiziana!"

They heard steps, then a spyhole opened. The woman's lips could be seen; she must have been bending down.

"Who's there?" she asked, revealing no particular regional accent.

"I'm sorry if this is not a convenient time," Petri said, assuming an impersonal voice. "But we've come from outside the city on the recommendation of a friend. If you are busy, we can call again."

"Where have you come from?"

"Caselette."

"Who sent you?"

"No-one sent us, but a friend of mine works like me here in the city, freezing food for shops. My friend suggested this would be a good place for me to come –" he paused like a ballet dancer balancing on the point of his toes – "for an initiation."

"An initiation?"

Petri crouched, bringing his face close to the spyhole, which must once have related to the letter box of some commercial organisation. It looked as if the use of the building had not changed much.

"I told the boy here –" he used his eyes to indicate Corso still standing beside him – "to come here on his own, but inexperience and embarrassment, you know. Even though my friend assured him that he would really feel at home here, and there was no need to be too formal. I mean, that by calling on you he could even gain a bit of self-confidence."

"I have no idea what you're talking about," the woman said.

Petri cut her short: "It's just that the boy needs to learn to be a man."

The woman thought about this. Standing between her door and the outside shutter, they could sense confusion in her breathing.

"Both things together could be worth ten thousand lire to you."

Petri looked at Corso, as though expecting this comedy would convince him too.

"Entirely my own fault if I haven't made myself clear." He shook his head. "All I need to do is to come in to check for hygiene and whether the premises are peaceful, and then make the financial settlement, of course."

The woman seemed to be considering the matter.

"Just the boy?"

"Just the boy. I shall simply be here to keep him company."

The little window closed and the shutter, presumably operated by a handle, opened. The woman was dressed just as she had been when Corso left her at the door of the block of flats after the tram journey a few hours earlier. Though her face seemed more tired and shrivelled than he remembered. He shuddered at the thought of having to get into bed with her, even as a ploy.

"How old is this boy?" she asked, closing the door after them.

"How old are you?" Petri asked him.

"What? Don't you know the age of your own son?"

"Of course I do, he's twenty; but I shall be the one looking after everything."

Clearly, the place had not changed much since the time when it had been used for electrical repairs to cars, or as a garage where two cars could be worked on at the same time, one in front of the other. The cement floor was still stained with motor oil and the pit under the cars had not been filled in, just covered with boards partly concealed by an elegant double bed. At one end was a toilet, probably once accessible from the yard outside. That access had now been closed to make a self-contained one-room flat, though one without windows.

"This is the premises," the woman summed up. "And the bathroom is over there. With its own water."

"With its own water?" Corso thought, noticing a chest of drawers that presumably contained linen. On its marble surface were a few bottles of perfume and some cheap jewellery. And a vase of flowers. The unassuming simplicity of the place unexpectedly made him feel faint.

Petri tool a few steps towards the main part of the former garage, which was decorated by nothing but a little floral inlay work at the far end. He tested the strength of the wooden boards over the pit and fingered the mattress, clearly enjoying himself.

"Everything seems entirely suitable," he said, "and hygienic." Then, taking out his wallet, he added: "Now let's agree on a price; the boy and I have a bus to catch at three."

"Oh!" The woman thrust out her chin. "At three! That'll be five thousand lire, then."

She took the banknote that Petri held out to her, folded it in four and stowed it inside her bra, where there seemed to be plenty of room for it. An action imitated from a film, perhaps.

"Good," Petri said. "Now that we've done what we had to do, there is something I must show you."

As the woman studied Petri's police identity card, her eyes faded from chestnut to grey.

"A case of seduction," Petri said, reverting to his natural deep, slow voice, "and not perhaps entirely legal, as it involves a minor, and is aggravated by the mature years of the seducer in view of the innocence of the boy in question."

The woman gave Petri a blank look, then turned to Corso.

"So you're not really his son?"

Corso shook his head. The woman sat down on the bed. For a long time, she sat motionless, then lay down as if dead. All that was missing was a rosary for her fingers. She had closed her eyes, not making clear whether this was a free offer or a threat. Perhaps to some extent a bit of both, it occurred to Corso.

Petri sat down by her feet – she was in any case a short woman – at the foot of the bed. She was wearing pantyhose, and before lying down had been careful to throw off her shoes.

Petri spoke: "Who was around last night when they started that fire across the road?"

"No-one!" The woman sat up abruptly, her feet meanwhile having, it seemed automatically, slipped back into her pattens. "I have no clientele of that kind!"

"What do you mean?"

She scratched her neck.

"Anyone who would do anything like that."

Petri put a reassuring hand on hers.

"But you can't really believe we had that in mind. We only want to find out if there was anyone here who could have wanted

167

to take advantage of the situation by realising it is possible you may have seen something. We just we need to do things properly. Or at least do the best we can."

She looked at him uncertainly. Perhaps she had been in a similar situation before. As can easily happen to any prostitute sooner or later. Preferably, when you are young and bold, with more time still ahead of you to recover, smoother skin, and more value. When you get older it's not so good. Experience won't help, unless you can turn things to your advantage by working to collect information. But you have to be intelligent to do that. More intelligent than beautiful. Above all, more intelligent than greedy. Those who end up in a ditch with their throat cut and their dress over their heads have usually miscalculated the relative measures of these three essential ingredients.

"How old are you now, Tiziana? Sixty? Sixty-two?"

"Sixty-three."

Petri looked at his feet, which were close to hers.

"Sixty-three years old, but you scarcely look it." He nodded. "Now we're going to take you to the police station, where checks and so on may take at least a week, if all goes well, because in October there will still be a backlog to catch up on after the holidays, then everything will be passed on to the judge who will give you . . . let's be optimistic, a year. By the time you come out your steady clients will have found other women, so you'll need to create a new circle for yourself. Money aside, what little you possess will have to go on rent while you're inside, or you won't even have anywhere to live when you come out." He had a quick look round. "You'll be paying something here too. In fact, you'll have to find somewhere else for your business so as not to get a bad name, which seems fair enough to me."

Tiziana seemed to be thinking about it. Probably, she had not understood everything Petri had said, but it was like the opera *Madama Butterfly*, you don't need to know the music or even understand the words, to weep when you get to the "wisp of smoke".

"I do have one client who has been coming to me for some time, but I don't know his surname."

"Let's start with his first name, then."

"Alberto. He works in a bank near the station. Very respectable and clean."

"Was he here when they broke the windows?"

She nodded. Her false eyelashes were reddish too.

"And then what did he do?

"He went to the door and looked out through the spyhole."

"And what did he see?"

"I don't know, he never told me."

"But he must have said something at the time?"

"Just that they had broken the windows at the front of the house."

"Is that all?"

"Yes, I swear it."

"And where were you then?"

"On the bed. We'd just finished. Then he came back to the bed, because he still had to put on his shoes. He said all this politics is disgusting. That Cossiga is the only politician who can control the students."

"The students, he said that?"

"Yes, but I wasn't interested. Then we heard shouting."

"Shouting from the house?"

"My client went back to look through the hole and said there was a fire. And that someone inside was shouting. Then he opened the shutter and ran away."

"And what did you do?"

"I wanted to run after him because he hadn't paid, but I saw the smoke and closed the shutter again."

"And looked out through the spyhole."

She nodded.

"You saw him?"

She nodded and started weeping.

"Sometimes," she said, still weeping, "his wife and child used to come to fetch him. You could see how much they loved him."

Petri put an arm round her shoulders and gave her a couple of shakes, apparently more to be sure she was solid than to comfort her. Then he got up and, without looking at the woman, went to open the shutter, indicating to Corso that it was time to go.

"But don't disappear," he told the woman, before lowering the shutter in front of her tear-filled eyes.

They walked to the car. The last fire at the market had gone out, and people were rummaging among the broken boxes for firewood.

"You don't like this kind of thing, do you?"

Corso deliberately didn't answer. Petri lit a cigarette.

"It just means you can make wine without treading grapes."

21

"Alberto Lessona?"

Everyone at the big table, made from four little tables moved together, stopped talking. Regular customers nearby were affected too. Only at the counter did the automatic lunch-hour routine proceed unchanged: cold dish, single dish, cannelloni, milanese with potatoes, coffee and water; wine not included.

A man stood up from one of the furthest chairs from the door. When he saw Petri, the police sergeant and Corso, he shook his head as if responding automatically in the negative, the kind of movement that might be produced by contracting nerves in a person newly dead.

"Would you be so good as to come outside for a moment?" the sergeant called to him. Lessona pushed back his chair so that it scraped the floor, picked up his jacket and came out of the restaurant, slipping between the backs of his colleagues and other people. He turned out to be an exceptionally hairy man of middling height and weight. Hairs sprouted from the collar of his shirt. The female colleague he had been sitting next to, perhaps not a close friend, turned on him, possibly for the first time, a look of serious interest; he showed no sign of appreciation.

They went out into Via Sacchi, with its pretentious high porticoes, handsome buildings with elegant entrances and two or three banks – but even so nothing more than a street next to the railway. Petri had planted himself in front of the window through which Lessona's colleagues were staring at him, forks in the air, mouthfuls of food in suspense. The day was beginning to seem wintry, not so much from the temperature as the low sky, the dim light and the mood of the city.

"You know why we're here, don't you?"

"I've no idea," the man said; he had the beginnings of a stutter and was almost completely bald, though his face was far from ugly. His little remaining hair was curly.

"I think you know perfectly well."

Alberto Lessona looked first at Petri, then at Corso, and finally at the police sergeant.

"No need to worry," the sergeant said, not famous for his wit.

"You must promise me something," Lessona said.

"Promise you something?" Petri repeated.

"My mother thinks I spend Sunday evenings at the chess club."

Petri looked at his two subordinates. Bramard had the same expression on his face as when they were with the prostitute, unsure for the second time that day whether he was really in the right career. In contrast, the sergeant's expression was entirely neutral as he concentrated on Lessona.

"You are aware that if you don't help us you could end up inside; for sending secret signals, for exploiting a prostitute despite the lady being of venerable years, for duping a handicapped person, for using a telephone for criminal purposes, and for arson, not to mention culpable homicide? And before the judge even gets round to reading out all these charges, you will have already been in jail for a week. How will your mother react to that? Will she just think your chess match went on rather longer than usual?"

The man's soft outer skin seemed to cover sterner stuff. Petri was impressed, realising that, assuming more than was justified, he had almost certainly jumped to a wrong conclusion because he was in too much of a hurry. He took the last cigarette from his packet, stuck it between his lips and lit it with exaggerated calm. He did not often lose his head. But to go back to the crossroads and take another turning was the first lesson he had taught Corso, without ever having even tried to teach him anything.

"Do you smoke?" he asked the man.

Lessona said yes. Petri indicated someone should give him a cigarette because his own were finished, but when Corso pulled out his Gitanes, Petri stopped him with a look and turned to the sergeant.

"Better let the man have one of your cigarettes, Vitaliano, now that we no longer have the death sentence in Italy!"

The sergeant offered the man one of his Ambassadors. For both him and Petri, who smoked Dianas, the brand preferred by Corso was far too exotic, and as something beyond their understanding, was dismissed as harmful.

"There was nothing I could do." Lessona shook his head, while the sergeant gave him a light. "I can guarantee you that."

"Of course," Petri agreed. "No-one's blaming you for anything." We just want to co-ordinate your impressions with our own. You said on the telephone 'they've started a fire'. That interests us."

Lessona turned back towards his colleagues. They had resumed eating their lunch, but were still watching events through the window even so. He turned back to the policemen.

"They had already turned the corner. I don't know how many there were exactly."

"And if you can't be exact, how many would you say at a guess?"

"Three, or maybe four."

"Were they young or old?"

"Young, I think, but I couldn't see their faces."

"Then why say young?" Petri's voice had resumed its earlier tone. Lessona registered this. Petri looked left and right. His switch to a more relaxed tone of voice seemed to have done the trick, but it might still be worth giving the key a few more turns in the lock.

"So they seemed young," Petri said. "What about their hair and clothes?"

"Jackets and trousers." Lessona nodded as if agreeing with himself. "The last one had a grey coat."

"A grey coat."

"He was the one I could see best, because he was limping, so he lagged behind."

"He was limping?"

"Just a bit."

"Anything else?"

"He was tall and had a bag on his shoulder."

"What sort of a bag?"

"A sports bag, reddish-rose in colour and with a number on it in white. Twelve."

"Twelve?"

"Twelve."

"That's all?"

"Twelve, and that's all."

Petri was thinking, and smoking while he thought.

"Nothing else?"

"No," Lessona said. "I ran to the phone box and made that call. Then I went straight home. Mother was waiting for me."

"No," Corso said gently. "You stood in front of the house leaning on a notice about loading and unloading. You were wearing a multicoloured hat and the glasses with dark frames that you keep in your pocket. No harm in that. You were just curious, like everyone else, and afraid someone would blame you for what had happened."

Lessona took two last pulls on his cigarette in rapid succession, staring at Petri since Corso had already turned back towards the traffic as if Lessona and what he had to say were of no further interest to him. The sergeant was shifting his feet impatiently. All this nonsense was too much for him. With a list of telephone numbers, he could have discovered it all in two minutes, in the warmth of the interrogation room and without wasting cigarettes.

"We'll go to the police station and examine everything in detail," Petri said, crushing his cigarette into the pavement with the toe of his shoe.

Lessona nodded. "But preferably not before four o'clock," he said.

"I'm not so sure about that," Petri said, turning to his colleagues. "Vitaliano, I think you have a barber's appointment at four, don't you? Bramard, I seem to remember you've scheduled a blow job at Ponte Sassi and I . . . well, by four o'clock I may even have gone into retirement. No, I'm afraid we all have other commitments. Waiting till after four won't do at all."

Lessona understood; he wasn't stupid, even if he was convinced that everyone else was. And he knew nothing whatever about chess. That much was obvious.

"If you don't mind," Lessona said, "I'll just go and get my briefcase."

"Good. And Vitaliano, who has a sensitive touch, will let your mother know you may be home rather late. How does that sound?"

22

In those years, the city had brief and breathless moments of transition between day and night. Once it must have been different and perhaps one day it will be different again, but this is how it was at that time, and there was nothing either people or inanimate objects, and still less the city herself, could do about it, so they had to accept light and darkness just as they were.

The end of this particular day found Corso standing in front of the university, leaning on a street lamp with the air of one doing nothing more than enjoying the rapid onset of darkness. The building where they all pursued their studies, regressed and paired off, was displaying in that light something human and maternal, where it usually seemed more of a father, a factory or a bawdy house. Sometimes your best friend can be the one to put you to the sternest test.

Not many students were coming down the stairs at this time, and none were now going up them. Lectures had finished a couple of hours before, and the few still coming out had been using the rooms for seminars, to demonstrate that one could stay in the building even when one had nothing more to do there, or for no better reason than to give oneself a hard time, if one didn't even have so much as a handful of small change to spend in the bar, on the jukebox or on anything else.

He could recognise them by their faces and clothes. They came in groups, a few skipping down the stairs. He waited for them to reach the street and fan out before letting himself admit that *she* was not among them. The group split in two, some making for the city centre, and others, a group of girls with a guy old enough to be their father, though dressed just like the others, heading towards Vanchiglia. A caretaker bustled about doing something behind the doors, before disappearing in the direction of a concealed service exit. The lights of Palazzo Nuovo had been switched off.

Corso passed through the arcade and found himself by the river. Leaning on the balustrade, he gazed at it, the traffic behind him no longer having any meaning for him. "Where there's a river," he was thinking, "nothing else seems to have any meaning at all."

The interrogation at the central police station had not added much: the session with the prostitute, three or four people running away, among them the boy with a limp, a grey coat, and a bag with the number twelve on it, and the phone call. Alberto Lessona had not been hiding anything. All that bothered him was his mother finding out that he had been playing chess with a woman on a double bed at the cost of five thousand lire a time.

Corso thought of his own mother. Small, thin and ethereal, even if she did in fact till the earth. Mysterious – rarely speaking or making demands and never complaining. Something the destitute family she came from and the more comfortable family she had married into must have accustomed her to. When her husband died, she had continued with her uncle to involve herself in country matters, though she was aware that her husband would never have approved. When Corso had told her he was joining the police and studying at the University of Torino, she had said "good" as if his whole life had already been mapped out for this purpose, and that this was simply the next stage and not likely to cause him any problems.

He went back through the arcade from the other side, feeling in his legs the upwards slope that those who had designed the arcade must have deliberately intended to be deceptive. Recently, he had not been sleeping well, and the image of his attic with its bed, dormer window, chair, table, books and shared bathroom on the same floor had not pleased him much. He turned down a couple of streets until he found himself outside a cinema, face to face with a poster of the film actress Stefania Sandrelli.

She is more beautiful, Corso thought.

He was breathing the atmosphere of the city, its gloom, its shyness and its car exhausts. Corso and Torino were fundamentally similar, like two virtually lost languages, that once deciphered are seen to express the simplest concepts with clarity.

So that was why he was there.

23

He had his first coffee of the morning in the bar facing the central police station.

He had no love for the place, because it was too full of faces and talk connected with his work, but the old man in the waistcoat who placed the little cup on the counter in front of him and said "Served" was a relic of a past that would soon be forgotten. He liked to see him once a week, and this week it was Wednesday morning.

Passing through the police station entrance hall, he climbed the stairs to the large room that at one time or another over the centuries had hosted Savoyard dragoons, Napoleonic artillery-men, friars, pilgrims, consumptives and polling booths. Now it contained the desks of a dozen coppers. The smoke of a thousand cigarettes collected under its high ceiling like a dense hypnotic sky. He headed for the adjoining office at the far end where he would be sure to find Petri.

"Come in!" came the voice from the other side of the door. The room was over-furnished, with an armchair, a table and two sets of shelves, similar pieces of furniture that had never belonged together. Petri was on his feet with a map spread out on the table and Vitaliano at his side. His bottle of fizzy water had been moved to the windowsill.

The commissario looked up.

"What are you doing here?" he said, nodding towards the

courtyard. "Don't you know you have friends waiting for you out there?"

Corso turned towards the window.

"Friends?"

Petri pointed to a place on the map and Vitaliano scribbled something on his notepad.

"You may go, I've authorised it," Petri said. "Even in our own small world we have other things to do."

Corso went down the stairs and cut across the yard, where five patrol cars were lazing in the modest sun together with the dark car belonging to the questore, and went through the small door that led to the basement.

He found himself in a narrow corridor lined with doors with no names or numbers on them. From further off came voices and an occasional metallic sound. Through a half-closed door he could see a woman sitting with her back to him in the dim light of a lamp. He had the impression that neither she nor the man speaking to her knew there was daylight outside. A coffee machine was bubbling on an electric plate; no-one paid it the slightest attention.

A man appeared at the far end of the corridor. Corso recognised him as the one with a moustache who had been driving the green Alfa Romeo Giulia that had arrived on the night of the fire. Now he was wearing a cream-coloured polo-neck sweater and an armpit holster. Not correct at all, in fact distinctly out of order.

"Are you Bramard?" the man asked.

"Yes."

"Come with me."

The man swung his head slightly as he walked, like a dog insisting on being led to interesting smells. Without altogether stopping, he slowed down in front of one of the doors.

"Go in," he said, still walking on.

Corso went in.

A familiar figure with white hair was circling the room with his hands behind his back, as if the ten square metres available to him were a long drive leading to some summer residence. His cheeks, though healthy and virile, were faintly pockmarked.

"Shut the door," he said.

Corso did so. The blue suit Fiore was wearing was the same one he had worn on the night of the fire, though he had hung the jacket over the back of a chair, leaving him in shirtsleeves, tie and waistcoat.

"Do you know anything about music?" he said, revealing a faint Abruzzo accent.

Corso shook his head; he knew no more about music than he did about fishing, a failing that seemed about to become a problem. Fiore took a few steps towards the skylight that gave little air and even less light to the neon-lit basement.

The office's rough cement walls bore no relation to the glass-topped desk, expensive armchair and antique filing cabinet, which were much as you might expect to find in an old country police station.

"But you do understand about perfect pitch, don't you?"

With a movement like a wading bird, Fiore scratched one knee with the sole of his other foot. It was only then that Corso noticed that he had neither shoes nor socks on his feet.

"Beethoven, Mozart and Bach," Fiore said. "And Schönberg too; they could all identify a note the moment they heard it. It's a gift, not something you can learn. Not much use to a baker or a lawyer, but if someone puts a piano before you . . ."

Taking a packet of cigarettes from his trousers pocket, he offered it to Corso.

"No, thank you, I smoke my own."

Fiore put the packet back in his pocket. Then he opened the only file lying on his desk.

"Father an early fascist, joins the X Mas, Barberigo battalion in 1943 ..." he read out, then turned the page, making no attempt to conceal the irritating banality of having to do this. "His partisan brother in the Justice and Liberty Party saves his skin at the end of the war, but they kill him anyway in 1958, when you were still a small boy. A hunting incident, case closed. After college, you study to be a surveyor. Mother and uncle take an interest in you, no brothers. You're not exactly drowning in money, but you do own a little land. After that you would have done national service and then found work as a surveyor, but you read in an advertisement that it's possible to join the police and continue studying at the same time. You are one of the few qualified applicants, and you are selected. Ascoli Piceno, then the school for trainee policemen at Bolzano, then Torino where you enrol at the university to study literature. Suspected of left-leaning sympathies, favourable to reform, but no official party or trade union membership. Barely up to scratch on the shooting range. Service with neither particular praise nor blame, until Commissario Petri asks your opinion on the spot on an investigation at Santena. It could have been sheer luck, but when the murder at Moncalieri brings you further success, they realise it was no accident. So Petri makes a special point of selecting you as his assistant, takes you under his wing, etc., etc. ..."

Fiore closed the file and threw it down on a corner of the desk.

"All very nice, but do you know why you're here?"

He picked up half a Toscano cigar that had been lying abandoned on his ashtray and stuck it between his lips without lighting it. They were probably what he offered to those he interrogated.

"Contradictions," Fiore continued.

Corso moved no part of either his face or body.

"Everyone thinks we must be a pack of conspirators down here: retrograde, nostalgic, masons, even monarchists, but do you want to know what the real truth is? Everything is here. Myself, to start with, if I really had to choose . . ." He took a pack of wax vestas from his trouser pocket. The air was full of the smell of burning plastic, halfway between wax and disinfectant, then the acrid scent of tobacco.

"To understand how things are today –" Fiore made the Toscano dance between his big square teeth – "one must understand these contradictions. One has to have grown up with them. To have them in one's blood. This is why I want you to work with us. For you to play our pianoforte. So it's up to you to decide . . . but even Luigi Riva never wanted to play for Cagliari."

Corso stared at what was presumably a fairly new wooden floor. Fiore's bare feet were balancing on it with an oriental lightness.

"What does Petri say?" Corso asked.

"What do you expect him to say? Molotov, MSI, students . . . You don't need Mozart to understand our kind of music. In any case he won't be short of work, there will always be murder victims to keep him busy. And as for you, you will be here on loan; once this business is over, you can always go back to playing for Cagliari if that's what you really want."

Corso made no comment.

Fiore smiled. "Come with me," he said.

They went out of the office and down the corridor, heading away from the exit. Fiore's bare feet hit the floor heel first, then toe. A sophisticated, studied, rolling gait.

"This would do you good too," he said, realising Corso was watching his feet. "You should try it."

They went down some stairs. The atmosphere got colder, smelling more strongly of coal. There were several steel doors, while others were similar to those on the floor above. They stopped in front of one of them. Fiore knocked with a single blow of his knuckle.

"Yes?" someone answered from inside.

"Snow white," Fiore said and smiled.

Inside, lit by neon, were six people, all except one of them in white shirts. Surrounded by numbered keyboards, needles and timers, cabinets with spools of magnetic tape, electric plugs and cables. On two of the walls hung large maps of Torino, one studded with black pins, the other with red. Round these were snapshots taken in the street, showing the interiors of houses and cars and bars. All high-quality black-and-white prints.

"Everything OK?" Fiore asked the thin man who had opened the door to them.

"Yes," the man said, going back to the blackboard to resume writing on it.

Fiore went up to the man wearing jeans and a chequered sweater, who seemed the oldest, and like the others was wearing large headphones. From the moment they entered, no-one had turned towards them or paid them the slightest attention.

"And that man from the bank?" Fiore asked.

"No big deal," the man said.

"No matter," Fiore said. "But let me hear the latest." The man pushed several buttons, causing the reels to whirl rapidly, stop, then start again. Metallic sounds came from a loudspeaker, followed by the voice of a woman saying, "Hello?" to which a man replied, "I'm here, have they come?" "Yes, they've just left, there was a piece missing, the son will be back next week." "How do you mean, next week? Couldn't they make it any earlier?" "Says the washing machine's an old one, the spare parts aren't stocked anymore, so we have to put in an order." "You haven't made a down payment, have you?" "Yes, of course I have, otherwise . . ." "I told you to call me if they ask for anything." "Yes, I know, but I'm never sure if actually doing the job . . ." "But if I told you! But I can hear them now, there's no need to . . ."

Fiore indicated that was enough, and the man stopped the conversation.

"You know who that was?" Fiore asked Corso.

"Alberto Lessona. But I didn't think Petri had passed on the file."

Fiore lifted a corner of his mouth. Corso noticed he wasn't wearing a wedding ring.

"You don't believe that, do you?"

"No, I don't."

"Then what do you believe?"

Corso looked at the dilated pores in the man's bright skin. His wet lips. There was something spontaneous though at the same time sharp about him. Something dangerous.

"I believe you have control of the telephones, including the public ones, even Petri's phone."

Fiore took a few steps, passing in front of the big cupboards full of reels rotating slowly and simultaneously. His broad white feet grasped the floor.

"When Bach was invited to inaugurate the organ at Arnstadt he found himself facing an instrument with two manuals, twenty-two registers and a wheel mounted with little bells. He had never seen or played anything like it before."

"I don't understand music, I told you."

Fiore nodded to indicate that he knew that, but that they understood one another even so. "Lessona has nothing to do with it, nor does the prostitute, and there are no other witnesses. If you had to come to a decision, what would you do?"

Corso took a few steps towards one of the maps of the city and looked at the young and not-so-young faces that framed it. There was not much difference between those faces and the ones on the opposite wall, and yet at the same time there was all the difference in the world.

"The bag," he said.

He listened for a few seconds longer to Fiore walking round the room, probably enjoying the rough freshness of the floor against his feet. Corso became aware of an urge to experience the feeling himself and it terrified him.

"Call Barbicinti," Fiore told someone.

After a minute in which no-one said or did anything, the door opened, admitting the man in the cream polo neck that Corso had met in the corridor.

"Yes? Do you need something?" the man asked Fiore.

"Check every sports club in the Torino district with the number twelve in its name or postal address. And find out if any of them have had any sports bags made and if so whether the bags are magenta in colour."

"OK. How many men can I take with me?"

"Gianni and two more. I need the others."

The man nodded and went away.

Corso did not move, attracted by the fine lines drawn with a pen linking distant points of the city on the map. Words, names and dates had been added in tiny writing, like winged creatures.

He was aware of Fiore approaching, a smell of Toscano, and the man's hand landing heavily on his shoulder.

"This is a place where subordinates give orders to their bosses!" he sneered. "Down here we have created a revolution!"

24

During the ten hours passed in the basement listening to tapes, verifying timetables, checking names already listed in police records and registering other names without reaching any conclusions, night had imperceptibly enveloped the city. The air was cold though not freezing.

Corso leaned against a car to light himself a Gitanes, reflecting that ten hours earlier he had possessed nothing but a gun on loan, a cupboard he could hardly open, two uniforms and a single piece of soap, whereas now he had an office of his own in a hole under the stairs, with a desk with a green vinyl surface, eight drawers, and a telephone. True, this little room with its sloping ceiling had no windows but, dating back to the days when it had been used as a place to store chloroform and disinfectants, it did have a grate for ventilation that led through a duct to the courtyard. He spent much of the first day in his office trying to work out whether the footsteps on the stairs above his head might include those of Commissario Petri himself.

Out in the street now, he smoked calmly, feeling very much alone and not entirely at ease: two circumstances that often go together.

A few cautious cars passed him, almost touching his feet. He looked at the drivers: people who worked in the city centre, professionals whose homes were down by the river or up in the hills. As soon as they caught his eye they immediately looked away, because anyone smoking in front of police headquarters at that hour of the day had to be either a policeman or a delinquent.

The familiar bar was now closed, and he imagined the old man with his invariable "Served" now resting in a little domestic nest after his working day. His elderly wife would be a dressmaker, sharing with him two rooms and a kerosene stove facing an internal yard, like in some song by Nino Oxilia from the early twentieth century: ". . . here I am, all hands and eyes and sperm/ and know it/ though I never was a poet/ and I'm sad".

"Are you following me?"

He swung round, and it was *her*.

"No," was all he could say.

"Then why were you waiting for me in front of the university yesterday? If it was because of your work . . ." She raised her shoulders and snorted. "Look, I'm not going to piss myself over it, but it would be nice to know."

He went on smoking, staring at her. She had a boy's coat, a man's sweater and a pair of boots mostly hidden inside corduroy trousers, yet he had never seen a woman look more feminine. Not even the city of Torino itself, and until that moment Torino had been more feminine for him than any woman.

"What do you mean by my work?" he asked.

She pushed back the long black hair a gust of wind had blown into her eyes. In the few instants her face was unobstructed, he noticed big slanting eyes, a small, slightly irregular nose, and perfect cheekbones.

"Oh, investigations, inquiries . . . all your usual police nonsense."

"I wasn't working, no," he said, nodding towards the building he had just left, "but all kinds of things happen here."

She looked away as if the matter were of no further interest. When she opened and closed her jacket a couple of times, Corso saw that her breasts, if she had any at all, must be extremely small, and the body under her clothes thin and bony, with the harmonious toughness of an insect. Her gentle but not unassuming profile reminded him of the French singer Françoise Hardy.

"How was the film, then?" she asked.

He scratched the side of his nose, not knowing what to say.

"If you didn't notice me following you, you can't be much good as a cop." She twisted her mouth. "Because I've never been any good at trailing people."

They headed for the river, down the narrow and discreetly dark road parallel to the arcades. Occasionally, her shoulders brushed his because parked cars left them so little room. Corso assumed she must be so used to moving in a group that this did not disturb her.

"What do you do when you're not working?"

Throwing away his cigarette, he told her he read or watched films and went to the mountains.

"What do you do in the mountains?"

He gave the question serious thought, but he couldn't think of any presentable explanation.

"Let's go this way," she said as they passed close to the university. "I catch my tram in the square."

At the tram stop they stood apart from the other people waiting. Unpaved, Piazza Vittorio was dark. Beyond the bridge the tramlines seemed to vanish into some netherworld ruled by the Great Mother.

"Why don't you like people following you?"

"No special reason." She leaned with a slight swagger against the barrier. "I suppose because of the odd joint, demonstrations, the usual things." She took her left hand out of her pocket. "And this."

Corso looked at the watch on her wrist. It looked like an antique.

"Stolen," she admitted.

"How do you know?"

She looked to see whether the tram was coming.

"I bought it from someone who sells stolen goods and it cost me next to nothing."

He took hold of her hand to get a better look at the watch. His thumb on her pulse registering a consistency, warmth and rhythm he could no longer imagine not keeping close to himself.

"It would be best to give it back," he said. "Or get rid of it. It could land you in trouble."

She thought about this. He imagined her having an analytical mind and being quick on the uptake, but having once acted being inclined to let things stay as they were. She took her hand back from him and thrust it into her pocket.

"For all I know it may even have belonged to Hitler," she said. "But it's just so beautiful."

The tram's headlight appeared on the bridge, quickly followed by a metallic clangour. She pulled herself away from the barrier, and when she passed close to him, Corso was aware that her clothes smelled like a carpet, but her hair had a scent of the sea. The green tram stopped before them, and she climbed in.

"We'll meet again," he said into a blast of air from the closing doors.

It never occurred to him to ask her name because something had filtered out of his head anything remotely connected with films.

25

Fiore called in Corso at about ten.

Entering the other's office, Corso saw that Fiore, wearing canvas shoes, was smoking in his armchair, with a game of chess set out on his desk. The room also contained two canvas chairs with folding metal frames.

"Barbicinti will be here in a moment," Fiore said. "Meanwhile, take a seat."

When the door opened and Barbicinti came in, Corso noticed that he had trimmed his moustache, but his face was still that of a predator lacking weapons adequate for expressing its malice. No doubt the reason why his gun was so unorthodox, and why the bulge in his tight trousers seemed to be nothing more sinister than his genitals. He did not sit down, but approached the desk.

"Shall I be brief, or do you want details?" he said, addressing Fiore exclusively.

"Make it brief."

"Nothing, then."

Fiore made a steeple of his hands in front of his mouth and asked for the details.

"We checked every club, society or firm with a twelve in its name or address. There are of course people who manufacture bags, but none with the number twelve printed on them. Except one where this is part of the postal address of the firm, but in this case the number is very small and the bag in no way resembles what we are looking for. In fact, it must merely be a shopping bag."

A noticeable silence filled the room.

"Should we extend our search to the whole of the north of Italy?"

"I must give some thought to that," Fiore answered. "Otherwise, how have things been going so far?"

"Nothing much to report."

"How long have they been on the job?"

"Since yesterday evening."

"And the files?"

"The man is clean, not even a fine against his name. The woman's an old acquaintance from the streets: extortion, two or three times in prison, but nothing political. Once she was run by a pimp who used a pistol now and then, but he's been dead ten years now."

Fiore moved his chair ninety degrees so he could look straight at the skylights. They gave enough light to emphasise the dilated pores in his skin and his mastiff-like profile.

"Who've you got on the job?"

"Velluto and Salmerino."

Fiore nodded as if to indicate nothing could be better.

"Right, I'll come along myself."

It took Barbicinti a couple of seconds to realise their conversation was at an end, after which he gave Corso a self-important look and went out. Fiore lit himself a strong Toscano from the rustic wooden box on his desk, and looked up at the little windows, the natural destination for the smoke he was producing.

"And where do you think you yourself would best come in?"

Corso kept his elbows on his knees, one hand inside the

other. He imagined his posture looking both ridiculous and innocuous. It was only years later he realised that no posture of his had ever been innocuous.

"I'd like to be out and about," he said. "Best of all, near the action."

"So your office is no use to you?"

"No idea. I've never had an office before."

"Even when you were a surveyor?"

"I've never been a surveyor." Corso could hear himself beginning to argue.

Fiore nodded and turned to look at him.

"They could amputate one of your kidneys without using an anaesthetic, couldn't they? You would never even turn round to see what they were doing behind you."

Corso waited for Fiore to stop laughing, then glanced up at the windows. Today the neon lights had not been switched on.

"I think best in bare feet," murmured Fiore to himself. "Or sometimes just in my underpants, but here . . ." He tapped the glass surface of the desk with his finger. "That's why I had this chess set brought here. The office is best at night and in the early morning, when no-one else is around. But I authorise you to go wherever you like. All you have to do is report to me each morning at this time and bring me something. You know how to play chess?"

"No."

"It doesn't matter who you play against, it just helps you to discover yourself."

Fiore got up and walked round the desk. "Learn the rules and tomorrow we'll have a game."

They went out into the corridor, where, after a few steps, Fiore took Corso by the arm. The man's temple brushed his shoulder, as if he were a master leaning on his disciple. It occurred to Corso how seldom people touched him. He had had a couple of girls, then there was that country festival when Carla grabbed him from behind in front of everybody. Then his uncle's hand on his shoulder in the corridor of the hospital where his father died, and of course as a child he had been touched by his mother. Now he became aware of the strength of Fiore's arm beneath his light wool jacket and cotton shirt, and of the apparent confidence of his gesture. And the smell of cheap but attractive aftershave, double strength like everything else to do with Fiore.

When they stopped before a door, Fiore took his arm back. Voices could be heard coming from inside. Corso recognised one of them as Lessona.

"So you've established that neither Lessona nor the woman had anything to do with it, have you?"

"Probably," agreed Fiore. "But in chess you mustn't forget to move your pawns! If you do your game will get nowhere. Only a knight can jump over pawns. And whether that can happen will be up to you!"

Fiore pushed the door half-open. Peering through the gap, Corso saw the prostitute and Lessona sitting together at a table, the man with his back to them. The woman was in tears. Corso forced himself to believe that the black mark under her eye had been caused by mascara that had run.

"Bishops and rooks," Fiore whispered. "Just let me introduce a modicum of judgment! If the king can only move one square at a time, there must be a reason for it!"

26

The house with its blackened walls and gaping windows resembled the shell of a dead insect that still retained the appearance of the life it had once contained. Or like an old photograph that brought back a memory of little girls in pinafores on their way home from school, or of elderly couples, or of long forgotten cars, transactions or quarrels.

When Corso had been walking round the area for a couple of hours, it began to rain.

He sheltered under a balcony, where he exchanged a few words with an old man who told him of trains in Calabria, sheep-farming and village injustices. "Here in the factory, they complain," the old man summarised, "but do you think it was ever any better down there?" He spat.

When it stopped raining, Corso wandered on, bought a banana and ate it, while watching a small boy score a fantastic flying goal in the entrance to a garage, then went into a couple of shops in search of cigarettes without finding his usual brand.

Nothing else happened before evening, which found him with a bread roll with butter and salami and a glass of red wine in a bar. The wine, passed off as a Barbera, had clearly been mixed with something else from further south. The bar was living through the hour of transition between its afternoon customers and those who would come in for the evening.

At the next table, two men whose faces he could not fix in his mind even while he was actually looking at them, were arguing that no boxer worth the name had entered the ring since the famous Benvenuti.

That was all Corso needed.

27

"Have you ever boxed before?"

"No."

"Not even outside a gym?"

Corso tried to understand from the man's expression what that was supposed to mean.

"In the street, brawls and so on ... Don't you ever enjoy getting into a fight?"

"No."

"Is that because you suffer from heart problems, haemorrhage or diabetes?"

"No."

"Do you do any sport?"

"Only in the mountains."

"Such as? Skiing?"

"No, I walk."

"You walk. Can you touch your toes?"

Corso tried, but it was an effort even to reach his ankles.

"How often do you try to do anything like that seriously?"

"I've no idea."

"Never mind if you've never been serious about it, you have no problems. But it would do you no harm to work out a bit. You could even go around telling people you're doing a bit of boxing, but if you were ever to think of taking it seriously, you would either need to strengthen your back or become a good punchbag, because avoiding blows with that stalk that's serving you as a spine at present would be impossible. Is that clear?"

Corso nodded.

"Did you read the name of the gym outside?"

"Yes."

"Do you know who he was?"

"An anti-fascist worker who commanded a pro-communist SAP brigade during the resistance."

"Good, but now forget it. Even if they'd like to fuck us up as though we came straight from the Kremlin, we don't do politics here – we don't even talk politics. Outside you can come to blows for any reason you like, but boxing is another matter. Whatever political views you have, you leave them in the changing room. OK?"

"Yes."

"In the ring you may find yourself against a student, a fascist, a boss, a Marxist, a priest or a copper, but to you he must never be anything more than your sparring partner, is that clear? If boxing was the only thing in the world, politics wouldn't even exist. Have you brought a tracksuit with you?"

"Yes."

"The changing room's over there. Go and get changed."

"What's the charge?"

"We'll discuss that next time. In any case, this evening the boiler's not working so there's no hot water."

Corso headed towards an area with benches arranged in a U-shape and several small lockers. The changing room was empty, its tiled floor was wet and the shower had no curtain. The place smelled of the saltpetre on its walls.

He sat down and began to unlace his boots.

A few pieces of clothing on clothes hooks, three pairs of shoes and two small lockers fastened with padlocks explained the rapid blows on a punchbag and slaps of a skipping rope that were coming from the wide space where the man he had just been talking to was standing.

With his small, nervous physique one might have mistaken this man for a former jockey, but his nose, which turned in several different directions before finally deciding which way to go, left no doubt that he had been a boxer, and indeed a pretty energetic one. His small, hollow crystal-green eyes were the only individual thing about him.

When Corso had donned his tracksuit and well-worn Lotto sports shoes, he rejoined the man.

"You're much too stiff!" the man was telling a young lad with shaved head who was working at the punchbag.

The boy seemed not to hear, but started moving his feet more.

"Rule number one: in boxing your feet are more important than your hands," the man said loudly enough for the words to reach Corso. "Rule number two: you may be brilliant, but even so some of your opponent's punches are bound to find their mark, so you must prepare your head and body to take them. There are other rules, but they don't apply to you yet. Do you know how to skip with a rope?"

"I've never done it."

"Do you see how he's doing it?" The man indicated a guy of about forty in a singlet, with a sweaty body that looked as though it had been sculpted. "Take a skipping rope from the nail and you try doing the same."

For the whole period of training, which lasted an hour and a half, the man watched Corso without making any further comment, and did the same with all the others, including the boy with the shaved head and another a few years older, who were the only ones to climb into the ring and fight a few rounds. Then he dismissed them one by one, going up to each in turn to say, "That'll do for this evening, have a shower then go."

In the changing room, Corso waited his turn for the cold shower, which the others all accepted without comment. He made the most of his time by calculating heights and studying walks and clothes. All the men were shorter than one metre seventy, the only coat was blue, and none of them had a limp. The oldest and most muscular man asked him if he came there often; Corso told him it was his first time. Nor did the others say much to each other, discussing a dive where you could dance without having to buy a drink, a new model of car and a tree which had fallen that afternoon in front of the railway station and blocked the traffic. Comments that revealed no profound thought, hardly surprising in view of their ages and the hard work they had been putting their bodies through.

When they started to leave in exactly the same order as the trainer had sent them to change, Corso understood what the man had meant when he had told them they should shower and go.

The trainer spoke to each in turn for about ten minutes on the bench at the entrance to the gym. The old man did all the talking, while the boys restricted themselves to nodding and changing their expressions in response to the criticisms, corrections or compliments meted out to them. To celebrate this sacrament the man had assumed a fisherman's blue beret and spoke calmly, hardly moving his hands at all. He seemed to have spent a long time preparing everything he had to say, so that things could only be exactly as he said they were.

Corso came last. By this time the man had crossed his legs and put on linen slippers.

"Do you dance?" he asked Corso.

"No."

"Not even modern dancing?"

"No."

"Then you're not doing too badly with the skipping. But you've been hard at it all evening and you haven't produced a single drop of sweat. Are you really a student? Quite sure?"

"I study literature."

"Do you plan to be a teacher?"

"I haven't made up my mind yet."

"You don't have much to say for someone who wants to be a teacher. But we could work on your back, if the effort involved doesn't frighten you off. The back is the most difficult thing to change because it is the most individual part of the body. It needs time and patience. The first thing that needs changing is the way you hold yourself. Is there anything you'd like to ask me? Otherwise, I'll see you next time. I just have to pass a cloth over the desk."

Corso looked at the shelves behind the desk, which was actually a woodturner's bench that had not been much adapted from its previous function.

"How much do those bags cost?"

"Three thousand lire each."

"Could I buy one?"

"If you have three thousand lire to spend. Do you know what the number on the cloth means?"

"Does it refer to punches?"

"One-two. Right, left." The old man mimicked two alternating jabs. "The simplest combination. I could have put the name of the gym on it too, but that would have pissed off anyone who wanted to show it to anyone outside. But at least now, if anyone asks you, you'll be able to tell them what's written on it."

Corso looked round the empty basement, the lights already turned off on the side where the punchbags and the ring were. The ropes round the ring were held up by rods covered with foam rubber. That too had probably been used somewhere for something else before.

"Why did you give your gym that name, if you didn't want political problems?"

The man took time to think the question over despite the fact that he must have answered it many times before.

"The man who founded the gym gave it that name," he said finally. "I decided to keep it. I agreed with him about everything, so I saw no reason to change it."

Corso took his wallet out of his bag. The man watched him count out three thousand lire, but when he offered the money, the man made no attempt to take it.

"Was it you who rang a few hours ago to ask if we had any grants to offer, and wondered how much they might be worth?"

"No," Corso said; in fact, he had bought a bottle for some guy in the bar to ring round all the gyms listed in the phone book.

One, two, three seconds passed, during which the man must have been mulling over various hypotheses and their many possible consequences; then he took the banknotes and put them in his pocket.

"My name is Duccio," he said, getting to his feet. "Not a name I've ever liked myself, but that's how it goes."

28

The man in the guardroom took time to recognise him because of the time of day, his plain clothes and his hair, which the dark autumnal air had failed to dry; then he recognised his mountain knapsack and saluted him.

"So it's started raining again, has it?" the man said.

"No, I just walked here quickly after having a shower."

"Ah!" the other said, not understanding.

"Is anyone still there in the political department?"

"Can't say. That lot use the courtyard exit. But Petri's around."

Corso walked past the main staircase and took the second passage, to reach the courtyard. When he left the building, a couple of colleagues greeted him, something they would not have done a few days ago, but now Corso had been elevated to the political department, and it was always a good idea to keep the political people sweet.

Entering the basement, he headed for Fiore's office.

A strip of light could be seen under the door. He knocked: no answer. Opening quietly, he saw the man slumped in his armchair, eyes closed, headphones over his ears and bare feet in full view on his desk.

He moved closer. Fiore opened one eye, signed to him to sit down, and closed his eye again.

For a couple of minutes Corso listened to the light hiss of stylus on a long-playing record. Time enough to sort out what to say, but instead he concentrated exclusively on the gentle rocking of Fiore's great white feet to the rhythm of this inaudible music.

When the record came to an end, Fiore removed his headphones, took an already half-smoked Toscano from his wooden box, and stuck it between his teeth without lighting it. His eyes were shining as though he had just left some place it had been difficult to drag himself away from. The record continued to spin, with the stylus now raised from its surface. Corso began unlacing his kitbag.

"We have one name," Fiore said. "Edoardo De Maria." Corso clenched his fists.

"A bit of wiretapping?"

Fiore shook his head.

"An anonymous phone call. You had just gone out. Barbicinti has verified it: a student, upper-class family but enjoys playing the subversive. It all adds up."

"Have you arrested him yet?"

Fiore gave him the look of a manager finding himself still in his office at eleven at night, discussing the progress of a case with a subordinate whose quality he must have overestimated.

"We never arrest anyone here," he said. "I just need to find out what this one does, who he phones and who he talks to, when he craps and what he thinks about while he jerks off. I need the whole gang, the cretins!"

At this time of evening, with a single neon light, the office was once more a place to clear things up, all the more effective with such limited lighting. Fiore's eccentric furnishings now seemed even more paradoxical. A joke in questionable taste.

"And what if this man escapes us?" Corso asked.

Fiore shook his head at the very idea that any such thing could happen. Something far-off, sad and theatrical passed over his face.

"When the Duke of Köthen went off to the spa at Carlsbad, he asked Bach to go with him to organise some spectacular music. So Bach said goodbye to his wife and seven children, got into the carriage and left home. The duke was his employer, so he had no choice. When he came back three months later, his wife was dead and in her grave. An infection, a haemorrhage, no-one ever knew. The only certain fact was that Bach had not been there for his wife in her hour of need."

Fiore pointed to the stereo and the record still silently revolving.

"That was when Bach wrote the sonatas for unaccompanied violin. One of the most demanding tests for any violinist. The violin is like two instruments, a he and a she, forcing a single instrument to act as both soloist and accompaniment. Bach's way of begging his wife's pardon and saying goodbye to her."

Fiore went on contemplating the disc for a few seconds more, then brought the conversation to an end with a wave of his hand, a benevolent reproach to his own sensibility. Wiping his eyes on the back of his hand, he lit his Toscano.

"And you, what have you been up to?" he asked.

"This De Maria, does he go in for boxing?"

Fiore stared at him.

"Why boxing?"

Corso became aware he was hugging his kitbag to his chest with unnecessary force and made himself relax.

"Just an idea." He lifted his shoulders.

The folder that Fiore opened contained a single typewritten page and a photograph. He studied this sardonically for a few seconds, then showed it to Corso: a boy with smooth hair cut in a bob was just coming out of a shop, or it may have been a bar. A girl with very short hair was at his side and they were both laughing.

"A boy like that boxing?" Fiore laughed scornfully. "Tennis would almost be too much for him!"

Corso waited for half an hour in front of the joint, then went in, walked round the room and an inside yard, and came out again. Then he stood for an hour in front of a second place that he thought equally promising. Through its large plate-glass window, he could see a counter and tables. He recognised a couple of the boys who had been taking the exam two days before and other faces familiar from the university, but that was all.

The third joint he came to was nothing but a hole in the wall with very loud live music. *She* came out alone just after one in the morning with her crash helmet under her arm and made for a Honda CB bike which was chained to the nearest lamp post. Seeing him standing across the road she smiled, left the key in the padlock and walked over to him. Corso could smell the smoke from the dive on her and dreamed of replacing it with the smell of his own Gitanes. One way the street led towards the centre, the other way to the River Po.

"If it's not your work that's making you follow me, it makes things even worse," she said.

"I have to admit, it really is worse."

"Good God!"

"Good God indeed."

They walked round the block, one side of which was Piazza Vittorio. It was difficult to assess the few people still standing around at that hour of the night. On another occasion, they might both have made an effort to do so, but now they took refuge inside their own bubble. When they had walked round once, they realised they had both said too much to continue in such close proximity any longer, without either quarrelling or starting to explore under each other's clothes. She bent to remove the key that was still in the padlock of her bike, but he forced her to walk halfway round the block once more before he let her open the lock.

"Will you take me to the mountains sometime?"

Corso reached into his pocket for a cigarette, but the packet was empty.

"I'm not sure," he said. "You have to be the right type."

"Oh yes? And what if I'm not?"

"If you're not, it would be very sad."

"Sad for me?"

"No, sad for me."

She went off on her Honda, and he went home to his attic near the station. Before getting into bed, he opened his kitbag, took out the magenta bag with the number on it, put it on the table and contemplated it.

One-hyphen-two, which from a distance could look like 12.

He had done three things that evening: found the gym, kept his discovery to himself, and gone to look for *her*. The only question was which of the three would now come next.

29

For anyone watching the ring from the outside, a punch has something in common with a painting by Caravaggio: easy, violent, instinctive and theatrical. Only someone standing in the ring can know how much work lies behind it, the extremely unnatural position of the fingers, the angle of the wrist, the preparation needed to convert chaos into a model of harmony. An ugly punch, like an ugly picture, is a pointless waste of energy and exposes its perpetrator to ridicule.

Such thoughts passed through Corso's mind as he exchanged the punishing blows he received for the relatively feeble and seldom accurate ones he managed to hand out himself. In addition to his painful nose, battered sides and choked breathing, he was aware of a new and not entirely disagreeable knowledge. Though at the same time, it seemed nothing more than a new aspect of learning.

"That'll do for today," Duccio said. "Have a shower, and come back to me for some ice."

In the changing room Corso collapsed onto the bench. He took out his gumshield, and rotated wrists that still seemed obstructed by gloves he was no longer wearing. His legs were the only part of his body that did not feel different.

"Who's the sparring partner today? Enzo or Garrincha?"

He looked up to see a boy he had not noticed when he came in. Sitting at the other end of the bench, he was lacing up a pair of boxing shoes. The real thing, not mere gym shoes like Corso's.

"I don't know," he answered.

The boy pulled wraps out of a magenta-coloured bag and concentrated on the first turn round the knuckles of his left hand. Corso judged this boy's physique to be similar to his own: tall, with elongated muscles and an elongated face. They could be the same age.

"Mostly, he uses Enzo or Garrincha because they both have common sense," the boy said. "What did he look like? Short, sturdy, thick hair?"

"Yes," said Corso.

"That'll be Garrincha."

"Why is he called that?"

The boy shrugged: he didn't know. That's how the man had introduced himself and no-one had ever asked.

"By the way, I'm Stefano."

"Corso."

The boy gave him a half-smile.

"Don't take it to heart," he said. "All the new ones have to start with a round. That's how he finds out what you're made of."

"I've done three rounds."

The lad gave a whistle, pulled out two strips of ribbon and tied his hand wraps.

"He must have had a lot he needed to understand, then – or a lot to get you to understand."

He took the gloves and a rope out of his bag. The fake leather of the bag showed signs of long use. The two numbers on it were worn but still visible, the hyphen between them almost imperceptible.

"Have you been training long yourself?" Corso said.

Stefano threw the rope over his shoulder and stood up.

"Three years, but I had to stop when I got hurt in a car accident. I injured my right thigh and I still have a scar there. It's getting better, but I can't box again yet. Duccio won't allow it."

Corso noticed how tall the boy was. One ninety, or perhaps just a little shorter. He had the tough skin of someone who, like himself, came from hill country or the mountains. Something in his voice suggested he was basically composed and serious, though in some way lost.

"Good luck with your session," Corso said.

The boy nodded, as though this wish must conceal a greater truth he needed to reflect on, then he limped to the door and went out.

Corso showered without checking whether the boiler had been repaired. The cold water anaesthetised the pain in his body. Bag, height, a slight limp. As he dried himself, he came to the conclusion that the combination of these three features was enough.

Duccio was waiting for him at the old counter that he called his desk, in the part of the gym he called his office. He took a bag of ice out of the ancient Fiat fridge and threw it on the table. Corso was unsure where to start.

"Cheekbones and nose. Put the ice there first and keep it there even if it hurts."

Corso did so, leaning back a little because a little water was running out of the bag.

"Are you planning to come again?" Duccio said. "Because if not, we don't need to waste words."

Corso said he did want to come again.

"Alright, let's go ahead, then. The bad news is that you are rigid and slow on your feet and scarcely have the mobility of a kerbstone. But we knew that already. On the other hand, Garrincha says he can feel it when you punch."

"I didn't think I ever hit him."

"I told you, even when you're fighting a weak opponent something always gets through. The other positive is that you're a good punchbag. This will stand you in good stead since you're incapable of dodging blows or fooling your opponent."

Corso moved the ice bag slightly so as to be able to see Duccio with both eyes.

"Do you imagine you're the first of your kind they've sent me here?" Duccio smiled.

"No-one has sent me anywhere."

"I hope that's the truth; if not I really am on my last legs. But as far as I'm concerned, I'm happy for you to come and go as you like. I've told you already, we have no politics here. Here we box. Have three rounds been enough to make that clear?"

Corso nodded.

"Good. Now we both know I'm the communist and you're the cop, so have a think about it and make up your mind what you want to do. I never close the door to anyone."

Two hundred metres from the entrance to the gym there was a neighbourhood bar, with card players, braggarts, people nursing grudges, scroungers reading newspapers, and a couple of hardened drinkers still capable of carrying what they drank.

Corso went in and ordered himself water and a piece of cheese. Out of the fridge came a half-mouldy local cheese which they brought to his table with a few olives, some dry tomatoes and a bowl of wild hyacinth bulbs. The bread dated at least from the day before and may have been even older.

He drank a litre of water, ignoring the glass of red wine that they had brought automatically, then began chewing the bread and cheese and the rest of the food. He felt he must do this with extreme caution, for fear his mandible might otherwise come loose from his jaw and end up on his plate. Despite the fact that his was the only face new to the place, that he was the only person hunting for anything, and that he must look as though he was chewing glass, nobody took the least notice of him. Since it was also the only bar anywhere near the gym, he was probably presenting no unusual spectacle.

During the next hour no more than five cars passed in front of the bar, all small ones, and a dozen people walking, mostly workers and artisans on their way home, but also two women who, though clearly tired after their day's work, were taking their dogs for an evening walk.

Then a girl stopped in front of the entrance to the gym, lit a cigarette and leaned against a lamp post. It was very much like a scene from Berlin, as in the meantime dusk had fallen, bringing with it a cold vapour that threw the evening out of gear. She had short hair, a long wool sweater and a scarf that could have been silk. Despite his eyes feeling evermore swollen, Corso was in no doubt that this was the girl he had seen in the photo with Edoardo De Maria. Her hiking boots and trousers with their horsewoman's bulge completed the image of an upper-class rebel.

He saw Stefano come out of the gym with his bag on his shoulder, kiss her and move off with her away from the bar. The boy's grey coat was too short for him.

Corso paid, including for the wine he had not touched, and went out in time to see the couple turn to the right in the direction of Barriera, not the ideal direction if they were planning to take a pleasant stroll.

He followed them for ten minutes or so. The boy's arm was round the girl's shoulders and he kissed her a couple of times without stopping as they walked. She accepted his kisses and retuned them, but never took the initiative. She was smaller and shorter than he was, but her aristocratic proportions were harmonious and contrasted with the boy's rather graceless figure. Like one horse suitable for carrying packs and another for dressage. Not a bad combination.

The two came out on to Piazza Respighi and headed unhesitatingly for the rotunda of badly worn grass that during the day acted as a roundabout for the traffic, which was non-existent at this hour.

Three figures had gathered round one of the benches there. The one talking was clearly Edoardo De Maria. The other two, sitting on the back of the bench with their feet on the seat, were listening to him without any great conviction. Both were older; one, wearing a parka, had slightly curly hair, while the other, in a black leather jacket, had short hair and was the oldest of the group by at least ten years. But the atmosphere did not suggest they were students.

Corso hid himself round the corner, where the window of a shop allowed him a good view.

Stefano and the girl joined the others at the bench. The five greeted each other with signs Corso did not understand, but there were no embraces, kisses or handshakes.

The eldest, the one in the leather jacket, was doing most of the talking. The others listened in silence, apart from De Maria, who interrupted a couple of times. The first time he did this the older man shut him up, but the second time he placed a reassuring hand on his shoulder.

Corso searched for the agents and cars that Fiore had associated De Maria with, but the square and the roads leading into it seemed deserted, none of the cars parked there a possible candidate. There was not even a single passer-by. Shadows cast by the street lamps fell on the five in the middle of the rotunda.

When the man in the jacket had finished speaking, the one in the parka said a few words, after which Stefano and the girl moved away to retrace their previous steps. Corso was forced to slip hurriedly back to the next block to keep out of sight. He waited a few seconds until the sound of the girl's heels faded, then turned back to the square to buttonhole the eldest man.

But by then the rotunda was already empty.

Hurrying on, he explored the entrances to the nearby streets, but all he could see was the back of a Renault 5 that switched on its lights at the tram stop, then turned them off again, accelerated and disappeared in the direction of the municipal cemetery.

Looking around himself, Corso tried to establish whether he had been the only spectator. Nothing suggested otherwise.

30

"Shall we deal with this question at once or would you rather discuss it at greater leisure?" Fiore said with a meaningful smile.

Corso, summoned by telephone a few minutes earlier, thrust his hands into his pockets. Had someone he had never noticed at the time, someone more awake than himself, seen him in Piazza Respighi that evening? Barbicinti perhaps? That could explain why the man was now there in Fiore's office, when previously he had only ever seen him passing by, never stopping anywhere.

"Well?" Fiore urged him. "What's the problem? Something to do with women perhaps?"

Corso remained stubbornly silent.

"Just look at your face!" Fiore said. "Do you insist on playing the grand gentleman and keeping yourself to yourself, or are you prepared to be a friend and tell us what happened?"

Corso touched his face, which that morning he had discovered in the mirror to be swollen and livid, but which he had since forgotten about.

"I've taken up boxing," he said vaguely.

Fiore inspected the results.

"It looks to me as if, so far, all the boxing has been done by the other man."

Corso lifted a corner of his mouth, which he could feel right down to his navel. Even Barbicinti sniggered, clearly out of a sense of duty. There cannot have been many things that made him laugh outright, though they probably all involved other people being seriously hurt. Whatever had hit Corso was obviously not severe enough for him.

"Can we get to the point?" Fiore said.

Corso nodded. Barbicinti moved away from the wall, came to the desk and laid a few sheets of paper on it. Corso realised that what had been annoying the man was having to wait before speaking.

"He spent a classic day as a student," Barbicini started. "University, lectures and lots of chat at the bar. After exchanging a few words with some nobody distributing leaflets, he went to a dentist which his father paid for, and then to the rowing club on the river."

Fiore looked at Corso with his head on one side, as if to say: maybe not tennis, but just what you'd expect of a well-heeled student, even so.

"His rowing friends are as well-off as he is. One was caught a year ago with some cocaine, but none of them have political connections. At eight he went home and had dinner with his family. No phone calls, not even from public phones during the day; then he went out again. He took a car to the San Donato district where there's a left-wing bar, but he does not seem to have said or done anything relating to the subjects on the file index. There seems to be nothing we can draw particular attention to. At about one a.m. he returned home. At the moment, Manzon and Tonelli are on the job, but it seems that so far today he hasn't put his nose out of the door."

Corso studied Barbicinti's profile: resolute, sharp, unhesitating. If Barbicinti had seen De Maria in Piazza Respighi with the others, why didn't he say so? Why not admit he had seen him rather than throw away a chance to show him in a bad light? Or had Barbicinti lost the man he was supposed to be watching?

Was he now trying to conceal his negligence? Difficult to believe. Policemen of Barbicinti's type are like wolves and children: they are incapable of thinking about more than one thing at a time.

"What would you do if De Maria can't be exposed?"

Corso had spent all night trying to think how to catch him out. It must be something not too obvious. Fiore was not stupid.

"The blacks." Corso now said.

"How d'you mean, the blacks?"

"They know how to make use of criminal acts, loan sharks, ponces and prison contacts to find out who has done what. People who would never talk to us, but might say something to them. So long as we can control them . . ."

Fiore looked at him.

"Did you hear that, Barbicinti? Not all the wheels have fallen off yet."

Barbicinti gave Corso a look more murderous than a shot from a pistol.

"Right." Fiore clapped his hands. "Barbicinti can continue to keep De Maria on a short rein, OK? Constantly on his tits, but with a wider grasp too in case anything moves further away. Now, good people, let those of us who need to work get down to their work, and those who need to think, get on with their thinking . . . using their brains, I mean, not their bollocks!"

Corso went out into the corridor and deliberately walked off in the opposite direction to Barbicini, to avoid any possible suggestion from the latter that they might like to walk through the basement together.

Shutting himself in his little office, he took a sheet of paper, and to free his mind, began tracing lines on it. After a while he realised the lines he was drawing were parallel, though he had not intended this, and he understood that in some way they represented the relevant factors of the fire, the bag and the gymnasium. Of De Maria and his relations with Barbicinti. Clear lines, but not yet connecting to make any pattern.

Later in the evening, through the air duct, he heard the comfortable canvas shoes of Fiore passing softly towards the driveway. Getting up from his desk, he left his office and went up the stairs.

The big main office was silent, its desks just as their owners had left them for the weekend. He knocked on the relevant door and went in without waiting for a response. For as long as he had known him, Corso had seen its occupant there every Saturday, and sometimes even on Sundays. Apparently, the man had a sick wife who never left home. Nothing else was known of his private life.

Petri raised his head from his newspaper just sufficiently to see who it was.

"May I sit down?" Corso said.

"So you need me again already. Is it the reds, the blacks or Fiore himself that has screwed you up?"

Corso sat down.

"I'd like to ask you for a favour."

"You mean you want me to take you back already?"

"Not yet."

Petri went so far as to partially close his newspaper, though he continued to hold it in his hands.

"There's a name I'd like to check."

"So you come up here to ask us? When you lot down there already know everything it's possible to know about everything!"

"This is something personal."

"I don't believe that."

"Why not?"

"Because nothing is personal to you. So watch it! It would

be a good thing if you'd got into a state over a girl or something personal like that but ... You're twenty years old now, Bramard! At this time on a Saturday, other boys of your age are drinking in bars, dancing, or getting themselves dolled up for the evening."

"The only reason we are discussing this at all is that she's also here on Saturdays."

Petri looked at him with a serious expression, not wanting to tease him if he was desperate.

"Logic's not always the best solution, you know," Petri said.

"I can give you something in exchange."

Petri finally closed his newspaper completely and put it down on the desk.

"I agree it's true they are making a dog's breakfast of this in the political department! But what is there that you can give me in exchange? This?" He indicated the telephone on his desk. "To me? I was here when they had got no further than sweeping out that basement with a broom. Alright, give me the name! Do what you can!"

Corso left the office half an hour later, kitbag on shoulder, with a fistful of information: Stefano Aimar, born in San Damiano Macra, 1952, student of philosophy, height one metre eighty-six, living in Via Bava but still resident officially in the village of his birth. A militant leftist writing for several publications in the field: articles on sociology that are difficult to read, without precedent and yield no clues.

The moment he left Petri's room, Corso lit up, though he hardly ever smoked in closed spaces, not liking to contaminate his own smoke with the smoke of other people.

When the bike braked violently and pulled up in front of him, he thought for a split second that this must be the end. But if anyone had asked him in later days whether he had ever been afraid of dying in an ambush, he would have said no, because as soon as *she* took off her helmet everything else ceased to exist.

"Well?" she said. "What about those mountains, then?"

31

He opened his eyes as first light filtered into the tent, revealing Michelle's lightly sunburnt profile and the almost invisible blond hairs between her brown eyebrows and on her upper lip. He studied the precise slope of her nose as her breath disappeared into the cold air.

It was a sin that even that amount of vapour should be lost. He ought to have been able to prevent it. She turned over in her sleep without waking, perhaps sensing his thoughts.

Outside, the air was sharp, though the dawning sun was beginning to warm the grey rocks, but the little lake, barely the size of a basketball court, was still the dense pool of motionless mercury they had discovered the evening before.

There were still a few unburnt pieces of wood by the rock in whose shelter they had made their fire last night and heated their little cooking stove. The sight reminded him of Andrea Gonella's body reduced to carbon, though this image was immediately swept away by the smell of packet soup and the sound of the fire crackling when Michelle had held out her bare feet to be warmed by the flames.

They had ridden a couple of hours on her motorcycle, then walked as many more in the dark, guided only by a quarter moon, before lighting the fire, eating, washing the plates in the lake and putting up their tent. Throughout all this he had left her enough silence to show that such activities were not for her, but this had not happened.

Now, down at the lake, he washed his face and between his legs, dressed, filled the kettle with water and went back to the stove. While the flame gasped for oxygen, he sat and reflected on what he was experiencing, on his fears and hopes. He knew resisting the term people usually used to define what he was feeling was little short of superstition, but he resisted it nonetheless.

He dropped a teabag into the kettle and studied the surrounding mountains: ancient untamed summits rising to three thousand metres, like certain mongrel dogs kept not to impress other people, but because the owner can't do without them. He recognised the value of what they had come here for, as though it was some kind of mysterious beauty created from what could have been disaster.

And *her*?

There she was, on all fours, sticking her nose out of the tent, her singlet slipping off her shoulders, revealing her little tits.

"But if you're tired . . ." he said, to show he was aware of her.

"Why the hell should I be tired? How long did we sleep?"

Corso looked at his father's Cyma wristwatch, which he only ever wore when walking in the mountains.

"Four hours."

"No wonder I feel so well-rested. And how about you? What do you feel?"

"What I feel is that I love you."

She smacked her lips.

"A likely story! When I'm at my worst!"

Coming out of the tent, she walked a few steps then pushed down her pants. They continued to gaze at each other while she peed.

"What have we got for breakfast?"

"Tea and plain biscuits."

"Perfect. I've never felt more relaxed . . . and *you* are at your best!"

Dismantling the tent together, they accidentally folded the cloth the wrong way more than once, aware that the urge to start touching each other again was driving them both mad, forcing them to communicate in mute glances. A weak barrier that each defended to the best of his or her ability.

When they started walking it was easier, each body more independent, and the few words they managed to exchange made them both laugh. They realised they had already said most of what they needed to say in the tent during the night, with their mouths almost touching. How come you have a French name? And why is *your* name such an idiotic one? How can anyone like you possibly be a police officer? What about your father? And the rest of your family? And why me? Why you? What do you believe in? Do you have a dog? Then why do you taste of dog? Or is that a silly question? Are you scared? Shall we sleep now? Their answers took too long to digest, especially for whichever of the two happened to be speaking at that moment.

After they had been walking for an hour, Corso took the stove out of his kitbag and hid it with the bag and the tent among the boulders near the rock wall.

"This way we won't have to carry all this stuff – no-one's likely to pinch it."

She looked at the barren heaps of stones that stretched down as far as the lake they had left behind them.

"Then why not leave it hidden nearer to the lake?"

He looked back at the mirror of water and the grass that was putting forth its last shoots of green before the snow came. In the two thousand metres between them and the summit birds were cawing and fluttering.

"Because I'm a cop, I suppose," he found himself saying.

When they reached the top, they put on their jackets to protect themselves from the wind and huddled together near the pile of stones round the cross. She looked at the surrounding peaks, but even more at the plain below where she could imagine villages and roads stretching as far as the grey mass of the city where each had first set eyes on the other, and since neither tried to escape, had captured each other.

"Was this what you wanted?"

Corso poured her some tea from the thermos.

"This was it," he said.

The sun was about to reach its highest point, and anyone pure of heart could have detected a touch of sea in the wind.

"Is that mountain over there the Monviso?"

"It is."

"Let's climb it!"

Three hours later, back down where they had left the bike, they stretched out in the shade of a hazel tree and closed their eyes. Soon a herd of cows came to crop the grass round them, bringing cowbells and flies.

After a few kilometres on the bike Corso tapped Michelle's shoulder to slow her down.

"I'm hungry."

She stopped in front of the last building in the hamlet, notable for its yellow sign indicating a public telephone. Inside were a counter and six tables, but no diners. Just one man, smartly dressed and extremely old, with a hat on his head as if for an early-twentieth century wedding. He had a white moustache like King Victor Emmanuel and a tie knotted in the local style, and was sitting with both hands on his cane. On the walls were the heads of wild boar, steinbock, chamois and some smaller animals. The tiled floor had once belonged to some unimportant military barracks.

From the back of the premises came a tall, good-looking man of over fifty, whose hair, physique, difficult personality and intelligence had been dripping off him for half a century like water from a stalactite.

"You're a bit late for a meal," he said, confirming what already seemed obvious. "But the toilet's over there."

Ignoring him, Corso sat down on one of the bar stools, and Michelle on the stool next to him.

"A beer and some wild boar for me. Michelle?"

"Wild boar and some beer."

The man glared at them with old-fashioned malevolence.

"Luckily, people from the city are always telling us why we're lucky not to live down there," he said, wiping the counter with a rag so that Corso and Michelle were forced to lift their elbows out of the way. The man turned to Corso. "Who's this chick you've got with you?"

"My name's Michelle."

"French, are you? My wife upstairs is half French. Do you know why I keep her upstairs? Because when she comes down, I have to go up! *Fi-fi, scu-scu, pe-pe* . . . You French are a fucking insufferable lot. And there's only one portion of wild boar. There's a little sausage, but it's not fresh."

Michelle said that would be fine. The man pushed aside the curtain hiding the back area and disappeared.

"That's Cesare," Corso said. "He was once a talented Alpinist. Then his father died, and he had to take over the local trattoria. That was when he married. He's made a drama out of his marriage ever since."

"How long has he been married?"

"About twenty years."

Michelle greeted the old man with the Victor Emmanuel moustache, who acknowledged her politely, as if disappointed not to hear something much more important.

"Who's that?"

"The grandfather. A hundred and two years old, or maybe a hundred and three now."

Corso and Michelle ate as eagerly as young dogs while Cesare, watching them, remembered things that had left a hole in his stomach as large as a table centrepiece and impossible for him to fill. Then Michelle asked for the toilet and left them.

"It would be best if you say at once that it doesn't exist," Corso said.

"What?"

"What you're just about to say."

"What's that?"

"What you're about to say."

Cesare snorted, despite himself in an extremely French way, then took the first rag that came to hand and the nearest glass and began to wipe it. It happened to be the glass from which Corso had just been drinking his beer.

"Women who leave you make you suffer because they leave you, and women who don't leave you make you suffer because they stay with you. So the best thing is to never get married, and particularly not to a Frenchwoman. And the French always have dwarfs in their family."

"Dwarfs?"

"Eloise has an uncle and a female cousin who are dwarfs. Can you imagine anything uglier than a dwarf? Just imagine a female dwarf! When we got married, I was even forced to be photographed with them. Twenty thousand lire for photos I can never even show to anyone!"

Corso looked at his glass, which by now had been put away with the clean ones on the shelf. He took a swig of beer from Michelle's glass which was still on the counter.

"At least I hope this woman of yours is alright," Cesare said.

"She is."

Michelle's glass had a halo of lipstick on it, but not from Michelle, who never wore lipstick.

"Good. But take care not to waste money on photographs."

32

He had to wait till half past eight for the other to arrive, after which he waited another twenty minutes or so more to make his arrival look convincing, then hoisted his bag on his shoulder, paid for the six coffees he had drunk since three that afternoon, and left the bar.

He found Stefano Aimar bandaging his hands, a sign he had stopped to exchange a few words with Duccio or someone else before going into the changing room. They both said ciao. Corso put down his bag and started undressing.

"Hardly a mark to be seen on you," Stefano said. "I can see you're getting used to taking punishment."

Corso stopped halfway through pulling off his sweater and looked at the boy. The liquid melancholy of Stefano's grey eyes had settled into something sharper and more solid.

"Yes," Corso said, continuing to pull off his sweater. "Things are beginning to go much better now."

Stefano finished his hand wraps, tied his shoelaces and began palming ointment onto his scar, something that would have made more sense before he wrapped his hands. Evidence, perhaps, that he had something on his mind. For a few seconds there was no sound in the changing room apart from Stefano spreading cream and rubbing it into his skin.

"An old road accident," he explained as he closed the jar and threw it into his bag. "In June I had the plate taken out, but that must be obvious."

Taking advantage of the need to lace up his Lotto shoes, Corso kept his eyes to himself. Once in his tracksuit, he went to listen to Duccio's instructions and begin the physical exercises he had been given to increase the mobility of his torso, abdomen and muscles. All procedures that kept him on the side of the gym with the wall bars and slipping cord, while Stefano worked with the punchbags, from time to time sending across looks that Corso was careful not to respond to.

Towards the end of the session, he saw Stefano in close conversation with Duccio, and gathered that he must be insisting on fighting a round or two. Duccio allowed this, but Corso heard him say, "No serious punching," implying "just work on your timing".

Stefano got into the ring with Elio, who was a much shorter man, a tough industrial worker. But very soon Stefano was punching seriously. Elio let him for a while without either encouraging him or taking advantage of his limp; then lowered his fists, left the ring and went off to do a bit of skipping.

Stefano called to him to stop skipping and come back, but Elio took no notice. Eventually, Stefano shrugged, and without a word from Duccio went off to change.

Corso carried on for another half an hour, waiting for Stefano Aimar to come back, then decided that delaying any longer might be interpreted as deliberately avoiding him.

Going into the changing room, he found the lad in his underpants, busily cutting his toenails.

Corso undressed and went straight to the shower, keeping Stefano in view as the latter opened his locker, took out his clothes and put on his grey coat. Then Stefano moved towards the shower, one hand in his pocket, while Corso played roughly with his own balls to punish himself for having been so careless as to have left his pistol back at the police station.

Then Stefano Aimar said, "We need to speak. Outside."

The evening threatened rain, as the weather had been doing for days: it was still summer in the mornings, then gloomy afternoons were followed by autumnal evenings, as if from the very start the day did not want to accept what it knew it ought to be.

Stefano was waiting for him under a roof that Corso decided was too exposed.

But it was Stefano who said, "Let's move," as soon as Corso joined him.

Two similar young men, they walked a hundred metres or so further down the same pavement, until they came to a door with a notice forbidding entry on the grounds that the building inside was unsafe. The padlock had been broken, so Stefano opened the door and motioned Corso to go through.

They found themselves in the courtyard of a large building, one of many long-abandoned buildings now completely deserted, with a few rags still hanging from clothes lines, two demijohns under a roof and four or five ruined chairs where once there had been a rope-making business. One wing of the building still carried the scars of a bomb or a fire; it must have been hit in the war and since judged to be beyond repair while too expensive to demolish.

Stefano entered the roofed area, but Corso stopped on the threshold. Noticing this, Stefano turned back towards him, perhaps because he had wanted to speak at closer quarters.

"Why don't you just get out the handcuffs and stop fucking me around?"

Corso did not feel in danger nor particularly regret this turn of events. Perhaps this was what he had wanted from the start. Though there remained the problem of what to say at this moment; then he remembered that it had been Stefano who had decided to bring them here, so, presumably, since he had not already shot Corso, he must have something to tell him.

Corso pulled out his packet of Gitanes and offered them to Stefano, just as Petri would have done in his place.

Stefano shook his head in annoyance, then put his hands into his pockets and headed for the darkest part of the roofed area. Here the only light reaching the yard came from the street lamps outside, as though it too had been forced to find its way secretly past the main door.

"How did you do it?" Stefano Aimar asked.

Petri would have had no problem distinguishing between truth and theatre, but what about himself, Corso? It had taken Stefano two days to work out who he was, Duccio rather less, and as for Michelle . . .

"An anonymous phone call," he hazarded, choosing on the spur of the moment to pretend already to be the policeman he hoped to become. "And what about you?"

"You were the first new face in the gym for weeks," he shrugged. "I just put two and two together and asked Duccio."

Corso lit himself a Gitanes.

"Was she there that evening? The girl with short hair?"

Stefano took in how calmly Corso had spoken, and that he was now smoking. He shuffled his foot through the pieces of broken glass, small stones and dead leaves lying round them on the ground.

"How long are we likely to get?" he asked.

"I can't tell you that. I'm not a lawyer."

"But roughly?"

"A couple of years, maybe three, so long as you did not know there was anyone inside the building."

"Of course we had no idea!" Stefano looked up sharply. "The

whole thing was just a bit of bloody nonsense. We didn't even all agree to do it."

"Who hadn't agreed?"

"I and—" He interrupted himself, looking up at a vine growing above them with withered bunches of grapes.

"You'll all have to give yourselves up," Corso said.

Stefano nodded to indicate that he had already thought of that, and Corso, watching him, understood for the first time how important having to make choices could be when there was another person vitally important to you. He realised that before Michelle, this would have been another feature of the world that affected others but was meaningless to him. Now that had changed. And for the first time in his life, he felt afraid.

"I need time," Stefano Aimar said.

"Time for what?"

"To talk to the others. Convince them. Without her I can't do that. And in any case, I can't ditch them."

Corso was smoking in the dark.

"How much time do you need?"

Stefano was looking for an answer among the surviving fragments of the vine that thirty years before must have ruled this area. Sharing it with children's cries, busy craftsmen, women at windows, water splashing in shared lavatories with a balcony in the background. All gone now.

"I don't know," he said finally. "I have to find a way of talking to them, but we've decided to keep away from telephones . . ."

"Was that a collective decision, or an order from the man in the leather coat? Because he's the boss, isn't he? It was his idea to burn down the premises, wasn't it?"

Aimar gave him a fierce look.

"Never mind whose idea it was, we're all responsible."

Corso agreed that this was the case, and Aimar had done well to recognise the fact.

"I can give you a day," he said. "But I won't be able to do anything more for anyone who isn't here with you at nine o'clock on Wednesday morning."

He took from his pocket the notebook in which he had drawn the parallel lines that were not yet starting to form a pattern and wrote a phone number on it. Then he tore out the page and gave it to Stefano.

"If there's anything you want to add, ring this number and ask to speak to Commissario Petri and no-one else. Don't give any reason, just say that my aunt has been admitted to hospital and that I must immediately ring the number you give Petri. Use a public telephone. It must be a public phone, is that clear? Don't ring your friends, especially not De Maria."

Stefano took the piece of paper, studied it for much longer than strictly necessary for reading the number on it, then put it in his pocket.

"I'm risking my arse," he said. "So don't be so stupid as to fuck us all up."

Corso took one last pull at his cigarette and threw it away.

"And I'm risking my job, so don't be so stupid as to disappear."

They shook hands and Stefano Aimar went out.

Even if they had been able to live through exactly the same situation a second time, neither of them would have found again the youthful innocence they shared that evening.

33

The morning passed slowly till ten o'clock when he went down the corridor and knocked on the door of Fiore's office for the latest newspaper report. The previous night, before he fell asleep, and perhaps even after he was asleep, he had been rehearsing what to say.

When no-one answered, he knocked again and went in: the office was empty. At that moment Barbicinti came round the corner.

"I'm looking for Fiore," Corso said. "Is there any news?"

Barbicinti, who had just passed him, took several steps back. His moustache looked as if it was struggling somewhat, and this must have put him in a bad mood. Nature seemed to be unwilling to help him assume his habitual look.

"I don't give a fuck that the boss has stuck you up on a pedestal," he said, straight into Corso's face. "But it's me what's going to be sticking around here. So just remember: you come second to me and not the other way round, because with or without Fiore, I can bury you in shit up to your neck if it suits me. Is that absolutely clear?"

Corso nodded that he understood, but as always, the reality seemed quite different.

"You're nothing but a bloody prick," concluded Barbicinti, shaking his head and moving away.

Back at his own desk, Corso checked the time: quarter past

ten. It seemed a suitable time to ring the number Michelle had given him. A woman's voice said Michelle was out "at her studies". He assumed from her reverent tone when she mentioned this activity that she must be a domestic servant or perhaps a cleaner.

He started pacing up and down his little room, though it always meant crouching beneath the stairs above his head. The yard, so far as he could tell from the air duct, was quiet. Leaving the room, he walked back and forth a couple of times, smoking, but could not relax for fear of seeing the figure of Petri suddenly appear at the window. He worried that perhaps he should tell Petri everything. But what was everything? That he had told a suspect how far they had got in their investigations? Come to an agreement that they were not competing at his level? That he had decided on his own initiative to let the man go with nothing more than his word as a guarantee? One of those who had let an innocent Christian burn alive! And what if on Wednesday neither he nor the others were to show up? Perhaps at this very moment they were organising their escape! And what about Fiore? It was now quite clear that he was not tailing De Maria as he had said he would, but why not? What was going on in Fiore's mind?

He remembered a little story of Petri's that he had never understood: a man thrusts a cactus into his pants, and when someone asks him why, he says: "At first it seemed to me a good idea."

It still didn't make him laugh, but he thought he was beginning to understand.

During his lunch break he went for a walk under the arcades, and when he reached the river, it seemed to him more muddy and less like the Seine than usual. He bought a sandwich at the bridge and ate it walking up the Monte dei Cappuccini. It was hot for mid-October, but the stillness and greyness of the sky made sense. The evening would see the season reverting to what it ought to be, though Torino seemed in no hurry for that. Cars, pedestrians, trams and barges were out of harmony with each other. Far off was the great factory whose three shifts supplied the laborious carillon of the city.

When he turned back towards the centre, he avoided the university and the premises that seemed to be a sort of annex to it, the bars, trattorias and flights of steps where the students relaxed during their free periods, breathing a little fresh air before they returned to the classrooms for their next lecture. Basically, all he wanted was to see *her*. He knew this need was stamped on his every thought, but clearly this was not the right moment.

Back at HQ, the guy in the guardroom said, "Petri was looking for you."

"When was that?"

"Ten minutes ago. I told him you'd gone out."

Corso rushed through the entrance hall and climbed the stairs two at a time. When he reached the commissario's door, he knocked twice and went in.

"You were looking for me?"

Petri was writing something that would almost certainly have to be typed out later.

"I was indeed."

Corso shut the door and made himself step firmly towards the desk.

"Your aunt is not well," Petri said. "You need to phone her; they left a number." Saying nothing more, he continued with his neat writing. His handwriting was elaborate, akin to a relic of the Renaissance, and seemed in no way to relate to his frank unfussy nature. Finally, he marked a full stop, unhurriedly put the cap on his fountain pen and looked up at Corso, who was waiting without any attempt to hide his impatience.

"I've spent years making decisions that affect other people," he said, "and I can tell you there are two ways of going about it: if you worry about what might happen, you'll be an old man in no time at all, and if you don't give a damn, you'll very soon grow arrogant. There are not many other possibilities."

Corso nodded to show he was aware of this.

Petri opened a drawer and put the document he had been writing into it.

He said nothing more, except: "You're welcome."

Corso walked as far as Vanchiglia to be a reasonable distance from the centre. There was a roundabout there with a phone booth hidden by the low branches of trees. He exchanged a coin in a nearby bar for a couple of telephone tokens.

"Bramard here, I think you were looking for me?"

"There's a problem."

"What kind of problem?"

"Edoardo . . . One of us has noticed a car outside his house. He's certain he's being watched. He rang to warn me that you lot are on our tail. Do you know anything about this?"

"You have to give yourself up at once."

"I can't. We have a meeting this evening."

"Where?"

"I've already told you, I'm not going to let anyone down. I'd rather end up inside myself. But this evening I'll talk to them and try to convince them."

Corso allowed a pause.

"And what if they don't want to know?"

"Whatever happens, she and I will be in that yard tomorrow."

"But what if it turns out that she doesn't want to know?"

A pause.

"She will come with me."

Corso gave himself a moment to think.

"Alright, but I must have the name of the man in the leather jacket."

"No, we came to an agreement . . ."

"Things have changed, or you wouldn't have phoned. I need his name and where to find him, otherwise the agreement's off, also for you two and the girl."

Silence.

"We know him as Neocle. We don't have any other name for him, and we don't know what he does or where he lives. We came across him at the Circolo Garibaldi some months ago. He had just arrived from the north-east, from Verona, or maybe it was Vicenza."

"Was the attack his idea?"

"Yes."

"Did he know Gonella was inside that building? Did he know Gonella at all?"

"I've no idea. That's enough now."

Click!

Corso delayed his trip back to the centre, stopping to eat fried cod in a dive near Porta Palazzo. The phone call had excited a ferocious, even cerebral, hunger in him. He chased down the cod with a glass of white wine, balancing the glass on the crude board that did duty for a table in that little hovel. A few metres away the square was teeming with scavengers scratching about among discarded boxes in search of bruised fruit. Like the lively pilfering that might follow a cheerful bombardment.

At 4 p.m. he had a coffee and went to earth in his office hoping no-one would phone him or come looking for him. He made no attempt to ring Michelle for the same reason he had not tried to phone her during his lunch hour.

When at 5 p.m. he picked up his kitbag to leave, he found Fiore waiting for him in the corridor just outside his own door, back to the wall with one foot raised.

"Busy this evening?"

"No, why?"

"De Maria has just called the others from his home phone. So now we can nab the lot."

34

"Do you know the one about the old bull and the young bull?"

"Yes."

"That makes me think you can only be theoretically intelligent. How did they get here, in your opinion? Did they come in a group?"

"One at a time, so as not to attract attention."

"Good! So the first to arrive won't have checked around looking for the others?"

"He will have checked."

"And if he had noticed a suspicious car he would have called off the meeting?"

Relaxing in the back seat, Corso studied Fiore's head, as solid as one hewn on Easter Island. Barbicinti's voice croaked from the radiophone. "No movement at rear exit. Sent Tonelli and the other car to move in parallel. You never know, they may want to go past the garages."

Fiore raised his two-way radio to his mouth.

"So you really want to fuck the whole thing up for me, do you?"

"We haven't got that far yet." Barbicinti sniggered.

Corso checked the time on the dashboard: ten forty.

The appointment had been for ten o'clock, but Fiore had decided to give them an extra half hour. He had just explained why to Corso. There were four cars involved. And about fifteen men. All plain clothes.

Their base was a side street off Via Passo Buole. Those who lived there had been carefully checked. They turned out to include a one-time tart called Rossella Bastente, one Anfossi Paolo, a loan shark, and Domenichino Attilio, a receiver of stolen goods. All the rest had clean records.

So there could be no doubt that the person calling himself "Ciano" that De Maria had been talking to on the telephone must be Luciano Cau, a 28-year-old employed at the Fiat ironworks, who was already known in Cagliari as an agitator and had been arrested in Torino when carrying a flick knife; a "professional", Fiore called him. In his identification photograph Corso had recognised the curly head in the parka as one of those he had seen in Piazza Respighi. The meeting was to be held in rooms rented in Cau's name on the fifth floor at the top of staircase B.

Fiore lit a Toscano and opened a couple of fingers of window to let out the smoke. The man driving their car was as heavily built as a docker. From the moment they got in he had restricted himself to following Fiore's instructions without opening his own mouth. "Tell me about life at the university, Bramard!" Fiore said without turning. "How it is with all those easy modern girls? Do you boys have any spunk left for your studies?"

"I go there to take exams, but otherwise I'm never there."

"Did you hear that, Manzon? In my day we talked sex all the time, but actually did next to nothing. But Bramard never admits anything . . . that's just the way it goes!"

The radio gave a croak every few minutes, but reported nothing of note.

"They must have been in there an hour by now," Corso commented.

"Just relax, Bramard. Have a cigarette. This may take a long time. I'm sure those guys have a lot to discuss. Don't forget, they have a revolution to plan. The dictatorship of the proletariat!" He shook his head. "And since you're a teacher, let me inform you that there's more proletariat in these six cars of ours than in the whole of their movement. Even Pasolini has confirmed that! So Pasolini should be here now to defend us, shouldn't he, Manzon?"

Manzon lifted his shoulders twice to show he shared the joke, then returned to his imperturbable observation of the front door of the house. Compared to Manzon's enormous cranium, the ox-like head of Fiore was more like that of a small calf.

A volley of sound shot out of the radio, interrupted by Barbicinti's voice: "There's a woman coming down the stairs. She's heading straight for us."

Fiore moved his face closer to his radio, even though he was already holding the microphone right against his mouth.

"She seems mute so far as I can tell, hardly breathing."

The microphone caught the sound of a door being closed, then silence. They waited two minutes, three. The street was deserted, and not many of the windows facing it were lit. From a distance nothing was visible.

"We've got her," the radio announced unexpectedly.

"Good, is she co-operating?"

"Yes, she's being reasonable."

"Check if there are any documents on her."

"Tonelli's having a look. What did you say? There's a paper here that says Rossella Bastente, thirty-five, born in Settimo, resident in . . ."

"Alright, alright, that's the tart. She doesn't interest us. But hold on to her. Don't let her make any phone calls."

"Did you hear that? Just stay here with us and be a good girl. Over."

Midnight passed and Wednesday found them still sitting in

the car, damp and numb with cold. A dense mist was rising from the manhole covers and waste-water gutters, hiding everything lower than the second floor.

When Fiore looked at his wristwatch, Corso detected an impatience concealed until that moment.

"For fuck's sake," Fiore swore at his transmitter. "Let's go up now."

They got out of the car and moved towards the main entrance, their footsteps hammering on the damp pavement, those of Manzon loudest of all. Passing through it, they reached the courtyard, where six more officers, who had come in from the back, were waiting.

"My team goes up first or we'll get in each other's way," Fiore announced. "The rest, watch the exits. Bramard, you wait till last."

They climbed the five flights of stairs, making quite a lot of noise, though no-one peered round a door at them or disturbed the curtain over a window. When they reached the attic corridor, Manzon took a piece of paper from his pocket and checked it.

"Number six is at the end," he said. To Corso his voice sounded horribly childish, as though his huge frame must be no more than padding for his tiny voice.

Coming to a halt in front of the door to number 6, they stopped to listen. Those who had not yet drawn their guns, now did so. Corso thought it enough to rest his palm on his open holster. Silence. No light visible from the passage.

Fiore signed to Manzon to go ahead. Manzon kicked the door hard; it flew off its hinges and crashed down loudly inside. Corso was just in time to see that there was a light on, before his colleagues rushed in and blocked his view.

"Wait here," Fiore said. "No-one is authorised to go any further."

Corso and the others waited five, ten minutes. Nothing could be heard from the inside but the subdued voices of officers, and the sound of furniture being shifted, plates being broken and cloth being ripped. Then Fiore appeared in the corridor and signed to Corso to go in.

The flat's two rooms were in confusion but bore no sign of anything seditious. The floor was strewn with papers, books, cutlery and a few broken plates. Fiore lifted a chair that had been knocked over, moved it to the table, sat down on it and relit his Toscano.

"That De Maria made fools of us!" He emitted a huge cloud of smoke. ". . . Sometimes you win and sometimes you lose. But the revolution won't be over by tomorrow!"

Other officers were busily packing leaflets and other papers into several boxes. Manzon was lifting a duplicator. Someone else had put some books in a suitcase.

"If they're not here, where can they be?" Corso wondered aloud.

Fiore gave him a look as if to imply that his question had been more tasteless than ingenuous.

"How do I know?" He smiled. "Maybe drinking brandy at De Maria's house."

"Or wherever it is that Neocle lives," Corso added.

Fiore, still smiling, looked Corso straight in the eye.

"Neocle? Who's this Neocle you're talking about? Aimar, the girl, Cau and De Maria: there were four of them that evening. Unless you know more than the rest of us do." Fiore leaned over to pick up another chair and signed to Corso that he should sit down too. "In any case, Bramard, there can be no doubt that this was their den. For a first effort you haven't done too badly!"

Corso thought about this, then lit one of his Gitanes. He smoked it nearly to the end while he looked round the room: a damaged sofa, a small table, a map of Sardinia, an electric water heater, and an old plaid used as a curtain over the only window. But he refused to look at the chair Fiore had picked up for him.

"I shall go back to Petri tomorrow," he said.

Fiore drew in another lungful of Toscano, then nodded.

"Fine. There's even room for the likes of Gigi Riva in this world!"

Corso walked home with his eyes firmly on the ground. A long road for a penitent, but he had plenty of time to contemplate the various aspects of the lesson he had learned. Things that could help him in the future, because he knew he would never see Aimar and the others again. Neither at liberty, nor even behind bars. It was not logic that told him this, but something else he should have been aware of earlier, and that he would pay more attention to in future.

He realised where he was when he began recognising individual flagstones in the pavement, and the empty spaces that gave them their voice. And the gratings over basement laboratories, and the spit the rain was still not heavy enough to wash away.

A hundred years before, when the new railway station had been built as a point of entry for everything that arrived for the city by sea, the square area next to it had been filled with taverns for travellers, merchants, profiteers, thieves, fast-food sellers, swindlers, drinkers, theatregoers, gamblers, artists, brothels and religious orders, all dedicated to the lives of these sinful people. This had not worked particularly well, though the quarter had remained faithful to its beautiful if dirty origins.

He went through the main door, crossed the peeling hall and started up the stairs. Eight flights each consisting of twelve steps, at the very top of which, sitting on the ninety-sixth step, he found *her*.

She had a woollen hat on her head and was reading a book.

"This is not a good part of town," Corso said. "You shouldn't come here on your own."

Michelle went on reading to the end of the paragraph before she lifted her eyes.

"I'm a free woman. And in any case, I've got you to protect me, haven't I?"

Corso said nothing.

"You will protect me, won't you?"

Corso still took time before answering.

His life had changed. "Yes," he said. "I shall protect you."

35

Now that Corso has stopped talking, Arcadipane realises how full the darkness all round them is of humming, flying, slipping and whispering sounds. He reaches into his pocket for a sucai pastille and slips it into his mouth. The countryside has always made him want to shit.

"What's the time?" he asks.

Corso looks at his Cyma. It is some time now since Elena turned off the light in the courtyard, thinking perhaps that they had gone for a walk in the countryside. The moon has either gone behind a cloud or is simply not there at all.

"Let's have some coffee," he says.

"Won't that disturb everyone?"

"We can go to the library."

Arcadipane follows Corso's footsteps down and along the passage, then, just before the end of it, he turns and emits a sharp breath that is not quite a whistle. After a few seconds something lands in front of him.

The sound of their four feet and Trepet's three paws is amplified by the resonance of the courtyard, where the Alfa, sitting in the middle, is now covered by light condensation.

"Still excellent?" Corso asks as they pass the car.

"Still excellent."

They climb the stairs into the house. Trepet immediately lies down on the carpet.

"Here I only have the machine that makes Caffè Americano."

"Fine," Arcadipane says, suffering from the damp that reached him outside. "So long as it's hot."

As they wait for the machine to heat the water and let it drip through the filter, Corso and Arcadipane stand in silence near the standard lamp that Corso has turned on. Then he fills two cups to the brim and puts them on the little table. They sit down in the armchairs. Arcadipane looks at the walls lined with books.

"Before you ask me if I have read them all," Corso says, "I'm going to ask you something. What did you want to say that time I took Autumnal's letters to your office to be examined?"

"That after twenty years the chances of catching a killer are less than 0.3 per cent."

"And here we are now discussing a case from forty years ago. When you hadn't even become a policeman yet. So let me ask you the same question in a different form: why did you take that bone?"

Arcadipane takes a sip. The terrible quality of the coffee seems to reflect his own state of mind. He looks at Trepet, sleeping, unconscious of his own ugliness and disability, and of the fact that neither of these is his worst feature.

"I've lost the sining," Arcadipane says.

"The what?"

"The sining. Don't you know what that means?" Arcadipane says, indicating all Corso's books, which seem to make this possibility unlikely.

"I've no idea what you're talking about. Tell me."

"It's when someone immediately grasps what other people can't understand at all."

"'Shining', then, though that's not really what the word means."

"If you say so. Anyway, whatever it is, it's something I've lost."

"How do you know you had it before?"

Arcadipane considers this.

"Because you would never have given up your job to anyone who didn't have it."

Corso smiles, hearing the right answer. He takes a sip of coffee.

"And how do you know you've lost it?"

"No idea, but the simple fact is I no longer have it. How about you?"

Corso shrugs his shoulders.

"I work as a teacher now. If I've ever had it, I certainly don't use it anymore."

They drink, each considering the question from his own point of view. Outside, the darkness is changing. Not getting lighter, just less intense. A variation bringing the sense of promise that comes with every new day. Another ten minutes, then, as always, this promise will dissipate in a day no different from the day before.

"Well?"

"Well, what?"

"I've lost it, and you don't even know whether you have it or not. So what shall we do?"

Corso gets up and goes to the big window to confirm that dawn is almost upon them. He knows Elena will soon wake, go into the kitchen and make herself coffee to drink while reading a magazine about plants and gardens, in no way related to the untamed nature that surrounds them here. Then she will go back to bed and sleep for another two hours. Dawn is usually when they make love.

"Do you really want us to go on with this story?"

"Of course. Don't you?"

PART THREE

PART THREE

Third Prologue

She can remember the house perfectly, with the woman, the husband, the little girl and the old man who took a rifle from above the dresser, shouted at the others to get out of the way and fired out of the window. And the car driving off with squealing tyres, as she hid under the table with the glass of water they put on the floor, dying of thirst but not daring to touch it; then another car arriving, and a carabiniere with highly polished shoes bending down to ask her to come out from her refuge, holding out a hand to help her. A man with a young face but the eyes of a father. She took his hand. Then nothing more. She must have lost consciousness. She has no idea what happened next, how long the journey was or where they took her. For all she knows she could be down there again in the place she escaped from.

With her eyes shut, she sniffs the blanket under her chin. It does not smell of sweat or dirt. Nor does it prick or sting her. When she listens, she can no longer hear cockroaches plopping into a bowl. Or scrabbling busily for scraps of food.

"Nini!"

She opens her eyes at once, and there he is.

"No!" she cries, thrusting herself back against the bedhead. An animal reflex to protect at least one side of her body.

"It's alright, you're in hospital." He puts his hand on her shoulder. "There's a carabiniere outside. Look! You're quite safe."

Beyond the frosted glass is a dark figure, and the silhouetted head suggests a military cap.

"The doctor says you're fine. Now put on these clothes I've brought for you, and we can go." He strokes her cheek.

"But . . . you said I'm safe."

The man pulls a pair of jeans from a plastic bag and lays them on the bed.

"Of course, you're safe, but we have to go. I can't explain now."

She stares at him while he rummages in the bag.

"How did you manage to get in?"

"Come on, Nini, take off those hospital clothes. And hurry up."

She slowly slides her hand towards the emergency bell.

"Help!" she shouts, pressing the button. "Help me!"

The man puts his hand over her mouth, letting her continue pressing the bell, but no sound of a bell ringing comes from the corridor, nor is there any sign of anyone rushing past. The carabiniere turns towards the door, then after a second or two turns back and faces the corridor again.

"Do you think we could have done what we did without anyone knowing about it?"

She stops resisting, stops struggling. He takes his hand from her mouth.

"In a minute that guard will be off to get himself coffee from the machine. He'll be away five minutes, giving us time to get down the stairs and out of here."

"But where can we go? They're looking for me! And they'll be looking for you too."

The man takes her face in his hands.

"I've made an agreement, Nini, you have to trust me . . ."

"Agreement?" She raises her voice. "How can you have made an agreement with . . ."

He pushes his forehead against hers, holding her face in his hands.

"I've collected some documents together," he whispers a few centimetres from her lips. "And they know it. Downstairs we have a car, ten million, and two fake passports. But we must be out of the country by tomorrow. If not, the agreement will no longer be valid. It's our only chance. I'm not interested in spending the night in prison and as for you, even under protection . . ."

She looks towards the door. The carabiniere is no longer there. The two stitches they inserted in her forehead have come out. A drop of blood trickles down her nose.

"But the others?"

He shakes his head.

"We have to tell someone they're in there!" she insists. "Let's call them from outside, without—"

"We can't do anything about it, Nini." He wipes the blood off her nose with the edge of the sheet. "That was decided right at the start."

"Then why did you not do something then?" she shouts, pushing him away.

Her eyes fill with tears. The room is still full of distant noises from the corridor. And the hum of the air conditioner.

He takes her arm and gently pulls out the needle of her phlebotomy drip.

"The only thing left to us to decide now," he says, "is whether we want to do anything for ourselves."

36

Putting his key in the lock, Arcadipane assumes that for the next half hour he will have the place to himself. It is still open to him to go downstairs again and absent-mindedly get himself something to eat at the nearby bar, while keeping an eye out in case any of the three members of his family pass by, putting off until later in the evening what will undoubtedly be in store for him before calmly going upstairs again.

But the key has already clicked in the lock, so now it's too late for second thoughts . . .

He opens the door: the corridor is empty. One step forward, then two. He can hear cups rattling in the kitchen. He advances cautiously, without putting down either the basket under his arm or the bags in his hand, as if holding on to these objects could shield him.

Mariangela is at the coffee machine with her back to him, and Loredana is dunking in her tea a slice of bread without salt, sugar or pleasure. She is the first to catch sight of him, giving a half-smile before she looks down, thus quickly extinguishing even that faint suggestion of happiness. Her dunked bread softens with agonising slowness and slips down into her tea.

"What was that?"

Mariangela turns round.

"Where on earth did you get to, you could at the very least have . . ." Then she sees Trepet and goes quiet.

"Giovanni!" she shouts. "Papà has brought the dog!"

Arcadipane turns towards the dark part of the corridor at the same moment Giovanni peers out from his room. The boy sees Trepet, who, becoming aware of the difficult atmosphere, huddles against the legs of the only human being he is familiar with.

"Cool," Giovanni says. "What's his name?"

"Trepet."

"But . . . Vincenzo . . ." Mariangela's coffee stays under the chromium spout of her designer coffee machine. "Where did you get it?"

"I went to the kennels. And I've got his lead and some shampoo for him here, and some bowls for him to eat out of. But first he needs a good bath."

"I have no intention of touching that thing," Loredana says.

Arcadipane looks for support from his son, but Giovanni has already disappeared back into his room. Mariangela picks up her cup and drinks without taking her eyes off the dog.

"It can't be easy to find an animal like that," she says. "You must have spent all night at the kennels."

Arcadipane puts down the basket-cum-bed and the bags near the place where the keys are kept. He looks in the bag for the shampoo and moves away.

"Come on," he says to the dog.

Trepet gives the women a last look before following him.

Shutting the bathroom door, Arcadipane sits down on the toilet and searches his pocket for a sucai pastille, watched by Trepet, who has curled up on the fluffy mat by the bath.

Chewing the sucai, Arcadipane forces himself to try to think positive thoughts.

The first thing that comes into his mind is Bramard: not much aged, in peace now with a new woman and two children to keep him busy. No more drinking, no more suicidal climbing in the mountains. His past is now finally behind him; at least it was until he started giving Arcadipane hell over the only case during his whole police career that he, Bramard, ever failed to solve. And started to involve Arcadipane in illegal activities. Asking his help in throwing shit at the fan. If, as policeman, husband and father he disgusts Bramard, it's not very likely that he impresses him as a friend . . .

Weeping, Arcadipane puts the plug in the bath and turns on the water. Trepet moves himself just far enough away to feel safe. The passivity he has allowed himself in following Arcadipane is now beginning to seem suspect.

"Until now we have been doing things your way," Arcadipane tells Trepet. "But no longer . . ."

When there is a hand's breadth of water in the bath, Arcadipane turns off the tap and grabs him. The dog emits a tiny whimper of protest. Lifting him, Arcadipane feels the animal's wrinkled skin stretch over his compact and tepid body. He looks at his pink belly and his testicles, one white and one black, both covered with sparse hair. Where his missing leg must have been there is a small scar, as if the limb had somehow been sucked back into his body.

As he lowers the dog into the water, he hears the children say goodbye and go out, slamming the door behind them. He imagines that while he has been in the bathroom they will have talked about nothing else.

"Hello?" Mariangela knocks on the bathroom door.

"Come in."

Mariangela observes her husband lying in the half-full bath, his chest rising above the foam, with the dog's head at his feet, surrounded by bubbles.

"I really am beginning to worry about you now, Vincenzo."

"Really?"

"Yes."

On her shoulder is the bag she carries to school, a large satchel with straps and lots of pockets. Pens protrude from one pocket, her badge is fastened to another, and yet another contains the key she needs for the school coffee machine.

"Can you tell me what got into your head? Wouldn't it have been better to take the children with you to choose a dog? As it is you've managed to do what they wanted and annoy them at the same time."

Arcadipane shifts a little foam to conceal his belly and genitals. Trepet stares vaguely at the window, a bubble perched on his head.

"He's helping me to see if I can still get it up."

"The dog? What on earth . . ."

The bubble on Trepet's head bursts.

"I can't explain. It'll only need two or three weeks. If it works, it works; and if it doesn't . . ."

37

Corso steps out of the lift and turns right as instructed.

The corridors on the third floor are long and narrow just as he remembers them, but the colour of the walls, the glazed doors and the floor remind him of somewhere else. The only things that haven't changed are the scraps of paper stuck with Scotch tape to the doors of the closed offices, indicating times available for students to see the lecturer, and lists of texts and names. A habit he never liked, which now seems frankly pornographic. But this is not why he is here today.

There is a boy sitting on a bench in front of one of the offices. The only bench in the corridor.

"Are you waiting to go in?" he asks the boy.

The lad looks up from a football paper.

"No, my girl's in there at the moment."

Corso sits down next to him; two muffled voices can be heard from beyond the door. A discussion leading nowhere in particular. The boy would probably rather have been somewhere else, as it's Saturday morning and he is sure to have been up late last night. "Who the hell interviews people on Saturday mornings?" he must have protested, before realising his girl is determined to be there, and that it could damage their relationship if he is not willing to go with her.

"Are you still studying at the university?"

Corso, staring at the boy, has been contemplating him for some time and planning to ask him the same question.

"No."

"Good for you. But in any case, you would be in no danger."

"Why? What danger could there possibly be?"

"Sexual assault." The boy nods at the door. "She's so juicy they've already laid hands on her twice. That's why I have to come with her. Not to exams, because there are lots of people around then, but to one-to-one tuitions . . . Her parents wanted it reported. But that would have forced her to go through hell to get her degree. Naaaa! But I make sure he sees me when she goes into the room. I give her a kiss and I have a newspaper with me, and they know I'm here. What's the saying: 'Lord, be my shepherd . . . protect thy flock.' But it's disgusting, it makes me sick. After all, we pay these people's salaries, don't we?"

Corso agrees. The door opens, and the girl comes out. Attractive enough, apart from the fact that her looks are totally spoiled by her teeth. Too many, and not correctly spaced in her mouth. When the boy sees her, his expression softens. They leave together without a word. Halfway down the corridor he slips his hand into the back pocket of her jeans.

"Come in."

Sitting at the desk writing is a man roughly the same age as Corso, who, like him, has managed to retain a good head of hair. He is wearing a chequered shirt and corduroy trousers and looks to be putting on weight.

Corso sits down. The office is a modest one, in no sense the cell of a learned scholar lined with heavy tomes. Just a set of IKEA bookshelves and a few books. A couple of pictures, photos of the man himself with tennis trophies, shaking hands with his doubles partner beside the net, the woman in a short white skirt.

"Please excuse me, I must write a note on that last interview," says Edoardo De Maria. "There are so many students and it's not always easy to remember everything they say. There . . ." He files the paper away in a drawer. "But what can I do for you?"

"I'd like to have a word about Via Lampredotti."

De Maria shakes his head in incredulity and gives a half-smile.

"Are you a journalist? Or writing a thesis? Or have I done something to upset you, because if that's the case let me tell you at once that three years ago a student I failed had the brilliant idea of posting the matter on Facebook to discredit me. Do you know how many likes he had? Three. Most of the comments he got were either insulting or said who the hell cares. No, that's the truth! A couple of students wrote to me to ask if I could put them in touch with Commander Marcos. The answer I gave them was the same as the answer I'm about to give you now: that I'm not a terrorist and have never had anything to do with armed resistance. When I was twenty, I was guilty of a bit of stupid nonsense and paid the penalty for it. End of story. If you have any sensational revelations to make, take them to the police. They will be happy to hear you out. I said what I had to say at the time. Now, if you would be good enough to excuse me . . ."

Corso does not move or change his expression.

"I want to know about the meeting you all had the evening before you left for France. Tuesday, October fifteenth . . ."

"For what reason, excuse me?"

"Because I was one of the police on the case at the time."

"The case has been closed for more than thirty years now, and if you had followed it as you seem to claim, you will know that I was prosecuted in court and that Cau was jailed years later, while Aimar and Maria Nicole escaped abroad where they presumably made new lives for themselves. They would not have been the first to do so: Italy is not a country that tempts its exiles to come home, especially if they have made a good career for themselves abroad and have a sentence hanging over their heads."

"And what if I were to tell you that they never got any further than Chivasso?"

De Maria takes a moment to connect this information with what he may have read or half read a few days earlier in the local paper, and to process this. Corso, watching his face, recognises a calm man who has learned to conceal the good fortune of his birth, the one stupid slip during his youth, and his subsequent prosperity, behind a wall of modesty, sophistication and cordiality.

"The body of Stefano Aimar was in that ditch," Corso says, "and very likely the body of the Bo girl as well. I have no idea when they finished up there, but it was almost certainly that meeting that decided their fate. Which is why I've come to ask you to tell me what happened that evening."

De Maria stares at him with his mouth half-open. His eyes are chestnut brown, and there are a few broken capillaries on his cheeks; he probably eats too much and enjoys strong drink during evenings with his intellectual friends: the sort of people who write articles for newspapers – councillors, administrators, some of them hand in glove with the banks though they still see themselves as left-leaning. He is not wearing a wedding ring but there is a photo of two little girls on his desk. His divorce must have cost him a good deal of money, though cushioned by a family fortune he was probably able to afford it.

"Why not ask Cau?" he says finally. "After that evening, I neither saw nor heard anything more of any of them, but maybe since he spent so much time around the place, Cau . . ."

"I went to see Cau this morning."

"Oh yes? And what did he tell you?"

"A man who can spend so many years inside without opening

his mouth is not likely to start talking as soon as he gets out. I met him in an office like yours, except that in his case he was only there as the cleaner. Did you ever go to see him when he was in prison? Were you at all in touch with him then?"

"I wrote to him a couple of times." De Maria shakes his head. "That was years ago, but he never answered."

"To ask him to forgive you?"

De Maria leans forward from his chair, coming closer to Corso, who has not moved since sitting down.

"It wasn't Via Lampredotti that got Cau twenty-five years, but two other murders and six robberies. He could have re-established himself in the outside world eventually, just as I have. As could they all . . ."

"What did Aimar suggest to the rest of you that evening?"

De Maria looks out of the window. The city. The same city as long ago. Except that it is now utterly different. Clearly, the city Corso is now forcing him to return to is a place he had assumed he would never need to visit again. A place of dust, memories and guilt.

"It's all more than thirty years ago. You can't expect me to remember now who said what." He passes a hand over his forehead. "We were all confused and terrified. I need a little time to sort out my memories."

Corso gets up and goes to open the window a fraction. Modern windows that open, but not far enough for anyone to throw himself out of them, not even a child.

"There were five of you that evening when you threw the Molotov cocktail that killed Andrea Gonella. You, Aimar, Cau, Maria Nicole and Neocle."

Corso pulls the packet of cigarettes from his pocket, takes out a Gitanes and sticks it in his mouth. The smoke heads for the gap in the window, sucked out into the equally grey outside world.

"Thirty-four years have passed since then and, as you see, my memory is still in fairly good nick. The only problem is that there must have been five people, not four, at that meeting. That's why I'm here."

He smokes calmly, his eyes on the city, but his attention concentrated on any movements and noises that may occur behind him. Once he has established that the other man is also unlikely to move, he turns around.

De Maria is staring at him, his manner clearly showing that he is rattled.

Corso continues to smoke. Now that the door is open, he notices he is no longer so anxious, no longer so eager to see again these rooms he had looked forward so much to returning to.

38

By the time Arcadipane has finished putting Isa in the picture about the connections between Bramard and Aimar, between Fiore, the break-in, the empty attic and everything else, a good half hour has passed.

Isa puts a piece of bread in her mouth while looking at the ancient photos of old stars like Totò, Fabrízi and Alberto Sordi that are hanging on the walls, including someone in a picture now so totally faded that it is impossible to identify them.

"The whole story's a load of crap!" she says loudly.

Arcadipane looks around. The last time he sat at this table it was with someone in tears, while now . . . no-one seems to be listening to him or paying him any attention. Apart from the waitress, who has been giving them the occasional worried glance since they told her ten minutes ago they were waiting for one more diner to arrive. A major obstacle, throwing out of gear the progress of their smoothly planned three-course meal.

"Well then, what now?" Isa says.

"How do you mean, what now?"

"Have you told me this story just because you couldn't keep it to yourself any longer, or is there some other reason you wanted to meet me here?"

Arcadipane would like nothing better than to punch her or smash a plate over her head, but she would probably respond by giving him a kick in the balls. She had actually done that once to Oscar, who would never have been violent towards her . . . though who knows what got into him to make him tell her she was a "cunt with knobs on"?

"Because Bramard thinks you can help him."

"Why?"

Arcadipane too takes a piece of bread and chews it while looking around the place.

"Because he says you're a bit like us."

Isa stares at him.

"I don't give a fuck what either of you thinks of me. I just want my pistol back."

Arcadipane remembers he wants to punch her or smash a plate over her head. But he would also like to keep his balls.

"I'm going through hell to get you taken back."

"Then try harder and give me my gun."

Corso appears in the doorway and looks around. Arcadipane lifts a hand to attract his attention and escape from the embarrassing subject of Isa's pistol. Corso comes across, takes off his woollen jacket, which he hangs on the back of his chair, and sits down.

"Ciao, Isa."

"Ciao," she answers, without turning away from his gaze.

Arcadipane knows this is the first time they have met since the Autumnal affair, which had already destroyed Corso's life, his only reason for continuing to live at all being to find out what had happened. Isa was the eccentric girl who had helped him solve the puzzle. What Arcadipane can't decide is whether, after it was over, the two of them had talked, thanked each other and stripped naked before moving on, or simply parted with a nod, as might be expected from two such unusual people.

"Have you told Isa everything?" Corso asks.

Arcadipane hurries to confirm that he has.

"Well, then." Corso turns to Isa. "What do you think?"

She crushes a piece of bread. The arrogance on her face is not her usual expression. But the incomprehensible effect Bramard always has on people is something Arcadipane has long been familiar with.

Finally, she says, "All I want is to have my pistol back."

The waitress comes up. Today she is wearing trousers so tight that her bare belly is bulging over them.

"What can I bring you all?" she says.

Arcadipane goes for horse steak and fried artichokes, while Corso chooses spaghetti and tomato sauce. Isa decides on grilled octopus, linguine with squid ink sauce, kidneys and a Piedmontese valerian salad with hard-boiled eggs. Plus a half-litre of red wine for herself, while the two men make do with water.

The waitress leans through the fringed curtain to the kitchen to repeat the order.

"Have you spoken to Cau?" Arcadipane asks.

"He didn't bother to tell me he knew nothing, just kept silent. But I have an idea that after thirty years he knows many more incriminating secrets than Via Lampredotti. Things that might have even secured him a reduced sentence. So if he's never mentioned any of this before . . ."

"And De Maria?"

"Needed oiling, but softer. In the end he told me what he knows. Which must be more or less the same as what Cau knows."

"And that means . . . ?" Isa says, dropping her eyes to snap off a piece of grissino.

Corso takes the remaining piece and puts it in his mouth.

"It must have been Neocle who decided the time and place for the meeting on the fifteenth. A bedsit on Corso Svizzera that might even have been where he was living, but De Maria had never been there before and isn't sure. However, nothing in the telephone calls ever mentioned any particular place for this meeting."

"And Fiore? All that business of the break-in to Cau's attic?"

"He knew perfectly well the three boys wouldn't be there. He only took me there because he didn't want me interfering with things if there had been a meeting."

"But that was the meeting when Aimar promised to convince the others to give themselves up. That was the agreement you'd made with him, wasn't it?"

"De Maria says Aimar tried to, but Neocle had other ideas."

"Which were?"

"That a group was being formed to take the fight to a higher level. De Maria came to the meeting already determined to escape to France, while Cau was already in contact with Lotta Continua; but Aimar and the Bo girl—"

"Who were there."

"According to De Maria, apart from Cau, who was already an experienced campaigner, they were all fascinated by Neocle. He was the one who had got them together, convinced them to take action, and chosen the house in Via Lampredotti for their target. It seems the Bo girl was a bit of a hothead, maybe there was even something going on between her and Neocle. Perhaps Aimar was only there out of jealousy or in an attempt to protect her."

"But who the hell was Neocle?"

"Almost certainly a *nom de guerre*. None of them knew his real name. De Maria says he must have been over thirty and he once let something slip about training in South America, but of course he may have invented such stories merely to impress them. But he was certainly experienced and knew all about taking action. This is more or less what Aimar told me thirty years ago.

I think De Maria is being honest when he claims that when first interrogated he mentioned five people being responsible for what happened at Via Lampredotti, without omitting anything. Then he noticed that the questions he was being asked tended to leave out Neocle, that any reference to him tended to elicit either indifference or irritation from his interrogators. Ultimately, he could only lose if he tried to row against this tide, so he played along and the name of Neocle disappeared altogether from the reports."

The waitress puts two plates in front of Isa, and only one each in front of the two men. Isa immediately eats a forkful of pasta with a slice of octopus. The two men watch her, the black squid ink on her lips matching her black hair and black eye make-up, with the ferociously shaved left side of her skull offering a stark contrast. Corso suspects that even if a heavy lorry crushed her, she would still be beautiful when they pulled her out.

"Do you think you can find out any more?" he asks her.

"I could see if there's anything on this Fiore," she says, energetically dismantling her food. "It depends whether it's been marked as classified or not, and if it has been, at what level."

The fried artichokes arrive. The three eat in silence for several minutes.

"I say we should go back to the beginning," Corso says. "Find friends, relatives and fellow students of Aimar and the Bo girl. The police will have spoken to them at the time, but today we may be able to see things that weren't clear back then. What do you think?"

"Fine by me," Arcadipane says, glancing at his watch. "But tread carefully. Don't forget you're supposed to be a teacher and a temporarily disabled police officer. Now I have to run." He is already on his feet, searching for his wallet. "Up to my eyes in work."

Corso signals to him to put away his wallet. Arcadipane makes a gesture of thanks, gives a single ciao for the two of them, then goes out, followed by Trepet, who has been lying under the table.

Corso watches the street door slowly close.

"Have you really been helping him so you can get taken back to HQ?"

"Uh-huh." Isa sips some wine while still chewing.

"Then why are you still making such a fuss? Don't tell me it's just for the gun."

Isa swallows another mouthful of food.

"Two years ago, I asked you if my father had been fucked up by his work, remember?"

"Yes, you did ask me that."

"And do you remember your answer?"

"That those were difficult times."

"Well, I carried on digging around, and the only thing I could find out was that in 1972 he was involved in a judiciary squad that never produced any files or made any arrests. I don't know what this squad actually did, or what it was expected to do. Because from 1975, till they killed him in Barcelona in 1982, he spent ten days every month away from Torino. I have no idea if my mother knew where he went, or why he was so ready to leave me with a woman who spent all day in bed stuffing herself with pills. And I don't know why the person who killed my father started by making him hand over his wallet and then fired two shots, one to his heart and one to his head, but ignored the Rolex on his wrist and the gold cigarette case that in his pocket. Nor did I know why the Rolex, the cigarette case and the cash he seemed to have been carrying when he was killed, had always disappeared before he got back to the shitty suburb where he forced my mother and me to live. Nor do I know why his body was cremated without any authorisation from his family, and why not a single one of his colleagues was there at his funeral. And I don't know why following up this case of a murdered policeman was never entrusted to the senior police officer at HQ at the time – that is to say you."

"A matter of correct procedure. Since it happened in Spain, all we could do was give support."

"And who did we send as support? A useless fucker who signed a couple of documents and then went home. And you want to know why I stick my nose into every bag of shit they shove in front of me."

Corso finishes his pasta in silence. When Isa's kidney and salad arrive, she starts eating as before without any allowance for Corso's seniority.

"The Bo girl had a brother," she says. "He's her only living relative now. There's no-one left related to Aimar."

"Does the brother live far away?"

"In the hills, near . . . Fuck me!" She strikes her forehead with her hand.

"What's the matter?"

Isa rummages in the black bag she has hung on her chair and pulls out a long, narrow box, the sort of thing in which someone might keep a single greatly valued flower. She leans the box against the table.

"Does that contain what I think it does?" Corso asks.

"Do you plan to take it back to him?"

"Maybe not."

"And are you going to eat all the steak and artichokes Arcadipane left?"

39

"What's that?" she says, pointing at Trepet already curled up on the carpet. "Is that one of the noes I told you to change to yeses?"

Arcadipane nods. "His name is Trepet."

"A hideous animal, well done. Well, are you still whimpering? Still feeling wishy-washy? Things getting worse rather than better, eh?"

Arcadipane speaks for about ten minutes, looking out of the window and explaining in his own words how he feels, sighing and feeling his shoulders sinking ever lower. Ariel, sipping her tisane, listens, also looks out of the window and scratches a knee hidden under her travelling rug. Now he knows what she hides under that rug he cannot help thinking about the withered legs she must drag behind her without them making her any less beautiful in her strange way of being beautiful, though Arcadipane has not yet made up his mind whether this is real beauty or not.

"All this is quite normal," she says finally.

"How do you mean, quite normal?"

"*The times they are a-changing.* The important thing is for the orchestra to play on, because if the musicians also run for the lifeboats, the story loses its beauty. Do you understand what I mean?"

"I don't understand English."

"That doesn't matter. Just make yourself comfortable and listen. Would you like a tisane?"

"What's in it?"

Ariel fills a cup and holds it out to him. Arcadipane sips it cautiously: it tastes like the fibre sole of an espadrille, but the smell is 100 per cent cannabis.

"How d'you like it?"

"Could be worse."

"I was born in 1981, during the night of June the eleventh, at the very moment people were trying to pull little Alfredo Rampi out of the well he had fallen into at Vermicino. How old were you at that time: twenty-three, twenty-four? Do you remember it?"

"Yes, I'd just been promoted to be Bramard's deputy."

"Maybe you remember that it was a time when everyone in Italy was obsessed with television! A little boy six years old fell into a well eighty metres deep, with people lowering themselves down inside in an attempt to pull him out, and a digger simultaneously excavating another well beside it in a battle against time. Firemen, journalists, thousands of people all waiting round hoping to see the little boy brought out, even the President of the Republic; it was like a film! And do you know why that story will always affect everyone who hears it? Keep drinking your tisane, don't stint yourself! Because it's like a Greek myth, and the Greek myths have survived for thousands of years because they're about the things that happen inside us all."

Arcadipane watches her shake a disorderly lock of hair loose from behind her ear, nod, and turn firmly back towards the dormer window.

He turns too, perhaps thinking that there may be some explanation in the mainly green hillside now brought closer by the grey sky. Then he turns and looks at Ariel. Then back at

the hillside again, and then at Ariel once more. He is about to
say that he has not understood, that he needs her to explain . . .

"What happened?" she asks him.

"About what?"

"To the child?"

"What child?"

"The one you threw down the well."

"Down the well? What well?"

"The well in the bathroom at that hotel in Andora."

"But . . . there was no well there."

"Of course there was, and you knew it perfectly well. That's
why you took him there and told him, 'Go for a little walk, see
if you can find any flowers'. The child didn't understand. He
believed what you told him, went to look for flowers and fell
into the well. And you did the just same as everyone else; you
covered the well over. Using a cover strong enough to support
your weight for the rest of your life, while only the cover can
be seen."

"What cover?"

"Except that one day, my dear, you heard the boy crying, and
it got more difficult to continue to pretend there was nothing in
the well. Because you know the boy is down there, alone in the
darkness. You've always known that. Everyone knows it. A child
who wants nothing more than to be hugged, soothed, caressed
and taken to see the base so he can see the radar and dream of
being a soldier."

Arcadipane doesn't understand what she means, but he finds
he is weeping.

"Don't cry," she says. "It's the price we all pay for taking our
Martha of the moment and screwing her stupid; for making
money, reproducing ourselves, buying a car and growing up
to be adults. And children don't listen and don't understand;

275

they're all egoists – all they think of is playing, but even so they end up shitting themselves. What comes nearest to saving them is that they're darlings when they're little, but as soon as they sprout a few hairs they begin to feel shame like thieves, and to understand that a moment will come when they will have to make a choice: either him or us. In your case this happened in the bathroom at that hotel. And you made the same choice as we all do. Anyone who doesn't end up in a mental home, a prison, a museum, or on the sleeve of a long-playing record. Though the fate of most is like that of little Alfredo, the child who died alone in the dark, while the grown-ups outside whimpered, appeared live on TV, and in the end resigned themselves to what they had done. That is what they were all really watching on television that day: a child dying. It was a loss of innocence, a collective rite of passage. The fact is that since that child fell in that well, nothing in this country has ever been the same. But these things are too complicated for you to understand, and in any case, they are no use to you. Is that clear now?"

"I don't know." Arcadipane wipes his eyes on the sleeve of the coat his in-laws gave him. "I'll have to think about it."

"Think about it for as long as you like, but leave the money in the usual place. You'll have never spent a hundred euros better. I doubt you have ever heard so many truths in a such a short time. And I'll give you another for free: go to a chemist's and get some charcoal for that dog to stop him farting so much! If you haven't noticed it, that's just something else that's not been working for you, besides the things we already know about. Your homework for this weekend: don't leave the house, don't work, don't think, don't do anything at all. Just sit back and stare at the ceiling."

Exhausted, Arcadipane gets to his feet and makes his way to the door.

"Just a moment!"

"Yes?"

"One more thing. The porter won't be here on Monday; just ring twenty-four and come straight up."

40

No sooner are they past the hills, than the view from the road opens on to the Monferrato plain, with its monotonous series of villages in the haze. Corso remembers other trips down that road: the body he is grasping now not so very different physically from that otherwise utterly different woman's body on those first motorcycle trips long ago. He had himself been different then, not only because he had not yet been a man, but still a boy.

Isa takes the curves tidily, accelerating smoothly out of them, as if investing in her driving all the common sense she possesses. She has already studied the route on her phone and has kept it clear in her mind, and before they reach each warning road sign, she has already adjusted her speed ready for the curve. Five hundred metres of road cutting through the hillside, following its lines horizontally, and suddenly there they are, in front of the gate. They get off the motorcycle.

"Do you often ride a motorbike?" she asks him, unstrapping her helmet.

"No, but there was once a time when another woman used to give me lifts on hers."

"She must have been happy with you. Not many people know how to ride pillion properly."

Corso tries to remember whether that other woman had in fact been happy about it. He has no idea. In those days he had not known how to tell the difference between what made them happy and what upset them. Both emotional states had been one and the same. After all, that's how relationships always start. It's only later that you begin to separate things into you yourself, the other person, and happiness. And unhappiness, truth, lies, using and being used. That's when courage and judgment have to come into play. And you nearly always find that you don't have enough of either. Or that you have too much. But that was not how things had developed in his case. He had lost the other woman because she was dead. And she had died because he had not been as clever as he thought he was.

"Will you do the talking or shall I?" Isa says as they contemplate the bell on the gate.

"I will, but if they ask for proof of our identity, you'll have to take over."

When they ring, the gate opens automatically, giving them no time to say more. A gravel drive leads them to the house, a two-storey building around fifty years old, which in its day must have seemed audaciously practical in design, but now, surrounded on three sides by trees, simply appears square and lifeless. The hillside has been deforested to make room for several paddocks and a wide area where horses can move freely. Apart from two racehorses, those visible are robust black beasts with powerful legs.

A man of about sixty approaches them, his trousers suggesting a professional horseman dirty from doing the hard work himself. A man of medium height, with an actor's face and clear eyes. His sparse, dishevelled hair in no way detracts from the elegance of his appearance. He is wearing a cheap jacket.

"Are these Mérens horses?" Corso asks.

"Mérens ponies from the Pyrenees. You're here from the co-operative, aren't you?"

"No."

"No? They rang to say they were coming this afternoon. We go in for a bit of horse therapy here, you know. But if all you want is a ride, you have to book in advance."

"We'd just like to ask you a few questions."

"Please go ahead."

"We need some information about your sister."

Marco Arturo Bo's face has been closely shaved. Which is perhaps why a sudden stiffening of his jaw is immediately noticeable.

"Why should we talk about my sister?"

Isa produces her police ID. This seems neither to reassure nor disturb him.

"Over the years," Corso says, "the police must have asked your parents and you many questions . . ."

"My parents have been dead many years, and even when they were alive, I had nothing to say. My sister and I were very different, luckily for me. We were never close."

Isa takes a few steps towards one of the paddocks.

"Don't scare that horse," the man says to her sharply. "They don't like people in glasses, let alone whatever those are that you are wearing."

Isa goes to the enclosure and lightly touches the muzzle of the nearest horse, which remains suspicious but does not try to escape.

"What's the name of this horse?"

"Kabul."

"Why Kabul?"

"Because there's a letter for each year, and horses born in that year all get a name beginning with that letter. Five years ago, it was K."

Corso asks, "Did you know Stefano Aimar?"

"No."

"But you know who he was."

"I read in the papers that he was with my sister, but none of us in the family knew she had a boyfriend. My sister was not the sort of girl to have a boyfriend, and in any case, she never told us what she did outside the home."

"Why? What was she doing, in your opinion?"

"I didn't know and I didn't want to know. The only thing I was aware of was that she was capable of spending days lying on the sofa in a state of depression, and then suddenly becoming euphoric and playing nasty tricks and being either horrible or affectionate according to her mood. When we were little, we both loved horses, but even then she was unstable and spoiled. As soon as I developed a modicum of sense I lost patience with her. Then she got interested in theatre, yachting, racing cars, fashion and revolution. It depended on who she happened to be friends with at the time. The fact that she was beautiful didn't help. She could always find some man to pay her attention. At first my parents supported her and let her win all the arguments, but even they eventually gave her up as a lost cause, a bottomless well."

"From the point of view of money?"

"Money and other problems. She kept disappearing."

Corso looks at Isa; the horse has come a step nearer. She now has one hand firmly on his muzzle.

"When was the last time you saw her?"

"A few days before the police came looking for her. Officially, she was living at home with my parents, but in fact she would only pass by to fill her purse and take food from the fridge. I think one of her friends must have been looking after her. Maybe this Aimar, I don't know."

"Did you never ask yourself what happened to her after the fire in Via Lampredotti?"

"Why should I? I was already on bad terms with her before

that, let alone after that poor man was killed. Later she phoned my parents a couple of times, but with me she didn't risk . . ."

"She phoned your parents?"

"A couple of times."

"When?"

The man squashed a horsefly that had been buzzing around his face.

"The first time was about a year after the evil deed. She told them she was abroad, that she was fine and that they shouldn't believe anything the police said because it wasn't true. My parents obviously asked her if she was short of money, and she said she didn't need anything. She had only called because she wanted to hear their voices."

"What impression did she give of herself?"

"I don't know if she was dealing, perhaps taking them herself, but to me it was obvious she must have some connection with drugs. When she phoned, my parents said they thought they could hear someone speaking something like Arabic in the background. I tried to persuade them to tell the police everything, but they didn't want to. In the end they did nothing."

"And the second time they heard from her?"

"That was in December 1976. She rang one night to say she was in hospital in Vercelli. She seemed confused."

"In Vercelli?"

"That's what she told my parents, but it probably wasn't true. She cried out that she was scared and begged them to come and pick her up. The call broke off, and my parents phoned me at once, but my wife was about to give birth at the time, and I didn't want to leave her and drive off at three in the morning. But my parents insisted on me going because my father had poor eyesight and my mother couldn't drive. I didn't want a lot of nonsense or other people getting involved, so in the end I agreed to go.

She had been admitted to hospital a few hours earlier, but when I got there a nurse told me she had already discharged herself."

"Why had she been admitted to hospital?"

"It seems she was found wandering naked in the countryside in a state of shock, though she was able to give her name. She had some injuries, I don't know what kind. Perhaps she'd been attacked, or perhaps they were self-inflicted. Probably she'd already forgotten what had happened."

"And that was the last time you heard from her?"

"The very last time. After that, my parents went on looking for her. I think they may have even used private detectives without telling me, but nothing was discovered. By the time they died they were sure she must be either be dead or living who knows where with no identifying documents. It was a shame they had nowhere to go to mourn her, but in my view that was for the best."

"I understand."

"I can tell you nothing more. And, as I've explained, I'm expecting some people from the co-operative to arrive here at any minute."

"Can you remember the date of that phone call from Vercelli?"

"Yes. It was the first of December 1976. I remember because my son was born exactly a month later."

Corso looks at Isa.

"My colleague was born in the same year."

The man looks at her.

"But my son has no resemblance at all to this lady."

41

"Corso speaking."

"I know."

"You sound terrible. What's wrong with your voice? Where are you?"

"At home, shut up in the sitting room."

"Shut up?"

"The others won't allow the dog in any of the other rooms. They say he stinks."

"And does he?"

"It's a complete muddle. His diet has changed, so it's only natural he . . ."

"Well, why not put him out on the balcony for the time being?"

"It's raining and it's cold, and the old lady next door wanders around half-naked. But what can I do for you?"

"Yesterday we talked to the brother of the Bo girl. It seems that in December '76 she called her parents from hospital in Vercelli. Isa has checked and confirmed the fact that a girl was found naked with no identification around that time in the countryside near Vercelli. The woman at the infirmary said she claimed her name was Maria Nicole Bo."

"Why would she have been naked?"

"I have no idea, but it seems the carabinieri were involved. Isa and I are going to make a trip to the place where they took the call."

"Where was that?"

"A village known as Livorno Ferraris. Are you coming?"

"You want to take a blind man to look for mushrooms?"

"Stop talking nonsense."

"But the fact is, I can neither go out nor get to work."

"Till when?"

"Till Monday. I've committed myself."

"With Mariangela?"

"No. Mariangela's shut up in her room correcting students' homework. She says it's bad enough to live with a despot, but a despot who's taken leave of his senses is even worse. What the hell can that mean?"

"You told me the two of you were getting on well."

"But I didn't have the dog then and I didn't know I was a despot."

"Well, we're just about to start out. Sure you're not coming?"

"I can't."

"But do we have your authority to go?"

"If I can't work, I can't grant authority."

"Fair enough, but I'll keep you up to date."

"I can't even think, not much point keeping me up to date."

"I will anyway. Courage, my friend."

"Courage my arse."

42

They spend a couple of minutes staring at the carabinieri station building at Livorno Ferraris, exchanging views on bad taste, statistics, the army and the random construction of small-scale housing in the 1960s.

Otherwise, the village seems reasonably full of life, bearing in mind how small it is and the fact that it's lunchtime. There are shops, a public weighbridge, a hairdresser, a stationer and a few street stalls. Even a trattoria.

They ring the doorbell and in a few moments they find themselves in what looks like a school entrance hall, even down to the furniture. The first carabiniere they meet smiles and says *buongiorno*. They are struck by the indefinite age of these young men from the south, who are always boys and always efficient, even when past thirty. This man's voice, like his nose, is so thin as to seem transparent.

They follow him to the office where the local carabinieri chief, Brigadiere Salvatore Bresciani, is at his desk, concentrating on his computer. He gets up, welcomes them in, asks them to sit down and dismisses his underling. An extremely fat man, his neck is piglike but his expression intelligent. His fingers are fat too, though, no doubt long ago, he managed to fit two rings onto them, including his wedding ring. Perhaps one reason he has not divorced is that he would never be able to get it off again. He has a Swatch on his wrist and seems to be around Corso's age.

"Well now," he says. "This Cascina San Lazzaro business you're interested in. Can I ask you whether this is in connection to other enquiries, or to relatives, insurance premiums, journalism, that sort of thing . . ."

"Other enquiries," Isa says, getting in before Corso, who had intended to say rather more.

"That's what I thought," the brigadiere says. "I've looked for the record of the case, but the carabinieri station has moved since then, and it's not the only item that has gone missing. You'll have to trust my memory, if that'll do you."

"It'll have to," Isa says.

In the brief pause that follows, Corso grimaces, as if to say, please take no notice of her. The man smiles in complicity: young people don't always know how to behave, but being impetuous can also be a positive factor. He locks his hands over his stomach, an achievement that needs to be seen to be believed with such fat fingers, and proof of unexpected elasticity.

"I myself took the phone calls that evening," he begins. "It was in early December, a Tuesday or Wednesday if I remember rightly. At that time, in '76, I hadn't yet brought my family here and was looking at the calendar with a view to buying railway tickets to go down and see them. A man phoned from Cascina San Lazzaro, I can't remember his name, but he said there was a woman there with them in a sorry state, and could we come over and pick her up. I said it would probably be better if he got on to the Red Cross, but he added that some men had come there and someone had even fired a gun, so it would be best if we could come because the situation was confused. So I made him give me the details and passed everything on to the lance corporal who was on duty with me that evening, and we set off."

Bresciani pours himself a drink from a bottle on his desk that contains a greenish substance resembling stagnant pond water, with bits floating about in it.

"For my back pain," he says. "Can I have something brought for you?"

"No, that's alright, we've only just had coffee," Corso lies. "You were saying that you and the lance corporal . . . ?"

"Yes, he was a southerner, from Cerignola, but had been here some time and he was familiar with the local roads, so we had no difficulty finding the farmhouse, which was out beyond Saluggia though still within our district. We drove into the courtyard, got out and went to the door." The carabiniere grimaces with disgust as he swallows half the contents of his glass. "Oh, it took us ten minutes to convince them who we were! 'Show us your identification . . . the other people who came here also said they were from the police . . . and of course ID can be faked . . .' In the end the lance corporal lost his temper and told them if they didn't open the door at once they'd be prosecuted for obstructing public officials. So they opened the door: a terrified father, mother and daughter, and a grandfather with a gun. We tried to assure them that they were safe and asked to see the injured woman. They took us to the sitting room, but I couldn't see anyone. 'She's under there,' they said. I got down on the floor – in those days I weighed much less than I do now – and I saw her. She was under the table, completely naked, scratched and covered with blood. A young girl, scarcely a grown woman. When I asked her name and how she was feeling, she just looked at me with big eyes and said something that sounded like 'isondo', 'rai isondo', 'isondo', 'rai'. I couldn't make out if she was a foreigner or off her head, and when I offered her my hand to help her out from under the table, she just started screaming as though she was mad. We put a glass of water on the floor for her, but it took us a good quarter of an hour before we finally managed to pull her out. She was disgustingly filthy, all covered with shit and blood, but I soon realised her wounds were superficial and not recent, so we asked if they could give her a bath. The woman of the house took her away and wiped her down with a wet cloth, but as soon as she tried to turn on the shower, the girl started screaming and kicking. While she was being washed, we interviewed the others: they had heard battering at the front door, and when they opened it the naked girl rushed in, instantly hiding under the table. After ten minutes in which they tried to understand what her 'isondo rai, rai isondo' could mean, a black car drove into the courtyard. Two men in plain clothes got out and said they were police. The people in the house, guessing something wasn't right, refused to open up, and the men outside threatened them and tried to break down the door. It seems one of them had a pistol, so the grandfather, a hunter, took his legally owned rifle and shot out of the window into the air, shouting that the carabinieri were coming. He watched them go back to their car, say something into a radio, and drive off."

"Did the family give any description of these men?"

"Only that they were quite young and dressed in jeans and jackets. Also that they hadn't been able to see their car very clearly. The woman put a bathrobe round the girl, and we hurried her to the hospital in Vercelli. On the way we continued asking her questions about what had happened, but she just constantly repeated 'rai isondo, rai isondo'. Though at the hospital she told them her name was Maria Nicole Bo. I heard that myself."

"Nothing else?"

"Not another word. They gave her a sedative and she fell asleep."

"What did the doctor who examined her say?"

"That she was in a state of shock and had been subjected to

violence: she had a lot of livid scars, had lost the nails from one hand and one foot, and had a broken nose, an open wound on her forehead and cigarette burns all over her body."

"Any sexual violence?"

"Not that I know of, but the doctor said she was pregnant."

"Pregnant?"

"I hadn't noticed, but when they told me, in fact I realised that . . . meanwhile the lance corporal had checked her name and we realised who she must be. That business with the fire in Torino, of course, and since you're here you'll know what that was about."

"And she had no documents?"

"No, but I had previously seen an identification photograph of her, and I thought that even with her face messed up, it did look like her."

Corso looks at Isa whose eyes are fixed on a broken electric fan above the filing cabinet. He asks himself what she must be thinking, and how far her inattention is down to the fact that she obviously finds this man extremely disagreeable. In Corso's opinion the Bo brother was far more disagreeable, but he seemed not to have irritated Isa.

"I hope I've been able to help you," Bresciani says, taking another sip of his potion.

"You have, very much, though we'd like to know about the rest too."

"How do you mean, the rest?"

"This fugitive from justice was being guarded in the hospital by a carabiniere on the door of her ward. This being the case, how did she manage to escape and cover her tracks?"

The brigadiere rocks himself very gently on his chair, careful not to subject its four feet and its back to excessive strain. He glances at Isa, who is now staring at him, and tries to move to a more comfortable position on the chair as if it were suddenly obstructing them.

"Do you know where I spent Christmas that year?"

"No."

"Here, with the train tickets I'd already bought in my pocket, because I couldn't get them to give me any money back. And where I was a month later?"

"Still here?"

"No, I'd been transferred to a little village near Domodossola on the Swiss border, the sort of place where not even Mussolini would have imprisoned Lenin. I had to rot for six years in that dump before I was transferred to Santhià and promoted. Then, at last, I was able to settle here where I had already brought my family, and do you know why? Because on the second of December '76 I had the brilliant idea to ask that lance corporal how a pregnant woman who had been beaten up and was being guarded by a sentry could contrive to escape from a hospital without being seen, hiding all traces of her departure."

Corso and Bresciani look at each other in silence, then Corso indicates he would like to smoke. The brigadiere does not respond, but takes his own cigarettes out of a drawer. They light up almost in unison. Corso does not offer Isa his cigarettes but puts the packet on the desk in front of her. She ignores it.

"Who was this sentry?" Isa asks.

"A kid who had nothing to do with the matter. The lance corporal had told him to go and get himself a coffee."

"And where's the lance corporal now?"

"Accounting for his sins in the next world, but he was not called there until he had been transferred a couple of times and promoted to maresciallo."

"Couldn't you have put someone else on the door?" Isa says sharply. "Someone more senior and responsible?"

The brigadiere draws in a lungful of smoke at enormous length as if to demonstrate the huge capacity of his chest. Finally, he releases the smoke, and lifts his chin at Corso as if to say, Did you hear that? Clearly, this girl was not around at that time. She doesn't know that in those days, right or wrong, you just had to get on with whatever you had been told to do. Like it or lump it.

"Thank you, brigadiere," Corso says.

Fifteen minutes later Corso and Isa are in the Vauxhall Zafira, stopped by a traffic light, perhaps the only one in the village. Isa is smoking with the car window closed.

"There's always so much to learn when you lot of the old school get together," she says.

Corso glances at the traffic light, which is still red.

"There is no old school. And you were wrong to attack the brigadiere. He was under no obligation to tell us anything at all."

"As he has been doing for the last twenty years. The fat slob!"

"He already sacrificed half his career. And besides, it would have changed nothing."

"How do you know?"

"Because the same thing happened to me."

"Well done, both of you." She claps her hands twice. "How brilliant you both are!"

"The man has been useful to us, end of story. If you want to find the heroes from those days, go and look for them in the cemeteries."

Isa shapes her lips to say something cutting, then shuts her eyes and tries to calm down. She thinks of her father, of her fading memory of a tall, dry man with immensely strong hands, though perhaps he only seemed tall and strong because she had been a little girl of five when he died. She can remember him coming home from his travels to his room and stretching out on his bed, closing his eyes and going to sleep beside her without saying a word or even hugging her. When she woke in the morning he would have already gone out, leaving her breakfast and lunch ready on the table, on plates covered by other plates upside down, and marked by tickets with numbers on them: 1 for breakfast, and 2 for lunch. He would be back around four, look into the room where Isa's mother would still be sleeping, then come into her own room where they would read together stories about d'Artagnan and about rebels. Just before six, summer and winter, they would go out and walk round the park, then have supper outside, usually pizza. It would be like this for two days. Then her father would go back to his natural timetable as a working man, eight to five, until, every two weeks, he would bring home a supply of medicines, put them on her mother's bedside table, pack his suitcase, come into the room he shared with Isa, sleep fully dressed beside her, and in the morning be gone with his suitcase before she woke up, leaving no more plates with numbers on them in his absence.

Isa takes a last pull at her cigarette, which is already beginning to taste of filter, and crushes the stub in the ashtray.

"Don't forget, the autostrada's on the other side."

"We're not taking the autostrada," Corso says.

"No? Then where are we going?"

"To the Cascina San Lazzaro farm."

The woman who opens the door is a little over forty years old. She is in jeans, overalls and a white top, her curly black hair held in place by wire hairpins. She introduces herself as Angela Tomatis. She has the strong arms of a working woman, covered with a light blond down that rises from the cold or some form of electricity, and prominent veins on the back of her hands.

She listens at the door to what they want, then beckons them through the kitchen and some kind of workshop, to sit in the garden.

It is not warm, and the sky threatens rain, but Angela is wearing a low-cut singlet.

"These are pretty cool," Isa says, looking in turn at several two-metre-high metal insects that have been placed standing about on the lawn. Most of these sculptures are mosquitoes, but there are beetles and dragonflies among them too, and the only one without wings is a solitary ant.

Angela Tomatis tells them that she created these insects. She is stained with cooking fat and metal filings, and her breasts stand out so extraordinarily firmly that Isa can't take her eyes off them, realising at the same time that the woman very much expects her tits to attract attention.

Angela says she remembers the evening well, even if she was only a child at the time. Her parents would certainly have been able to tell them more, but they are dead now, as naturally is her grandfather.

Corso and Isa have already heard most of what Angela has to say from the brigadiere, but she adds that the two men who tried to get the family to hand the girl over said they were her friends and claimed she had escaped from a care home and was not at all well. On the other hand, the girl had been naked, terrified and covered in blood, and the family had never heard of the existence of any care home anywhere in the district. Angela mostly addresses Corso, though at the same time moving her hands and lips and touching her hair, as if to make sure that Isa doesn't stop looking at her. When Corso asks whether the injured girl said anything, Angela says nothing but meaningless words.

"Do you remember her saying 'isondo rai' or something like that?"

"Could be," Angela says, drawing their attention back to her tits with a dirty finger that leaves a halo of grime on her cleavage. "But as I told you, what the girl was saying meant nothing to me, and in any case, I can't remember now what her exact words were, I'm sorry."

When it's time to leave, Corso starts the car, and looking back at the house sees Isa still standing with the woman on the doorstep. When Isa speaks Angela laughs, but Isa, presumably remembering that she is supposed to be working, does not share her laughter but scribbles something on a piece of paper "just in case you remember anything more". She raises her arm in farewell, even though the two women are almost close enough to touch each other, then, thrusting her hands into the pockets of her studded jacket, she walks to the car. Angela watches her get in, and only then goes into the house and shuts the door. The large farmhouse has been tastefully decorated to make a striking home even though at present it is surrounded by featureless countryside under a grey sky.

"I left her our phone number, in case she thinks of anything else."

They drive off. The intermittent raindrops on the windscreen are threatening to turn into something heavier, and there are no other cars to be seen.

"I don't mean to stress the obvious," Isa says, "but the auto-strada's that way."

"We'll be taking the other road home."

Isa lifts one foot, props her boot on the dashboard, and crams herself sulkily into her seat. Corso slowly turns to look at her. Feeling his gaze, she takes her foot down again.

"Have you got the foggiest idea where you're going? I have no intention of spending the afternoon staring at fields."

"The high-speed railway's over there beyond the autostrada, and all we need is to keep parallel to . . ."

Corso brakes abruptly, throwing Isa's knees against the dashboard, where a compartment flies open, disgorging a handful of toy soldiers.

"What the hell are you doing?" Isa struggles to regain her balance. "You must be half asleep!"

But Corso is staring at a road sign a few metres ahead of them, which indicates two cart tracks leaving the main road in opposite directions and heading through the fields.

On one is written CASCINA CRISTOFORO, and on the other CASCINA ISONZO.

43

Once upon a time, when a steward, sharecroppers and attendants lived there with their families, the great square farm, with its two covered entrances and solid brick wall, must have looked like a fortified citadel specially constructed to cram in together and protect for all eternity the farm's produce and those who were responsible for growing it. But now that the wall built round it has begun to collapse, the whole farm has been violated and had its life taken away from it, like an old fortress that has lost its battle against time.

Perhaps this is why it has not recently been inhabited or even been demolished, but has simply survived, accessible to the vagaries of the weather. That its gates are still sealed with locks and chains is proof of that. And the partially breached surrounding wall, which allows anyone to get in just by climbing over a heap of rubble, gives further evidence of this.

Corso and Isa climb over a small pile of bricks to reach the main farmyard. There they find no ancient agricultural machinery or tools, or any other surviving relic of the activities of bygone days; just an empty yard cluttered with leaves, branches and the detritus of time. A few puddles are forming under the light rainfall.

"Could Isondo stand for Isonzo? Meaning this place?"

"Possibly."

"What would that mean?"

"The Isonzo is a river. In the north of Italy, after the First World War, they renamed farms in memory of places where they had fought against the Austrians: Ortigara, Piave, Isonzo . . . It was a way of celebrating the fact that they had won the war and been lucky enough to get home alive."

Isa moves off towards the main house. Through the windows, some open and others broken, rubbish can be seen, the ashes of old fires, scraps of cloth and attempts by vegetation to reclaim lost ground. Corso follows her in. They walk through the kitchen, much of it taken up by a massive chimney breast, then through what must once have been the dining room. Upstairs they find six bedrooms. All is in ruins.

Going back out they pass through more modest accommodation, with small, cramped rooms where the sun would not have reached the servants who lived there until the evening. Apart from the low ceilings and beaten-earth floors typical of this area, natural levelling has reduced everything to a sameness.

A few rooms show signs of more recent temporary habitation: toxic, roofless places, where some stranger may have looked for shelter, far from the city centre where too many others were searching for the same. Full of tin cans, syringes, excrement and scraps of old newspaper, but nothing to interest the two visitors.

"Let's try the stables," Corso says.

Outside, the rain is falling more heavily. The stables occupy the whole of one side of the yard, with the upper floor forming a hayloft. Geography familiar to Corso, but not to Isa with her more urban background.

He goes in first and she follows.

The stables extend the full length of the building, with a vault for casks. There are intact mangers still on the walls, two drainage channels for effluvia, a central pathway and strips of metal from which buckets would have been hung, together with equipment and pulleys for the more complicated animals. At the far end are small separate enclosures for bulls and a collective area for calves.

Corso and Isa hear their steps reverberating on the compact tile flooring as they turn at the end and come back the same way. Nothing organic is left apart from a few last remnants of straw or hay, and encrustations of dried dung.

"Maybe they kept the girl in here with the other junkies," Isa says, "and she came to a bad end."

Corso says nothing, but stops and stands still. Walking back a few steps he passes again over the last three metres. His final step brings a different note out of the ground. Not markedly different but not quite identical, like when the same note is played first by a violin, then by a cello.

This hollow note leads him to the wall. He runs his hands over it but finds only patches of damp plaster which comes away under his fingers. With his foot he pushes aside some straw covering the floor. Then he bends down to shift some tiles, discovers a large ring and, pulling it, lifts a metal trapdoor.

"Let's go down," he says.

The steps are narrow but not steep. Halfway down, Isa turns on the light on her mobile phone.

"Turn on yours as well."

"My phone has no light."

"Nonsense, of course it does, give it here."

Corso, who has already reached the floor, passes his phone to Isa. She fusses over it and eventually a light comes on. She passes the phone back to him. Together they look around. The walls and floor are rough concrete, with six reinforced pillars to support the ceiling. The place is empty.

"When can they have made all this?" Isa asks.

"No idea, but when they built the farm, reinforced concrete had not yet been invented."

In the darkest part of the cellar, they become aware of a corridor. On two sides of this are steel doors, each with a spyhole. Peering in, they see windowless cells, no bigger than a cubicle in a public lavatory. On the floors of some are blankets and grey military garments. There are twenty of these cubicles, ten on each side. Towards the far end of the corridor are two larger rooms. One with a metal writing desk, and cables for telephones or other electronic gadgets. In the other, six military camp beds without mattresses. There are also two baths and a shower. A smaller room holds an air pump linked by a large pipe to the outside world: the cellar's lungs.

Going back to the corridor, they follow it as far as the door at the end. This door is ajar: opening it they find another broadly similar area, with the same pillars, but no exits or stairs rising out of it. There are two small rusty hospital beds, an electric generator, and several now-oxidised car batteries. From the ceiling hang chains, bars and rings, all of which, though rusty, still carry a threat. Here and there on the bare concrete floor, a figure seems to be lying curled up, but on closer examination this proves to be a scrap of material, a hank of rope or a chain or blanket.

"What the hell can have been going on down here?" Isa says.

Corso feels a strong sense of imprisonment and pain.

"They were doing what the carabinieri found had been done to Maria Nicole Bo."

This is not the first time he has been in a place like this. Not underground last time, but in a small hut in the woods. The place where Autumnal used to take his victims. Where he took Michelle. He senses the adrenalin that evil can draw out of people spreading through the surroundings here. Not a stink or even anything liquid, more a vibration. A vibration that will never fade, that has pervaded the universe ever since the Big Bang. He knows that a tiny quantity of it emanated from Michelle and still circulates now, mixed with the misery of whoever was tortured here in this prison, and everywhere in the world where evil flourishes. The faint light of their two improvised torches is too weak to outface it.

"Let's go," he says.

Back in the courtyard he walks up and down very slowly and quietly, smoking, for about ten minutes. Isa has understood or sensed his mood and keeps to one side. She too is smoking. She waits for Corso to decide what to do next and when, whether to go now or stay longer. Corso passes a hand over his face, brushing away the rain that is still falling on all this evil as indifferently as it would fall on anything else. He sticks his tongue out into the rain, though this satisfies no thirst and has a mechanical taste.

"We've had enough", he says.

Isa watches as he makes his way back to the ladder leading up to the hayloft. She throws away her cigarette and follows him. They climb up, but the great open space contains nothing but ancient hay; even so they examine this. From the loft a little door leads to what turns out to be a small chapel. Nearly all the larger farms once had such a chapel where any child born during the night could instantly be baptised, and where adults could take the sacrament and at the end of their days receive the last rites.

This little room was probably the first part of the farm to be plundered. Benches, kneelers, fittings, lamps: everything has gone. Corso climbs the small ladder to a tiny bell tower, the highest point on the farm. Isa joins him.

They look out over a countryside bowing its head under the rain. Far off, a long grey train passes in the mist: the Milano–Torino high-speed express.

A couple of kilometres away, or it may be three, a building site is clearly visible, with a yellow bulldozer, a lorry and a container vehicle, and, towering over the rest, a crane.

"This farm is where they were, all of them," Corso tells Isa.

44

Isa watches the outskirts of Torino rush past the window: expanses of sheds and stores, apartment blocks, hotels, freight warehouses and old factories.

"What are these toy soldiers?" she asks, pointing at the drawer under the dashboard.

"They belong to Matei."

"Who's Matei?"

"One of Elena's children. Ani, the other, is older. Ani doesn't play with toy soldiers."

Isa takes something out from between her teeth and fiddles with her tongue stud.

"Elena. Is she the woman you were seeing two years ago? The Romanian?"

"She is."

Isa studies the saliva on her finger. The note of the Zafira's engine changes as the road rises for a banked curve. Now the two tall buildings that announce central Torino appear in the distance, grey and windowless. Old-fashioned skyscrapers that are in fact working-class homes, ideal for displaying billboards because they rise so high.

"Is she the reason you got rid of the Volvo?"

Corso keeps his eyes firmly on the road.

"I got rid of the Volvo because it was too old to be worth servicing anymore."

"Pity. It was brilliant, while this coffin you have now isn't worth a fuck."

"It's capable of taking you home. Which is all it needs to do."

They descend towards the great roundabout, surrounded by a depressing district the developers have tried to improve, only succeeding in making it uglier than ever. Corso recognises the blocks of flats where the tart who used to live in Via Lampredotti used to ply her trade. She must be over ninety now, if she has lived so long. Isa gazes with disgust at the Auchan hypermarket car park on the far side of the road. Families and their trolleys in the rain. Mothers with pushchairs and umbrellas and children with their mouths open, presumably either in supplication or reproach.

"To be honest," she says, "a coffin would do a better job."

Corso ignores her. They enter a suburb crowded with huge buildings full of miscellaneous agents, poisonous fast-food outlets and insurance companies. The main road, with its three lanes, seems to have been planned specifically to encourage drivers to go as fast as possible so as not to notice their surroundings. Though today it is crammed with Saturday afternoon traffic.

"Are we going to tell Arcadipane about the farmhouse?" Isa asks.

"On Monday."

"Why not now?"

"Because people with families like to keep their weekends free, to have some time for themselves."

No sooner have the words escaped him than Corso realises he has said the wrong thing. Isa has no family, and her weekends must be very different. To punish himself for his insensitivity, and to give himself time to make up for it, Corso moves into the slow lane behind a blue Piaggio Ape three-wheeler loaded with junk. This is the area known as Barriera di Milano, an old quarter of Torino where the side roads have obscure names and are now full of Chinese bars, fruit-machine arcades and poky little shops run by artisans and unremarkable shady individuals of no particular significance, speculators who operate through telephone advertisements, African retailers, and a few southern Italian immigrant survivors from the age of transistor radios.

Corso suddenly recognises the entrance to the road he is looking for and moves to the left to give himself more room to turn.

"This was where the headquarters of the MSI used to be," he explains.

Isa glances at a building blocking their light from the right. A low grey house with two large ground-floor shop windows displaying photocopiers. It is now a sales and repair centre.

"And that's where the former garage used to be, where the old tart was living thirty years ago."

Isa can't be bothered to look. They sit there in silence, she wanting something she knows she can't have, he wishing he could find a way of giving it to her. Waiting here for a while could be a good compromise. The rain is pattering on the car like a gentle anaesthetic. Corso scratches a little farmhouse dirt from his corduroy trousers.

"If, as her brother told us, the Bo girl was not living with her parents, maybe she was spending much of her time with Aimar. The student Aimar shared a flat with must have known her. Do you think you could track him down?"

"That would need . . ." Isa shrugs. "There may have been a contract between landlord and tenant."

Two young boys pass close to the car with a mobile phone, on which they are watching a film featuring a lot of shouting in metallic voices. The boys seem neither amused nor impressed by their film, but look exhausted, as if watching it is hard work.

"Are you annoyed with me?" Isa asks Corso.

"No, why should I be?"

"I don't know, maybe it annoys you to see me flirting."

"How do you mean?"

"With the woman who made those metal insects. Maybe you think I shouldn't mix sex and work."

"That wasn't work. Anyway, it's entirely your own business."

For a moment an unusually sweet expression passes over Isa's face. Then she opens the door.

"Don't forget, I'm doing you a favour," she says, getting out of the car. "And if I feel like flirting with a woman, that's my own fucking business."

By the time Corso has taken in her last words, Isa is running away down Via Lampredotti.

45

The coffee percolates slowly in irregular drops, occasionally ending up too far across, so that it just misses the cup. This does not detract from the fact that the machine is a fine one, its red and chrome finish frankly magnificent in the early morning light. Mariangela was right: "It's beautiful ... contemporary too." Even the coffee it makes is reasonable. Not as good as the moka, but acceptable.

He hears footsteps behind him. Female, not wearing heels.

"There's tea on the table," he says without turning.

"Thanks, but I have to come by again with Elisa before school."

It's Loredana, taking something from a drawer.

"What about breakfast?"

"At the bar, on the way back."

"Then why are you taking the biscuits?"

"Just a few. They only serve fatty food at that bar."

Loredana closes her knapsack over the biscuits. He opens his mouth to say something, but really only wants her to stop a moment so he can admire her black hair and her face, the exact image of her mother's. It is inside that the two women are different. Like two cars identical till you start the engine, then you can hear that one runs on diesel and the other on petrol.

"What is it?"

"Nothing. Were you studying late last night?"

"Quite late. I'm going now."

"What's this oral you're preparing for?"

"A Greek test."

He puts on the face of someone about to watch a boring curtain-raiser in the theatre. When she smiles it's only to please him. Her teeth are beautiful. Also her mother's.

"You're doing alright in Greek, aren't you?"

"Seven and a half at the moment, but last year they gave me eight."

"Not quite so good, then."

"I know." She looks at Trepet who is sitting near the door leading to the balcony. "But I'm in good company."

"I thought I might take him to have his hair done today." Arcadipane is testing the water. "He and I could both have those . . . what do they call them . . . ?" He reaches for the few surviving hairs at the back of his neck.

"Extensions."

"Extensions. Then perhaps I could start working undercover."

"Are you pretending to be his father?"

"That's the sort of thing your brother might have said."

"A bit sharp for him. I must go now, or I'll be late."

He nods and takes another sip of coffee. This machine-made coffee gets cold so quickly. The moka keeps it hot longer. Loredana heads for the door, her short but solid figure tightly enclosed in jeans that draw attention to the legs inside them. In the corridor she runs into her mother for a rapid kiss. They have already been in the bathroom talking and doing their make-up. Over the years Mariangela has developed her strategies, rewards and the way she communicates with the children. When something no longer works, she changes it. This comes naturally to her, perhaps because she is more intelligent than her husband. More attentive. Better adjusted to life.

"Why are you perched up there?"

"Having my coffee. It always gets cold when . . ."

"Then why not make it with the moka, if that's what you prefer?" Mariangela adjusts an earring. "I shan't be upset if you do."

"No, it's fine as it is. There's a little tea here if you want it."

"No, I think I'll make myself some barley coffee." She switches on the kettle.

Arcadipane contemplates the table: three cups, two packets of biscuits and the teapot, with the threads of two teabags dangling over the side like ropes for hanging a man.

"Since when has Loredana given up eating breakfast at home?"

"Quite a while now."

"I didn't know."

"Strange," Mariangela says, pouring hot water into her cup. "All the newspapers have been talking about it."

Giovanni comes in, goes over to the table and puts one foot up on his chair to tie his shoelace.

"I could use ten euros."

"What for?"

"A museum visit, and there's something on at the theatre."

Arcadipane looks from his wife, who is stirring her barley and water, to his son.

"At least sit down for a moment and eat something."

"No, I've got to go on foot today, the scooter won't start."

"What's wrong with it?"

"Don't know, I'll have a look at it later."

"But there's always someone else to give you a lift, isn't there?"

"What do you mean?"

"Nothing." Arcadipane finishes what's left of his coffee. Stone cold. "How's it going?"

"We're top in the league."

"I know. I see your matches too. What I mean is, how are things in general?"

"Same as usual."

"Same as usual!"

Giovanni takes a biscuit from one of the two packets. He is wearing the dark grey trousers of his tracksuit with the cord round his waist hanging loose, and a bright green military-style jacket with no words on it.

"These ones taste better," he says, showing the biscuit to his mother.

Mariangela has been looking on for some time, her hip poised between sink and cooker. She nods.

"They're honey biscuits," she says.

Giovanni puts a couple in his pocket, then changes feet to tie his other shoelace.

"Can I have that ten euros, then?"

"It's good they get you to do these things."

"Compulsory," Giovanni says, taking the banknote. "I'm off now, ciao."

A moment later they hear the sound of keys being snatched from the wall bracket, the front door slamming and the clamour of the lift.

Arcadipane contemplates the teapot in the middle of the table, the untouched teacups and the fragments of biscuit.

"Well, that didn't go too badly." Mariangela smiles, turning to the sink to wash her cup.

"Considering you're top of the class. Do you know why he came back an hour late from training last Wednesday?"

"I could have told you he'd be an hour late home, but you weren't here."

"But do you know why I was late?"

"I assumed you were at work."

"I was, but he came home an hour late because he was seeing a—"

"A . . . ?"

"A girl. She went to meet him at the training ground. I saw them have a kebab together, and she brought him home on her scooter."

"Then it's true that having a policeman for a father really is a misfortune."

"Would you rather not know what he's doing?"

"But I do know what he's doing."

"You do know."

"Uh-huh. Her name is Eleonora Pedullà, and she lives near Piazza Sabotini. She's in the language fifth and plans to do economics next year. They've been an item since the end of last year, and on Wednesday he sent me a text to say not to keep supper for him because he would be staying out and eating a kebab with her. Do you need to complete your official report by adding the registration number of the scooter he came home on?"

Arcadipane scratches his wrist.

"What does the boy do for money?"

"Money?"

"Going out, buying the girl pizza, going to the cinema. Does he ask you for money?"

"Things have changed a bit since your day, you know."

"What things?"

"Well, for example, when they go to the cinema or eat pizza, she's with her friends and he's with his friends. And neither group pays for the other."

"But when they're alone together?"

"That hasn't changed, and you should remember that."

Arcadipane feels a sharp pang, but Mariangela's expression tells him she has not been trying to hurt him deliberately. Rather,

her eyes are saying, You and I must keep talking, or this kind of nonsense is bound to happen again.

"Well, I have to be off now. There's a mountain of work waiting for me at the office."

46

"I'm getting through now . . . I told him we'd ring him at this time."

"What do I have to do?"

"Nothing. Just watch the screen. The camera's up there."

Corso looks up, but can't see any recognisable video camera.

"Can't we just use voices?"

"Just don't bugger it up! All you have to do is make the call. We're there now."

Corso stares at the screen from which a sound not at all like a telephone emerges, something that reminds him more of light music.

"What time is it out there?"

"Evening. After ten. Here he is!"

A distorted face appears on the screen, the size of the nose exaggerated because it's so near the camera. Loud noises, like someone touching a microphone.

"Good evening," the man says, manoeuvring to find a flattering angle.

"Good evening," Corso answers, moving closer to the screen at his end. "I'm Bramard."

Isa intervenes: "Don't get so close, it's not a mobile phone. He can hear you perfectly well."

The man smiles.

"Your assistant has explained everything to me by email. You could say she was extremely direct."

Corso turns to look at his 'assistant', who has made herself comfortable on the mattress flung on the floor she uses as a bed. Compared with his previous visit, the attic has not changed much, but at least the two windows are no longer hidden by black cloth. Isa indicates with her head that he should watch the screen and speak.

"I'd like to start by asking you how you came to know Stefano Aimar. Were you already friends before you shared the same flat?"

"No. When I started at the university I was commuting, then I rented a room from friends of my parents, and it was only after I began selling newspapers at night and had saved a little money that I looked through advertisements at the university to find a place of my own. Stefano's flatmate had just left so he was looking for a replacement. We met and got on well."

"How long did the two of you share the apartment?"

"A couple of years. Outside the university we moved in different circles, but we became good friends all the same. If I found him still up when I came in from work, we'd often go out for a walk together. Two boys from the provinces who both loved Torino. And we shared a passion for philosophy, cinema and books."

"But not for politics?"

"No, I had no special commitment in that direction. And as I told the police years ago, Stefano was not one for the barricades either. He was left-leaning, voted Proletarian Unity and wrote for a local paper, but he would never have done anything politically violent. He was too reasonable, too gentle, in some ways too innocent, for his own good."

"But he joined the group who threw the Molotov cocktail."

"My only explanation is that he must have wanted to protect his girl. He may have been trying to get her to change her mind about them."

"Maria Nicole?"

"Yes."

"You knew her?"

"Not well. As I told you, he and I moved in different circles. But I did speak to her a few times."

"What was she like?"

"Extremely beautiful. Definitely the type a man could lose his head over. Nice girl too, but very spoiled. Perhaps the world she had grown up in had something to do with that. The sort of girl who can get everything she wants without making the slightest effort herself."

"Did you ever hear them mention the fire? Or name any of the other people involved?"

"No. Stefano carried on going to the university and boxing at the gym, just the same as usual. But on the night of the fifteenth, I noticed when I came in from work that he'd taken away his clothes and a few books. I assumed he must have been given a lift home or that something had happened with his family. Four or five days later, I learned what he had been accused of when the police came to see me."

"The police never found him, you know. Did he give you any clue about where he went?"

"None at all, but unless Nini dropped him, they must still be together somewhere."

"Nini?"

"Yes, that's what he called her."

"Was he the only one who used that name?"

"I don't know, but to him Maria Nicole was Nini."

Corso imagined them walking together under the porticoes

where he and Michelle used to walk. Embracing or holding hands, dressed the way kids of twenty were dressed at that time. Perhaps with their arms round each other, gazing into each other's eyes and smiling, astonished to see the experience that had brought them together reflected as though in a mirror.

"Some years ago, I scanned some old photos," the man says. "Some of them show Stefano with Nini. I could email them to your assistant, if that would help, but I'd like to ask you something first."

"Go ahead."

"What happened at that time must fall under the statute of limitations. Can you confirm that? Stefano and I shared some happy times. Wherever he may be, I wouldn't like him hurt in any way."

"There is no way you can hurt him now, I can assure you of that."

The man looks round as other voices, including a woman's, can now be heard, speaking English.

"Well, if that's everything, I'm expected for supper. I'll send you the photos. If you find out anything else, let me know. And give me an email address that will reach you."

Corso asks Isa if he should do anything to end the connection. Isa shakes her head. Her shirt has a parachuting logo and its sleeves have been cut off. She has a tattoo on one shoulder – a primitive design.

Corso thinks for a few seconds, then gets up and goes to the door.

"No great shakes, eh?" he says, his hand on the door handle.

"No great shakes," she confirms, her last word coinciding with what sounds like a bouncing ping-pong ball.

Isa goes to the monitor where a feeble light is glowing from the rectangular screen. Corso studies her gypsy figure from behind as she bends over the desk, and admires her broad hips.

"Is that the photos arriving?" he asks.

She continues to stare at the screen.

"Best you phone Arcadipane now," she says. "In any case, the weekend's over."

47

Arcadipane has used up ten minutes listening to the news bulletin, but when the weather forecast follows, he turns off the car radio: he does not need the radio to know the weather in Torino, he can look up and see it directly in front of him, and who gives a damn what the weather is in Rome or anywhere else. Added to which, the weather forecast on the radio is always followed by the sport, which interests him even less than what the weather in Rome might be.

Trepet, exhausted, has fallen asleep on the seat beside him. He too, having this chance to close his eyes, is making the best of the spare quarter of an hour. Their attempts to sleep together in the sitting room have been a disaster. For Arcadipane because the seventies armchairs with their electrically welded structure conspire to torment him with painful lumps and respiratory problems; and for Trepet because the neighbours' cat, having discovered that Trepet exists, has extended his nightly excursions, forcing the poor dog to open his eyes every time it suits the cat to pass in front of the roller blinds, and after that to fall asleep again, miserable with guilt for not having been able to do anything about it.

So now, as they are wait in the car, Arcadipane lowers the driver's seat another couple of notches, but even so, after a few seconds he is forced to open his eyes again. Too nervous, too many worries, too much irritation. The sessions with Ariel are doing nothing to support him or help him stop weeping. At least before he started listening to that madwoman, he still used to have a wife to sleep with even if he no longer had any inclination to do anything with her in bed. At least his children didn't detest him, even if they did hold him in contempt. But now he has inflicted on himself this canine monster with all its intestinal problems.

He looks at the time again. Still ten minutes to get through. Yes, he might as well deal with the dog. So he reaches into the dashboard for the pills and reads the information leaflet to find the appropriate dose for a dog of this weight. But the writing is so tiny as to be illegible. Still, the pills are fairly large, so surely for the moment one will suffice.

"Trepet!"

The dog refuses to move a muscle.

"Trepet!" He touches the dog's back lightly then rapidly pulls his hand back again.

The dog opens one eye, which he rolls so as to be able to see his master clearly.

Arcadipane takes the pill from its blister pack: a perfectly round black capsule. Placing it on the palm of his hand, he holds it out to the dog. Trepet stretches and sniffs it, then turns away and goes back to sleep.

"You bastard!" Arcadipane hisses.

He changes his position to free up both hands, then with a quick movement grabs the dog's head. Trepet, though taken by surprise, does not kick, scratch or try to bite him. Arcadipane opens the dog's mouth and places the pill inside it. He then holds it shut for what he considers a reasonable length of time before rapidly pulling both hands away.

Trepet gives him a look that combines pity with condescension, then with a couple of jerks of the head, spits out the pill.

"Absolute bastard!"

Arcadipane looks at the time. Five more minutes to kill. His phone rings. He looks at the number to see if it's important.

"I'm in a bit of a hurry," he tells Corso. Best get that straight from the start.

"Go on with you! Just imagine if you had come to me to ask help with a case which, among other things, you were not responsible for yourself."

"OK, then. Tell me, what's the matter?"

"There's something I'd like you to see. If you have email, Isa can send it to you at once, but she says you'd better not use your work phone."

"That's the only phone I have."

"Then you'll have to come and get it in person."

"Where?"

"At Isa's place. Do you know where that is?"

"More or less, but first I've got to do something else. I can be at Isa's in an hour and a quarter."

Arcadipane rings off and looks at the time, two minutes to go now. Trepet has gone to sleep again.

Arcadipane takes the little Swiss army knife from his pocket, makes a small cut in a sucai lozenge, and pushes the pill into the sucai.

"Trepet!"

Having done this, he hurries across the road with the dog, climbs the steps and rings the bell. No answer. He rings again. Again nothing. Then he remembers: "The porter won't be here on Monday; just ring twenty-four and come straight up."

When he presses the button for 24, the outer door springs open. As usual, he walks up the stairs. The door of 24 is ajar. He knocks lightly and goes in. Trepet, panting behind him as they reach the landing, sniffs the air and follows.

Both armchairs are empty.

Thinking the woman may be in the bathroom, he sits down, trying not to speculate on how she must struggle when she wants to reach her tea kettle. But for a minute or two he can think of nothing else. He listens, but there's no sound of flushing or taps running from the bathroom. Nothing but a faint murmur, perhaps the draught from a window not properly closed.

Arcadipane goes cautiously back to the corridor again. The folding door to the bedroom is ajar. That is where the sound, as if of breathing, is coming from, together with tiny noises of shifting and rubbing or scraping.

He knows he should alert Ariel by saying something loudly like, Oh, there's no-one here, but instead he can't stop himself leaning round the edge of the door and looking in.

Ariel is stretched out on a white sheet on the single bed.

Her face is turned towards him, but her eyes are closed. Her dress has been pulled up almost as far as her throat, and the grey head of the porter is moving calmly between her open legs like a horse licking salt. He is caressing her spindly naked paralysed legs as if that is his true pleasure, and any other action merely a duty he must get through before he can go back to stroking her. She has a finger on her lips and her tongue half out of her mouth.

The man's head moves more slowly as he presses his face more deeply between her legs. Ariel, emitting a sound like a small animal, turns her head to face the other way, still without opening her eyes. Arcadipane can see her nostrils dilate as if she can smell what is stimulating her genitals. She moves her hand from her mouth to the man's shoulder, then onto his green pullover, with its usual smells of fried food and turpentine.

Arcadipane becomes aware of a stiffening between his own legs and closes his eyes so as not to miss an instant of this remarkable experience.

When he opens them again, he sees that Ariel is observing him calmly, with what seems like a faintly mocking expression.

Turning abruptly away, he leaves the apartment and rushes down the stairs, aware of Trepet hobbling after him, his three legs scratching the floor which that bugger probably waxes twice a week in the old-fashioned way, mercilessly polishing the marble with his woollen rag. He is aware he is sweating beneath his vest and pullover, with his rubber shoes and the tracksuit he bought in the market. "Bloody hell!"

He runs out of the building and into the road, aware of the uncaring sun beating down on his bald head, on the cars, on the plane trees, and on everything else.

Hearing barking, he turns: Trepet must be trapped in the hallway of the building.

Leaping back up the steps, he is just in time to grab the door before the lock clicks shut. The dog rushes out.

When he reaches the Alfa, it takes him a moment to find the car keys in his pocket, and then to fit the correct key into the lock. Finally successful, he grabs Trepet, flings the dog into the car, then falls into it himself feeing like an empty sack.

He makes an effort to breathe slowly, as they say people in a panic should always do. Then looks at Trepet, whose mouth is wide open, his belly alternately swelling and contracting like a pair of bellows.

The animal's having a heart attack, he thinks. Bloody hell!

He is on the point of turning the dog belly up to massage his heart when Trepet opens his mouth so wide as almost to dislocate his jaw and spits out a small black pellet.

The charcoal pill rolls across the seat, wobbles for a moment on the edge of it, and falls off.

48

The Countermovement

Imagine a country where they hold elections at regular intervals in which the people choose between a very large centrist party, another large party of the left, a smaller left-of-centre party and a mass of minor parties that are politically close to the large centrist party.

Imagine that this is the way it has been for thirty years, not that long if you remember that before this the country was ruled by a single dominant party of the right that was only ousted by a war. But what happened after that to those who had formed that single major party of the right which had been governing for so long without recourse to elections?

Some, still living in private homes, lamented the old days; others adjusted to voting for the new parties; and some even went so far as to recycle themselves within the new parties; but there were a few from that old single major party who believed that things could go back to what had been better for them before, using the same methods that had created that party in the first place – violence and the complicity of the State.

Imagine that a determined, audacious and bold few had attached a cable to the tower and for thirty years had pulled, pulled and pulled from their side until it was leaning over far enough for those who had adapted and recycled themselves inside the tower to start pushing hard enough from the inside to cause the tower to fall.

But the situation was in fact more complicated than that, because those who in their time had struggled against that single great party of the right and had won their battle against it, now wanted to create a country in their own image. A land of the left such as had never before existed and which even now they could not succeed in creating. What had happened to all those who had been struggling, hoping and winning, and then feeling deluded? Most of them were inside the tower with the great communist party and the other sizeable left-leaning party, and were going in for "one step at a time" politics, though there were others who had stayed outside and, together with young lads who had received their inheritance, had also attached a cable to the tower and pulled and pulled and pulled using weapons and violence in the hope of toppling the tower in their direction.

Now imagine things going on like this for years without the tower shifting because neither side had the strength, sufficient numbers or enough wind to bring the tower down in their preferred direction.

Besides, nearly all those inside the tower wanted to keep it standing. This despite the fact that every day someone inside would pass in front of the windows and watch those outside pulling either one way or the other, and say: "It would be no great harm if it fell that way!" Or, "Rather than have it fall that way, I shall join those pulling the other way."

So, in spite of bombs, ambushes, executions, demonstrations and the murders of those working as members of the forces of order, the tower stayed standing.

But imagine also that one day a great veteran from the

former single great party of the right collects both young-sters and veterans from his great single party and tells them, "We must help those who are pulling on the other side to pull harder, even though they are our sworn enemies!" This would result in a great murmuring and whispering: "The old man has gone mad!", "The old man is off his rocker!" and "I've always seen him as an infiltrator!"

Now imagine the old man does succeed in calming everyone down and asks them, "Why in all these years have we failed to make the tower fall in the direction we want?" Murmurs and whispers: "Because there are too few of us", "Because we are not pulling hard enough", "Because there are cowards inside the tower pushing the other way."

Then the old man might say, "It is for all those reasons, precisely! But how can we convince the people inside the tower to push in the direction we want?" Still more murmurs and whispers, until a young man at the far end of the hall stands up and says, "By making them believe that the tower is falling the other way. That must be the only way to make them all push our way. On top of that we shall only need the slightest extra effort. And they'll even thank us for it!"

Then imagine the old man's eyes filling with tears. He calls the young man over to him and says, "My dear young man, go out among those who are pulling the other way and make them strong and determined enough to force the tower to lean in their direction. Just enough to make it tremble but not fall, so that those inside beg us for the help we shall then be able to give them. Go as a wolf among the wolves to transform those other wolves into lambs. Then you tell them your name: Neocle."

Imagine that the old man and all the others will then

have a name. And that what happens will have a place. And that all those who have been killed will be able to have a date of death. And every one a worthy burial.

Arcadipane looks up from the three pages he has just read.

"What is this?"

"An article that came out in March 1982 in a publication called *Torero*," Isa tells him. "Someone scanned it and sent it to me a couple of hours ago."

"*Torero?*"

"Isa has checked it," Bramard says, his elbows on the sill of the half-open window. "*Torero* was a review of music and culture that came out in Bologna every two months back then. There were ten or a dozen issues in '81 and '82, then it ceased publication. The column the article appeared in was headed 'Imagine', after the song. It was used to discuss ideas that in a more serious column might have brought prosecution for libel. The piece is unsigned, but was probably written by Pietro Arru, the editor."

"And who is he?"

"A journalist who later worked on other periodicals. Nowadays he specialises in European cultural issues. He lives in Bologna. Still writes pieces from time to time for a local paper."

Arcadipane goes back to staring at the printed pages and changes their order.

"And he sent us this article?"

"No, I don't think it was him," Isa says, scratching her bare foot. "The email came from an encrypted address. A system used for online viruses and cons. The only thing that's certain about it is that it was sent from abroad."

Arcadipane puts the pages back in the right order.

"And what the hell is this all about?"

"Now or when it was originally published?" Corso asks.

"Now."

"Maybe it's meant to help us. Someone wants to help us to understand what really happened. Or, of course, it may just be a red herring."

"But why?"

"A warning. A threat. Or just to muddle us up."

Arcadipane puts the papers down on the desk and starts walking round with his eyes fixed on the linoleum floor. The fire, Petri, Fiore, the boxing, the tall slender figures of Aimar and Bramard in the courtyard, the agreement, the meeting in the attic, the break-in, Fiore again, the bones, the building site, the mud, the Bo woman, the carabinieri and the farmhouse . . . all apparently pell-mell, but at the same time there is something precise and rhythmical about the way the elements fit together, like marks on the hands of old men who use their hands to play the traditional game of morra. Trepet, bored, watches from the bed as Arcadipane strolls about.

"What was this Stefano Aimar really like?" Arcadipane asks.

Isa, sitting by the dog, stops massaging her feet.

"In what sense?" Corso asks.

Arcadipane stands still and raises his right hand, then rests it on the other window. He looks at Bramard.

"A young police officer discovers a man is guilty of a crime, follows him, makes friends with him, closes in on him, persuades him to confess and then . . ."

"Are you asking me if I saw something of myself in Aimar? If I let that influence me?"

Arcadipane shakes his head to make clear this is not what he is asking.

"The Bo girl was naked," he says, "and there was no scrap of clothing found with any of the other skeletons. Which makes me think that Aimar was probably naked too when they shot him in

327

the basement at that farm. What I want to find out is whether he was someone who might think along the same lines as you."

"You mean like swallowing a button?"

For some minutes Arcadipane's fingers have been playing with the button-like rivet in his left-hand pocket in pleasurable proximity to his balls. He now takes the rivet out and hands it to Corso.

"What would you have done if you had been shut up in a cell naked, watched by a guard, certain you'd never get out alive?"

Corso studies the little chromium-plated object.

"I would have hidden a small object where somebody might one day find it and trace it back to me."

Arcadipane lifts his head towards the square of pale blue sky beyond the window. The darting flights of the last swallows seem to trace a mosaic that will need a little more time to reveal its design.

49

Once again, the Barriera di Milano, with its Chinese bars, call centres, Arab bakers and money transfer shops; its three fast lanes running past agencies, insurance companies, roundabouts, Auchan and McDonald's, after which the Zafira drives onto the flyover and accelerates, leaving behind skyscrapers advertising banks and coffee.

Arcadipane is sitting up front, next to Bramard.

Isa, in the middle of the back seat, is eating a ham and mustard roll grabbed in haste from the bar next to the hardware store. Trepet stares at her from the mat on the floor, only distracted when she lets an occasional fragment fall. Beside her is a nylon bag holding three torches, three pairs of gloves, a pair of pincers, a screwdriver and a pair of pliers, bought from the hardware store next to the bar.

"Do you remember little Alfredo?" Arcadipane says, when the industrial zone is at last behind them.

"Vermicino's little boy." Corso nods. "Of course I remember him."

"Who's that?" Isa says with her mouth full.

Arcadipane takes another bite of the tuna and artichoke roll Isa bought for him. He chews calmly. By now, day has faded to a glow behind the mountains running past them on their left. On the other side, night is advancing beneath an apparently transparent moon.

"I've been seeing a psychologist," Arcadipane says.

Corso uses one hand to brush from his trousers the poppy seeds that his spiced bacon sandwich has been depositing on him. He has slowed down imperceptibly, as if to give himself time to find the right thing to say. Something between "That's what we all need" and the let's-talk-a-bit-more-about-it of "How's it been going?"

"I did that too," Isa says, rescuing Corso from his embarrassment. "From the age of fifteen to eighteen."

Arcadipane turns towards Bramard, as though it were he who had spoken. He holds his back rigid.

"You don't say!" Arcadipane comments.

"Uh-huh," Isa confirms. "I was a social case. Social services paid for it. Optician and dentist too, and schoolbooks. All paid for by them. And my clothes and shoes."

"And how did it go?"

Isa crams the remainder of her roll into her mouth in one go.

"The first one –" she chews her food – "was a little old lady who knew her stuff, but she had a stroke and had to give up. The next two were both too young. I hit the first and I was too much for the second one to cope with. Then I was classified as an adult, and they stopped paying for me."

Inside the car the short silence that follows this is broken only by the sound of Isa chewing, then Arcadipane also starts eating again.

"How far is the farm from the building site?" he asks.

"Three or four kilometres by car," Corso says, "or as the crow flies, I'd say half that. Maybe thirty years ago there would have been a cart track leading straight there. If they decided to bury them where they did, they must have had a reason for it."

"A cart track." Arcadipane nods, then bites into his roll and checks the progress of night; by now it has swallowed up half the sky. "Best leave the car at the building site and see if we can go the rest of the way on foot."

By the time they get to the farm it's pitch dark.

Their route from the building site never became a cart track or even a path. Just fields, irrigation ditches and mud. Nothing and nobody except a row of five mulberry trees, a votive pylon and the bed of an old canal lined with bricks. Nothing in the canal and nothing on the trees. With their torches they examine every centimetre of the pylon; words have been written on it: SHOK, ULTRA DRUGHI (a reference to Juventus football), and PAMELA E LEO, none of which seems recent, or from their point of view, relevant. Trepet has kept up with them, making the most of the chance to get his breath back when they pause. His only problem comes when they have to cross a roughly ploughed field.

"Will he be able to make it?" Corso asks, as the dog struggles over uneven sods.

Arcadipane shines his torch back over the route they have come by so far, lighting up Trepet struggling along twenty metres behind. Isa goes back to rescue the dog. Corso and Arcadipane ignore him after that, but by the end of the ploughed area Trepet is once more with them, his one not entirely unembarrassed eye shining in the torchlight.

Reaching the farm, they climb over the ruins of the outer wall at the familiar place where they already know it has collapsed. The only lights to be seen come from a distant group of small houses, together with the red safety light of the crane on the building site, and the lights that mark the railway line. The bright halo from the autostrada on the far side of the embankment is out of view.

Isa leads them across the farmyard to the stable and opens the main door. Once inside, Trepet, presumably excited by ancient animal smells, runs around with his head down, sniffing at scraps of straw. Occasionally, one of the three humans, distracted by his snorting, shines a light on him.

"Shall we take him down with us?" Isa asks at the manhole.

"He could be useful," Arcadipane says, hoping no-one will ask him how.

They raise the metal trapdoor, and Corso goes down first followed by Arcadipane; then Isa carrying the dog under her arm, like the pétanque bag carried by the old man from Marseille who frequents the police club.

Arcadipane shines his light on the concrete walls and pillars of the extensive but oppressive space in which they now find themselves.

"What a job!" he comments.

First, they check the large hall, rummaging among the camp beds and chains and the rest of the rusty rubbish. They look at the walls, discoloured by humidity. The cold has set its signature on everything, visible and invisible alike.

"Why don't we go on to the cells?" Isa asks after a while.

Corso and Arcadipane work on methodically in silence. The truth of it is something they do not need to tell themselves, and they know it would be useless to try to explain it to Isa: if you are searching for something you want to find at all costs, you start at a point where you know you are not likely to find it. This prolongs your feeling of being close to the ultimate climax. A sort of collective awareness the men can feel in their balls, as ageing male policemen who are not so much impatient as fragile, and conscious of being to some extent fools. And Isa is none of these things. She is only partly a policewoman, just as far as her backbone.

When they have finished with the main hall, they divide the cells between them on a random basis. When Isa comes out after finishing the first, she sees that the other two have only inspected half the floor of their own cells. She understands that they are taking this really seriously, so she goes back inside and adjusts herself to the situation. She can sense a train passing on the railway, something halfway between a vibration in the walls and a puff of air.

Corso is thinking that for Aimar, Maria Nicole and the others down here, the passing trains may have been a way of counting the hours, of imagining themselves for a moment among the men and women on board. Young people who, as they themselves had once been able to do, were going home from the city after a day at the university. Corso can sense the pain and relief this may have given them. He knows that Arcadipane and Isa, searching other cells, must at that moment be imagining something similar. This is the reason they are all three here now. They are the only real family I shall ever be able to have, he thinks. Then he feels ashamed and turns back to those rough walls, where it is so difficult even to graze the surface . . .

It is Arcadipane who calls out: "Here!"

Isa and Corso join him in his cell without getting excited: he is kneeling on the floor, beside a horizontal mark, perhaps made on the wall by the edge of a camp bed, and staring at a point a little lower down, almost at floor level.

"Here," he repeats.

Corso pushes Trepet aside so as to be able to crouch down beside Arcadipane. Isa, still on her feet, points her torch in the same direction. Some by now almost invisible lettering has been traced on the wall. Arcadipane puts his torch on the floor, pulls off his gloves, and takes a pen from the pocket of the sheepskin coat that his in-laws gave him. He puts it near the closed triangle at the top of a capital A, and lightly scratches the wall.

A little piece of what had seemed to be concrete falls off,

revealing a tiny cavity no bigger than a small beach ball. Before extracting whatever the hole may contain, Arcadipane picks up the patch of wall that came away and turns it over with his fingers, collecting the fragments in the palm of his hand.

"Bread," he says.

Corso picks up the pen Arcadipane has put down on the floor and pokes it a couple of centimetres into the hole. When he takes it out again there is a rivet on the point of it similar to the one in Arcadipane's pocket, but with half of it missing.

"Fuck," Isa says, without emotion.

Corso takes the small metallic object in his fingers. It is dry, not particularly cold, and has a cutting edge. He holds it just as Aimar must have held it when he became aware of its potential. A wealth of hope, rage and revenge enclosed in a few grams of alloy.

He scrapes it on the wall, higher up than the point where the word has been written, and draws a line there altogether similar in colour, thickness and consistency to the line of letters lower down. The rivet and the word it has written resemble each other as closely as a father and daughter.

"Yes, but what the hell does this word 'Benjamin' mean?" Isa asks.

Arcadipane cleans his hands, picks up his torch and gloves and gets back to his feet.

"If I don't know and you don't either, the little object we have found is obviously intended for Bramard."

Isa looks at Corso, still crouching over the word they have discovered.

"Well? What does it mean, then?"

Corso switches off his torch, as if to close the tomb again. What was there to be seen has now been seen, and what was there to be found has been found.

"I don't know," he answers her, "but you and I are going to Bologna tomorrow. Meanwhile . . ."

"That bloody commissario," Arcadipane cuts in. "He's got hold of the call logs for Marco Arturo Bo's number and he's checking every call made to and from it since Friday afternoon."

50

Isa and Corso stare at the gash the glass made in the wall, and at the stone with the eighty-five names on it, and at the square of old flooring cordoned off like a relic, on which the grey mark made by the explosion can still be clearly seen. They have just got out of one of the fast trains that come and go from underground tracks beneath the old station, their legs not yet recovered from the vibrations of the journey, despite two comfortable escalators and a short walk across the entrance hall.

Isa is reading the names. Corso imagines she must be asking herself how many of those men were fathers and whether their children were given better answers than she was given herself when her own father died. But this is not important, because neither she nor Corso has any intention of saying anything. Isa is the first to move towards the exit. Corso, for the sake of completeness, finishes his thought, then follows her.

Their appointment is in a small arcade five minutes away. Pietro Arru is waiting in front of a bookshop, sitting on a bench and reading a newspaper. He is in the uncertain zone between sixty and seventy, with a few brown hairs surviving among the grey. He looks at and greets Isa first, perhaps because her appearance amuses him or because she reminds him of something. She responds with the relaxed attitude of a dog anxious to offer its paw to a newcomer.

"You've done well to come," Arru says. "Not something easy to explain on the telephone. May I offer you a coffee?"

They sit down at a table in the bar under the arcade, a modern structure with too much green ironwork.

"Well then," Arru says. "Where shall we start?"

For all Corso knows this man may be one of those who is always ready to launch into memories from when he was young. Nostalgia for people he had met through his work or elsewhere, for how he once hoped to change the world, for what people had or did not have at that time. All of which could be summed up in the chance that you may have missed at the time when whatever you chose to wear actually suited you. A matter of small importance in his case, since he was clearly already an old man when he was young, and the trousers that suited him then still suit him now. All of which would be fine but for the fact that Corso and Isa need to catch their return train in less than two hours.

"What interests us is that article you wrote. How did you get the idea for it?"

Pietro Arru has the grey skin of a man who spends most of his time indoors, but his eyes are full of life.

"A group of friends and I started that magazine in '81. One of us had a passion for music, one for cinema, others for books, and so on. Our editorial office was my house, and our printing office was on the nearby corner. We sold five hundred copies of our first issue, which we distributed to friends and relatives, then mainly because of 'Imagine', the whole thing became more serious."

"Was that particular column one of yours?"

"Yes, it was, and after an issue in which I discussed the so-called Ustica Massacre of 1980, hinting – and I think I was the first to do so – at the possibility that a Libyan MiG having been involved, people started taking notice of us and writing

337

to us, and our sales doubled and then tripled. Several national papers got in touch with me, but I had started out with that particular group of friends and hoped that *Torero* would grow with us."

The waitress puts three coffees on the table, together with a cream doughnut for Isa.

"Can we smoke here?" Corso asks her, showing his cigarette packet.

"I've never understood why they make a problem about that," the waitress says, looking up at the open windows. "I always smoke when I have a break. And the security guard is always high, so . . ."

Corso watches her walk away, then lights up, leaving his cigarette packet in open view on the table.

"I used to smoke those too," Arru says, "but ten years ago I had to stop. Presumably, they can still be found?"

"Not everywhere. Well? The idea of the tower and the lambs, and the name Neocle, where did it come from?"

Arru takes a sip of his coffee, holding his little cup like a goblet.

"In 1982 I was working as a middle-school teacher. One morning, it was in February, the secretary came to tell me a phone call had come through for me. It proved to be a man who did not introduce himself, but said he thought I was the right person for a story he wanted to publish. I made it clear to him that we did not normally publish stories that came to us by telephone. He said he understood, but that in this case we ought to make an exception. He seemed a cold fish to me, but determined and very sharp. We made an appointment to meet next day at a cinema which I knew showed films in the afternoon. He told me to sit in the penultimate row with a torch and notepad. Could I have one of your cigarettes after all?"

Corso offers the packet to him. Arru shakes one out with an easy gesture. Corso gives him a light.

"Next day the man came and sat down behind me. He told me to switch on my torch, write down what he said, and not to turn round under any circumstances."

"And you didn't?" Isa asked, her lips sugary with doughnut.

"The man's manner was pretty convincing. It was obvious he was someone used to moving in a furtive, perhaps outright clandestine atmosphere. Or if it was all a sham, it was a very convincing one. At all events, I believed what he said."

"Did he say anything that you eventually left out of the article?"

"No, despite the fact that his story was full of gaps and I was given no names or dates that I could check. I made it clear to him that at the very least I did need to know whether what he was telling me was first-hand or second-hand information. He said if I agreed to publish the article, we could meet again when he would be able to provide the necessary documentary evidence. I told him he was talking about a project that involved some very prominent people, so how could he expect me to trust him and publish such a story? Then he started talking about a Palestinian training camp where some of the 'wolves' had spent four months. He said I could verify this because the matter was 'within my capacity'. During the next few days, I called several contacts of mine in the tribunal, and they confirmed that adherents of the far left, armed communists and members of Lotta Continua interrogated at the end of the seventies had indeed referred to such a camp. Elements of the German Red Army Faction had also made use of it. Perhaps even the famous Carlos, though this had never been acknowledged in public. It was confidential information. This convinced me that Neocle, the name by which at the end of the interview he told me I should call him, was a trustworthy source and that I could take the risk of publishing his article."

Pietro Arru watches Isa also light a cigarette.

"My daughter too went through a dark period when she was around twenty. She's a teacher now and has two children, so when we look through our old—"

"I'm not twenty and there's nothing dark about me," Isa says, interrupting. Then she wipes cream off her lip before darting out: "So you never saw this Neocle face to face?"

Arru looks at her without resentment, as if this remark also belongs to the minefield of an affection familiar from his own life.

"No. Before he left, he said it was important that the article should be published in our March issue, and that his name, Neocle, should be mentioned in it, but not as the author of the article. I asked him how I would be able to keep in contact with him, and he answered that once the article had been published, he would find a way of getting a dossier to me. But I never heard from him again."

Corso puts his packet of Gitanes by the ashtray, and watches as the other man unhurriedly continues to smoke.

"What was the reaction to the article once it was printed?"

Arru shakes his head.

"There was no support and no criticism. Maybe it was taken as an exercise in fantasy, a provocation; the fact is that no-one was indignant about it, found fault with it or accused us of poor journalism because of it. The whole thing simply made no impact at all. In any case the atmosphere was changing: we won the World Cup, and people were no longer interested in plots, obscure conspiracies or investigations that led nowhere. Everyone seemed to be increasingly ready to take what was rotten for granted. To accept it as all part of the game. A necessary evil in this country. After three more issues we called time on our periodical. We too needed something more stable and better paid. I was the first to go, taking a job with a newspaper with a much wider circulation."

"Have you any idea who the person who sent the article to us now could have been?" Corso asked.

"I seem to remember that issue sold about two thousand five hundred copies at the time. It must be someone who knew the article had been published and then kept a copy for all these years."

"Neocle?"

"Perhaps, but how can you tell? And, anyway, what does it matter? I write for a local paper now that sells ten times as much as *Torero* ever did. Do you know what people want to read about now? A neighbour caught with a prostitute, a restaurant closed down because mouse droppings have been found there, local policing . . . as for politics and more fundamental filth, no-one gives a damn about that anymore."

"But you do go to the cinema, don't you?" Isa puts in. "Then why write such stuff?"

Arru takes a last few pulls on his cigarette, puts it out and studies the filter with a melancholy expression.

"Because it amuses me." He smiles. "And when everything has gone to pot anyway, what more can you do? Nothing much. Do you know what my editor passed on to me today just before I came here? A story about undertakers paying those who care for the sick to call them when the hour of death is imminent, and people offering sexual favours to hospital staff in exchange for recommending them as carers to patients. Why would I go to the cinema to watch films?"

51

For the last half hour, Arcadipane has been resting at his desk with his head on his crossed arms, trying to sleep. He had hoped that last night at home would have been an improvement on the nights before it, but at 2 a.m. he was still awake and staring at the ceiling, listening to the rumbling of Trepet's stomach and inhaling the scent of those friends and relatives, many of them now dead, who over the years had propped themselves on their elbows when lying on the sofa which was now his bed. At dawn he was still restless, so he had got up, washed and dressed without waking anyone, and gone out to walk beside the Dora River until the first bar rolled up its shutters and could make him his first filthy coffee of the day. And when you are convinced in advance that something will be filthy, you don't imagine that . . .

A knock on the door.

"Come in," he calls, trying to smooth out any creases in his sleeves.

Pedrelli enters in his faded suit and chamois-leather shoes, the hair on his small head well combed as always. Pale, unhealthy and good-humoured as ever, until he glances at the desk.

"What's happened, commissario? Did you sleep here last night?"

"Mind your own bloody business, Pedrelli. What's the matter?"

"Certainly, commissario. We've checked those call logs . . ."

Arcadipane's mobile phone rings; he had flung it down carelessly on his desk, one of the many habits that contributed to the disorder in his life and work.

He ignores it. "Well, let's deal with them," he says. Pedrelli takes a step forward, but the phone rings again. Arcadipane takes it over to the window and turns his back on Pedrelli.

"Why do you keep phoning me, woman? The reason I don't answer is because I don't wish to talk to anyone at all."

"So sorry to disturb you if you're in the middle of beating someone up, arresting a thief, or extorting a bribe from some miserable trader or other. But how are you keeping?"

"That's what I should be asking you! What's the matter? Are you ill? If so, I hope at least you have someone to look after you."

"We can discuss that later. Meanwhile, tell me: has our experiment had any effect?"

"What?"

"Did you notice any recovery of sensation, either above or below?"

"You are utterly mad!"

"That too is something we can discuss later. I'll say goodbye for now. Don't try to ring me back, I'm extremely busy. You'll hear from me again at a more suitable moment. I'm just calling now to say that I shall pass by to pick you up."

"I'm going nowhere with you."

"Oh yes you are, you certainly are. Not least because you owe me a hundred euros. It was entirely your own decision to run away after two minutes yesterday, but the session must still be paid for. That is the first principle of psychology."

"You're no psychologist, you're just a . . . a problem! I don't want to hear from you ever again. Don't phone me! Don't . . ."

"If your sensation is returning, enjoy it, but for the present only in moderation. Remember you are still in the middle of a process of readjustment."

The woman rings off. Arcadipane goes on holding his phone to his ear a little longer, grinding his teeth. He knows Pedrelli is watching.

"Yes, well? The call logs?"

"Certainly, commissario, here they are. But if I may permit myself . . . there are times when these things can happen to any of us. That's understandable, but . . . you have such a fine family . . ."

"Pedrelli?"

"Sir?"

"Just bugger off."

52

"Are you both still on the train?"

"We are."

"I've got the call logs for Marco Staminichia Bo, or whatever the man's name is."

"Marco Arturo Bo."

"That's him. On Friday, just after you had gone, he made a call from his landline phone to a landline in Spain."

"Whose phone would that be?"

"You've got that phenomenon there on the train with you, haven't you? Get her to find out."

Corso touches Isa's knee. She has been asleep on the seat facing him for the last hour. Very slowly, she opens her eyes.

"Hello?"

"We have a phone number for you to check."

With the enthusiasm of a child realising it's time for school, Isa lifts her feet off the seat next to Corso. Since being ticked off by the guard on the train, she has removed her boots to reveal striped socks that are not identical in colour or even in thickness.

She pulls her laptop out of her black bag, crosses her legs and props the computer on them. A couple of seconds later, her olive-coloured face turns bluer in the light from the computer screen. Near them a few other passengers look up. A man of about fifty is sitting on the other side of the corridor. He is wearing round spectacles, and a jacket and bow tie.

345

"Well, what's the number?" Isa says to Corso.

"I need the number," Corso tells Arcadipane on the phone.

"Prefix 0034, then . . ."

"0034 . . ."

"97239018."

"97239018."

Isa types in the number, quickly but without hurrying, and waits.

"How did you get on with the journalist?" Arcadipane asks Corso.

"A few scraps of interest, let's see if they fit."

"It's a number in the north of Spain," Isa says. "On the border with France. Two hundred kilometres from Barcelona."

Corso puts a hand over his phone. "Portbou?"

"How did you know that?"

Corso's forehead puckers in a way that conveys nothing to Isa.

"In whose name is the number?"

Isa strikes keys again.

"Nini Nuvolari," she says with a half-smile.

Corso lets slip the hand he had over his mobile phone.

"I'm here," he says into the phone.

"What was that? A tunnel?"

"No, but we have to go to Spain."

"Where?"

"Spain. To Portbou."

"And where the hell's that?"

"I'll tell you later. How soon can you leave?"

"How are we going to get there?"

"By car."

"You must be mad! How long will that take?"

"About as long as driving to Calabria."

Silence.

346

"OK, we can leave tonight, but first I have a couple of things to sort out. But I don't trust my car for long journeys."

"Then we'll take mine."

"Good, then we'll all four be comfortable."

"No."

"Not comfortable?"

"Just you and me."

"What about Isa?"

"She won't be coming."

"Why not? And Trepet?"

"We'll discuss that later. The reception on this train is terrible."

Corso rings off.

"I've found it!" Isa says, reaching under her sleeveless vest to scratch her belly. "Walter Benjamin, Berlin, fifteenth July, 1892. German philosopher, literary critic and translator. An eclectic thinker interested in . . ."

While Isa is reading, the guy sitting on the other side of the corridor shifts his position to get a better view under the armpit of her vest.

". . . after an amazingly bold escape, he committed suicide in the Catalan town of Portbou on the twenty-sixth of September 1940. Why not me?"

"How do you mean, 'why not me'?"

"Why can't I come with you?"

"Because her brother has warned the woman that we're looking for her, so we may yet hear more from them. And if they try to meet, you will be needed to follow the brother. And we need to know who owned the Isonzo farm. Then there's Pietro Arru: I would like to know why, out of so many thousands of journalists, Neocle chose to make contact with him."

Isa looks out of the window; they are nearing Torino now.

"Nini Nuvolari must be Maria Nicole Bo. We've found her."

347

"I'm not so sure."

Isa suddenly swings round to face the man sitting near her and pulls down the top of her vest to give him a full and perfect view of what he has for so long been struggling to see.

The man turns abruptly away in embarrassment and stares straight ahead. "Yes, but as you well know," Isa says, pulling her vest back up and closing her eyes, "the real reason is that you two just want to be boys together."

53

Arcadipane slips his hand under the bedclothes to check himself.

Nothing to speak of, but at least it's not the usual semolina.

He pulls it back, clasps his hands behind his head and spends the next ten minutes staring at the lampshade with its crystal tears, a wedding present from his uncles in the south. When they gave it to him he didn't like it, then he gradually grew to like it, then didn't like it again, and now he feels for it something like what he might feel for a sebaceous cyst he has lived with for a long time: he only occasionally notices it at all, but when he does he thinks he must get rid of it, but never finally makes up his mind to act on his decision because it's really not that much of a nuisance. He wonders whether Mariangela might not feel the same way about it.

He sits up, the electro-welded netting beneath him reminding him of the existence of his trunk and buttocks. His idea of snatching a couple of hours' sleep before leaving was not a bad one, but . . . He gets up amid all the squeaking of the sofa, goes into the bathroom, calmly washes and shaves, and goes back into the sitting room to get dressed, take the sheet and blankets off the sofa bed and close it up.

"Trepet!"

The dog turns over in his padded basket.

"I'm off to work now." Trepet follows with his eyes as Arcadipane reaches into the wardrobe for the dog food and pours some into the animal's bowl. Trepet gets up lazily and sniffs. Not much of a meal, but perhaps suitable for his age. Arcadipane leaves the room, crosses the corridor and opens Loredana's door.

The light from the street lamps passes through the curtains with their large floral designs and illuminates the bedroom of this obstinate, disciplined and mysterious adolescent who sleeps with her bedclothes pulled over her head. A girl of fifteen who has realised that the most beautiful girls are those ranked eight or above, while she herself is a mere six. Or six and a half when she takes a bit of trouble over her appearance. In summer maybe even seven, when the sun tans her and the sea lends more substance to her flesh.

Which is not the fickle classification of an adolescent, but the estimate of her realistic and sensible mother. Who realises things could be better but also worse.

Arcadipane looks at his daughter's still childish body under the covers.

He sits down on the bed and puts a hand on her shoulder, searching through the bedclothes for the warmth that he used to hold in his arms or carry on his back or shoulders, a warmth her body must one day give to another man, or at least be dispersed or treated in any other way that may eventually suit her.

"Loredana!"

His daughter turns abruptly, as if already awake.

"What's the time?"

She has her hair pulled back, not the way she wears it by day. A tall, pale forehead, and jet-black eyes that make up for all the rest of her.

"It's early," Arcadipane says. "But don't worry. Just that I have a favour to ask you."

She follows the direction of his eyes to the dark motionless heap in the middle of the carpet.

"I have to go away for a couple of days, and I need you to look after Trepet." She throws her head back onto the pillow.

"Why me?" she asks.

"Because Mamma has it in for me, and Giovanni . . . you know what he's like."

"I have it in for you too."

"I know, but that has nothing to do with Trepet. All he needs is food to eat, and to do pee-pee and stay close to someone."

"You mean me."

"Yes."

Loredana raises herself on her elbows to take a closer look at the dog. The light hits the white streak on his head, turning him into a small clown who has not yet finished taking off his make-up.

"But what if he bites me?"

"Come on, Trepet!" Arcadipane murmurs. "Show Loredana you don't bite."

Trepet stares at him without making the smallest movement.

"Anyway, I know he won't bite you. And at night he has his own basket in the sitting room, so you can shut him in there."

Loredana moves her head slightly on the pillow. She stares at the ceiling, where her alarm clock projects the time in red on quartz: nearly one in the morning.

"Alright, but I have to sleep now, or tomorrow morning . . ."

Arcadipane looks at her, unable to think of anything else to say, then reaches out and puts his hand on her face in what could be the beginning of a caress or a game, but he simply leaves his hand where he has put it: heavy and rough and smelling of shaving foam. His daughter does not move or speak, but he feels her imperceptibly adjust her lips and nose and the hollows of her eyes to fit the pattern of his hand.

They stay like this for a couple of minutes, then Arcadipane stands up.

"You stay here now," he tells Trepet.

He goes out into the corridor towards the main bedroom, expecting to see Trepet following him out of Loredana's room, but this does not happen.

Mariangela is asleep. She has never had any problem lying in bed until late in the morning. On the other hand, she does sometimes have trouble getting to sleep at night. For him the opposite has always been the case.

He walks round the bed to see her better. Her face seems far away, her skin damp with sweat, the large breasts in her nightdress resting heavily on the mattress. He has no idea if she is beautiful. It is like wondering whether your stomach or liver is beautiful. Stomachs and livers can't be beautiful or ugly, they just exist; either they function well or they cause problems. There can be no doubt that Mariangela functions well. And this is what he lives for. He has no need even to touch her face to know it. He has touched her face so often, that it is as if his hand has moulded her face, rather than her face being the mould that shapes his hand.

Crossing the corridor on his way to the kitchen, he notices Trepet is no longer on Loredana's carpet. Going back to her room, he looks under the desk, in the wardrobe and in the dirty-clothes basket, then finally sees the dog's disproportionately large round eyes staring out from among the folds of the blanket on her bed. When he goes closer, Trepet lowers his snout, curling up more tightly into the angle formed by the knees of the sleeping girl.

Arcadipane compares the height of the bed with the short stumpy legs of the dog, smiling at the realisation that he could never have got up there by himself.

In the kitchen he puts on the moka, and while waiting for the coffee to rise, covers two pages of a notepad with a quick scribble.

Then he drinks his coffee, tears off the pages, and looking for an envelope, finds only an old one that contains a letter in memory of an elderly aunt. He takes out the contents, folds in four the pages he has just written and slips them into the envelope, which he then leaves on top of the barley-coffee machine, after writing on it: *For Mariangela, that she may never need anyone else.*

54

He recognises the car even through the heavy rain beating down on the parking area by the motorway snack bar. Corso recognises him too: the headlights of the Alfa Romeo have a style and colour long out of date.

Arcadipane comes to a halt in the marked space next to the Zafira. He gets out calmly, and ignoring the rain seeping in under his collar, walks round the car, making sure all the doors are closed, takes his knapsack from the boot and gets into the other car. Before speaking he throws his bag onto the back seat, next to a similar shape that at first sight seems to have something to say to him, but he does not examine this more closely. Then he takes off his sodden jacket and throws it in the same place.

"You have got heating in this car, I suppose?" he says, moving the palm of his hand towards a small air vent.

"Yes, but I never use it except when the children are with me."

"Well, let's pretend they are here now, shall we? Have you eaten anything?"

"A roll, and I've got one here for you too." Corso indicates a slim packet on the dashboard. "Will that do you?"

"You could have added a few biscuits . . . Why isn't Isa here?"

Corso ignores this. He starts the engine and backs out of the parking space.

"You have a sleep now," he says, passing between petrol pumps. "I've set the alarm at four thirty for the changeover.

After that we'll have four more hours on the road and plenty of time to talk."

"I suppose I can smoke?"

"No, eat your roll and go to sleep."

Arcadipane is asleep before they have even got as far as Susa. Corso drives without exceeding 120 k.p.h. through the heavy rain which continues to beat down diagonally. The autostrada comes to meet them unannounced, offering new signs of resistance, such as slogans attacking the proposed new railway link between Torino and Lyons.

Near the French frontier Corso switches on the radio at the lowest possible volume. Glenn Gould is tackling Bach's *English Suites*. Corso imagines him bent over the piano as if lying back on a deckchair contemplating his own navel, genitals and internal organs. If he, Corso, had known back then as much as he does now about classical music, fishing, chess and himself, Stefano would perhaps still be alive, he thinks, living in his own home, just like Isa . . .

After four hours, during which Corso has listened to Arcadipane snoring in three different keys, changing position a couple of times, and muttering something in his sleep, the alarm on his mobile phone rings.

He drives on for another ten kilometres or so until he sees an autoroute snack bar indicated, then leaves the dual carriageway. For a good while now the radio has been French: Georges Brassens, Jacques Brel, the Vartan woman, Johnny Hallyday, and a couple of songs by Françoise Hardy that have as usual disturbed him emotionally. Mawkish stuff crammed with regret, but what else can you expect with the French? And since they are in France now, he can allow himself such sentiments.

He pulls up behind the autoroute bar, choosing a shaded area so as not to disturb Arcadipane. Leaving the engine running and the radio on, he gets out. He drinks an Americano coffee, eats a muesli candy bar and uses the toilet. Then he buys a takeaway double coffee and a bottle of water, which he takes back to the car.

Getting in, he bangs the door to wake Arcadipane.

"Use the loo and get yourself something to eat, I've already had something myself. And here's a double coffee to start you off."

Arcadipane gets out of the car. Beyond the fence there are a few container vehicles, garage buildings, a refinery and some advertisements which are illuminated by day, even in what seems to be an unpretentious small town. Further off, higher up on a hillside, is the historic nucleus which must once have been the focal point of this area, with the remains of a castle lit up by white lights. A few sluggish footsteps take Arcadipane to a prefabricated building where travellers can relax a bit.

He returns after a dozen minutes, with a reheated hot dog on a cold plate. Corso has already reclined the passenger seat and closed his eyes. A satellite navigation device has now appeared for the first time on the dashboard.

"How long have you had a satnav?"

"Ever since we went to Romania and Elena had to drive," Corso says without opening his eyes.

"Then she's not a good driver, I suppose?"

"She's an excellent driver, but she has no sense of direction. Once she woke me up at Rimini, of all places."

"Pedrelli's the exact opposite. I wish I could set fire to that Peugeot he insists on driving."

"But he has other qualities."

"Yes, he's an encyclopaedia of information on dogs."

As soon as they are back on the autoroute, Arcadipane looks at the little image of a car on the satnav. He checks the time and the number of kilometres still ahead of them. Bloody hell, he thinks, but nothing more. And feels no craving for a sucai.

What's on the radio now doesn't piss him off quite so much. French songs have always seemed to him a load of interminable wank with no variation of feeling or pace. But he still ends up by turning the radio off, because the news in French is even worse. He looks at Corso, whose shoulders are turned towards him, his head against the door and his eyes closed.

"What kind of a dog would you say Isa is, then, an Alsatian?"

"No."

"Then what?"

"A Rhodesian ridgeback."

"Never heard of it. But since we're on the subject, will you tell me now why she didn't come with us?"

Corso settles more comfortably on his seat.

"Just drink your coffee and let me sleep. We'll both need to be wide awake tomorrow."

55

Corso opens his eyes to blinding sun shining in through the car window. Hillsides covered with wild irregular vegetation stretch down to the sea. The water is blue, as it always is when seen from above, and a pebble beach is visible perhaps a couple of kilometres away.

"Have we been here long?"

"A while, but it was fun watching you sleep," Arcadipane says, sipping coffee from a small glass. "Here's some coffee for you. The village here's a dump. Two bars where they speak nothing but Spanish, so no need to bugger around with your American English. We're lucky I found any coffee at all. You realise you fart in your sleep? And not just now and then, but like a full orchestra."

Corso shifts his seat to an upright position.

"I don't think so. Elena would have told me."

"She's probably just being polite."

"She would have told me. Where are we heading now?"

Arcadipane points to a group of houses about a hundred metres ahead, none of them more than fifty years old. The narrow village street plunges down so steeply it looks as if it will never rise up again.

"The satnav says just over there, but I didn't like to risk it."

Corso drinks his coffee in little sips.

"We'll leave the car in that wider bit of the road and walk from there."

Outside it is still uncomfortably cold, but there can be no doubt that morning has come. Putting his hand on the roof of the Zafira, Corso can feel that the sun has begun to warm the world here, even things this sun has never seen before, like their car and themselves. Looking down, the sun shows them Portbou, flattened against one side of the beach, with a striking disproportion between living space for a mere one thousand five hundred souls and the vast train station into which dozens of railway tracks dive. Even more railway lines also emerge from the tunnel that pierces the hillside, but these turn to the north, unusual among these frontier towns.

Corso's eyes rather than his thoughts lead him to the cemetery on the outskirts of the village. On a cliff is the rusty monument that he has only ever seen in a photograph before.

"I'll just freshen up," he says.

He takes his bag from the seat behind them. He can feel Arcadipane watching him as he weighs it in his hand, but neither man speaks. He takes out a small toiletry bag with washing materials. Using water from his bottle he washes his face and cleans his teeth, then smooths his neck and hair with wet fingers. He dries himself on an old cloth from the days when he used to go up into the mountains.

"Like some water?" He shows Arcadipane that there is still a little left at the bottom of his bottle.

"No, thanks. I didn't bring my swimming trunks."

They set off down the modest main road, Corso carrying his bag and Arcadipane smoking. The village seems not to be much of a tourist haven, its shutters still closed and blinds down, with lines of washing few and far between, as one might expect in October by the sea. No people to be seen.

"A great reception!"

Finally, an elderly lady walks down the little road, says

"*Buenos días*", and passes by. A man leans out of a window to water flowers, and a car appears, a kind of van with words written on its doors. Its two occupants, clearly on their way to work, register the fact that the two visitors must be strangers but show no particular interest in the fact: presumably, every so often some tourist comes up here from the beach to enjoy the view or eat at the trattoria, which at this early hour must still be closed.

The road divides into two smaller streets. The lower of these is the one they want, with the house they are looking for on the right. They stop in front of number 18. White like the others, behind an iron railing and small front garden with roses and a neat lawn. A young woman is watering the flowers with a hose-pipe; she looks as if she could have come from India.

"Is this where Nini Nuvolari lives?" Corso asks her.

"*Ciertamente.*"

"Can we speak to her, please?"

"*Creo que sì.*"

The girl puts down her hosepipe and turns off a tap at the wall. She dries her hands on her apron, changes her slippers for some canvas shoes lying ready by the door, and goes in.

Arcadipane and Corso wait in silence. Meanwhile Arcadipane finishes his cigarette, extinguishes it on the little garden wall and leaves the filter there as if he plans to pick it up again when they leave. The village is clean and bare, as if no rubbish is ever allowed to linger long. The girl presses a button to open the gate for them.

"*Ahora llega,*" she says.

They follow her into the house: the entrance hall has a brick floor, a small table and a place to hang up coats. The walls are coloured lavender, and the house is uncluttered, with everything in the best of taste. Through the open kitchen door to the right they see a tiled work surface, an old stone sink, copper pans, wooden spoons and a vase of basil on a windowsill; beyond this is a glimpse of garden, and, far off, the sea.

They are led down a corridor to a large room with a piano, two sofas, several mats and lots of shelves full of books. Three big windows overlook a terrace, where a woman with short hair is sitting with her back to them at a wooden table. The maid who has shown them in leaves without another word. Corso and Arcadipane go through to the terrace. Nini is finishing her breakfast; on a part of the table covered by a cloth are bread, butter, marmalade, a half-eaten piece of fruit and a glass coffee pot.

Corso's first impression is that she is still remarkably beautiful and has a not unattractive expression, despite the fact she must be sixty and the left side of her face appears to have been paralysed, perhaps by a stroke. Nothing seems to have changed her much, even if things that have happened to her must have made all the difference in the world. His second thought is much more banal: let's hope we can understand what she says. And his next thought, which he chases away at once, is that Michelle too had that kind of beauty that, if she had lived, would have survived the passing of time in the same way.

"Please do sit down," Nini says. "I've asked Manuela to bring two cups; you might like a little coffee." Her words are distinct and clearly pronounced, if spoken with an unfamiliar accent.

Arcadipane sits down in a large wicker armchair, Corso on a stool. The terrace opens towards the metallic roof of the train station, the railway tracks, the tunnel and the village. Only a tiny bit of the sea is visible.

She smiles when she sees they have noticed this. "We could have planned this house so as to give ourselves a better view of the sea, but we thought that would be overdoing things."

The Indian girl brings two cups and saucers. Also some lumps of sugar, which Nini evidently does not use. She pours their coffee without asking, about as much as a cappuccino each, and indicates the sugar.

"Not for me, thank you," Corso says.

"I'll have three, please," says Arcadipane.

Nini takes her own cup, and before drinking lifts it past her nose as if about to make a toast.

She has on a white collarless tunic in a style that would now be unthinkable even in places where such tunics are still worn. Her body has clearly not been exposed to the recent summer's sun, but her strong shoulders and smooth arms reveal that she must be a swimmer and a walker, a woman clearly comfortable in her own skin. In any case, her face confirms for Corso something he has always known: that it is only the poor who age, while the rich simply get older. This also applies to the hand with which she now points to the bag that Corso has put down on the floor, with the indistinct 1-2 on it.

"Strange to think we were so close to one another that evening so long ago. Perhaps, if we had been less formal . . ."

"Would that have made a difference?"

"Heaven knows." The woman's smile is mischievous. "But it means nothing now."

Her mouth, now twisted, is the only part of her appearance that has changed; her eyes are still mobile and restless, her brow intelligent, and her cheekbones youthful.

"I expect you'd like to know what happened after that meeting."

"That certainly is one thing I'd like to know."

She sips her coffee.

"For some weeks we lived in a horrendous warehouse in the Sesto district of Milano, then we went to the Veneto, to an isolated house in the mountains, I can't remember exactly where. But that's where we met the others. Given how things went, it will seem blasphemous for me to say this now, but those were glorious days: learning to shoot, sharing everything . . . We did not yet know why we were there, but we felt there must be a reason for it."

"How many others were there?"

The woman stops to think, as if she has to remember their names in order to work out the number.

"Sixteen or seventeen, including Stefano and me. All of us were between twenty and thirty years old. Students mostly, but there were a few workers and tradesmen too, and the son of a university professor."

"Was Neocle with you?"

"No. The camp was directed by a man known as Settembre, together with another guy who was our contact with the village. There were no shops, newspapers or telephones. Just a single radio. We met Elia again in Syria, in Damascus."

"When did you get to your training camp?"

"When did we get to our camp?" she repeats with a trace of distaste. "Apart from no baths and filthy food, we had some fantastic months there too. Meeting comrades from other countries: German, Spanish, Portuguese, a couple from England."

"Is that where Elia took his own group from?"

"The camp was a day from the nearest telephone by jeep, but Elia would go to the city once a week to keep up our contacts. I asked if I could go with him. When we got there, I said I wanted to phone my family to let them know I was still alive and well. He said it wasn't a good idea, but he didn't stop me. We were away three days. That was where my relationship with him started."

"Then you broke with Stefano?"

She looks out at the village as she must have done for the last thirty years, but apparently without boredom. And shakes her head.

"By the time Stefano told me about the agreement you had made with him, we were already back in Milano. Not that that would have changed anything, I had made up my mind much earlier, but I began to think that like Stefano himself, you must be an unusual person. The kind of person who would ask the sort of questions you have just asked me now. Maybe that's why you and he liked and trusted each other. But the answer to your question is no. I never broke with Stefano. Though with Elia it was entirely different."

Arcadipane picks up one of the traditional rusks lying on the table.

"But who is this Elia?" he asks, dunking a corner of the rusk in his coffee.

"Neocle," Corso says.

"Ah!" Arcadipane nods. "So Neocle is Elia."

"Yes," the woman says. "Neocle was Elia Mancini."

Arcadipane holds the rusk close to his lips. The woman stares at him for a moment, enjoying the spectacle, then switches her eyes to Corso, who has looked away to watch a goods train that has just emerged from the tunnel. A long earthworm of yellow cadmium wagons with a darker head.

"Was it Isadora who was with you when you went to see my brother?" Nini asks.

"We'll come to that later," Corso says. "What came after your training in Syria?"

Nini pours herself more coffee and asks the others if they would like some more too. Corso shakes his head, while Arcadipane continues to stare at her speechless, the rusk still suspended from his fingers. She tops up the cup he holds out to her.

"We moved to another camp in Yugoslavia to learn about explosives and methods of interrogation and detention. Then we lived for several months in Hamburg. With false identities, but apart from that life was almost normal. I even had a job in an ice-cream parlour."

"Did Stefano never try to get you to change your mind?"

"He was too polite to raise his voice, and too much in love to threaten to leave me. In any case, I would never have followed him. And he knew that. When I remember the depressions that afflicted him, the songs he listened to and the books he read, I think he knew somehow that there was no future in our relationship. I and the others were too excited by all the secrecy and the guns in our belts to pay any attention to Stefano. Settembre gave us each an envelope once a month. Nothing much, but enough money to make us feel we were salaried guerrillas."

The goods train has now stopped under the station roof, and all that can still be seen is the grey engine at the front.

"Who was Settembre?"

"I never found out. Certainly Italian, with an accent from the Emilia region. About forty-five years old. Someone said he had worked as a courier for the partisans, and that for him the war had never ended. It was he who got us into Italy. We crossed the Austrian border in a delivery van, and when we arrived in Verona, he handed us over to a man they called the Accountant and we never saw Settembre again."

"The Accountant."

"This man divided us into cells. Elia was the head of our cell. There were thirteen of us counting Elia, and together with two other cells, we were made responsible for Torino. We split up for travel, some going by train and some by car, on different days and at different times. Our meeting place was a house in the woods in the hills near Ivrea. The Accountant had told us we would be given our weapons in a few weeks, including explosives. A liaison figure would then give us our final orders. Our particular nucleus was to take over the Rai radio and television headquarters in Torino and block its transmissions, then broadcast a series of announcements over the air. Other groups would simultaneously break into the civic centre and other public buildings. The same thing was to happen in Milano, Verona, Bologna, Firenze, Napoli and other smaller cities. The Accountant spoke of three thousand comrades including some foreigners, half of them in Rome. But the important thing for us to remember, he said, was that other organised groups would join us: workers, students, sections of the trade unions, even some police. In the south of Italy, several corps of foresters would surround the occupied buildings."

"And did you all believe that was possible?"

Nini runs her eye over the table with its coffee and crumbs, remnants of pleasure.

"At that age you believe love will last for life, so you can believe anything. And we were too charismatic and honourable not to believe that destiny would be on our side. Italy had been waiting so long for us. We never mentioned it, but most of us assumed we wouldn't need to fire a single shot."

"Not a single shot."

The woman sips her coffee, her eyes shining. Corso notices a long faint scar on her forehead.

"Manuela!" she calls.

The girl comes immediately.

"*Liévate la jarra, por favor, y prepara más café. Y también algo de comer, unos bocadillos con jamón. Ve a la panadéra y trae eos pasteles que hace con almendras. Y zumo de piña, gracias.*"

The girl collects Corso and Nini's cups and stands for a moment in front of Arcadipane before the commissario notices her, dunks what is left of his rusk in what is left of his coffee, gulps it down and puts his cup with the others on the tray. The sun lights up a part of the terrace behind the railing: miscellaneous pieces of wood of different shapes and sizes with a variety of markings, arranged by someone with an eye for design.

"Fragments of wrecked fishing boats," Nini says. "The sea brings them ashore years later. We felt we ought to make use of them." She turns to Arcadipane. "How do you come into this story?"

"This is Commissario Arcadipane," Corso says, by way of introduction. "It was Arcadipane who found a bone at Chivasso and traced it to Stefano."

"Brilliant," she says, perhaps not entirely without sincerity. "Excuse me a moment."

She gets up and goes into the drawing room, where they see her dial a number on the telephone on the desk.

"Ciao, Arturo."

She opens a drawer and takes something from it.

"Yes, they've come. Two of them. Nothing. No, I just wanted to tell you, I'll call you again later."

She comes back to the terrace with a small coral box, which she puts on the table.

"When my brother read in the press about that mass grave at Chivasso, he rang me at once. I never knew exactly where they had been buried, but I assumed it was not far from the farm." She opens the little box. "Was solving the mystery difficult?"

"Not particularly," Arcadipane says.

"Arturo had his illusions, but I . . ." She shakes her head. "When they decided they were bones dating from war . . . I won the bet and bought myself a beautiful coffee machine with my winnings. It does make good coffee, don't you agree? No need to give me that look, Bramard! Like it or not, we nobles are even capable of sneering on the gallows! That's how you think of me, isn't it? A spoiled upper-class brat who amused herself by playing at being a guerrilla."

"How did your brother get the money to you?"

Nini takes from the little box a cigarette paper which she fills with marijuana. When she has nearly finished doing this she looks up, as if only now remembering that she is being watched by a policeman and an ex-policeman.

"Purely medicinal." She smiles. "I have a prescription. It would certainly be ironic, after a lifetime on the run, if I should—"

"Don't worry," Arcadipane says. "We have no authority outside Italy . . ." But feeling Corso's eyes on him, he cuts himself short. Nini licks the paper to seal it. Her small, rapid tongue protruding from the good side of her mouth is profoundly sensual.

"Until 1980 my money came from the source you would expect, but when Elia died –" she lights up and draws in a mouthful, paying no attention to the smoke, which the wind blows at her visitors – ". . . Arturo had the idea of starting a non-profit organisation for the painless liquidation of dogs suffering from incurable diseases. I am its president, I am the one to dispose and administer. Arturo makes a couple of substantial donations each year. All legal and above board: Marco Arturo Bo and Nini Nuvolari are officially unrelated, and have no other connections in common. In any case, the money belongs to our whole family, not to Arturo alone. And living here is cheap. My son Libero is an adult now, he works in Madrid and earns good money. His wife is about to make him a father for the second time. Apart from grass and occasional trips to see my grandchildren, I have few needs."

Corso gives her the blank yet offensive look that has made his fortune, but at the same time has condemned him to a largely solitary life.

"You loathe me, don't you?" Nini smiles, displaying perfect teeth. "Why? Because I managed to save my skin? Because the other twelve ended up in that grave? Or just because of Stefano? Two taciturn working-class Piedmontese boys; both strange and melancholy, yet at the same time both noble and chivalrous, and both dedicated to the noble art of boxing . . ."

"I have never been a serious boxer."

"No, of course not, it was just a way to get round Stefano." Her fingers are gripping her cigarette very loosely. "I believe I have neither the arguments nor the willpower to alter your view of me, but I'd just like to remind you that we are here today, both of us about sixty years old, on a terrace overlooking the sea, while the two great loves of our young years, our soulmates, have both been dead for thirty years or more. So I'm sorry but I have to tell you that if you're looking to find someone similar to yourself . . ." She turns her head and looks into the streaks of light passing through the closely woven curtain.

"Go ahead," is all Corso can find to say. "But why didn't you carry out your plan right to the end?"

Nini continues to stare at the curtain, as though searching for an error in the stitching.

"Because we were the chrysalis a caterpillar must experience before it can become a butterfly, that's all. If we had tried to take over those public buildings as we planned, in a few hours the forces of order would have come and wiped us out, followed by a real coup involving soldiers, curfews, special laws, opposition parties being outlawed on suspicion of having supported us, and arrests . . ."

"But none of this ever happened."

Nini nods, turning to watch Manuela removing her shoes in the corridor before carrying some shopping into the kitchen.

"From the very start they had an alternative, and when the moment came, they had probably worked out that this was more suitable to the situation that had evolved in the intervening two years. What was this alternative? Elia always said it would be better for me not to know, but there's nothing to stop me trying to fit the pieces together now. Curcio was captured for the second time, the leadership of the armed communist movement passed to others, the struggle took a different turn, up to the Moro affair, but perhaps these are only . . ."

Manuela brings in a tray with ham rolls and more sliced white bread and puts this on the table.

"*Muy buena esta manteca de cerdo!*"

"*Pero el zumo de piña se ha terminado.*"

"*Da igual, trae el de naranja.*"

The girl nods unhappily and leaves them. Nini takes one of the bread rolls with ham. The roll is as small and shiny as the cap of a mushroom. Sweet bread. She indicates they should help themselves. Arcadipane glances at Corso, then reaches for a ham roll because he has no idea what the hell may be in the others.

"Now," Nini says, chewing her sandwich. "We are left with the tear-jerking bit and the amazing bit. Which would you like first?"

"The Isonzo farm."

"The tear-jerking bit. Have you been there?"

"Yes," Arcadipane says, his mouth full of food.

"In our case we got there in three vans halfway through March," Nini continues. "They told us the basement had been built as a detention centre, and that after our action it would be used for high-level political prisoners, key figures that they would interrogate and force to reveal state secrets. In the meantime, we could use it as a base while we waited for the order to take the city. That is exactly what the man who took us there said: 'Take the city'. So we walked happily enough into the cells, and before we went to sleep that first evening, someone started joking and made up a rhyme about ghosts. But in the morning, we discovered we had been locked in, and no-one came out alive except Elia and me."

"So he must have known what would happen? Elia, I mean."

"Of course he did! From the start! He was one of the 'recruiters' who formed the groups, tested them in action, secretly checked their reactions and finally inserted them into the structure. It was the recruiters' job to test the strength of our conviction. Perhaps you would call that our 'stupidity'. They needed to be sure they could rely on us to go the whole way."

"But why keep you all shut up in that cellar if you were of no further use to them? Wouldn't it have been less risky to wipe you out immediately?"

"Less risky, but less fun for them." Nini wipes her lips with a napkin. "After all, we were communists, and the torturers needed to test things out. They kept us three months in there, and subjected us to five different kinds of torture. But the man who was in control and advising us was still the same."

"Was it Elia who helped you to escape?"

Nini took another bite from her roll.

"One night I found the door of the cell open. There was no-one in the corridor. I realised at once it must have been Elia who had unlocked it. I would have liked to free the others too, but I had no keys. Stefano told me to run and look for help, but I knew at once that the moment they knew I'd escaped . . . the others knew that too, but said nothing. One or two were in tears, but nothing worse than that. I was fully aware what was happening, but I went off without a backwards look."

"Did Elia save you for the sake of the child you were carrying?"

"I never asked him, and he never told me. In any case, he knew Libero was probably not his child. I think what he did that night was for my sake alone. Ridiculous, wasn't it? Stockholm syndrome in reverse. He had been preparing that dossier for a long time, but he knew our only chance was for me to escape. That was the only thing that could have forced them to come to terms with him. Once we had escaped from that hospital we left the country, and since then I have not set foot in Italy again. Elia's dossier has been our life insurance."

"But Elia did go back to Italy."

"That's the amazing part." Nini looks back into the house. "Or the sentimental part, depending on how you like to look at it. But I need a snooze now. I always wake at three in the morning . . . You two can either stay here, or come back in a couple of hours, whichever you prefer. And ask Manuela for anything you need."

Corso looks out at the countryside. The goods train has slid out from the station, while two others, shorter and greyer, have arrived. Now, at midday, the sea has a clearer look.

"Why did you come here, of all places?" Corso asks.

Nini gets to her feet.

"In two years at the university I only ever took one exam, and that was on the subject of Benjamin. Stefano used to love his writings. We often discussed the paradox of his death and told each other that sooner or later we would come here together and live in Portbou. In fact, I never had much to offer Stefano, but at least I did do this for him. I think it must have some kind of meaning. You've been a university student, haven't you? You know that if you suffer the misfortune of having to make definite choices in those years, you end up clinging to one of the few subjects you've studied."

Corso nods. Nini picks up a pair of spectacles that have been lying unnoticed on the table, puts them on and goes away. With bare feet.

Left on their own, Corso and Arcadipane look at each other.

"What shall we do now?" Arcadipane asks.

"I'd like a swim, but I've no intention of saying a single word."

"Just imagine! I'd like the exact opposite."

56

They float motionless with arms and legs spread out, about fifty metres from the shore where the bottom is all seaweed and rocks. Corso tall, slender and harmonious like a kite that has just landed on the water, Arcadipane short, compact and awkward, like a similar kite shrivelled up.

"How long have you known about Elia Mancini?"

Corso, his eyes half shut, looks back at the place where they left their clothes, just below the low wall of the cemetery, where there are a few poplars together with the rusty iron monument that commemorates the escape from the Nazis of the German philosopher Walter Benjamin, together with the sheet of glass that prevents it falling into the sea. The current is pushing the swimmers westwards, but without taking them further from the shore.

"Before my train journey with Isa yesterday, I had come across Portbou twice," Corso says. "First, when I was studying Benjamin at university, and then in 1982 in the report from the Spanish police that said that when Elia Mancini was shot dead he was carrying among other things a bus ticket from Portbou to Girona, a trip he presumably had to take every time he went to Barcelona to catch the plane back to Italy. Of course, it could have been a coincidence, but that's why I thought it better not to have Isa here when this was revealed."

Arcadipane watches Corso beginning to make his way to

the shore with his ridiculous doggy-paddle. He remembers first seeing this many years before near Albissola, where they had come from Genoa on the way back from being called to court as witnesses. They had bought themselves bread rolls from a kiosk; it had been near evening in early summer and the street lamps had been shining with a pink light. Corso had stripped off most of his clothes and launched himself into the sea. He himself, Arcadipane, had followed him. They had floated there in their underpants while the village lights came on.

Now, getting out of the water in Portbou, they spend an hour on the rocks. The sun quickly dries Corso's hair, while the little hair Arcadipane has left stands on end at the first puff of wind. Both smoke a couple of cigarettes. They have a warm bottle of orangeade buzzing with small wasps that have come down from higher ground. They gaze across the sea at oil tankers, vast container ships, a couple of cruise liners heading for Barcelona, and a miscellaneous mass of yachts, rubber dinghies and motorboats.

"Should we get back now?" Arcadipane asks, feeling his balls to make sure his boxers are dry.

"In a minute," Corso says.

They finish the sandwiches and orangeade Manuela packed for them, and before the gentle lapping of the sea can lull them to sleep, make their way to the car.

By three they are back at Nini's door and ring the bell.

"She must be eating now," Arcadipane says, but the gate snaps open at once. Nini is in an armchair in the sitting room with the curtains closed to shade her. She has a magazine in her hand and was probably half asleep when they came in.

"We'll stay inside, if you don't mind," she says. "A glorious day, but a little on the hot side, don't you agree?"

Corso and Arcadipane sit on the sofa facing her. Corso

recognises rows of Italian books in editions published by Einaudi and Adelphi. Plus a lot of Spanish books unfamiliar to him.

"They say the Spanish and the Italians have a lot in common," Nini says, "but that's not true. Here in Spain, there has always been a sense of tragedy, and a taste for suffering seriously felt and seriously endured, a great sobriety that remembers all the terrible things that have happened in this country; while for us Italians . . . so many things end up seeming ridiculous, don't you think? Perhaps not immediately, but after a short time . . ."

"Are you thinking of Elia? Of his life in Italy?"

"That too! Elia could have died anywhere without having been able to say a single word. The same could just as well have happened to me. Instead, he came to an agreement that ensured he could continue to work for the other lot. An exquisite form of cruelty."

"Work in what sense?"

"That was another thing he said it would be better for me not to know about. We agreed never to discuss the twenty days each month he spent in Italy."

"And that he had a daughter in Italy? Did you discuss that?"

"He told me as soon as he knew he had made the mother pregnant. To him it was just a trivial accident, but apparently the woman was determined to keep the child at all costs. Elia didn't want to marry her, but he said he must take some sort of responsibility for mother and child, rather in the same way as he continued to be involved with Libero and me. His real punishment was probably the simple fact that two separate families can never add up to one real family. He had no-one to give him exclusive love."

"Why did he make contact with that journalist in Bologna in 1982? Wasn't it in the interests of both of you not to attract attention? So people would forget all about you."

"The money we had agreed on wasn't reaching him anymore. Perhaps those who had signed the agreement were no longer in charge. In any case we knew it wouldn't last for ever, but Libero was growing up . . . Elia asked for a sum to settle the matter once and for all. He needed to get away from Italy for ever. To stop working for the other side. Leading a double life was destroying him."

"And what about you? What did you want?"

"Being his wife for only ten days each month was a fair price to pay for having been able to survive and bring up Libero. But apart from that . . . I told him to think hard about it and not to take risks. I was thinking of my own interests, but he was sure the other side would give way, as had happened on the previous occasion. He agreed to a minor revision of the agreement because he wasn't interested in creating a scandal, only in getting his message across. The message clearly did get through to them, and a month later he was dead."

"Weren't you afraid for yourself?"

"After those months at the Isonzo farm, fear had become a rather vague concept for me. I talked to my brother, the only person who, in his own way, has always been close to me, and we reached the conclusion that the best solution was to do nothing at all. They would understand that things were good for me as they were, and that they had nothing to fear from me. After that it was my brother who looked after us."

"Does your son know about this?"

"He knows his father's work often took him to Italy, and believes he was killed by a thief in Barcelona. I suppose that must be what Isadora thinks too? Once they were too little to be told the real truth, and now they're too big to be told it."

"Then why did you send us that Neocle article? And why specifically to us?"

"Do you want the truth?" She smiles. "It had to do with wills. You know the kind of baroque furniture uncles and aunts pass down thinking you will greatly value it? Stuff you have no idea what to do with, and goes with nothing you already have. I can't leave such stuff to Libero, and remembering the relationship you once had with Stefano, you seemed the most suitable people I could think of to inherit it."

Nini stares at Corso to see how much this statement is either moving or amusing him. It does neither.

"But come with me," she says, struggling up from her armchair.

Corso and Arcadipane follow her to a wooden cupboard Arcadipane would describe as reddish and Corso as "cherry-coloured" – a well-preserved handmade antique.

Nini opens it with a key from her pocket. Two shelves are packed with folders all identical in colour, each one held together with elastic, while the two lowest sections of the cupboard hold crockery and embroidered table linen.

"So we come to the famous dossier of Elia Mancini," Nini says with neither irony nor reverence. "In multiple copies."

She weighs one of the folders in her hand, but does not take off the elastic.

"Fifteen years ago I sent the first copy of this to a left-wing newspaper, and then immediately invented an excuse to get Libero to come with me for a few months to a house in the Asturias region, a place where no-one could possibly track us down, because I was afraid that once the article was published people would come and look for us, because some of the original names survive in the dossier, and they are not the names of unimportant people. But after six months the article had still not been published. So then I sent other copies to newspapers of the centre and right, and they too ignored it."

Arcadipane intervenes: "It's hardly likely that if a thousand young people vanished, no-one even noticed!"

"There were probably nothing like that many of us. Perhaps at most a few hundred. The fact was, we were never expected to take over the whole country, we just wanted to give the impression that that was our aim. Nowadays, in these years of heroin addiction, it is not particularly difficult to account for the disappearance of a hundred or so young people, when so many just escape to India or South America, for example."

"Do many people know about this dossier?"

"I sent copies to a couple of police chiefs, a carabinieri general, four members of parliament, a magistrate, various journalists and a prominent television newscaster ... in fact, apart from you two, I think everyone has now had a chance to read it. It even reached one old family acquaintance in the Vatican."

"And no response at all?"

Nini took a letter propped up inside the cupboard.

"Only this, which reached me five years ago." She opened it. "From the president of one of the many commissions set up over the years to investigate such murders. An extremely polite letter, even a sincere one, so far as I can tell. I'm not going to let you read it because it's a bit like the ring one intends to wear on one's finger in the grave, even if most of the people mentioned in the dossier are either already dead or on their last legs, or at the very least long retired from public life. The writer claims that such concerns are now irrelevant from the point of view of justice or current affairs; they are merely a matter of history. And history has a different sense of time from ourselves."

Arcadipane and Corso wonder if Nini will now burst into tears, but when she looks up from the letter, they see she is smiling.

"Stefano was an innocent and gentle man, as good as anyone

could wish to be, but Neocle was something else, truer to life as a complete human being. I would have liked to be like Stefano, but in the end, I was forced to admit that I had both men living within me. And the two did not mix."

She takes from the pocket of her tunic a ready-made joint, which she lights with a small cigarette lighter. On the red plastic body of the lighter is the pirate logo of a Spanish *taberna*.

"This answers your last question, I think, doesn't it?"

57

When Corso wakes Arcadipane it's the middle of the night.

"What's the time?"

"Half past ten. Your turn now."

"Have you already eaten and had a pee?"

"Yes, go and get yourself a coffee?"

Arcadipane takes his bag, orders an espresso in the motorway grill, and goes to the toilet to wash his feet, where the sand between his toes had been bothering him. In the grill he also asks for a hot dog but they have none, so he makes do with a cold sandwich containing what seems to be roast beef with several sauces. And he adds a bottle of water.

He finds Corso already stretched out, hands behind his head, eyes fixed on the roof of the car.

He throws his bag on the back seat, between Corso's magenta one and the dossier that Nini entrusted to him, and gets into the driving seat, sliding it closer to the wheel so he can reach the pedals more easily. Then he starts the car, lighting up the instrument panel. The satnav begins to explain their route.

The screen shows the time and distance in kilometres, and a violet streak that will guide them home.

"Do you think you'll tell her?"

"I don't know."

Arcadipane lifts the clutch, and the car moves forward.

"I think you should."

Now he has spent half an hour sorting out the pieces in his head, everything seems more or less in order. The overtaking lane is occupied by the usual minimal Thursday night traffic: cars full of young people heading for haunts along the coast, plus a few workers either on their way home or on their way to work. On the far side of the hedges, the presence of the sea can be imagined from time to time in the glittering moonlight. The deeply French, and thus to Arcadipane deeply offensive, radio is hissing at its lowest volume.

Arcadipane switches it off altogether, and as if the two things are closely connected, his mobile phone immediately rings. He takes it out cautiously, thinking of Mariangela, then recognises the number. He glances at Corso who is leaning to one side, already asleep. He answers the phone.

"It's late and I'm abroad, what is it?"

"Abroad where?"

"On my way home from Spain."

"The sanctuary at Fátima, eh? Never despair. Or did you go there to lock someone up? By the way, how are things with your lower parts?"

"I asked you what you want!"

"Nothing special, unfortunately, but I'll come and pick you up at eight in the morning."

"You're utterly mad! Why should I listen to you for a second?"

"Without wasting words, let's just say because you've been having a hard time for years, because you've stopped sucking sweets, and because you owe me a hundred euros, is that enough to be getting on with?"

Arcadipane stares at the non-continuous white lines either side of the car.

"Come on now, no need to shit your pants!" she goads him.

"As we arranged, this will be our final session. It couldn't possibly go worse than the last one!"

Arcadipane scratches his already bristling cheeks. He glances at the satnav to check their estimated time of arrival.

"Do you know the autostrada grill at Bauducchi West?"

"I'm aware of its existence."

"I'll wait for you there, but that will be the last time."

Arcadipane rings off, then drives on for another few kilometres before stopping the Zafira in a lay-by. For a minute or two all is silence and darkness, then a passing lorry buffets the car with displaced air before drawing away in a rectangle of red lights, like a small votive picture abandoned in a sea of night and swept onwards by an invisible current. As it passes, Arcadipane just manages to read on it the words TODO FRESCO.

He checks his phone for messages. The most recent is two days old: *Giovanni taking scooter to be fixed. Expected cost 100. Can I allow for a Papal Bull?*

He writes back: *Home early afternoon. Hope no problems with Trepet.*

He stares at the cursor pulsing at the end of the phrase. The sleeping Corso emits a modest fart.

A matter of radar and a child in a well, Ardicapane texts. *Will explain properly when we meet. Yours, Vincenzo.*

58

Knuckles tap on the window of the Alfa.

Tock, tock.

Arcadipane opens his eyes. Ariel is driving her coffee-coloured Golf, one arm hanging out of the window. She has pulled her hair back to make a ponytail and stuck a hat on her head.

"I bet you once had a car like this," she says, her voice muffled by the glass.

Arcadipane sits up and winds down the window.

"I bet . . ."

"I've got the point. Must go to the toilet. Be back in a minute."

He returns a few minutes later. He has peed, rinsed his face and bought himself a coffee. And two takeaway coffees. Getting into the Golf, he cannot resist looking for the paralysed legs under her skirt. They look like the normal legs of a woman driving a car. Any young woman in her sports car, apart from her huge black shoes. Is it possible she can't allow herself anything better? Or is this part of a game? Part of her incongruous way of being a human being in this world? But what the hell does the word incongruous mean, anyway? His brain is streaking away ahead of his instructions.

"Thanks, but I don't drink coffee," Ariel says, turning in her seat to back the car up. "As you'll have noticed, I'm too excitable as it is."

She giggles. Arcadipane lets the matter drop, and in the mirror follows her perfect driving. The Golf has no pedals; all its controls work through the steering wheel. He removes the tinfoil lid from one of the two coffees and swallows a mouthful.

"Where are we going?"

Ariel ignores him and accelerates, guiding the car onto the ring road. With her skirt and hat, she is wearing a man's white shirt and, over it, a green leather reefer jacket. With a tight waist and long sleeves.

"Do you know the first thing men think of when they see me?"

Arcadipane can imagine several answers, but says nothing.

"Whether I have any feeling at all in my legs. Or if having sex with me would be like sticking themselves into a piece of rubber. They have no idea how many others must have had the same idea. You'd never believe how many sexual advances cripples get."

"Good for you."

She takes a small sweet that smells of rose from a round tin she keeps near the wheel.

"Help yourself."

"No, thanks."

She puts the sweet in her mouth and sucks it without chewing.

"I should explain myself: I have a fiancé and a couple of lovers. They like me in spite of my legs, while Ferdinando, you saw him last time, only likes my legs. In fact, I'd go so far as to say that he only licks me out of politeness since he wishes he could spend all day just stroking me. We have tried other things, but it gets too embarrassing, so the fact is . . ." She moves the sweet across her mouth, where it makes her right cheek swell. "That does make sense to you, doesn't it? Even you wouldn't expect a barber to file your tax return or check your eyesight."

Arcadipane finishes one coffee and starts on the second.

"But all this is your private life," he says. "It has nothing to do with me."

"Naturally, I'm only telling you about it in case you can somehow benefit from it, if you're capable of that much."

They drive on for about twenty minutes in silence, as far as the autostrada for Piacenza, where Ariel makes a signal and takes the exit for Asti. After passing through the toll gate, they head north for the hills.

"Would you mind if I lower the window?"

"Why?"

"I'd like to smoke."

"Don't be so self-indulgent. We'll be there in a minute."

The occasional villages the road passes through are neither large nor beautiful: church, bar, small sports field, little else. Every so often a level crossing stimulates expectation, until they get near it and realise it has long been obsolete and is now permanently open to cars. After they pass a brown sign, Ariel leaves the main road. A couple more turns, and they see a church tower beyond some trees and what seems to be a sanctuary.

Stopping here in a wide-open space, they find themselves in the middle of a complex of religious buildings. Many of the surrounding trees have now turned brown with autumn and a few have already lost their leaves. The sky is a crystalline blue and there is no-one about.

"What are we doing here?"

"Have you never been to a Sacro Monte, or Sacred Mount, before?"

"Never."

"After today you'll never be able to say that again."

Arcadipane gets out of the car and throws the two coffee cups in the nearest waste bin. When he gets back, Ariel has taken the crutches from behind her seat and is getting to her feet. Instinctively, he reaches out a hand to help her find her balance, but she shakes her head.

"No, later," she says. "Now's the time for you to have a cigarette, while your hands are still free."

Arcadipane sees her swing herself towards a green wooden shed with a notice announcing a variety of prices. The glass door to it is half-open. He lights his cigarette and follows her.

Before he can reach her, a man emerges from the ticket office. A man of about forty, with a thick beard, brown hair and the physique of a mountaineer, in a chequered shirt and close-fitting trousers that end at his knees above naked calves as plump as plucked chickens.

"Ciao, Ariel," says the man, kissing her on both cheeks. "Do you need the motor-chair today?"

"No, this man's going to carry me."

The newcomer looks at Arcadipane with an expression that mixes solidarity with sympathy. Arcadipane offers his hand.

"A pleasure," says the other with irritating politeness. "But please be careful; it's been raining and it's easy to slip."

Arcadipane smiles as though from long experience, though he has no idea what the man is talking about.

"I'll leave these with you," Ariel says, handing her crutches to the man. "And these too, which will make me lighter."

The man bends down to unlace her medical boots for her, while Ariel leans on his shoulders.

"And my socks," she says.

"Quite sure? It's rather chilly today!"

"Don't piss me off."

Laughing, the man pulls off her substantial tights, then, making sure he is still supporting her weight, twirls her quickly round and grabs hold of her again.

387

She turns to Arcadipane. "Coming?" He throws away his cigarette and moves closer to her, still not understanding.

"I need to climb on your back. You must have carried your children like that often enough."

"Only when they were little."

"I weigh no more than forty-nine kilos. I'm sure you can do it."

Arcadipane turns and bends over so Ariel can drape her arms round his shoulders like a shawl, then stands up, lifting her. She is light and warm and spreads comfortably across his back.

"The first group will be here at eleven," the man who looks like a mountaineer says. "Have a good time!"

Arcadipane continues to stare at him as he goes back into his green shed.

"Take hold of my legs."

"What?"

"My legs. Pull my legs up!"

Arcadipane turns his head to see Ariel's left leg hanging as if dead inside her skirt, blue gravel just a few centimetres below its very white foot.

"Come on!" she says, encouraging him. "We need to be up there before the others arrive."

Arcadipane grasps her under the knees, lifting her legs up to the level of his hips.

"Do we have to go up?"

"Well, it's a Sacred Mount after all! What else would we do?"

When they have gone about fifty metres a path begins, and after about ten more it starts rising. Arcadipane's breathing becomes laboured and his heart begins pumping rapidly, as though his blood has somehow been contaminated. Racked by tears of cold and fatigue, he looks up, and is relieved to see that the chapel is not far away.

Once they have reached this building, he leans forward to free one hand and mop his forehead. He can see behind a grating the statue of some guy dressed in white down on his knees praying, while a dozen other people are threatening him and insulting him, and one of them is just about to drop a huge stone on his head.

"What is all this stuff?"

"The first chapel," Ariel explains, "illustrating the martyrdom of Saint Eusebio, sometime Bishop of Vercelli. The Arians dragged him out and smashed his head and limbs with rocks, so that his brain came out, and freed of his body, his soul was able to ascend to glory. Amen."

Arcadipane studies the grotesque toothless and goitrous faces of the persecutors.

"How many chapels are there?"

"Twenty-three. Let's go on."

Up to the fifth chapel they see suffering pure and simple, then after that the suffering gradually becomes familiar and apparently less extreme. But the questions raised by the suffering are always the same: why me, for how long, and for what reason? Which has the effect of making the suffering begin to evaporate into a sort of stupefaction, almost a kind of somnolence.

He is increasingly conscious of the fragility of Ariel's legs in his hands, her warm arm firmly round his neck and her soft skin against his rough beard.

As she shifts her position on his back, her breasts, small but full, press against him like the little fists of a small child.

"Have you been bathing?" she says. "Your hair smells of the sea."

Arcadipane does not answer; already for a minute or two he has been caressing the little blunt bones of her knees, without asking himself whether she can feel his fingers, and if she can, what it is that she may be able to feel. By now he has lost count of the chapels. His eyes are fixed on the path, his thoughts on the trunks of the trees on either side, and he is conscious only of her body.

"Here we are," Ariel says. "All that is left now is the stairs."

Arcadipane looks up at the circular building like a cork or stopper on the summit of the hill. Dropping his eyes again, he climbs the stairs up to it, and when they are about to enter the chapel, he imagines dozens of statues of angels, saints and putti on the walls. But Ariel, with a light touch from her hips, directs him instead to the colonnade surrounding the building. A few steps more and the plain opens beneath them; fields, roads, woods, railways, smoke, factories and reflections of glass and water that stretch as far as Milano and beyond.

"Set me down here," Ariel says.

"But you could fall!"

"That would be my own sodding problem. Just set me down."

Arcadipane swivels round so he can rest her buttocks on the wall. He senses Ariel's hands grasping the balustrade and taking her weight. When he turns round her legs are hanging out over the void with an uncultivated area of woodland fifty metres below them.

"Have you had a look?"

Arcadipane follows Ariel's finger which is pointing towards the hills rising from the plain. A sight he could never have imagined in relation to the dimensions of the place to which they have come. The plain, then land rising to the mountains. Just that.

"I had thought there would be some low hills to begin with," Arcadipane admits. "Then higher hills and then . . ."

"But it happens quickly and unpredictably, like everything else. So it's something one has to adapt to. And that concludes our final session."

Arcadipane sticks a cigarette between his lips and lights it without asking himself whether he has enough breath left for smoking. He looks at her neck, at the little blond hairs that divide on either side of the vertebrae like the backbone of a fish. And her white feet dangling into space.

"I'm so sorry we've reached our final session," he says, expelling smoke with a half cough. "Maybe I was beginning to—"

"Don't talk rubbish. In any case, you won't get a discount."

Arcadipane's eyes sweep over the plain, the mountains, the houses and the infinite roads down which people hurry towards other equally infinite things. He thinks of Pedrelli, Isa, Mariangela, Giovanni, Loredana, Nini, the porter, and of Ariel herself as though she were not the woman there with him at this particular moment. For an instant he has the impression that he understands them all. Trepet too. Even Bramard, who, considering all that he has seen and incorporated into his life, remains the most mysterious of all.

"You're right," he says. "That's not really what I think."

"I appreciate your honesty. That doesn't change the fact that you now owe me two hundred euros."

Arcadipane takes a long, powerful, cancer-laden breath.

"That doesn't change anything."

59

The bar has a huge glass window behind which the male subject has been sitting for the last quarter of an hour. He has just ordered and drunk a Caffè Americano. He is wearing a heavy old jacket with checks in various shades of grey over a winter shirt. And his usual trousers.

As soon as he sees the girl come in, he bends forward as if to get up, but stays sitting. She joins him at the table without sitting down, takes off her own black leather jacket and throws it over an empty chair. Her hair is now tinted orange, which is new. She is wearing a black shirt with its sleeves cut off, and he notices that one arm, just above the elbow, has been dressed with a Domopak pad; this is probably to hide a new tattoo still protected by vaseline.

The man asks the girl something, perhaps whether she'd like to order anything. She speaks directly to the woman behind the counter, then sits down. Apart from this couple, only two tables in the bar are occupied. The place is a favourite haunt of students, but at this hour of the morning most students are still asleep.

The proprietor brings the girl a glass of dark liquid, perhaps Coke or Chinotto, but the girl does not look like the type to drink Chinotto. The man watches her take a few sips. He seems to be assessing how much her appearance has changed recently. It is difficult for an observer to interpret their non-verbal communication. There is a considerable difference in their ages, though this cannot exclude anything.

When she puts her glass down, he begins speaking.

He speaks for ten minutes without interruption, then stops. The girl does not interrupt or ask questions. She waits in silence. Then he speaks again for several more minutes, during which he seems not to change either his tone or the expression on his face. Before interrupting himself, he turns and for a moment gives what is probably an entirely casual glance at the street, from where they could be seen. Then he stops speaking.

The girl continues gazing at her own hands lying on the table. She may well be crying. Finally, she asks the man a question.

He nods, then bends to pick up a magenta-coloured bag which until then has been on the floor under the table, on one side of which the figures 1-2 in white can be identified (exhibit 3).

Opening the bag, he takes out a blue folder held shut by elastic, which he puts on the table (probably a copy of exhibit 7). The girl spends a long time gazing at this, as if trying to come to a decision. A boy sitting in a corner of the bar, though accompanied by another girl, has been eyeing the female subject intensely for some time, perhaps in the hope of a response from her, but no such response ever comes.

Suddenly, the female subject opens the black knapsack she is holding on her knees and takes out a long narrow box which she places on the table (contents probably exhibit 15). After which she picks up the blue folder and slides it into her knapsack.

Standing up, she leans towards the man and gives him a lingering kiss (not easy to say at this distance whether on the cheek or on the side of his mouth), and then leaves the bar.

The male subject continues to stare at the chair in which the girl was sitting, but does not follow her with his eyes, even when she passes on the pavement outside the window of the bar. A lack of interest she reciprocates, as if everything between them has now been stated, discussed and settled.

The male subject continues to sit at the table for ten more minutes, drumming his fingers on the long narrow box that the girl has left behind. Then he puts it into his magenta sports bag, pays for the two items they ordered, and goes out.

Operator: 16 AoB, bar indicated by the male subject in telephone call 12, ref. Tape 56 ctex. Begins: 10:26. Ends: 10:53.

60

"I'm home!"

Trepet, clean and combed, sticks his snout out from Loredana's room, peers at him for a few seconds with his squinting eyes, then pulls his head back in again. Staring down the empty corridor, Arcadipane listens for any other possible reaction until he recognises a familiar rustling sound. Then he drops his travel bag, puts on his boiled-wool slippers and goes into the kitchen.

Mariangela is sitting at the table which is covered with densely written pages featuring true and false, multiple choices and questions either left blank or answered in the margin. Her coffee cup is on a corner of the table.

"I'm back," he says quietly.

She looks up and studies him over her glasses.

"How did it go?"

"A long drive and terrible food. Have you been waiting long?"

Mariangela puts down her pen and looks first at the table covered with students' homework, then round the kitchen, at the coffee machine, and at the unfinished puzzle still on the wall. Then at the man she married, with his sparse and uncombed remaining hair, his unshaven beard, and his large and typically southern eyes.

Only then does she say, "Quite a while."

DAVIDE LONGO was born in 1971 in the Province of Torino. In addition to novels, he has written books for children, short stories and articles, and his texts have been used in musical and theatre productions.

SILVESTER MAZZARELLA is a renowned translator from Italian and Swedish. His translations include novels by Michaela Murgia and Marcello Fois.